All Guns Blazing
A Wild West Omnibus

Alan David

© Alan David 2016

Alan David has asserted his rights under the Copyright, Design and Patents Act, 1988, to be identified as the author of this work.

This edition published in 2016 by Pioneering Press

Bullets at Sunset

One

When the shooting was over in the wide street of Santa Maria, Texas, and the gunsmoke had drifted away, there were three dead men stretched out in the dust, and Steve Jory and his pard, Hank Penner, were still on their feet. Jory had dropped his left-hand six-gun, and blood showed on his left sleeve just above the elbow. Penner was hung over a little, with a splotch of blood on his right side about level with his bottom rib. The watching townsmen on the sidewalks were motionless, scarcely daring to breathe, for this was a showdown that had been coming ever since Jory and Penner hit the town three days earlier and made it known that they were trouble-shooting for the owners of the vast TL ranch. The three dead men on the street were nesters on TL who had refused to move out.

Jory bent and retrieved his fallen sixgun, returning it to its ornate leather holster, and his slitted brown eyes watched the street about them for more trouble. The stinging pain in his left arm informed him that he had taken a flesh wound, and he paid it no heed as he glanced at his older companion.

'You okay, Hank?' he demanded, his tones brittle. He had noted the blood stain on Penner's red check shirt.

'Just a scratch, I reckon. But I figure we better get out've here now. Our job is done.'

Jory nodded. It had been a fair fight, with the odds of three to two in favour of the nesters. He did not even glance at the sprawled dead men as he moved back to where his bay stallion was tethered to a hitchrail. He mounted and whirled the bay, waiting for Penner to side him, and there was still menace in the atmosphere despite the fact that he no longer held his guns. The watching men on the sidewalk were waiting for the appearance of the local law, but Jory figured the sheriff would not show his face until after he and Penner had left town. He set his teeth as an extra sharp twinge of pain stabbed through his left arm, and eased his big frame in the hot leather of the saddle. He was twenty-eight years old, and had seen a lot of smoke and flame and dead men in the past eight years, since he had taken to the gun trail with Penner, his dead father's old pard.

They had sold their gun services to a number of hirers over the years, and bullet wounds were all part of the risks a gunslinger faced.

Penner seemed to take a long time to get mounted, but eventually he sided Jory, a short, stocky man of forty-five, with weathered features and sandy-coloured eyes that were enveloped in wrinkled pouches. He was a sombre, stolid man, and his manner and appearance betrayed his way of life. He nodded at Jory and they started along the street, their pay for the shooting in their pockets, and as they drew level with the sheriff's office the door opened and the local lawman peered out at them, having taken the precaution of removing his gunbelt first.

'So you got your gun chore done!' the sheriff commented as Jory reigned aside to face him. 'I saw it all from here. I guess the law would call it a fair fight, but I know it was murder. If there had been six of them nesters you two would have beaten'em. They weren't in your class. You're nothing but a couple of low gunslingers. You got twenty-four hours to get out of my county.'

'We're leaving now,' Jory replied seriously. 'You've seen the last of us.' He reined back to Penner's side, saw the older man was bent over in the saddle, and asked anxiously, 'Are you okay, Hank?'

'Mebbe the slug struck deeper than I thought,' came the cautious reply. 'I reckon I got me a broken rib.'

'Let's take a look!' Jory halted the bay, but Penner kept moving.

'Not here! Are you forgetting everything I taught you? We got to make ourselves scarce before any friends of them nesters decide to do something about us. Let's get back to the hideout.'

'There should be a Doc here in town,' Jory said, glancing around. 'We're not leaving until you're patched up, and I got a hole in my hide that's letting me know it's there.'

He saw a doctor's shingle hanging over a porch of a house along the street and moved in that direction. Penner made no protest, and Jory had to help the older man out of the saddle. They went into the doctor's office, and when the medico appeared Penner was made to lie on the padded leather couch, his shirt ripped carelessly open.

'Busted rib okay,' the doctor said. He went to work expertly, but his manner suggested to the observant Jory that there was no sympathy here. He smiled grimly, for sympathy was not what they wanted.

When Penner was made comfortable Jory stripped off his shirt and had his wound attended to. It was slight, a mere gouge that ran across the fleshy part of the arm, and a bandage stopped the bleeding.

'Thanks,' Jory said, reaching into his pocket to pay for the medico's services, but the doctor shook his head.

'I don't want your money,' he said harshly. 'It's got blood on it. Those three men out there on the street were not breaking the law.'

'Suit yourself!' Jory was in no mood to argue. 'We gave them the chance to ride out. They figured to stay and fight. They hit us, so it couldn't have been so one-sided as you folks around here figure. Come on, Hank!'

They left the house and mounted again, riding out of the little town, and Penner favoured his right side, his squat shoulders hunched, his face pale beneath its weathered exterior. Jory kept watching their surroundings, tall in his saddle, his handsome face pulled into a scowl as he considered the situation. He didn't figure his work as murder. They always gave their targets the chance to pull out, or offered an even break if it came to shooting. His brown eyes glinted warily. They would drift north now, probably make for El Paso. There would be other jobs in other places. He looked sideways at Penner, and a stab of concern struck through him.

'Hey, you look ready to pitch out've your saddle,' he said. 'Let's get down and rest for a spell, huh?'

'When we get to the hideout,' Penner retorted in chesty tones. 'I don't wanta get caught out in the open.'

'Okay, suit yourself.' Jory looked around again, certain they would not be pursued. They were bullet-toughened veterans of many cattle wars, and worked together as a team. With one backing the other they were almost unbeatable, and they were never short of work in a violent land where the law of the gun ignored justice and the man who could handle a gun was the kingpin.

They rode in silence, as was their habit, through semi-desert, and grains of sand stung their faces. The distant ridges were blurred with dust and haze. The country was inhospitable, barren and aggressive, and high summer was a period of drought and sandstorms. The sun was a merciless, brilliantly white orb that blazed down from a cloudless sky, drying up all living things. The rocks were burnished by the constant heat, and what vegetation there was seemed wild — cactus, thorn bushes, tracts of mesquite that was high and dense as an adobe wall. The only movements other than their own were made by the few buzzards that hovered high above the ground.

Jory narrowed his eyes against the glare of the sun. His gaze was never still and he was always alert. Now he kept glancing at Penner, who was hung over in his saddle, his right hand pressed against the wound in his side. They hit an arroyo and followed it, then emerged upon hard rock, and Jory dropped back and blotted out their tracks. When he went on again, riding faster to come up with Penner, he found the older man on the ground, unconscious, and the horse was standing with trailing reins.

Compressing his taut lips, Jory dismounted and took his canteen to Penner's side. Turning the man over, he frowned when he saw a trickle of blood at a corner of Penner's mouth, and he eased his pard into a more comfortable position and moved both horses around to afford some shade for the old gunman's face. Penner opened his eyes when Jory poured a trickle of water into his mouth, and he grinned faintly. There was a greenish pallor under the tan on his grizzled features.

'Sorry, Steve,' he said slowly. 'I figure I got more damage than the Doc reckoned. Feels like a lung is punctured. Mebbe that slug splintered a rib, huh?'

'I'll take you back to town,' Jory said instantly.

'Like hell! Let's go on to the hideout. I'll be okay if I can rest up for a coupla days. I'm a tough old goat and it'll take a lot to kill me. When I'm able to ride again I figure we oughta quit this neck of the woods for good. We've picked the place clean, huh?'

'Anything you say,' Jory retorted. 'Do you think you can ride now?'

'Sure! Push me into my saddle, and rope me there if I can't hold on. Let's make that canyon, huh? I'll be glad when the sun goes down.'

'Sure is hot as hell,' Jory commented, and helped the older man to his feet. He was careful pushing Penner back into his saddle. This gaunted man was the nearest thing to a father he'd ever had. His own father had been killed when Jory was a shaver, and Penner brought him up. There was an uncle, somewhere in Kansas, who had prospered as a rancher, but he had not been keen to take on his dead brother's son, and Steve Jory, with the pride that had finally killed his father in a gunfight, never pushed himself upon his reluctant kin.

They rode on, and Jory was concerned about Penner. When they reached a waterhole they rested for thirty minutes, and Penner lay inert under the sparse shade of a dry acacia tree. The water was bitter, alkaline, but good enough to sustain life, and Jory bathed Penner's face.

'Stop fussing around me, Steve,' the older man said. 'Hell, this ground is hotter'n the top of a cookshack oven at feeding time. Help me up and let's get on. We got a couple more hours before we hit the hideout.'

'That's a fact,' Jory replied, squinting around. 'You think you're gonna make it.'

'I'll die trying,' Penner said, and grinned. His eyes were slightly glazed, and Jory, who had seen men in many different degrees of injury, did not like the look of his pard.

When they went on Penner had to be roped to his saddle, and they finally reached their hideout just before the sun went down. By then Penner was delirious, and Jory hurried through the ritual of blotting their tracks in order to get to camp as quickly as possible. He was filled with relief when he finally had Penner bedded down under the shelter of a ruined adobe wall that stuck up out of dense undergrowth, and he began to boil water in a pan. He ignored his hunger as he attended to his pard, and with some grease-wood burning on a small fire he unfastened the bandaging around Penner's side and laid bare the inflamed wound.

There was nothing he could do! That much he knew as soon as he looked at the wound. The ugly-looking gash was several inches long, and in itself should not have been dangerous, but the doctor in Santa Maria had said a rib was broken. He had not discovered that a splinter of the rib had pierced a lung.

Covering the wound, Jory unearthed the cache of valuables they had buried before riding into town to handle their gun chore, and he smiled grimly as he weighed the two heavy saddlebags which contained much of the money they had saved from their high gun wages over the years. Between them they had twenty thousand dollars, but money could not help them now, and Jory placed the saddlebags by Penner's head. He made a meal, and ate it alone, for he could not rouse his companion. Afterwards, he made Penner as comfortable as possible, killed the fire, and turned in. He slept fitfully until morning.

When the sun came up Jory was on his feet and preparing to scout the area. He looked at Penner, who was sleeping uneasily, his face flushed, his body twitching, and walked off into the undergrowth, carrying his Winchester, his twin sixguns in their crossed belts around his lean waist. He took his time checking out the area, and satisfied himself that they had not been followed from Santa Maria. He went back to the camp.

Penner came to his senses while Jory was cooking breakfast on a low fire, and he seemed strangely weak and unstable. He glared at Jory with unfocused gaze, and did not answer when Jory asked how he was feeling.

'You want some coffee?' Jory demanded, reaching for Penner's cup and the coffee pot. Penner shook his head. He lay slackly, as if his strength had gone. Jory saw a slowly moving shadow on the rough ground, and looked up to see a buzzard sailing effortlessly through the clear sky. He tightened his lips, for a circling buzzard was a dead giveaway. 'We better pull out of here today,' Jory went on. 'Them buzzards are marking our presence.'

'I ain't going anywheres,' Penner said suddenly. His eyes held a sharpness now, and he was breathing shallowly, with a harsh rattle coming from his chest. 'Steve, I figure I'm cashing in!' He sounded surprised.

'Don't talk like a fool!' Jory retorted, getting up from the fire and taking the cup of coffee to Penner's side. 'Drink some coffee, then have some grub. You'll feel better.' 'Nope! I don't want anything.' There was resolution in the faint tones. 'I laid awake some during the night, and I been thinking, Steve. You got to listen to me!'

'Thinking ain't your strong suit, Hank,' Jory retorted, trying to sound casual. 'But tell me what you got on your mind.'

'I been thinking about the way I brung you up! I been your father since your Pa died. I made you what your Pa was, Steve. There weren't many could beat him when it came to gunfighting. But it killed him in the end.'

'The odds against him were five to one!' A trace of bitterness mingled with the pride in Jory's voice.

'He still wound up dead, even though he took most of them skunks with him! Now it's my turn, son!' Penner pushed himself over off his back and lay on his right side. A trickle of blood showed at the corner of his mouth and dripped onto the hard ground beneath him. 'What have I got to show for a lifetime of living off a gun?'

'You got a half-share of twenty thousand bucks,' Jory said. 'You wouldn't have saved that up punching cattle.'

'I'm forty-five, and I'm finished. I wasted my life, Steve, and I've moulded you in the same image. I ain't done you any favours, son, though I didn't realise it at the time.'

'Cut out that kind of talk,' Jory snapped. 'You're gonna be fine, Hank. Just rest up. A couple of days will see you on your feet. Heck, you been shot before! I've been down like you are more than once, and we both got over it.'

'Mebbe so, but I know my time has come,' Penner retorted. He slumped then and lost consciousness, and Jory sat back on his heels and wondered what to do.

But he was helpless. He checked Penner's wound, saw that it was badly inflamed, and knew that, short of riding all the way back to Santa Maria for the doctor, he could not help his pard at all. He bathed the wound frequently, and the long day passed. Nightfall brought some measure of relief from the discomfort of the day, but Hank Penner did not show any signs of reviving. Jory slept badly that night, awakening before dawn to check on Penner, and he found the older man's condition had deteriorated during the hours of darkness.

Penner opened his eyes around midmorning, and Jory could tell that his pard was clear-minded.

'Coffee, Hank?' he demanded, forcing his tones to remain unemotional.

'Nope!' Penner shook his head. 'How long we been here, Steve?'

'This is the second day since we left Santa Maria.'

'They've done for me. Listen, son, when I'm dead you own everything I got, which ain't much excepting the dough.'

'I ain't listening to that kind of talk,' Jory said.

'Don't be a fool all your life,' Penner snapped, trying to sit up. His cheek bones were pushing up through the taut skin of his face and his eyes glittered feverishly. 'I steered you wrong, Steve. I can see that now. You got to quit this business. It's no good. You're still young. You can get out've this! Don't wind up like me and your Pa. Do me one favour, Steve, will you?'

'Anything you say, so long as you quit talking like you was loco,' Jory replied.

'Get out've Texas. We done too much helling around here to give you any chance of settling down. Why don't you take a ride up to Kansas and see your Uncle Silas? I been keeping in touch with him over the years, although I ain't heard from him in the past six months. He often wrote saying we could go spend some time with him. Now you've growed up he'll give you a home on his spread.'

'Now I've growed up I don't need his help,' Jory said with some bitterness in his voice. 'When I was a kid I could have done with a hand. He'd have me now because I could sweat my guts out for him! No dice, Hank. I don't want nothing to do with him.'

'You're his only kin. Have you thought of that?' Penner was fighting for breath, and his pale face had mottled. 'Silas must be pushing sixty! He ain't gonna live for ever, although he always was a careful man! You could get something out've him at that!'

'You talk like you're already dead and I'm alone,' Jory protested. 'Cut that out, Hank!'

'I'm good as dead! I seen too many men die not to know when my time has come, and I can tell by your face that you know it too.' Penner sighed and laid back. 'All these years,' he mused softly, more to himself than to Jory. 'Everything I did, it all led me to this spot. It's right here where I'm gonna kick off for them pearly gates.' His face hardened. 'We've sent a lot of men on ahead of us, Steve. I reckon I got to face'em all right now! I hope they ain't got guns where I'm headed. Do yourself a favour and put away your hoglegs. Get out of this place and go somewhere your face and rep ain't known. Your best bet it to make for Kansas. Silas Jory owns the Broken J ranch in Bowie County outside of a town called Sunset.'

'Hank, I told you to quit talking like that!' Jory spoke in harsh tones, concerned about his pard's condition, for Penner's long discourse had begun fading about halfway through, and finished in a low, hoarse whisper that barely came through the man's stiff lips. 'You ain't ready to die yet. Me and you have got a lot more trails to ride before you cash in your chips.'

He broke off, for Penner's head suddenly lolled sideways, and something like a long sigh came in the ensuing silence. Jory felt a pang stab through him, and he reached out quickly, pressing a hand against the older man's chest. Fear hit him when he failed to find a heartbeat, and he bent over and pressed his ear against Penner's chest. He heard nothing, and sat back on his heels. Hank Penner was dead!

Jory had seen many dead men in his time, and had killed fourteen men during his bloody and violent career as a gunslinger. He had never shot a man in the back or given less than an even chance, but he was no stranger to death. But those corpses of his own making or victims of range wars had never been more than acquaintances. Some he had known and ridden with for short periods, having been brought together with them by the lure of gun wages. Their deaths had left him unmoved. His conscience never suffered because his own life had been down on the line in the hot action of a fight. Now he gazed down upon the lifeless face of the man who had been like a father to him for many years, and unaccustomed emotion hit him hard. He was stunned, shocked into a sense of unreality that cushioned his mind against the sharp agony of grief. That might come later. But he sat staring down at the dead man, unable to comprehend that Hank Penner was dead, had finally paid the penalty for his way of life.

Time lost its sense of proportion, and Jory found himself in a daze. The heat of the sun bore down upon his bowed shoulders and sweat dripped off him. His thoughts seemed to tick over remotely, and his memories of the past that had been spent with this old gunman came fleeting through his mind in a nightmarish race.

A fluttering sound near by alerted him and he swung around, his right-hand Colt's.45 leaping into his fist. The glaze left his sight and he saw a buzzard hopping in ungainly fashion on the ground only yards away. Uttering a curse, Jory thumbed off a shot that tore away the revolting bird's head, and the heavy string of echoes reverberated through the desolate region. Jory got to his feet, shaking his head, breathing heavily. He saw other buzzards sailing around in lazy circles far overhead, and thinned his stiff lips. His instincts told him it was time to get moving.

He buried Penner under an overhang, wrapping the body in its blankets after making a pitifully small pile of the personal items that Hank Penner had carried in his pockets. He piled rocks atop the grave, and stood for a timeless period staring down at it, picturing the man beneath it. But by degrees his mind came out of the initial stages of shock. He began to move around the camp, thinking of pulling out. He cooked a meal and ate it automatically, his face set in harsh lines, his eyes holding a grim glitter. When he was ready to leave he saddled up both horses, and a pang stabbed through him when he looked at Penner's riderless mount and imagined his pard sitting there waiting for him to lead out.

But where was he to go? In the back of his mind he could hear Penner's hoarse whisper. The oldster had been dying, and reviled their way of life. It was as if Hank Penner had suddenly attained a wisdom far beyond his mortal ability, as if the knowledge of death itself had come to his aid. Penner had asked for a favour with almost his dying breath. He had wanted Jory to give up their violent way of life. He had talked of Uncle Silas, up in Kansas. But Jory had no wish to see his only kin. Silas had turned his back upon him when he'd needed help. Yet Penner had corresponded with the only other member of the Jory family alive, and Silas had intimated that he would be glad to see them.

Jory shook his head as he rode out of the canyon without looking back at the solitary mound he had built over Penner's grave. He rode to the north, his harsh face turned towards the purple mountains in the distance, the green countryside beyond. If he did not go to Kansas, to Sunset, the town in Bowie County where Silas Jory had his cattle spread, he would quit Texas and this desolate wilderness of drought and heat hell. He would at least follow part of Hank Penner's dying advice. He would move on, and now he was alone he might quit the grim business they had followed together over the years. He had enough money to start a cattle ranch of his own. But right now he needed time to get over the shock of Penner's death and to adjust himself to the drastic change that had entered his life. He no longer had human contact. His only friend was gone. He was alone in a hostile world that was merciless towards the weak and the incapable.

Two

It took Steve Jory just over two months to reach Bowie County in Kansas. He followed a winding route north without the slightest intention of going to the Broken J ranch, but somehow he headed through Indian Territory and eventually crossed the border into Kansas. He rode into the cowboy's capital, Dodge City, got himself a room in a small hotel, and made inquiries of the local law. A town marshal informed him that Bowie County was a hundred miles to the north and west of the city, and Jory turned in, to arise next morning intending to push on for the town of Sunset. He had subconsciously decided that if his Uncle Silas had been unwilling to help him out when he had been orphaned as a boy then he might see if he couldn't get something out of the old man now.

He travelled for another week before finally spotting the town he sought, and reined up one evening as the sun was preparing to disappear behind a western ridge to take his first look at the objective a dying man's words had placed in his mind. Sunset! What a name for a town, he thought, but when he threw a cursory glance at the flaming sky and saw the sunset overhead he nodded to himself. Someone must had stood on this very spot and picked the name for the town.

He rode into town and dismounted in front of the livery barn. He still had Penner's horse, and most of Penner's belongings were wrapped in an oilskin tied behind the saddle.

Penner's gunbelt was buckled and suspended from the saddlehorn, and the dead man's Winchester 44-40 was in the saddleboot. A stableman appeared and studied Jory's hard, bitter features, and felt a shiver of apprehension at sight of the glaring expression in Jory's brown eyes. He could not know that Jory was suffering grief and loneliness, and mistook those outward manifestations as signs of violence and aggression.

'Take care of the hosses,' Jory said harshly.

'A dollar a day!' the stableman replied. He was a tall, thin man of fifty, with a bent back and a badly-set broken leg that had healed crookedly to leave him with a pronounced limp. He looked at Penner's horse, saw the gunbelt and holstered Colt's sixgun, and wondered what had become of its rider. But the expression on Jory's face warned that it might be dangerous to ask questions.

Jory reached into a pocket and produced a dollar. He flipped the coin into the stableman's ready hand, and read the expression of doubt and uneasiness showing on the man's weathered face. He did not want to give the wrong impression, and tried to relax a little.

'The bay is mine. The black was my pard's. He died a couple months back. I can't bear to part with his belongings.'

'Sorry to hear that!' The stableman nodded, smiling now. He breathed a little easier. In his business he had met all types, and learned by hard experience to only answer questions of some of his customers and never to ask any of his own.

'I never been this far north before,' Jory went on. 'Mebbe you can give me some information. Is there a spread called the Broken J around here?'

'Sure is!' A frown touched the stableman's lean face, and Jory noticed it.

'Something wrong?' he demanded.

'Don't get me wrong, mister!' the stableman said hurriedly. 'But I can't help noticing that you sure look like Silas Jory, who owns Broken J.'

'Is that a fact? Well I ain't seen my uncle in a coon's age. But him and my Pa were alike as two peas in a pod, so I figure I would show some of his features. How do I get out to Broken J? I plan on riding there in the morning.'

'You reckon on seeing your uncle?' A note of uneasiness sounded in the stableman's tones.

'Uhuh! He gave me the invitation a long time ago but I never got around to making it.'

'Then you ain't heard the news!'

'What news?' Jory's tones hardened, and he saw by the stableman's expression that it could only be bad.

'Silas Jory died about six months ago.'

'The hell you say!' Jory almost stopped breathing. His face stiffened and his teeth clicked together. His thin lips twisted as bitterness welled up inside him. 'Jeez! That's the helluva note!'

'I'm sorry I'm the one got to break it to you,' the stableman said slowly. 'Look, son, mebbe you better go along the street and talk to

Lawyer Marsh — Nick Marsh. He handled your uncle's business affairs. It's local knowledge that Silas had kin someplace, and Marsh has been trying to trace them.'

'There's only me,' Jory said.

'Well there's been a lot of speculation round here. Some folks figured you'd never be found. The Broken J is yours, but there's been a lot of ranchers asking about it. If you figure to sell out you could get top price. Ben Sharkey wants to buy, and Woody Arlen let it be known that he'd snap it up if he got the chance.'

'Where does the lawyer live?' Jory cut in.

'I don't figure he'll be at his office this time of the evening, but his house is along the street on the left. Just past the Doc's place. Third house past the Doc's. Nick Marsh. Just ask for him.'

'Thanks. Take care of the hosses!' Jory turned away, then paused. 'I'll take the saddlebags off the bay. Can you put the rest of my gear in a safe place?'

'Sure thing! You'll find everything still here when you come back.'

Jory nodded and took the saddlebags containing his money. He went along the sidewalk, looking around the town through narrowed eyelids, and the knowledge that his uncle was dead stuck in his craw and filled him with bitterness. Now he was completely alone in the world. He still missed Hank Penner badly, and that was the prime reason why he had followed the oldster's advice and come to Kansas. He had not known his uncle at all, and hated the man for years because Silas Jory had turned his back upon him. But the old man had been kin, and now the last link with his origins was broken and gone.

There were a great many folk on the sidewalks, and Jory frowned as he looked around, until he realised that this was Saturday night, and that was why Sunset was throbbing with activity. Horses were standing at hitchrails, especially in front of the several saloons, and Jory guessed the cow-punchers were in from the neighbouring ranches. He could recognise them easily enough. They were brash, carefree, sun-tanned men with the unmistakable gait of horsemen, and their loud voices echoed around the street as they hailed each other and greeted the men from other ranches with ear-splitting yells and whoops.

Jory was hungry and thirsty, but he needed to get news of what had happened to his uncle, and he left the busier area of the street and passed the Doc's house, with its shingle outside. He approached a large, white-painted house with a wide porch in front, and on the porch a large table was set for supper. There were two men at the table, and three women, and they were being served with their evening meal. Jory paused inside the gate, not wishing to interrupt these people, but as he turned away one of the men arose and came to the edge of the porch, calling sharply to him.

'Something you want, Cowboy?'

'It's all right,' Jory replied. 'I don't want to bust in on your supper. I'll come see you in the morning in your office.' He paused. 'That's if you're Nick Marsh, the lawyer!' The man on the porch nodded, eyeing Jory, taking in the details that marked Jory not as a cowpuncher but something more dangerous. The twin Colts in their crossed cartridge belts and tied down holsters seemed as if they had grown on Jory's hips, and Jory's easy manner and instinctive alertness, his tall, powerful figure and brooding manner, all added up truthfully to a perceptive man.

'I'm Nick Marsh!' The lawyer was tall, with smooth features and a complexion that bespoke of his long hours spent in an office or courtroom. He was wearing a store suit of light brown material, a frilled white shirt and a black string tie. His eyes were blue, hooded by lids that sagged at the outer corners, and his forehead jutted like a cliff over his lower features. 'You in some kind of trouble, mister?'

'I hope not!' Jory let his hard gaze flicker to the other man at the table, who was expensively dressed in a suit and had the manner of someone with authority. He took in the women there, saw one was fairly young, and obviously the daughter of the older woman on her left, and let this attention return to Marsh. 'I just got into town. I'm Steve Jory. I came to look up my Uncle Silas, and the stableman told me he died some months ago.'

There was a chorus of surprise from those others at the table, and interest betrayed itself in their faces. Marsh himself came off the porch quickly, advancing to where Jory was standing, and the lawyer extended a soft hand.

'Am I glad to meet you, Steve! I've been making enquiries everywhere for your whereabouts! This is a stroke of luck. You've showed up just in time to save Broken J.'

'Save it?' Jory demanded. 'From what?'

'Your uncle has been dead six months, and the ranch was about to be put up for auction. What money your uncle had in his bank account paid the taxes and other running expenses of the ranch, but that money is almost exhausted, and some of the neighbouring ranchers are ready to fight each other to get their hands on Broken J. But come and meet Mortimer Dillon. He's the banker in Sunset, and can tell you exactly what the financial situation is. If you haven't eaten perhaps you'll do me the honour of dining with us. We were about to start supper.'

'Thanks, but I don't want to bust in on you. I'm feeling pretty tired. I need to get cleaned up. I'll go rent a room at the hotel and drop in to see you in the morning.'

'I won't hear of such a thing.' Marsh shook his head. He was a man in his fifties, and had the suave manner of one accustomed to winning arguments. 'Silas Jory was a good friend of mine, and I was upset when he died. No kin of his will stay in an hotel while I have a guest room empty. Please stay with us!'

The man at the table had arisen when he heard Jory's name, and now he came forward, hand outstretched. He was of the same type as Marsh, well dressed, smooth-faced, polished in manners, and with a disarming smile.

'Mortimer Dillon — Steve Jory!' Marsh introduced, and Jory shook hands with the banker.

'I'm happy to meet you, Steve,' Dillon said in booming tones, a wide smile on his face. 'This is indeed a happy chance that you have shown up. Had you heard about Silas dying?'

'Not until a few moments ago, when I reached the stable,' Jory replied. 'But like I said. Our business can wait until the morning. You folks go along with your supper and I'll get myself a room at the hotel.'

'You'll be lucky to get a room at the hotel this evening,' Marsh cut in. 'Being Saturday, the place is usually filled to overflowing. I would be most happy if you would avail yourself of my hospitality. Come and meet my wife and daughter, and Mrs. Dillon.'

Jory met the womenfolk, without putting his attention to them. He saw smiling faces but calculating eyes, and then insisted upon departing despite Marsh's effusive attempts to get him to remain.

'I've spent a lot of time in the saddle over the past two months,' Jory said finally. 'I've been alone too long. I don't feel like company, and my presence here would only dampen your pleasure. I'll come talk to you in the morning in your office.'

'If you say so, but let me go with you along the street and try to find Shorty Craille. He's the foreman of Broken J, and he'll be in town with the few men still on your payroll. You'll want to talk to Shorty. He'll tell you all about the ranch.'

'Thanks, but I can ask around for him, although it's Saturday night and he'll be in town to enjoy himself.'

'That's right. Tomorrow is Sunday. I won't be in the office,' Marsh said.

Jory grinned tightly. 'I guess I've lost all track of time on the trail,' he said. 'But there's no hurry for my business. I can look in on you Monday morning.' He hefted the saddlebags on his left shoulder. 'Except that I've got around twenty thousand dollars in these bags that I'd like to put somewhere safe.'

'Twenty thousand!' Dillon whistled softly. 'You certainly don't want to carry that around over the week-end. If you'd care to walk along to the bank with me I'll put it in my safe. If you plan to run Broken J then that money will come in mighty handy.'

'I don't have any plans right now,' Jory said. 'I don't know what kind of a shoestring spread my uncle was running around here.'

'Shoestring spread!' Marsh echoed. 'Hell, man, you can't ride across Broken J in two days. It's one of the biggest cattle spreads in the county, and already the wolves have moved in to try and grab what they can.'

'Nick, you shouldn't talk like that. You'll give Steve the wrong impression about his neighbours.'

'Is there trouble on this range?' Jory demanded harshly.

'No more than cattle ranges usually have. There's a little rustling and hoss stealing going on. Nesters get chased off and now and again a badman gets shot or lynched.' Dillon spoke softly. 'These are hard times we're living in.'

'How did my uncle die?' Jory went on sharply.

'Heart attack, so the Doc told me. Silas was ailing for a long time. He couldn't sit a horse during the last six months of his life.'

'And he died six months ago?' Jory questioned.

'About six months! He was a tough man.' Dillon took Jory's arm. 'Let's go along to the bank. I'm sure you'll excuse me, Nick. I'll be back in a few moments, but you'll agree that Steve shouldn't tote that money around with him.'

'I'd like to meet the man who can take it away from me,' Jory commented.

'You look like a man who's had a tough time making a living,' Marsh observed. 'You can take care of yourself.'

'I've managed to get along. My father died when I was a boy, and Uncle Silas didn't want to take me in. Said this place was not right for a growing youngster. An old friend of my Pa brung me up, and he died a couple of months ago. But he kept in touch with Silas Jory, and that's why I'm here now.'

'Your appearance is going to put a few noses out of joint,' Dillon said. 'But let's attend to your business, Steve. Give me ten minutes, Nick.'

'I'll entertain the ladies until you return,' Marsh promised. 'Come and look me up on Monday morning, Steve.'

'I'll surely do that,' Jory retorted, and accompanied the banker to the gate.

They walked back along the sidewalk, and Jory saw that more and more riders were coming into town. The batwings of the various saloons were working ceaselessly as men entered the establishments. Then a stocky man dressed in a brown suit and wearing a law star appeared from the mouth of an alley, and in the growing dusk he looked like a boy. But Jory saw a big Colt's .45 holstered on the lawman's hip, and the man's right hand was down by the butt of the leathered weapon.

'Ed, here's someone you'll be glad to meet,' Dillon said loudly, and the lawman turned his dark gaze upon Jory. 'This is Steve Jory, nephew of Silas Jory. Steve, here, owns Broken J now.'

'Glad to know you, Jory. I'm Sheriff Ed Conway! Your uncle was a tough but honest man, and I'm sorry he's dead. I hope you'll handle Broken J the way your uncle did.'

'Thanks!' Jory shook the hand that was extended to him. 'But I'm out of my depth right now!'

'Be seeing you later then,' the sheriff said. 'This is my busy night, and I'm a deputy short right now.'

'Ed, if you see Shorty Craille around will you tell him his new boss is in town? I'll get Steve in at the hotel, so Shorty can report to him there.'

'Not tonight,' Jory said. 'A man is entitled to his time off. I'll go out to the ranch on Monday, after I've seen Marsh again.'

The sheriff nodded and went on his way, and Jory followed Dillon to the bank. He stood gazing around while the banker unlocked the street door, then lit a lamp just inside. They entered, and Dillon counted the money in Jory's saddlebags, gave him a receipt for the amount, then unlocked the large safe and deposited the money inside.

'I'm sorry to trouble you at this time of a Saturday night,' Jory apologised as they left the bank.

'I'm available for business any time of the day or night,' came the reply. 'I expect well have to get together shortly to sort out the mess your uncle's account is in.'

'Mess?' Jory frowned as he looked into the banker's shadowed features.

'Complications might be a better word to use,' Dillon said. 'Nick Marsh has been drawing from the account since your uncle died to pay the ranch expenses. But you've inherited a sizeable ranch and a great deal of stock.'

'Well I don't need to bother myself about details right now.' Jory turned slowly to peer around the street. Night was closing in and lanterns were burning, throwing pools of brilliance into the shadows. 'I'm tired. I need to get some sleep.'

'I'll walk with you to the hotel and ensure that you get a room,' the banker offered.

'Thanks, but I can take care of myself.' Jory smiled, and saw Dillon's smooth face tighten a little.

'Then I'll look forward to seeing you when the bank opens for business on Monday morning,' Dillon said. 'It's been a pleasure meeting you, Steve. I hope you'll be happy here in Bowie County.'

'I may not stick around long enough to see all of it,' Jory commented. He turned around on the sidewalk and made his way to the hotel which stood isolated by two alleys from the other buildings in the row that fronted the main street. It was the tallest building in town and lights burned in many of its rooms. The lobby was carpeted and there were fancy drapes at the front windows. The woodwork was polished, giving the place an air of luxury, and Jory nodded as he glanced around. There was an old man standing at a reception desk, and Jory paused before him. 'I'd like a room for a few days,' he said.

The clerk looked him up and down, nodding slowly. 'You must be Steve Jory,' he said.

'Does that make any difference?' Jory countered. 'What about a room?'

'Sure, Mr Jory! Just sign the register. I guess you'll want a real good room, huh?'

'Anything will do,' Jory said. 'How'd you know me?'

'Word soon gets around, and you look a lot like your uncle!'

'I hope not! He's been dead six months,' Jory retorted, grinning at the shock which showed in the clerk's wrinkled features. He signed the register and took the key which the clerk handed to him.

'Up the stairs and it's the first door on your right,' the clerk instructed. 'Best room in the joint. It overlooks the street. But, say, there's a man in the bar would like to talk to you. Soon as he heard you had arrived he left word for me to tell him when you booked in. Can I tell him to come on up to your room?'

'Not tonight,' Jory said firmly. 'I just got into town and I'm tired. I don't wanta meet anyone or talk to anyone. You got that?'

The clerk nodded, his keen gaze taking in the two guns belted around Jory's lean hips, and there was much in Jory's manner to indicate the type of man he was. Jory turned to the stairs, and was ascending them when a voice called to him from the open doorway of the hotel bar.

'Steve Jory?'

Jory paused and turned his head to find himself looking at a tall, lean, dark-featured man dressed in good range clothes. A rancher, Jory thought as he nodded.

'Yeah, I'm Jory,' he said.

'I'm Woody Arlen. I own Box A, which makes me a neighbour of yours.' The man came to the foot of the stairs. He was wearing a sixgun on his right hip and carried his grey Stetson. 'I know you've only just got into town, but I'd like the chance to talk to you. I was a good friend of your uncle and we had made plans to get together to face the trouble we got on the range.'

'I might not be sticking around here,' Jory said instantly, 'and I'm not interested in trouble. I keep my nose out of that kind of thing.'

'If you're planning on selling up Broken J then perhaps you'll give me first offer.' There was eagerness in Arlen's tones. 'I wouldn't like to see the place fall into the wrong hands!'

'Your idea of the wrong hands might not be mine,' Jory pointed out. 'But I ain't gonna consider business until Monday at the earliest.'

'I'll be in town over the week-end. I have a room upstairs. If you feel like talking then okay. Perhaps you'd care to have supper with me and my daughter Sue!' The eagerness was obvious in Arlen's voice. He glanced past Jory and looked up the stairs. 'Ah, here's Sue now!'

Jory looked upwards, and caught his breath at sight of the woman descending the stairs towards him. She was wearing a blue dress with a hoopskirt. Her long, slender arms were bare, and she was tall and curvaceous. She had the prettiest face Jory had seen in a long time, olive-skinned, and the dark tint of her cheek bones gave an added lightness to the glint of her wide eyes. Her black hair was braided and fixed in a bun on the top of her head, held in place by a Mexican comb. Her teeth glistened as she smiled down at her father, but her gaze was upon Jory's tall figure, and Woody Arlen hastened to make an introduction.

'Glad to know you, Miss Arlen,' Jory said quickly. 'You'll forgive my appearance, I'm sure. I just got in off the trail.'

'It's a pleasure to meet you, Mr. Jory,' the girl responded, her dark eyes gleaming. 'You do look like your uncle, if I may say so.'

'I didn't know him well, hadn't seen him in years,' Jory retorted.

'Will you have supper with us?' Arlen pursued.

'Thanks, but I'm not fit to be seen in company like this. I don't have a change of clothes. I guess I'll rest up in my room over the week-end, and on Monday I'll come out and take a look around.'

'Okay, and I'll be here to see you on Monday,' Arlen said. 'But watch out for Ben Sharkey, Jory! He owns Bar S, and he'll be no friend to you if he treats you the way he treated your uncle.'

'I can look out for myself,' Jory replied, and stepped aside for the girl to pass him.

She smiled at him as she did so, and Jory caught the tang of whatever perfume she was wearing. It was heady, and for a moment his senses whirled. Then her father held out an arm to her and they departed, entering the dining room. He stared after them for a moment, half sorry that he had not accepted Arlen's invitation. But he smiled tightly and went up the stairs and let himself into his room. He had no wish to become involved with any of the locals, he told himself as he began to unbuckle his gunbelts.

His ears caught the sound of heavy footsteps in the passage outside, and a frown touched his lips when they paused outside his door. By the sounds he judged there were at least two men, and then a heavy fist smote the thick wooden door.

'Hey,' a hoarse voice bellowed. 'Steve Jory! You in there? Open up. I'm Ben Sharkey of the Bar S, and I wanta talk to you!'

Jory stiffened at the words, but it was the tone of the voice that grated upon his nerves. He recognised arrogance and contempt, and without seeing Sharkey he could guess at the man's character. The Bar S rancher was the type who rode roughshod over anyone and anything in his way, and was accustomed to getting what he wanted. Jory smiled thinly as he moved towards the door, his right-hand gun still holstered on his hip. He paused a couple of feet from the door and suppressed a sigh as he replied.

'I'm Jory,' he said. 'But I'm not opening up for you or anyone tonight, Sharkey! I'm tired and I'm turning in.'

He heard a low muttering outside, and then the stamping of booted feet. The next instant the door shuddered and crashed open, almost hitting Jory in the face, and a big man came blundering into the room. Jory's reactions were razor sharp and he swayed sideways, moving the upper part of his body only, and the blundering man who had shouldered open the door went staggering past towards the bed. There were two other men outside. One was evidently Ben Sharkey, a massive figure in a gaudy red shirt that was stretched across a barrel chest and wide shoulders. A gleaming cartridge belt was buckled around a paunch, and grey eyes glittered as they surveyed Jory. Hatless, the rancher exhibited a mass of greasy yellow hair that was bunched at the nape of his neck and thick around his ears.

The other man in the doorway had a tall, angular figure dressed in a store suit, and he was wearing two black-handled .45's which were tied low on his thighs. His pale eyes glinted from under the brim of a flat crowned plains hat.

'I'm Ben Sharkey,' the bigger man rasped angrily, 'and nobody says no to me. I didn't even send my boys to bring you to me, Jory. I came to you.'

Jory turned his head and looked at the third man, who had finished his charge at the door on his knees by the bed. He was scrambling up now, a tall, heavy redhead with a shaggy moustache that covered a great deal of his mouth. His eyes were a pale green colour and there was a contemptuous grin on his heavy features. He was wearing a Remington. 44, butt forwards, on his left hip.

'I'm Steve Jory.' A spurt of anger flared through Jory as the redhead came back towards the door, and when the man was within reach Jory lifted his left hand and grabbed a handful of the man's shirt. Moving his feet quickly, Jory went to the right, swinging the redhead around. Then he bunched his right hand into a fist and slammed his hard knuckles against the redhead's stubbled jaw. At the same time, Jory thrust the man backwards through the doorway, where he collided with Sharkey and the gunman. All three went sprawling across the passage to crash against the opposite wall. Jory moved into the doorway, his right hand down at his side, the butt of his gun touching the inside of his wrist. 'Nobody busts into my room when I say I'm going to bed,' he rasped. 'Get to hell out've here, Sharkey.'

The trio staggered, and the gunman went down on the bare boards. But the redhead was out cold, and slumped into Sharkey's heavy arms. For a moment the Bar S rancher held his man, then released him and let him fall to the floor. Jory's dark eyes were glittering, his lips pinched as he fought to control his anger. The gunman on the floor was pushing himself into a sitting position, and his right hand suddenly streaked towards the butt of his gun. Jory tightened his lips, let the man almost clear leather before making a move, then drew his Peacemaker with a flick of his right hand. The big gun came out of leather and levelled, then blasted as Jory squeezed the trigger. The crash of the shot seemed to rock the hotel, and a plume of gunsmoke billowed in the doorway.

Jory had aimed for the man's right shoulder, and he saw the hole that sprang into the cloth of the man's jacket. The impact of the heavy bullet slammed the gunman back against the wall, and he jerked and twisted, to fall upon his face on the bare boards. Then Jory transferred his attention to Ben Sharkey, and the big man was instinctively reaching for the handle of his holstered gun.

'Go ahead and try it,' Jory said through his teeth. 'That's if you wanta have a funeral tomorrow!'

He stood breathing heavily, his feet apart, his pulses racing, and the excitement of the action warned him that since Hank Penner's death he had missed the thrilling suspense of life and death situations. But it seemed that he had walked into one right here in Bowie County and he meant to follow it up to its lethal end.

Three

Ben Sharkey was paralysed with shock as he stared down into the black muzzle of Jory's big .45. At his feet his bully-boy, Buster Pollard, was stretched out cold by a single punch, and to his left his top gunhand, Lou Bragg, was on his face, groaning with a bullet in him. Sharkey stared at Jory's tall, powerful figure, and saw a lot of the indomitable Silas Jory in this nephew who had arrived to put a spoke in the wheel of all Sharkey's selfish plans. Sharkey lifted his hand from the butt of his gun and drew a quick breath. He was a man who had fought his way to the top with ruthless efficiency and callous indifference. He had bought what he had to and stolen what he could. There were dead men on his back trail, and some of them had gone out with a bullet in the back. It was all the same to Sharkey. He was big and tough and did not know the meaning of fear. But for a moment he was staring death right between the eyes, and he could tell by Jory's impassive features that here was a man who had seen it all before and could handle it.

'I don't like you, Sharkey,' Jory said thinly, his ears still ringing from the crash of the shot. Gunsmoke was raspy in his throat. 'If you treat folks around here like you tried to handle me then I guess they deserve all they get. But you made a big mistake trying to stomp me. Now you better get those two polecats out've here, before I really lose my temper and do something you might be sorry for.'

Sharkey took a grip upon his temper and glanced to left and right. He saw scared faces peering out of doorways at the scene in the passage, and realised that his hard reputation had suddenly been seriously dented by this apparently tough stranger. His cunning mind flitted over the possibilities, but he saw no way out of this other than backing down, and that he tried to do, but with ill-grace.

'Okay, Jory,' he rasped heavily. 'So I made a mistake busting in on you. But I'm a mighty concerned man, and I needed to talk to you before anybody else could get to you. I heard you was here in town and I've been aiming to buy Broken J for a long time. I need that ranch because I'm expanding, and I'm the only cattleman in the county who can afford to do so. Look, you name any price you want for the spread and I'll pay it.'

'I don't do business like that,' Jory retorted. 'I ain't even seen the place yet. Get to hell out've here and stay out of my way. I don't like a grabber, and if you try strong-arm tactics around me again I'll put a bullet through you where you can't digest it.'

Boots thumped the boards of the passage and a big figure moved towards the doorway. Tory let his glance flicker to the right and he saw a law star pinned to the newcomer's lapel. He holstered his gun instantly and stood with his right hand down at his side. Gunsmoke seemed to linger in his nostrils, and he exhaled sharply to get rid of it.

'What in hell is going on here?' the newcomer demanded in grating tones. He was in his early twenties, a powerful, muscular youngster with dark features and brown eyes. His nose was hooked, had been broken, and his jaw was long, his chin prominent. There was an officious note in his tones, and his words were directed at Jory.

'You could call it a misunderstanding,' Jory said.

'Sharkey, here, figured I could be bullied like everyone else around here. He probably bullied my uncle before the old man died. But here's one man who can't be bullied, and I figure I've impressed that upon him. I reckon the whole county will realise it when word of this gets out.'

Sharkey's heavy face showed a flash of blind rage before the rancher managed to control himself. He looked at the deputy and spoke in placating tones.

'It's okay, Brad. It was a misunderstanding. I guess I'm a hard man and Jory didn't take it the way I intended.'

'You're Jory?' The deputy studied Jory's powerful figure. 'It's about time you showed up. The county has gone down since your uncle died and all the ranchers have been trying to snatch a piece of Broken J for themselves.'

'You talk like it was my fault I didn't show up earlier,' Jory said. 'I didn't know my uncle was dead until I hit town. Now perhaps you'll get these skunks out've here and let me have some peace.'

Another man came forward, a short, fleshy cowboy dressed in his Saturday night clothes, his fair hair slicked down with some kind of pungent hair-oil. He was wearing a holstered sixgun on his right hip, and his hand was close to the butt as he paused at the deputy's side. He had homely features, an open expression, and there was concern in his blue eyes as he looked around. His gaze flitted from Sharkey to the two men on the floor. Then he looked at Jory, and a grin broke out on his fleshy lips.

'I don't need to ask if you're my new boss,' he said cheerfully. 'I can tell you're a Jory. I'm Shortie Craille. I'm foreman out at Broken J. I did a good job for your uncle while he was alive, and I been doing my best to hold the place together since he died.'

Jory studied the foreman, and decided he liked the look of Craille. He held out his hand.

'Glad to know you, Shorty,' he said softly, ignoring Sharkey and the deputy. 'Come on in and let's have a talk. I guess you're the only man around here I wanta see before Monday morning.' He stepped aside and Craille entered the room. Then he looked at Sharkey, and his expression had changed imperceptibly. His eyes were cold and filled with a chill expression. 'Sharkey, if I never see you again it'll be too soon,' he said slowly. 'I don't like your manner, and you better not make the mistake of tangling with me again. If I do plan on selling Broken J then you can bet your bottom dollar I won't let it go to you.' His gaze flitted to the watchful deputy's face. 'Seems to me the law should keep a tighter rein on men like Sharkey,' he commented. 'Howcome he's allowed to stomp around town like he owned it?'

The deputy's heavy face showed surprise, and a flush came to his tanned cheeks. But he thinned his lips and turned angrily to shout at the gathering crowd in the passage. Jory looked down at the groaning gunman and the big man now sitting up and shaking his head.

'Sharkey, if these pet skunks of yours come sniffing around me again I'll kill 'em,' he promised, and stepped backwards into the room and slammed the door. He put the back of a chair under the door handle to keep the door shut, and turned to face the beaming Broken J foreman.

'Jeez!' Shorty Craille said in high pitched tones. 'I never thought I'd see the day when Ben Sharkey was treated like a maverick. And Bragg and Pollard put down. Hell, I knowed the Jory family was tough. Your Uncle Silas was a helluva man, even to work for. And I heard him talk about your Pa, and some of your doings down in Texas. But you're even bigger and better than he gave you credit for, Boss. You bested the two best men Ben Sharkey's got on his payroll.'

'I took'em by surprise,' Jory said. 'They figured I was a push-over. Next time they'll handle it different.'

'Next time? You know there's gonna be trouble?' Craille shook his head. 'I wish I could give you a good report of what's been happening, but you've been landed with a hatful of problems, Boss.'

'That much I guessed, after talking to Arlen and meeting Ben Sharkey. But Sharkey ain't gonna bother me none. If he tries to get tough with me I'll kill him.'

Craille frowned, shaking his head. 'Sharkey's got a real salty crew on Bar S,' he said. 'There's a score of 'em. The law can't do much about them. Ben Sharkey has got too much power. He's bullied every rancher in the county, run out a lot of the smaller cattlemen, and tried every trick he could think of to pull down Broken J. I figure it was Sharkey's tricks to get hold of Broken J that put your uncle in his grave.'

Jory threw a quick glance at the fat cowboy's expressive face. He breathed heavily.

'Was my uncle bullied by Bar E?' he demanded.

'Huh, that wouldn't have succeeded in a hundred years,' Craille retorted. 'Silas Jory couldn't be bullied. But Sharkey tried everything in the book short of that.'

'What did Silas die of?' Jory asked.

'Overwork and a bad heart.'

'He was over sixty. I guess he had a good life.' There was no gentleness in Jory's tones. 'I hated the old bastard, although I never knew him, and only saw him a couple of times when I was a kid. When my Pa died Silas wouldn't give me a home here. I was left to fend for myself.'

'He would have had you on Broken J any time in the past five years,' Craille said defensively.

'Mebbe, but only because I'd growed up and might have been some use to him.' Bitterness sounded in Jory's tones. 'The hell with him. He had no use for me and I got along without him. Anyway, he's dead now, finished, and I'm saddled with his problems.'

'You planning on running Broken J or will you sell out?' Craille demanded.

'I don't know what I'm gonna do. I need to look over the situation before I make up my mind. I've been a gunslinger for a long time, fighting the battles of other men, drawing gun wages, and I'm sick of it and tired of the whole damn business. I don't want to walk into gun trouble around here. I got plenty of dough of my own, and I'll sell Broken J for what I can get for it.'

'Ben Sharkey will get it,' Craille said.

'No he won't! I don't like Ben Sharkey! He's a bully. He's got no respect for anyone or anything that ain't carrying his brand. I've come up against his kind a lot of times. One thing I will do is see that Sharkey don't get what he wants this time.'

'If you sell out to anyone else, Sharkey will bide his time, and get Broken J after you've pulled out,' Craille said. 'That's the way he works. In the last five years he's forced out our neighbours on three sides of Broken J. If Woody Arlen quit we'd be completely surrounded by Sharkey's range. Sharkey has been putting a lot of pressure on Arlen, but Arlen won't budge. He's another man like your uncle was.'

'Yeah,' Jory said thoughtfully. 'Arlen spoke to me. He wanted first chance to buy Broken J if I planned on selling.' He pictured Arlen's daughter, and could almost smell the perfume the girl had been wearing. 'But this is Saturday night, Shorty, and you're in town to enjoy yourself. Me, I'm turning in. I've had a hard time of it lately. I'll be out to the ranch sometime on Monday. I wanta talk to the lawyer and the banker again before I make any decision. Now you get out of here, and don't answer any questions about me should you get asked.'

'You can trust me, Boss,' Craille said, moving to the door. 'I figure you're gonna liven things up around here, and no mistake. But watch your step. Ben Sharkey ain't the kind of man you can say no to, or get the better of. Watch out for yourself.'

'I've been watching out for myself for as long as I can recall.' Jory retorted, removing the chair from the door and letting the foreman out. 'Be seeing you, Shorty!'

The foreman departed and Jory replaced the chair, then went to the bed and dropped down upon it, his face showing a thoughtful expression. But it was the face of Sue Arlen that intruded most into his mind, and when he finally slumbered the girl was still uppermost in his thoughts …

Sunday was a quiet day for Jory. He took his meals in the dining room, going down late to avoid meeting anyone who might want to talk, and he spent the rest of the time in his room, thinking about his future, reliving some of his past, and attempting to settle his feelings about what should be done. The incident involving the two hardcases and Ben Sharkey had warned him that there would be trouble if he stayed in Bowie County. But that threat left him unmoved, for he had lived in the midst of such situations for almost as long as he could remember. But he could not forget Hank Penner's last words, and there was a strange reluctance in him to join any local issues that would bring him face to face with gun muzzles. But such was his nature and character that he could not face the thought of being forced out by circumstances. He finally decided, after much soul-searching, to look over the Broken J ranch before making up his mind about any of the questions looming in his mind.

On Monday morning he was up at daybreak, and after cleaning his guns and buckling them about his waist he went down to the dining room to eat breakfast. There he came face to face with Woody Arlen, and the Box A rancher was not accompanied by his daughter. There was a twinkle in Arlen's dark eyes as he greeted Jory, and Jory, hoping to see the girl again, invited Arlen to sit at his table. The Box A rancher sat down with alacrity, leaning forward to peer into Jory's harshly set face.

'Let me say how much I regret missing the sight of you teaching Sharkey a lesson,' Arlen said. 'I would have given half my spread to have seen it.' He grinned. 'Sharkey won't have the gall to show his face around town for a long time.'

'I think he's got enough gall to do anything,' Jory replied.

Arlen sobered a little, stared into Jory's impassive face for a moment, then nodded slowly. 'I'm afraid you're right,' he finally agreed. 'But you sure took him down a peg or two, which is what was needed. He got a lot too big for his britches. Pity you didn't hit him! Or shot him! That would have been better. But I heard tell you put Buster Pollard out cold with one punch, then beat Lou Bragg to the draw and bored his shoulder. You're something out of the ordinary, Jory, and that's a fact. But so was your Uncle Silas! He never let the grass grow under his feet!'

Jory resumed eating his breakfast. He studied Arlen's face for a moment, and the rancher gazed back at him.

'Are you planning to sell out, Arlen?' Jory suddenly demanded.

'To Sharkey?' Arlen smiled as he shook his head. 'Not on your life. Are you?'१

'Sharkey owns the range on three sides of Broken J, so Shorty Craille told me. I could be in trouble if you sold out.'

'Shorty is a good rangeman, and he's done your spread just fine. Nope, I ain't gonna sell out. The only buyer around here is Ben Sharkey, and I wouldn't sell him anything I didn't want. But to set your mind at rest I'll make a deal with you. If I ever figure on selling out I'll give you first offer to buy, if you'll shake on the same terms for me.'

'You've got a deal,' Jory said without hesitation, and extended his hand. They shook, and looked into one another's eyes. 'You got first chance of Broken J if I do sell,' Jory went on. 'But I'm going out there to look the place over. Before I came into the county I was thinking of buying a cow spread. Now I find I got a ready-made one. It's a lot bigger than I reckoned, from what I've been told. I didn't know Silas made such a big success of his business.'

'Maybe you'll drop over to Box A after you've had the chance to look around,' Arlen said. 'Me and my daughter would be real glad to see you.'

'Thanks. Give me a week to settle down, and mebbe you'll call on me sometime.'

'Be glad to.' Arlen nodded eagerly. 'If I can't buy you out then we've got to get together and stand side by side against the trouble around here.'

'Tell me about it,' Jory invited, drinking his coffee.

'Sharkey's outfit is behind it,' Arlen said firmly.

'You got proof of that?'

'Nope, or I would have done something about it. The law is pretty good around here. Ed Conway wouldn't let Sharkey get away with anything, you can bet. But nobody else around here is trying to hog the range. If you figure on staying in the county then you got to be prepared to do some more punching and shooting.'

'I don't figure to take sides in any range war,' Jory said. 'All I'm interested in is living a quiet life, and I'll shoot anyone trying to change my ideas. I've had a tough life until a couple of months ago. Now I wanta settle down.'

'Walking around with those two guns strapped around your middle won't give anyone the impression that you're a peace-loving man,' Arlen pointed out.

'I wouldn't leave my room without them,' Jory retorted. 'They're a part of me, and they're strictly for defence.' He sighed as he got to his feet. 'Well I got some business to attend to this morning. See you around, Arlen!'

'I hope I see you around for a long time to come,' the Box A rancher replied.

Jory left the hotel and paused on the sidewalk to look around the street. Monday morning was a quiet time in Sunset, although there were some saddle horses standing at hitchrails, and a buggy was already drawn up in front of the store. Looking down at his travel stained clothes, Jory started towards the store, and had to pass the law office to reach it. The door of the Sheriff's Office stood open, and Ed Conway thrust his stocky figure into the opening as Jory reached.

'Morning, Jory,' the sheriff greeted. 'Got a minute?'

'Always got time for the law,' Jory responded, pausing to face the sheriff. 'What's on your mind?'

'Just like to get your side of what happened in the hotel on Saturday night,' Conway said in a steady tones. His face was sober, but there was a gleam in his dark gaze.

'Three men busted into my room and I threw them out,' Jory replied, smiling thinly at the memory.

'Just like that, huh?' Conway nodded slowly. His voice was unemotional. 'You didn't know those three men were Ben Sharkey and two of the toughest bullies in the county.'

'I didn't know at the time, but it wouldn't have made any difference if I had known.' Jory was still smiling. 'Nobody pushes me around and gets away with it.'

'You don't figure you can fight the whole Bar S crew, do you?'

'I don't reckon I have to. If anyone riding for Bar S makes a play for me after this I'll go straight to Sharkey to settle it. He pays the wages, so he's the man I'll settle with.'

'You could spark off a range war!' Conway warned.

'Nope!' Jory shook his head emphatically. 'I could stop one flaring up, and I will if I have to. But don't try to put the blame on me for Sharkey's intentions. He wants me to sell Broken J to him. If I don't sell I reckon there'll be trouble. Well I'm not selling to keep the peace. That's your job around here. If I have any trouble I know how to handle it. That's all I got to say about it.'

'And you're right, at that!' Conway said. He smiled then, nodding slowly. 'I'd have given a month's wages just to seen what you did. Sharkey's bunch have had it all their own way around here for a long time. They allus stopped short of actually breaking the law, and men have been too scared to fight back. Not that I blame them. But you're something out of the ordinary, Jory, and I figure you might have given Ben Sharkey just the kind of a shock he needed to pull him up short. I hope it's worked that way. If he doesn't haul on his reins then there will be a lot of bloodshed on this range, and I can't do a damn thing about it until it starts.'

'I know that.' Jory glanced around the street. 'I've been in a range war or two, and I know what it's all about. But whatever comes up around here, you can bet that I'm on the side of law and order.'

Conway nodded. 'I wish you luck,' he said, as Jory went on his way.

Jory bought a new suit at the store, and a couple of shirts.

He also purchased some .45 and 44.40 cartridges. Then he went on his way, intending to call first upon the lawyer, Nick Marsh, and afterwards to see the banker, Mortimer Dillon.

He was on the sidewalk, making for the lawyer's office, when he felt an old familiar prickling sensation between his shoulder blades. He turned instantly, stepping into the mouth of a near-by alley, and his right hand dropped to the butt of his gun. As he did so a gun blasted from somewhere across the street, and a heavy .45 slug tore into the thick boards by his left shoulder. His instinctive action saved his life in the first instance, and he ducked back into cover as he drew his right-hand gun. He returned fire immediately, aiming for the two indistinct figures in an alley opposite, and his teeth were clenched, for this had come a lot sooner than he expected.

Four

The crashing blasts of sixgun fire ripped apart the heavy silence that hung over the town, and harsh echoes fled into every dusty corner. Through slitted eyes Jory saw the two men opposite, wreathed in gunsmoke, crouching back in the cover of an alley mouth, and he heard the ripping impact of their bullets striking around him. He returned fire instinctively, but in the back of his mind was the fear that some innocent bystander would get hit by a ricocheting slug.

Then another weapon joined in the shooting, and Jory recognised the flatter crack of a rifle. A string of shots hammered hard on the booming detonations of Colt-fire, but the rifle slugs were not directed at him. He saw with sudden amazement his two ambushers crumple into the dust, and the shooting that accounted for them seemed to come from Jory's right, from the roof of a building. But echoes trapped in the alley where he was crouched baffled his ears, and he waited, gun cocked, muzzle uplifted, while he awaited further developments.

As the echoes of the shooting died away the stocky figure of Ed Conway appeared in the street, making for the alley mouth, a gun in his hand. The sheriff was followed by the big deputy Jory had seen in the hotel on Saturday night. Heaving a long sigh, Jory straightened and moved out of his cover, looking up at the buildings on his right, and he spotted a big figure standing on the edge of the roof of the Mercantile, a rifle in his hands.

Jory ventured out to the street, and the sun was hot upon his shoulders as he walked across to where the sheriff and his deputy were bent over the two motionless figures stretched out in the alley. Conway straightened as Jory reached the spot. Townsmen were beginning to run towards them. The little lawman's face was set in harsh lines. He nodded slowly as he met Jory's level gaze, then turned and waved a small hand to the man on the rooftop opposite.

'Both dead,' Conway commented. 'Good thing I half expected something like this and put one of my deputies to watch out for your back. That's Chuck Reed up there on the roof, and this is Brad Terrill here.'

Jory's face showed his surprise, and a tight grin came to the sheriff's face.

'I'm sure glad you did figure this out, Sheriff,' Jory said slowly. His judgement of the little lawman was changing drastically. 'I would have got these two jiggers in another moment, but I was scared someone on the street might have been hit by a stray slug.'

'That's what we've got to guard against,' Conway agreed. 'That's why I'll be glad when you've gone out to Broken J, Jory —'

'I understand, and I'll be leaving town soon as I've seen the lawyer and the banker. Jory glanced down at the two dead men. 'You know either of them?' he demanded.

'Nope! They're strangers around here.' Conway's tones were decisive. 'Looks like they've been brought in for a particular job.'

'To knock me off!' Jory grinned tightly. 'So far I get the impression that Sharkey is the only man who really wants me out of the way.'

'They could be on Sharkey's payroll, and we'll check on that,' Conway said. He turned to his deputy. 'Brad, you saddle up and ride to Bar S. Talk to Sharkey. Warn him to pull in his horns. I'll check around town and find out when these two rode in and where they came from.'

The big deputy nodded and departed. Jory glanced around the street. He caught a whiff of gunsmoke and wrinkled his nose against its acrid bite. He saw curiosity upon the faces of the men pushing closer, and their attention was divided between himself and the dead men. Then the other deputy arrived, his rifle still in his hands. He came pushing through the crowd, grinning wolfishly when he paused to peer down at the two corpses. He looked at the blood splotches on the chests of the men and shook his rifle.

'This damn rifle is shooting a trifle high,' he commented, then turned to look into Jory's face. 'Howdy, Jory! I had you covered from the minute you stepped out've the hotel.'

'Thanks,' Jory replied. 'I'm grateful. You saved my life.'

'I saw them two hombres watching the street about the time you went into the store,' Chuck Reed said. 'I figured they was laying for you. I guess you've got this deal figured out, Sheriff! Good thing I was up there on the roof. But now what?'

'Jory is heading out to Broken J after he's settled some business here in town. I want you to ride at his back, Chuck, and watch him for a day or two. He's raised hell with Sharkey, and we all know Sharkey well enough to know that he won't take that lying down.'

'Pity about Sharkey,' Jory commented. 'The next time I tangle with him I'll kill him.'

'I guess you could do that!' the sheriff commented, 'and you got the right to defend your own life, but I hope you're gonna let the law handle this trouble.'

'Sure!' Jory nodded instantly. 'I'm all for law and order. I'll give you a chance to stop this. But I'm not gonna hold back if I get attacked.'

'I wouldn't ask you to.' Conway nodded. 'Okay, you get your business settled around here and then go out to Broken J. That way we might avoid a lot of bloodshed. You've got a crew out there who can take care of themselves, and your foreman, Shorty Craille, is a good man. Stay out on the range for a spell. If Sharkey is after you then he won't wait long before making his try. We'll be ready for him.'

'I'll go along with that!' Jory nodded. He grinned at the watchful deputy once more. 'I'm going to see Nick Marsh first, then Dillon over in the bank. After that I'll be riding out.'

'I'll tail you right into your own back yard,' the deputy said. He was a hard-bitten type with cold blue eyes and a grim manner. 'I hope Sharkey does try something now. We've been trying to put down his crew for a long time without success. Looks like you're a fuze, Jory. This whole county has been sitting on a powder keg for a long time, and you've come along and set light to it.'

'I'm sorry about that,' Jory retorted.

'It ain't your fault, and I'm glad it's happening,' Conway cut in. 'It's got to boil over, and now is as good a time as any. So far no one has got hurt, apart from hardcases, and if we can limit it so much the better.'

'I'll see you around,' Jory said, and heaved a long sigh as he turned away.

He pushed through the crowd and went on to the lawyer's office. When he glanced over his shoulder he saw Chuck Reed at his back, his deadly rifle held in the crook of his right arm. Jory shook his head. The two dead men were being lifted and carried out of the alley. It was a sign of what was to come, Jory told himself, and entered the lawyer's outer office.

Nick Marsh was in an inner office with the door open, and when he heard Jory's boots thudding on the bare boards he called out an invitation to enter his inner sanctum. When Marsh looked up from some papers on his desk and saw it was Jory he got to his feet immediately and came around the desk with outstretched hand.

'I hope that shooting didn't involve you,' the lawyer said, his dark eyes gleaming. 'Come and sit down. I've been going over the accounts for Broken J, and, of course, the will that your uncle made some years ago.'

'You're not interested enough in the shooting to find out what it was all about?' Jory demanded. 'Hell, I thought I was cold blooded about that sort of thing.'

Marsh smiled thinly. 'If someone's got a murder charge against him then I'll probably be called in to prosecute or defend him. I'll learn all about it then. But right now I got too much work on my hands to afford time running out to the street every time someone fires a gun. Sit down! Is it too early for you to have a drink?'

'Yeah, I don't drink much. In the line of business I've been carrying on these past few years a man who drinks usually dies pretty quick. Let's get down to business so I can get out of town. I don't mind fighting off a few hardcases, but not around here, where innocent folks might get hurt.'

'Admirable sentiments,' Marsh said. 'Did you have a talk with Mort Dillon on Saturday evening?'

'He just told me the accounts for Broken J are a bit complicated,' Jory said. He looked into the lawyer's dark eyes. 'He used the word mess at first. What did he mean?'

'There's no trouble, and your uncle left you a considerable property. Rustlers have been nibbling away at the stock on the ranch, but then every rancher in the county has had his losses over the past few years. Let's get down to the will Silas Jory left. I don't have much to tell you except that everything Silas had in this world passes over to you.' Marsh looked up from the documents before him. 'I suppose you can prove beyond all reasonable doubt that you really are Steve Jory!'

'I can.' Jory nodded. 'Let's get down to figures, shall we? What kind of a cattle spread is Broken J? How many head of cattle are being run on it? What money is in the ranch bank account?'

'Broken J is measured in miles, not acres,' Marsh said. 'At the last count there were seventeen thousand head of cattle on the range. I can't give you an accurate figure of the balance in the ranch bank account because there are some outstanding bills to be paid. But I figure, at a rough estimate, that you've got some fifty thousand dollars to your credit.'

Jory's brown eyes narrowed as he listened. He had not known that his uncle was so successful. He shook his head slowly as he thought about it.

'Since your uncle's death the wolves have been howling around Broken J,' Marsh said, breaking into Jory's thoughts. 'It's always the same. Some of your neighbours are trying to steal themselves a piece of the spread. But a strong man like you will soon put a stop to that. Silas Jory ran the spread with an iron hand. He kept out the nesters and he hanged rustlers where ever he caught them. A man like that can keep what is his. You're going to have to be as strong and ruthless or you'll be robbed of every last cow, acre and dollar.'

'Don't worry about that,' Jory said tightly. 'Nobody is gonna get away with anything. But you'll need to check on my origins before we go any further. You can get in touch with the sheriff of James County, Missouri, which is where I was born. There'll be folks there who will remember me. I've got a scar on my left shoulder which I picked up in a fire that nearly killed me. If old Doc Evans is still alive then he'll give you a physical description if you need it. Apart from that I got in my possession some letters Uncle Silas wrote to Hank Penner, who brought me up after my own father died. You can see them.'

'Fine,' Marsh commented. 'I'll need to run a check on you, but I'm quite satisfied that you are Steve Jory, and I suggest you go on out to Broken J and take up residence while I make these enquiries. You won't be able to touch any of the money in the ranch account until your identity has been officially established, but you said you have some money of your own. I don't see any problems arising to trouble you, apart from those stemming from the local situation. I heard what happened between you and Ben Sharkey on Saturday night. No doubt others have warned you against Sharkey, so all I can do is tell you to be on your guard.'

'I'm on my toes,' Jory said.

Marsh smiled and got to his feet, coming around the desk with extended hand.

'I wish you luck,' he said. 'I have the feeling you're going to need it. If you find any problems arising then don't hesitate to call on me or send for me. You can rest assured that we have a good, efficient law department in this county, and I don't think this bad patch will last much longer. Now you've turned up matters should come to a head. Then Ed Conway will pounce. A number of men around here have been pushing their luck for some time, but they're getting to the end of their rope now.'

Jory nodded as he shook hands. 'Thanks,' he said briefly. 'I shall be riding out to Broken J now. Will you give me directions for reaching it?'

'Come and take a look at this map.' Marsh turned to a large-scale map of the county, and his long forefinger traced out the trail Jory would have to take to reach his new home.

Jory studied the map, impressing details on his mind, and then he departed, with Marsh's good wishes ringing in his ears. He did not bother to see Mortimer Dillon, for he would have to prove his identity before he could handle the financial side of the Broken J. But he had enough money of his own and was not concerned. He went along the street, aware that he was being tailed by the deputy, Chuck Reed, and entered the stable. He quickly saddled his bay and led Hank Penner's black out of the stable. When he mounted to take the trail north he saw a number of townsfolk standing on the sidewalk to watch his departure.

There was a strange sense of uneasiness in the back of Jory's mind as he rode the trail north. The odds against him did not count. He and Hank Penner had always faced tremendous odds. That was why they had drawn such high gun wages. But now he was sorely missing his old pard, and his dark eyes glittered as he let the bay run for the first mile or so.

He glanced around as he rode, and spotted the figure that was trailing him. The local law was on its toes. He smiled fleetingly at the thought, for he did not need help to fight his wars. Then his face sobered, for there was dust on the trail ahead and he spotted five riders coming towards him along the trail. He kept riding easily, Penner's black cantering obediently at his left side, its reins tied to his saddle horn. He glanced at the gunbelt suspended from the black's saddle, and a sigh tremored through him for now more than ever he could do with Penner's backing and experience.

When the riders drew closer Jory recognised the foremost of them as Ben Sharkey, and alertness filtered through him, stiffening his musles and bringing his mind to concentrate upon the probable outcome of this meeting. He held his reins in his left hand, and kept his right hand on his thigh. He had spotted Sharkey and his riders before they saw him, and noted that when Sharkey did eventually recognise him the Bar S rancher twisted in his saddle and called urgently to his followers.

Moments later Sharkey was reining up in the centre of the trail, his four men halting behind him. They sat in a cloud of slowly rising dust, facing Jory, who continued until he reached the group. Reining in, Jory faced Sharkey with impassive features, although his eyes were glinting. He saw that the men with Sharkey were hardcases. Lou Bragg was one of them, his right arm in a sling, and another was Buster Pollard, his heavy figure stiff in the saddle, his fleshy face showing hatred and a desire for the chance to take up the fight where it had ended so disastrously for him on Saturday night in the hotel.

'So you're riding out to Broken J,' Sharkey commented harshly.

'Unless you're figuring on trying to stop me,' Jory retorted. He smiled as he saw the two unknown gunnies at Sharkey's back drop their hands to the butts of their holstered guns. 'You better warn your men that I'm in no mood for half measures today, Sharkey,' he said in the same even tones. 'Bragg was lucky I didn't plug him dead centre on Saturday. I don't usually let a man off the hook when he makes a play for me. But I was a stranger in a strange place, and I gave him the benefit of the doubt. That's over and done with now. Anyone trying to trade lead with me will get a bullet smack through the middle.'

'So you're a hardcase!' Sharkey's hoarse voice was edgy. 'I guess I made a mistake about you. I was keen to get Broken J off you. I know other ranchers around here have the same idea, so I figured to get in first.'

'And you tried to bully me into selling to you.' Jory chuckled harshly. 'Too bad I ain't the type who can take that kind of thing. You made a wrong play, Sharkey, and now I wouldn't sell to you even if I planned to sell out.'

'I'll give you a better price than anyone else around here can pay,' Sharkey growled. He was making an effort not to lose his temper, but his control was shaky.

'You couldn't get the place for a million dollars,' Jory told him.

'Howcome you're setting yourself up against me?' Sharkey demanded. 'You didn't come off worst in that encounter we had on Saturday.'

'What happened on Saturday don't concern me none. I guess two of your men are more worried about that.' Jory grinned as he let his sharp gaze flicker to Bragg and Pollard. He saw Bragg stiffen, and noted that the gunman was wearing his holster on the left. Pollard scowled heavily, and his big hands clenched into ham-like fists as he gripped his reins tighter. Then Jory changed expression, and he leaned forward in his saddle, holding Sharkey's gaze. 'But what does get to me is the fact that I was ambushed in town this morning by a couple of strangers no one had ever seen around before. So it looks like they were brought in specially to nail me.'

'You accusing me of handling that?' Sharkey demanded. 'I don't make accusations,' Jory went on. 'I got no way of getting at the truth of what was behind that attack. If I figured for certain you knew about it or paid those men to kill me I wouldn't waste time making accusations. I would have come out to your place and put a bullet through you!' Jory's steely tones cut through the tense atmosphere. He saw Sharkey's heavy face harden, and for a moment there was pure rage shining in the big man's pale eyes.

'Hell, I don't take that kind of talk from anyone,' the Bar S rancher said in a rasping voice.

'You're getting it from me,' Jory went on calmly. 'You figure you're the big wheel in this county, huh? That's okay by me, so long as you don't try to step on my toes. I know a lot about you, Sharkey, by the way you busted into my hotel room on Saturday. Mebbe you can bluster your way around the county and bully other men, but I ain't the type. You want trouble then you can have it. I've lived on that kind of thing since I was old enough to hold a gun. But I'll tell you this much. If you want a fight then you've got to do your own fighting. I ain't gonna stand still and let your pet bullies come at me. If anyone tries for me again and I figure you're behind it, I'll come for you. That's the way I stand. Now if you got any plans to take my spread over by force then make your play now. Let's get it settled. You're wearing a gun. Pull it and make like you're a man.'

Sharkey looked as if he had been struck dumb. He spluttered in anger. His eyes glared and his lips were pulled tightly against his teeth, making his mouth look like a steel trap. Jory sat easy in his saddle, unmoving, his tanned features impassive, and waited for developments. But it was Buster Pollard who broke the silence.

'Why, you damn, swaggering polecat,' the big man declared angrily. 'Who in hell do you figure you're talking to? You reckon you can take on the whole damn Bar S outfit? Nobody is gonna talk to my boss like that while I'm around!'

'You make more hot air than a pot-bellied stove!' Jory replied, smiling thinly. 'But you sound like you didn't learn anything from our meeting on Saturday. I'll bet Bragg wouldn't try to reach for his gun against me unless my back was turned towards him.' He saw the gunman scowl, but Bragg remained silent, the memory of Jory's swift draw beating his own fast play a nightmare in the back of his mind.

'Climb out've your saddle and I'll show you a thing or two!' Pollard rasped, making as if to dismount.

'Guns have been used,' Jory snapped. 'Bragg started that play on Saturday, and it continued this morning. I'm not going back to fists. And I don't figure to fight the whole of the outfit. When I pull my gun again it'll be aiming at Sharkey himself.'

'This talk is getting us nowhere,' Sharkey said, making an effort to control himself. 'I admitted I made a mistake by busting into your hotel room. Okay, so let it lay there. My boys came off worst in that. But I didn't set any gunnies onto you today, and I ain't likely to try. I don't fight that way. I'm interested in getting Broken J under my brand, but if you ain't planning on selling out then that's the end of it. You settle down on the spread and try and make it pay.'

Jory nodded and touched spurs to his mount. He rode at a small gap between Bragg and Pollard, and Bragg had to wheel his mount aside to avoid being run down. Pollard cursed and reached out for Jory, his right hand clenched into a big fist. Jory, aware that any trouble which might come from this meeting would certainly come from Pollard, was ready for it, and canted his head to the left, causing Pollard's fist to skim past his right ear. At the same time he drew his right-hand gun, and the weapon was cocked as the muzzle jammed up under Pollard's right armpit. Sharkey's big hard-case froze even as he tried to whip back from his missed punch, and when he turned his head and looked into Jory's face, saw the grim intent impressed in Jory's eyes, Pollard knew the fear of certain death. He caught his breath, his anger evaporating, and his heavy shoulders slumped.

Sharkey called out heavily, warning against trouble, but at that moment Chuck Reed's harsh voice slashed through the tension, for the deputy had ridden up unobserved. All eyes turned towards the lawman, and Jory grinned when he saw Reed's rifle levelled at the group of riders.

'I figure this has gone far enough,' Reed called. 'What in hell are you trying to pull, Sharkey? I figure you got some questions to answer. I was on my way out to your place to talk to you, but this has saved me a ride.' He paused, looked at Jory, and asked another question. 'You finished with this bunch, Jory?'

'Looks like it,' Jory retorted. 'There ain't no fight in them. I just wanta make it clear that if I get any trouble after this there will be some bloodletting.'

'You ain't through with me,' Pollard said in sullen tones. 'Put up your gun and climb out've leather. Let's see if you can back up your big mouth.'

Jory stared at the big man for a moment, then sighed heavily. He holstered his gun and stepped down out of his saddle.

'Okay,' he said. 'I guess you won't be satisfied until this is settled one way or another. Come on and try your luck.'

Pollard grinned triumphantly and dismounted with a rush…

Five

The deputy made no move to interfere as Jory stepped away from his bay and stood waiting for Pollard to join him, but Reed's rifle was lying across his thighs, ready for action, and there was a doubtful expression on the lawman's face.

'Kill him, Buster,' Lou Bragg said thickly.

'That's something you can't do, Bragg,' Jory retorted, slitting his eyes as Pollard came forward, his heavy shoulders stiff, a grin of anticipation on his massive face. There was a sadistic light shining in Pollard's pale eyes.

The big Bar S hardcase got within a few feet of Jory, walking determinedly, but then he made a diving rush, his huge hands outstretched, his fingers hooked like claws. He planned to get to close quarters and use his strength to crush Jory's ribs. Jory remained motionless until the last moment, then sidestepped, easily avoiding the clutching hands. He kept his weight upon his right foot and his right fist came up in a short punch that was perfectly timed. A sharp clopping sound cut through the tense silence as the blow landed, and Pollard ended his attack face down in the dust. Jory stepped back a couple of paces, letting his gaze shift for a moment to the watching men.

Sharkey was astonished, and his expression showed it. Buster Pollard had a big reputation for his bullying ways around the county, but now he was stretched out in the dust on his belly, his big head shaking slowly as he tried to regain his composure... Chuck Reed had a tight grin on his thin lips, and there was admiration in his gaze.

'That's twice I've hit you, Pollard,' Jory said, his hands at his sides, 'and each time I've nailed you. Are you satisfied you ain't the man you figured, or do you want a real lesson?'

Pollard came up off the ground with a bear-like roar of anger, and he sprang at Jory with fists flailing.

'You're a tricky cuss!' he raged. 'But I'll fix you.'

Jory clenched his teeth. He met the attack with his feet firmly planted, sending a straight left punch between Pollard's big hands and crashing his hard knuckles against the man's nose. Pollard was brought up short by the blow, and began to swing heavy punches, but Jory was not idle. He moved forward half a pace, sliding in, keeping his weight balanced. He followed with a right hook that skimmed above Pollard's left fist and smacked solidly against the jaw. Then Jory went in, hurling a succession of swift blows that smacked into the big Bar S bully. Lefts and rights blasted against Pollard's face and sank into his stomach. Pollard's hands fell away and his knees lost their strength. Jory threw a solid right to the jaw, felt it connect perfectly, and stepped back as Pollard went down on his face. He turned and walked towards his bay before Pollard stopped rolling over, and as he climbed into his saddle he looked around at the silent, shocked Bar S riders. Ben Sharkey looked pale and strained, his gaze fixed upon his champion.

Then Jory looked down at the motionless Pollard, and a grin came to his hard face. He let his gaze shift to the deputy's face.

'Well?' he demanded. 'Does that prove anything? Will Pollard be satisfied now?'

'It proves a lot to me,' Chuck Reed said admiringly. 'I reckon anyone trying to make trouble for you is in for a hell of a fight, Jory. What do you say, Sharkey?'

'All I got to say is that the men I hire are bigger fools than I figured them for,' the Bar S rancher retorted. 'All right, Jory. So you can handle yourself. Well you'll need all your skill to buck the trouble that's building up around here. I've got a tough crew and I'm finding it hard to hold onto what I own. I hope you'll have better luck than your uncle ever found.'

'I don't believe in luck and never trusted it,' Jory retorted. 'If I find trouble I'll rely on my fists and guns, and anyone coming at me had better be ready to face them.' He grinned at the deputy and gigged the bay forward along the trail, leading Hank Penner's black, and he didn't look back as he continued towards Broken J...

But despite his confidence, Jory was troubled as he finally breasted a rise and reined up to get his first glimpse of the ranch his uncle had left him. There was a good, two-storey frame house by a creek, and a huddle of barns, sheds and corrals to the right, surrounding a yard. A long, low bunk-house faced west across the yard; and a pang touched Jory's mind as he considered that this place might have been his home years ago if his uncle had taken him in. He rode down the slope, following the well worn trail, and rode towards the yard.

A board was nailed to two poles over the gateway to the yard, and burned upon it in wavering letters were the words BROKEN J — SILAS JORY. Jory reined up and stared bitterly at the sign for long moments, until a voice called to him from the nearer of the two corrals. Then he jerked himself from his harsh thoughts and looked around. He saw Shorty Craille swinging into the saddle of a horse tethered to the corral fence, and the foreman came riding quickly to confront Jory, a grin on his fleshy face.

'Found us then, Boss!' There was a glint in Craille's pale eyes. 'Glad to see you! What do you think of the look of the place?'

'It's bigger than I thought,' Jory replied cautiously. 'How many punchers in the outfit?'

'About a dozen right now, although your uncle used to run a bigger crew. But Mr. Marsh told me to run down the place a little because of the rustling, and some of the boys had to be fired. I think you'll find everything satisfactory. I've done the best I can, and there'll be an accounting for you to look over.'

'Don't worry about it,' Jory said as they jogged back across the yard. 'What I'm interested in right now is the trouble on this range. When we spoke on Saturday night you said Ben Sharkey was trying to grab Broken J, that he'd taken over a lot of the smaller spreads around. You mentioned that Sharkey had put a lot of pressure on my uncle. Do we have any proof of this?'

'Nope. That's the hell of it!' Craille shook his head as they dismounted by the corral. 'If there had been any proof then your uncle would have done something about Sharkey a long time ago.'

'Then howcome Sharkey's name is being linked with the trouble?' Jory demanded.

Craille stared at him when they stood face to face, and the foreman had to tilt his head back quite a way to gaze into Jory's glittering brown eyes.

'Well Sharkey is the only one doing the asking for the place,' Craille said thoughtfully. 'He's burned out nesters and hanged some rustlers.'

'So did Uncle Silas, huh?'

'Well yeah! You can't let that kind of thing go unchecked.'

'So it might not be Sharkey behind the trouble!'

'I don't know. We all took it for granted that he is. You saw the way he handled you on Saturday night.'

'The way he tried to handle me, you mean,' Jory cut in. 'Yeah!' A troubled grin touched Cradle's fleshy face. 'Well that's how he acts around the range. He's like a bull, plunging into everything and raising hell.'

'Yeah, but that don't mean he's causing the trouble we're getting. Has Arlen got any proof against Sharkey?'

'Not to my way of thinking. Ed Conway is a good sheriff, and he would step in against Sharkey if there was proof.'

'So where does that leave us?' Jory asked.

'You're not sticking up for Sharkey, are you?' Cradle countered.

'Nope. I just wanta get a true picture of events. Everyone around here blames Sharkey for what's going on. I admit that there's ground for thinking so. But it ain't good tactics to close your eyes to other possibilities.'

'You're a deep thinker,' Cradle said admiringly. 'But I figure you could be right.'

'So let's push it a little further,' Jory went on. 'Forget about Sharkey. If he wasn't on the range then who else might be trying to cause trouble?'

'You've got me there!' Cradle shook his head. 'Take Sharkey out of it and there's no one. Arlen wouldn't look for trouble. He spends most of his time trying to avoid it.'

'Okay, so let's look at it another way. With Sharkey in the picture, throwing his weight around like he does, could someone in the background be using Sharkey as a figurehead, someone to take the blame for what's happening?'

'Nobody could use Sharkey that way!'

'How about without Sharkey's knowledge? Sharkey says he's having trouble on the range. Say he's telling the truth! You give a dog a bad name and it'll stick. So Sharkey is getting trouble like the rest of us, and also the blame for what's happening. Who would be in a position to handle that kind of a deal?'

'Hell, I can't even begin to take that in,' Craille said slowly. 'Howcome you dug up such a thought, Boss?'

'Because I'm used to riding into a mess like this and getting to the bottom of it. I've made a living shooting this kind of trouble for ranchers.

I'm sure as hell gonna handle it for myself. Now tell me about the cattle losses we've had. Rustlers are hitting the range hard, huh?'

'You can say that again!' Craille scowled. 'I'd sure like to come up with them with the outfit at my back.'

'Have you tried to?' Jory demanded.

'Sure have, but there's some hard ground to the north and west, and the stock is trailed out that way.'

'On to Sharkey's range,' Jory commented.

'Yeah, it's got to cross Bar S unless it's taken south. Then it would cross Arlen's range.'

'You've followed tracks until they petered out.' There was patience in Jory's tones. 'Okay, so you've been looking at it with your eyes down on the ground. But what happens to the rustled stock? Where's it taken to? It ain't just stolen and moved off the range. It's got to go someplace.'

'You're right!' Craille shook his head. 'Why haven't I thought of that angle? Someone is buying that rustled stock, and it ain't only our steers being stolen.'

'Can we trust all the riders on our payroll?' Jory went on.

Craille looked startled for a moment, then nodded slowly. 'I think I can trust my life with the men we got now,' he said. 'I got rid of some of our riders because I had to, and I kept the best of the bunch. I think you can rely on them, Boss.'

'Okay, so I'll tell you what to do. Push a fair-sized herd out to graze on an isolated part of our range and leave it, but have it watched from a distance. Arrange for several of the men to do the watching, and one of them can get back to the ranch to raise the alarm if rustlers show up. We won't hit them immediately, but follow to check on their activities. That way we'll get a line to what is going on.'

'Boss, I wish your uncle could have worked it out like this. It would have saved a lot of trouble. I'll get this organised right now.'

'Don't make it too obvious, and pick a spot which will make it easy for our men to watch. I'll lead any pursuit that comes up.' Jory turned slowly and looked around at the buildings. 'Show me around the house first, Shorty. I want to make myself at home.'

'Sure thing!' There was eagerness in Cradle's voice. 'Boss, I think you're gonna beat this thing. I wish you had come when your uncle was alive.'

Jory nodded soberly and they walked across to the house. When they reached the porch Jory paused and looked around. Craille was silent at his side, aware that Jory was taking in all the details of the spread. Then Jory looked at his new foreman.

'Sure is some ranch,' he commented. 'Uncle Silas was a good cattleman, judging by what I can see, and he deserved better luck than he got. Let's get to it and try to flush out the snakes, huh?'

'You bet! I'll show you the house and then set this thing going. Will you be staying around the ranch now?'

'I'll be around today, but I want to ride around the range to see exactly what belongs to me, and I wanta know where the headquarters of the neighbouring ranches are.'

'I'll show you around myself,' Craille said eagerly. 'Maybe we can fix up some kind of co-operation with Arlen, Boss. If the two spreads work together then we'll have a better chance of beating this trouble.'

'I want to make up my mind about the folks on the range before I start trusting them.' Jory thinned his lips for a moment. 'You better have at least one man standing by around here with a rifle ready in case of trouble.' He paused and looked into the stocky foreman's troubled-lined face. 'It could get that bad,' he added slowly, and explained what had happened in town and mentioned his meeting on the trail with Sharkey and some of the Bar S crew.

Craille was disturbed by the report, but grinned when he heard that Pollard had taken another fall.

'I got complete faith in you, Boss,' he said, 'and the men we got riding with us are gonna fall over backwards to see you through. Nobody likes any of the Bar S bunch, and the next time you tangle with any of Sharkey's riders make sure our outfit is on hand to see it.'

Jory smiled grimly. 'I just hope it won't come to that sort of a confrontation,' he said. 'But let's get prepared for it, just in case.'

They went into the house and Craille led the way into the enormous living room. A huge, black-faced fireplace occupied almost the entire west wall. There were hunting trophies adorning the other walls. The floor was uncarpeted, but several animal skins covered some of the bare areas. A long board table and some heavy chairs occupied the centre of the room. Jory looked around. This was a typical male household, he thought. There were none of the feminine touches that could have made the place into a home. There were no drapes at the windows, no cushions on the hard chairs. The room had an atmosphere of utility about it, and Jory could imagine his uncle, a bachelor, lonely and solitary in this big house through the hard years of his life.

The rest of the house had the same image, as far as Jory was concerned. He felt a strange hostility in the place, as if the ghost of his uncle lingered on and resented his coming and taking over. But he knew he would not spend much time in the house until the trouble had been dealt with, and after a cursory look around he sent Shorty Craille out to give instructions to the rest of the crew. When he heard Cradle's voice addressing the men he went to a window and peered out at the yard. Half a dozen cowpunchers were standing in front of the foreman, listening attentively, and Jory let his gaze run over each man, weighing him carefully, sizing him against the experience that had come to him through many gun chores. He figured Craille had spoken the truth about the outfit. They looked honest cowpokes, and some of them were nodding in agreement with what Craille was saying.

Jory went out to the porch, calling for attention, and alert and curious eyes studied his big figure. He rubbed a hand across his chin as he gazed at the men. Shorty Craille introduced him, and Jory nodded slowly.

'Glad to know you, men,' he said. 'I figure to give you a few facts. There's trouble on the range, as you all know, and I think it's gonna get worse. Shorty will have told you about the shooting I was involved in back in town. And you know that Ben Sharkey and me ain't exactly on friendly terms. I know that most of you figure Sharkey is behind our trouble. Well I want you to keep that thought in the back of your minds, but don't take it as gospel. We'll get down to brass tacks and find out what's doing. That brings me to an important issue. This trouble is gonna get worse before it gets better, and that means you'll probably have to duck lead if you continue to ride for Broken J. Mebbe some of you reckon the job ain't worth risking your life for. If that's the case then I'll pay you off here and now. But anyone who stays and is ready to use a gun in defence of Broken J gets an extra twenty dollars a month. That don't make the wages anything like gun wages, but it's better than average, and I might be able to handle this trouble myself. How'd you feel about that?'

There was a concerted agreement to the offer, and Shorty Craille grinned as he looked at Jory.

'You got the whole bunch behind you, Boss,' the foreman said cheerfully. 'Just get to the bottom of the trouble and show us who's to blame and we'll take 'em on.'

'Okay. I've told you what to do as a start. You put that into operation and we'll see what comes up.' Jory looked across the yard as he heard the sound of approaching hoofs, and his dark eyes pulled into slits when he saw Woody Arlen and his daughter Sue coming through the gateway, riding saddle horses. 'Looks like we got company. I can do with a talk with Arlen.'

'He'll be anxious about you selling out, Boss,' Craille said.

'Well I ain't selling!' There was the flat note of finality in Jory's tones. He looked intently at Sue Arlen as the girl came across the yard. She was dressed in a brown divided riding skirt and a red check shirt. Her feet were pushed into calf-high black riding boots that were highly polished and decorated around the tops with a row of small white, hand-stitched stars. When the girl and her father reined up in front of the porch Craille and the punchers were moving towards the corrals, and Jory smiled as he moistened his lips. 'Glad to see you, Arlen,' he greeted. 'I was figuring on riding over to your place later today to have a talk. You've sure saved me a ride. I got a lot of things going right now, and can't spare the time to be sociable. But I need to talk to you.'

'I figured we would have to talk,' Arlen replied, dismounting and wrapping his reins around the hitchrail by the porch. He smiled at his daughter as she joined him, standing lithe and straight by his side. 'You did meet my gal Sue in town, didn't you?'

'I had that pleasure!' Jory said, smiling. 'Good morning, Miss Arlen!'

'We ain't gonna make much progress unless we become friends,' Arlen cut in. 'Call me Woody, and Sue, here, is just plain Sue!'

'She's anything but plain,' Jory retorted, and saw the girl's lovely face take on a becoming flush. Her dark eyes gleamed as she smiled at him. 'I'm Steve to my friends,' he ended.

'Fine, Steve.' Arlen was keen to talk business. 'Forgive us busting in like this, but I heard about your shooting trouble in town, and then you had a run-in with Sharkey and some of his crew on the trail here.'

'News sure does travel fast in this neck of the woods,' Jory commented.

'One of my riders was in town to watch how things panned out, and he came up with Chuck Reed and Sharkey on the trail just after you left them.' Arlen grinned. 'Buster Pollard was still dazed. I understand you figure on sticking here and running the place.'

'That's right, and I'm taking steps right now to find out who is causing the trouble on the range,' Jory said. 'But before we start gabbing let me ask you to step inside. The place is a bit dusty. It's been closed up since Uncle Silas died. But the shade is cooler than out here.'

They went into the house, and Jory led the way into the living room.

'First time I ever got into this room,' Arlen said slowly. 'I guess you know your uncle wasn't the most sociable of men!'

'I know that better'n most,' Jory said, shaking his head. 'But he's dead now. We got other things to think of. We're gonna be neighbours, and I reckon we'll have a better chance of beating this threat against us by getting together and pooling what we got.'

'That's partly why I'm here this morning,' Arlen said. 'If you don't plan on selling out then we'll have to help each other to survive. I got a feeling that you turning up here will make a big difference to the way things have drifted. Matters might come to a head now.'

'They will if I have anything to do with it,' Jory said harshly. 'But tell me first. Have you got any proof at all against Ben Sharkey?'

Arlen shook his head. 'I would have turned my crew loose on Bar S a long time ago if I'd had proof. I reckon he's playing his game close to his vest. We're gonna have to shift a lot of logs to see who's hiding in the woodpile!'

'Yeah, that's what I figured. But since we're trying to get to the bottom of it, tell me who you figure might be causing the trouble if it ain't Sharkey?'

'Ain't Sharkey?' Arlen grinned thinly. 'Couldn't be anyone else. He's been doing all the land grabbing. His men cause all the trouble in Sunset every Saturday night. He's run off nesters and hung rustlers.'

'That kind of thing you expect from a tough outfit,' Jory said. 'But you got nothing to connect Sharkey with the trouble.'

'Nothing at all.' Arlen sighed.

Jory was aware that Sue Arlen was studying him intently, and from time to time he let his hard gaze shift from her father's taut features to her dark-haired loveliness, his blood stirring.

'So we've got nothing to go on,' Jory said slowly. 'All you can do is what I've done — take steps to catch the next rustling raid when it happens. If we lay our hands on those cattle thieves it might give us a lead to the man running them.'

'You figure a local man has brought in strangers to make it impossible for us to get to him?' Arlen pulled a face and shook his head sharply, intimating that he did not like the idea.

'The two men who tried to get me in town were strangers,' Jory reminded.

'You're on your guard now!' Arlen got to his feet. 'I don't know how we can get together over this, Steve, but you seem full of ideas. Let me know what you think, and if you need any guns to back your play in anything that'll hit the crookedness that's spreading then you only got to send a man over to my place.'

'That goes for you too!' Jory said. 'Call my outfit in if you get anything you can't handle.'

'We'd better be getting back home,' Arlen moved towards the door. 'Perhaps you'll give us a look soon, Steve! You'll need to see what the range looks like, and we could do with the company.'

'Thanks for the offer, but I'm gonna be busy for a week or so. This place needs cleaning out, and if I knew a woman around here who could advise me on how to make the place look civilised I'd sure be happy to meet her.'

'I'd welcome the chance to help you out, Steve,' Sue Arlen said, breaking her silence. 'I don't have much to do at home, and I'd like nothing better than to be turned loose in a house like this with orders to brighten it up and make it into a home.'

'The chore is yours for the asking,' Jory said, smiling. 'You don't have to consider expense.'

'So you don't have a wife, Steve,' Woody Arlen said.

'Nope! The kind of life I've led, a woman would have been a hindrance. But I'm planning on settling down now, and when this trouble is over I'm sure hoping to be able to take it easy and look around. I figure there's got to be some good, home-loving gal around who might look kindly upon me.' He let his dark gaze search the girl's face, and saw a flush in her soft cheeks. 'I reckon you must be falling over the young men who call upon Sue,' he said, grinning.

'Sue ain't that way inclined yet,' Arlen said. 'She's got me worried, I don't mind telling you. Since her Ma died she ain't been easy to bring up. Sometimes I wish she would find a good man and get hitched. When she settles down I'll be the happiest man in the world.'

'Now, Pa,' Sue said chidingly, her cheeks coloured. 'You know you wouldn't be able to take care of yourself at home if some man came along and swept me off my feet. You'd have to get in a housekeeper, and that would cost you far more than I do. I'm nothing but a servant to you, and a cheap one at that. You only have to keep me in clothes. If you paid me wages like you pay your outfit I'd be well off.'

Jory ushered them towards the door, promising himself that he would make an effort to get to know this tall, long-legged girl. He could tell by Woody Arlen's expression that the Box A rancher would welcome any such event, and the girl was a real beauty. For the first time since he had come into the county, Jory felt that his trip was worthwhile.

But harsh reality jolted him as he opened the door leading onto the porch. Both he and Arlen stepped back to let Sue leave the house first, and as the girl's figure moved into the doorway splinters of wood splattered out of the post by her left side. Before the sound of the shot crashed out the silence Jory had realised what was happening, and he stepped forward quickly, seized hold of the girl's lithe body, and hurled himself backwards with her into the room. They fell to the floor in a heap, the girl exclaiming in shock, and as Jory rolled over and scrambled to his feet he heard a whole string of shots blast out hard on the heels of the first echoes. Woody Arlen ducked as windows splintered and sent shards of glass across the room, and bullet holes appeared in the door and the front wall.

Jory clenched his teeth, filled with anger because the girl had been exposed to death, and he started for the door regardless of the shooting. It was a rifle doing the shooting, but his horse was saddled by the corral, and he meant to get the dirty bushwhacker if it proved to be the last thing he did…

Six

Calling for the girl to remain in the house, Jory went out to the porch, followed closely by an equally angry Woody Arlen. But a bullet hummed past Jory's ear and he flung himself down on the porch and crawled to the right. A second bullet kicked up splinters just in front of his head as he angled to cover, and he fell off the end of the porch as a third bullet slashed across his left forearm, leaving a bloody furrow on his tanned flesh. The harsh echoes of the shots hammered away to the horizon and a short lull followed, but then the Broken J punchers, some of whom had been saddling up, swung into action. Rifles blasted, filling the uneasy atmosphere with more din.

Jory raised his head and peered across the yard. There was a ridge a couple of hundred yards beyond the gateway, and he saw a small cloud of gunsmoke drifting from a spot about halfway along its length. The guns of his outfit were directed at the spot, but Jory instinctively knew that they were wasting lead. He got to his feet as Arlen joined him.

'Take care of your daughter!' Jory rapped. 'I'm going after the ambusher.'

He did not wait for a reply but started running across the open yard to the corral, where his bay was standing with drooping head, unmindful of the shooting. He did not expect further shots to be aimed at him, and by the time he hit his saddle and was snatching up his reins he guessed that the ambusher had gone. It had been a hit and run attack!

Shorty Craille was swinging into his saddle, turning to yell orders at the rest of the crew, and Jory paused long enough to order the foreman to hold the outfit where it was.

'Could be a trick to pull us out,' he rasped. 'There was only one gun doing the shooting, Shorty. I'll handle it.'

The foreman began to protest but Jory was already turning away, and he let the bay stretch out into a run before he was halfway across the yard to the gateway. When he hit the open range he made for the ridge, and gained it in a couple of minutes. He reined up, his slitted brown eyes taking in the scene revealed to him, and a horseman was some five hundred yards away, making for another ridge. Jory set in his spurs, made the bay leap forward, and set off in pursuit. This was a chance he could not afford to let go by. He settled himself down to a chase, but did not make the mistake of letting all his concentration focus upon his distant quarry. This could be a trick to draw him out of the ranch.

The range was good for travelling, with gentle slopes and easy ridges. A thin banner of dust marked the direction taken by the ambusher, and Jory spotted the man a couple of times during the next fifteen minutes. But although he was well mounted, his quarry also possessed a good horse, and for a time it seemed that Jory was not going to make any impression upon the distance that separated them. He was close enough to take in details of the horse, which was a chestnut with a tan-coloured tail streaming out behind. But the man was indistinguishable, bent over in his saddle and riding for his life. He appeared to be heading in any direction that would take him clear of pursuit, and Jory soon realised that he was not going to be led into any hideout or lair that was used by these hardcases.

The bay was the best horse that Jory had been able to buy, and had served him well on many dangerous trips. Now it proved once again that Jory had a good knowledge of horseflesh. In the next thirty minutes it began to decrease the gap between both riders, and when the ground began to turn wild, with upthrusts of rock showing here and there and grass thinning out, the bay still maintained its mile-eating pace while the chestnut began to falter on the higher slopes. Jory did not press his animal to greater effort. He had all the remaining hours of daylight in which to come up with the ambusher, and he knew now that he would do so, unless something unforeseen occurred.

The rider ahead of him kept twisting in his saddle to stare at his back trail, and Jory was in plain view and moving closer. The man pulled his sixgun and thrust his right hand towards Jory, emptying the handgun ineffectively, smashing the heavy silence with a string of useless echoes. Jory grinned, for he knew he was beyond six-gun range, and the action seemed to indicate that the ambusher was in a panic and getting more desperate. He touched spurs to the bay to push it a little harder, and within minutes the decreasing gap between himself and his quarry had narrowed still further.

Ahead, the ambusher took stock of the situation and hit a slope that inclined sharply towards the crest. The man was still on the slope, well below the crest, when Jory reached its foot, and Jory, watching intently, saw the man reach out and grasp the butt of his Winchester. Knowing what was coming, Jory, setting his teeth, grabbed for his rifle and took it with him as he hauled the bay to a halt and vacated his saddle. He hit the ground hard and rolled into a depression, coming up on his elbows and jacking a cartridge into the breech of the long gun as his quarry turned for a look at him. The man took in the situation and redoubled his efforts to get over the crest. Jory lined up his sights, allowed for movement, and fired, sending a string of echoes across the wild landscape. He saw the man throw wide his arms before pitching to the ground, and gained his feet instantly while the figure above lay motionless and inert.

Shaking his head, Jory remounted the waiting bay and went on up the slope. When he drew nearer the sprawled figure of the man he returned his Winchester to its saddle-boot and drew his right-hand sixgun. He covered the figure as he moved in.

Before he reached the man Jory knew he had killed with his only shot. There was a splotch of dull red in the centre of the man's broad shoulders, and the careless jumble of limbs indicated that life had departed from the figure. But Jory took no chances. He dismounted carefully and moved in, stirring the man with a dusty toe before holstering his gun and bending to make a closer examination. His first impression was soon borne out. The ambusher was dead.

Jory rolled the man over onto his back and found himself looking into a stubbled face that was dusty and carried the unmistakable pallor of death. He glanced around before dropping to one knee beside the figure, and then he searched through the pockets of the dirty range clothes. He found a thin sheaf of dollar bills but little else, and no identification at all. Squatting back on his heels, Jory studied the figure, shaking his head as he did so. Here was a two-bit gunhand who had been hired to make a nuisance of himself at Broken J or to gun down the new owner. Jory knew his speculations would not help him solve the mystery of why the shooting had occurred and who had paid for it, and he stood up slowly, moving to the chestnut, which stood hipshot with trailing reins.

A search of the saddlebags revealed nothing significant in their contents, and Jory packed the dead man across the saddle and roped the body there, covering it with the blanket tied behind the cantle. He tied the reins of the chestnut to his saddlehorn and swung into leather, then picked his direction and started back to Broken J. He had barely covered a couple of miles when he spotted four riders coming towards him, and reined up when he recognised Woody Arlen and three of his own outfit.

Arlen's face carried an expression of wolfish anticipation as he came up, and the three Broken J cowpunchers hastily dismounted and came forward to take a look at the features of the dead man. Jory watched them impassively, and when he saw them all shaking their heads he knew he was getting no more than he expected. The ambusher was yet another stranger.

'Two of you take the body into town and hand it over to the sheriff,' Jory directed his men. 'Tell the law what happened. See if they can find out who he is. Then report back to the ranch. I'm going back there now. I wanta take a look at the ambush spot and see if I can back-track that hombre. He wasn't heading anywhere in particular when I chased him, but he sure must have come from some place definite.'

'That's a good idea,' Arlen said. 'I'll ride with you, Steve, if you don't mind.'

'What about Sue?' Jory demanded.

'She's staying on at your place. Shorty Craille will take good care of her! We've got the chance to bust this thing open now. I figure we got to take advantage of it.'

'I mean to,' Jory said heavily, and they rode back towards the ranch.

Jory had made a note of the prints the ambusher left behind in his bid for escape, and when they reached the ridge and stood looking down at the spot where the ambusher had fired his rifle they found plenty of evidence that the man had taken his time and tried to do a good job. There were five cigarette stubs in the dust, and a handful of spent 44-40 shells. The chestnut had been left several yards down the reverse slope of the ridge, off the skyline, and Jory immediately saw the tracks the animal had left during arrival. He pointed them out to Arlen, told his remaining rider to report to Craille and explain what was happening, and then set out to back-track the prints.

Arlen rode at Jory's side, and the Box A rancher was silent as they went on. It was obvious that the ambusher had not considered the fact that he might be back-tracked, and he had not made any attempt to conceal his route of approach. As the miles slipped by, Jory began to wonder if the trail was too easy to follow, and he glanced at a tight-lipped Arlen when they reined up to give their mounts a breather.

'What lies in this general direction?' he asked, cuffing back his Stetson and wiping sweat from his forehead.

'Nothing but Ben Sharkey's range! He's bought up most of the spreads in this area. There's just you and me left, Steve.'

'Yeah, I know Bar S surrounds me on three sides, but these tracks are not going off a straight line. That ambusher came across the range on a bee-line, it looks like, and we're gonna ride straight to the spot he started from. It looks too easy to me. If I was gonna shoot up a place I'd make damn sure I didn't leave tracks like this, and any gunnie worth his salt would make an effort to blot his trail.'

'You could be right. But perhaps he didn't figure on getting killed. He planned to kill you and get away with it.' Arlen sounded doubtful. 'But these tracks seem to be leading to the headquarters of the old Jameson spread. Sharkey bought Jameson out two years ago, and he's got a bunch of his riders on the place now.'

'So the ambusher could be one of Bar S?' Jory asked the question hesitantly, knowing that they could only guess at the answer. 'Let's get on and try to find the answer. Seems the tracks are leading us with no trouble at all.'

They continued, and eventually left Broken J range. Arlen pointed out the boundary, and announced, when they crossed a gully, that they were on Bar S. The tracks went on and on, and Jory shook his head as he looked ahead.

'How far to the Jameson headquarters?' he said.

'Eight miles from here. Last I heard, there was a gunnie name of Rourke bossing the place for Sharkey, with a dozen hardcases riding for him.'

'And you never saw our ambusher around before?' Jory demanded.

'Nope. He's a complete stranger to me.' Arlen spoke with decisive tones.

More miles fleeted by under their hooves, and finally they came in sight of a small spread that had its clustered buildings in a shallow valley.

'Jameson's place,' Arlen said needlessly.

Jory was looking at the tracks they had followed from the ambush spot. They led down into the valley. He drew his right-hand sixgun and checked it, returned it to its holster and drew the left-hand weapon. Satisfied, he pulled the Winchester from its saddleboot and examined it. When he looked into Arlen's face he saw anxiety in the Box A rancher's expression.

'You're not figuring on riding down there and bracing Rourke and the rest of the outfit, are you?' Arlen demanded.

'I'm not asking you to go with me,' Jory retorted. 'In fact I'd prefer it if you stayed up here out've sight and watched what happens. If anything happens to me you can make a report to the law.'

'Hell, I'm not gonna sit around here while you go down and stick your neck into a death trap. If Sharkey gave orders for one of this outfit to come for you then the others are gonna jump you soon as they get the chance.'

'Maybe!' Jory grinned tightly. 'But I'll have surprise on my side, and I doubt if any of these men have ever seen me. I'm going down there to give them a jolt, and I might learn something. You cover me from here.'

'I can't cover you. I'm too far out!' Arlen sounded unhappy. 'Why don't you stake out and watch the place while I ride back to your spread and fetch your crew? Then we'll have something to back our play.'

'No time for that. If Sharkey is at the bottom of this I want to uncover the fact and catch him unawares. I don't want a stand-up fight between two outfits. I've been in more than one cattle war, and I don't fancy one right here on my own doorstep.'

'Well pretend you're a drifter, and just check that those tracks do come from the place,' Arlen suggested.

'Leave me to handle it,' Jory said. 'Just make sure you ain't spotted, huh? I'll come back here after I've nosed around. Rourke is Sharkey's manager here, huh?'

'Yeah, Shank Rourke! He's a hardcase. Watch out for him, Steve.'

Jory nodded and gigged his mount forward. He moved down a gentle slope and found a trail that angled from left to right. It led into a yard of the small ranch headquarters, and as he neared the yard, Jory looked around with alert interest. He figured that not all the outfit would be here. Some would be out riding the range, and there might be others of them on his own range, handling the rustling and other trouble. But his gaze kept checking the ground, and the tracks he was following showed here and there in the dust, leading straight into the yard.

There was a sign over the gateway, announcing that the ranch belonged to Ben Sharkey and was under the brand of Bar S. It warned all trespassers to stay out. Jory rode under the sign, sitting easy in his saddle, slouched a little, but alert and ready for trouble. He passed a bunkhouse on the left, then a corral. There were a couple of barns on the right, and ahead of him, across the yard, was a small, one-storey ranch house that was little more than a cabin. It was solidly built, with a stone chimney rising up on the left-hand side. A small porch fronted the building, and a saddle-horse stood hipshot at a hitchrail before it.

The sound of a hammer beating metal on an anvil came from a small shed by the corral, and there was a man standing in the doorway of the nearest barn, gazing at Jory's approach with curiosity. Jory looked down at the dust of the yard, where there were a great number of different hoof prints, but he saw the ones he had been following, and they led to the corral. He eased towards the barn, and the man there came forward a couple of paces, his left hand close to the butt of the sixgun holstered on his hip. Jory reined up and stepped down from his saddle, trailing his reins.

'Howdy,' he said pleasantly, eyeing the man before him.

'What do you want?' The man was around forty, a burly, dark faced individual with surly tones that grated in Jory's ears. 'You see the notice over the gate warning trespassers to keep away?'

'I ain't a trespasser,' Jory retorted, smiling. His hands were down at his sides. 'Shank Rourke runs this place for Ben Sharkey, doesn't he?'

'What of it?' There was no hospitality in the heavy tones, and the man's brown eyes held a menacing glitter.

'Are you Rourke?' Jory demanded.

'Nope.'

'Then I'm wasting my time with you. Where can I find Rourke?'

'Over in the house, I shouldn't wonder, playing cards with the other galoots around here who don't do any of the work.'

'Gunhands, huh?' Jory grinned. 'They sit around all day doing nothing while others do the work.'

'You got the rights of it, and you look like one of that breed yourself. You on Sharkey's payroll?'

'I'll talk to Rourke!' Jory swung back into his saddle and turned the head of the bay towards the house. He did not look back at the man, but his ears were keened for any suspicious sound. He reached the house and dismounted by the hitchrail, trailing his reins instead of wrapping them around the rail. He stepped onto the porch and it creaked under his weight. Without pausing he went to the door and opened it, stepping into the building and pausing on the threshold.

He had entered a big room which had a door in the rear wall that probably led into a kitchen. The room was thick with cigarette smoke, and looked as if it hadn't been cleaned out in months. There were five men seated at a thick plank table, and they were playing cards. Whisky bottles, some empty, were standing on the table, and cigarette and cigar butts lay around where they had been tossed. The place smelled and looked like a pig-sty, and Jory thinned his lips. He turned his attention to the men at the table. Three of them had their backs to him, and of the two facing him, he immediately decided which one was Shank Rourke.

'What in hell do you want, busting in here like that?' the man snapped instantly, peering at Jory over the top of the cards he was holding close to his bearded face. 'Who are you and what do you want?'

'You Rourke?' Jory replied.

'That's right. What's it to you?' Rourke threw his cards face-down on the table and stared at Jory. He was a big man, with massive shoulders and heavy arms. His sleeves were rolled up well above the elbows, revealing that his forearms were covered with thick black hair. The same coarse hair covered most of his heavy face, and a straggly moustache half concealed thick lips. His hair was unkempt, thick and curly at the temples, and his dark eyes held a dangerous glitter.

Jory moved forward and closed the door at his back, his hands down at his sides. The three men with their backs to him twisted in their seats and regarded him with cold, calculating eyes, and a silence followed Rourke's truculent tones.

'You got a rider operating out of here who rides a chestnut hoss?' Jory asked. He pictured the figure of the ambusher. 'A man about five foot ten, lean, with a stubbled face and dark hair. He's got a small scar that cuts through his right eyebrow like a piece of white string.'

'Sounds like Al Burnett!' one of the men at the table commented.

'Shuddup!' Rourke snapped. 'Who in hell are you, mister, coming in here like you owned the place and asking questions about my men?'

'So he is one of your men?' Jory persisted.

'Burnett is the man you just described. What's it to you?' Rourke began to get to his feet, revealing that he stood well over six feet. He thrust back his chair with such violence that it toppled over with a crash.

'I killed him this morning,' Jory said, and a tight grin of anticipation came to his lips. His eyes glittered. 'I'm Steve Jory, the new owner of Broken J, and Burnett threw some rifle slugs into my place from cover. I nailed him and tracked his hoss to this place. Now you answer me one more question, Rourke! Who sent Burnett out to do the shooting? You run things around here, so I heard. Was it you?'

The challenge in Jory's voice was unmistakable, and yet he stood apparently at ease, his hands down at his sides, but his face showed the iron determination that was in him and his eyes betrayed the intention gripping him. The men at the table, able to read all the small signs in any situation such as this, saw a tall, powerful stranger wearing two low-tied sixguns on his thighs and recognised that here was one of their breed, and one who rated himself highly because he had dared to come alone and walk in on them. They made no move, aware that it was up to Rourke to take up the challenge.

Rourke's bearded face betrayed no emotion, but his eyes narrowed until they gleamed from slits in the pouchy sockets that surrounded them. He was wearing a Colt's. 45 on his left hip, butt forwards, and his right hand half-started into a crossdraw, but he halted the movement, and suddenly his teeth were glinting through the matt of black beard covering the lower half of his fleshy face.

'So you're Steve Jory!' he said in jeering tones. 'I heard about you. Old Silas Jory's nephew.'

'You heard about me all right,' Jory rapped. 'That hoss outside is carrying a Bar S brand. Which one of these polecats was sent by Sharkey to give you orders to nail me?'

'Is that what you figure?' Rourke grinned. 'You got more than your share of nerve, Jory, walking in here like this. You reckon you can take me and these four?'

'I came in here to get the answers to some questions bothering me,' Jory said, 'and I won't leave until I'm satisfied.'

'You won't leave, period!' Rourke snapped. 'Okay, so you bored Lou Bragg and beat Buster Pollard with your fists! That ain't such a difficult chore. I can beat Bragg with a gun and I've stretched out Pollard three times. He takes a lot of convincing! So where does that put you and me, Jory?'

'Right in line for a showdown!' Jory spoke in even tones, his voice pitched low. 'You sent Burnett out to nail me, huh? Answer that question and you've got a fight on your hands.'

'Yeah!' Rourke nodded his large head, and his grin widened. 'I sent Burnett out with orders to shoot up your place and make a general nuisance of himself. So he did a good job.'

'And got himself killed!' Jory's smile faded. 'Now what are you gonna do, Rourke? You got a choice. You can tell me what's going on around here or you can make a play for that gun your fingers are itching to grab. Either way, make up your mind right now.'

Rourke maintained his grin, but his eyes changed expression, and Jory, watching closely, saw the change and knew what the gunman's decision was. The next instant Rourke's big right hand was flashing across to the butt of his holstered gun, and the weapon came out of leather like greased lightning. At the same time the men around the table began to throw themselves out of the line of fire…

Seven

Jory had the advantage of having read the situation a split second before the action came, and as Rourke made a flawless draw Jory's right hand flickered and came up filled with the big Colt's .45 that had nestled in his right-hand holster. The gloomy interior of the room was momentarily lit with the blasting flare of the gunshot that hammered deafeningly in the confined space. A plume of gunsmoke spurted from Jory's muzzle and seemed to reach out towards the massive figure of Rourke, as if pointing the path the bullet had taken, but before it lengthened the .45 slug had struck Rourke in the chest. The gun bucked strongly in Jory's grip and Rourke's right hand, swinging up his gun, jerked wildly as he took the impact of Jory's bullet. The shocking smash of the speeding slug of lead caused the big man's answering shot to spout off wide and high, and Jory felt a searing burn across the top of his left shoulder.

Thumbing his big gun, Jory loosed a second shot, drilling it dead centre, and another splotch of blood appeared on Rourke's massive chest. The man was rocked back on his heels, then doubled forward across the table, sending bottles flying, his gun blasting once more, the bullet cutting a gouge across the heavy planks. Jory held his breath against the gun-smoke, hating the acrid stench of it, and he peered around in the smokey atmosphere, looking for more trouble. One of the four men was reaching for a gun, and Jory blasted a shot at him that cut the top of a chair before ploughing through the man's right eye.

Another of the men was peering at Jory from under the table, and there was a gun in his hand. Jory angled his gun muzzle, thumbing another shot that ripped through the man's gunhand, sending the weapon flying, and the man flung himself sideways, gripping his injured hand and signifying that he was out of it. Jory checked the other two men, saw them down in attitudes of defence, but with their hands in plain view and empty of weapons. He drew a quick breath then, and gunsmoke rasped in his throat. He moved away from the door, easing to the right, placing himself in a position from which he could guard against outside attack.

The racket of the gunfire began to fade slowly, leaving Jory with ringing ears.

The two men who had taken no part in the fight got slowly to their feet, shocked beyond comprehension by Jory's display of masterly gunskill, and the injured man sat groaning on the floor, gripping his right hand, with blood dribbling through the fingers of his left hand. Rourke was stretched out dead on his back, the two splotches of blood on his chest looking like gory eyes. The other dead man was huddled face down, his shattered head mercifully turned away.

Jory swallowed to rid his ears of pressure. His keen gaze swept around. He motioned for his two prisoners to get rid of their guns, and they obeyed without hesitation, tossing their weapons at his feet.

'Who rode in here this morning on the Bar S hoss tied to the hitchrail?' Jory demanded.

'Him!' One of the men pointed to the dead man on the floor.

'What instructions did he bring Rourke from Sharkey?' Jory's tones were even. He broke his gun and reloaded the spent chambers from the loops on his cartridge belts.

'We don't know anything about it,' the other man retorted. 'We draw gun wages. They tell us what to do, and that's all.'

'What have you been told to do in the past month or so?' Jory pursued.

Both men shrugged and made no answer, and Jory grinned thinly.

'Don't worry about it,' he said. 'I'm taking you into town along with Rourke and this dead man. You're witnesses to what happened here. You'll tell the sheriff.'

Hooves pounded out in the yard, and Jory closed his fully loaded gun and moved sideways to peer out through a dusty window. He saw two men afoot talking by the corral, watching the house, but the rider coming across the yard was Chuck Reed, the deputy, and there was a sixgun in the lawman's hand. Jory drew a swift breath, then sighed heavily. He had forgotten about Reed, about the deputy's orders to cover his back for a few days. But Reed hadn't been around when Burnett fired those shots at Broken J.

'Open the door and let's go out to the porch,' Jory ordered. 'Both of you go out with your hands up. Make it quick.'

One of the men opened the door and led the way outside into the sunlight. Jory followed closely, and moved to the right as he reached the porch. He watched his prisoners, and saw Chuck Reed's face register astonishment as he reined up by the hitchrail.

'I saw Woody Arlen back there on the ridge,' the deputy said, 'and he told me you'd ridden in here alone, Jory. Then I heard the shooting. I figured they'd done for you. What in hell happened?'

'Let these two tell you,' Jory retorted. 'But first you better round up the rest of the men on this spread. Far as I can gather, they're mixed up in the trouble this range is getting.'

He stood watching the yard while Reed dismounted and came forward to get some information from the two prisoners. Both men told the truth about the shooting, and Jory was satisfied. Then Reed went into the house, to emerge moments later leading the wounded man, who was in a semi-dazed condition, his right hand spilling blood freely. Jory looked at the man without emotion. Hoofs sounded in the yard and he looked up to see Woody Arlen coming in.

The Box A rancher's face showed wonder and surprise as he reined up. Then he shook his head.

'I guess Ben Sharkey will have to answer for this,' Arlen said after he had gained some of the facts of what had taken place. So he sent a man in here to tell Rourke to give you some trouble! Too bad for them you killed Burnett or you wouldn't have got on to this bunch.' He looked squarely at Reed. The deputy had produced two pairs of handcuffs from a saddlebag and was manacling the wrists of his prisoners. 'How does Sharkey stand now? What happens if you prove he sent Burnett to kill Steve?'

'We'll have Sharkey in for questioning,' Reed said, turning his attention to Jory. 'I missed that trouble out at your place because I stopped on the trail after you rode on from your meeting with Sharkey. I gave it to Sharkey straight and plain, but he insists he knows nothing about the trouble everyone around here is getting.'

'He owns this place,' Arlen cut in. 'Rourke is Sharkey's manager.'

'And we know that a Bar S rider came in here this morning with orders for Burnett to shoot up my place,' Jory commented. 'I figure we better ride on to town and see what Sharkey has got to say about this.'

'Why don't you leave it to the law now?' Reed asked. 'It looks to me like you busted this business wide open. We can pick up the pieces.'

'I don't figure it'll be that simple,' Jory replied. 'If Sharkey is at the back of this he's gonna have some excuses about what's happened. He's playing for high stakes, and he won't be caught this way.'

'Well we got more to work on now than we had before you showed up in Sunset,' Reed said. 'Just keep an eye on these two and I'll round up the other men here. I might as well take them all into town. Do something about this man's hand, will you? If we don't stop the bleeding he'll be dead before we can reach Sunset.'

Arlen took care of the wounded man, and Jory stood on the porch, his sixgun still in his hand, while Reed went around the spread and brought in three other men. They were all protesting their innocence, and Reed was telling them they would have a chance to prove themselves in town.

Rourke and the other dead man were brought out of the house, wrapped in blankets and thrown across the saddle of horses that were hastily prepared for travel. Reed roped his prisoners to their mounts, and some thirty minutes after the shooting had taken place the grim cavalcade started out for town.

'There's no need for you to ride in, Woody,' Jory said. 'Why don't you head back to my place to pick up your daughter and tell Shorty Craille what happened here and what I'm doing?'

'Okay, but I don't want to miss anything,' Arlen said. There was disappointment in his tones. 'After all this trouble, I want to be in at the death.'

'I'm sure the sheriff will need a big posse if Sharkey is back of this and we have to go for him,' Chuck Reed said grimly.

'Thank God we got a good law department,' Arlen commented. 'I don't know what would have happened around here if the law hadn't kept a tight rein on the situation.'

Jory made no comment, and they set out for town. Arlen rode off back the way he and Jory had come, and when the Box A rancher had disappeared from sight Chuck Reed led out. Jory rode behind the group, his guns in their holsters, but he did not relax. His thoughts churned over what had taken place, and although all the facts pointed to Sharkey's guilt, Jory could not help wondering if the Bar S rancher was completely responsible for what had happened on the range. His experience in this type of business, when he had sometimes operated against such range grabs, had given him an insight into the many devious ways men could work, and he fancied that here in Bowie County someone was taking advantage of the fact that a man of Sharkey's character and attitudes was in the process of building up his holdings by somewhat dubious methods. Anyone with such a scheming mind could easily make it appear that Sharkey was responsible for what was happening.

But he was a stranger to this county and did not know enough about the men in it to be able to form any conclusions. He knew that, given time, he would calculate who might be working under cover, but time seemed to be in short supply. Those strangers in town who had tried to gun him down proved that someone was trying to get rid of him quickly, and he wondered why his appearance should have caused such a panic. The attempt to get him had been badly managed, and seemed to point to the fact that a measure of desperation had crept into the situation.

It was a long ride to town, and most of the afternoon had gone by before they topped a rise and sighted the wide main street and the two rows of buildings fronting it. Jory suppressed a weary sigh, stiffening himself to peak alertness, for he would need to have his wits about him during the next few hours. There would be questions asked and answers to be considered. He didn't doubt that Ben Sharkey was intent upon picking up Broken J, and any way that it could be taken, but the unknown factor was what worried Jory, and he kept his suspicions of it in the forefront of his mind as they entered Sunset.

Their appearance in the street raised great interest, and a crowd began to converge upon the law office as Reed dismounted in front of it and turned to handle his prisoners. Ed Conway appeared in the doorway of the office, his heavy features set in harsh lines as he took in the scene that awaited his dark gaze, and when the sheriff looked at Jory there was respect in his expression. Brad Terrill, the other deputy, came along the street from the eating house, and Conway sent him for the doctor. The prisoners were ushered into the office and Jory followed, closing the door against the crowd that was clamouring for information and news.

'Okay,' Conway said. 'Lets get down to it. You better tell your story first, Jory. Two of your men showed up here earlier with Al Burnett's body. I've been expecting more trouble because of it, but I didn't figure it would be you causing the trouble.'

'As I see it I didn't cause the trouble,' Jory replied. 'I merely tried to put a stop to the trouble you already got.'

'Sure, sure!' Conway nodded. 'I didn't mean that you've been out raising hell on your own account. There is trouble in the county and your appearance on the scene has sparked off more. It had to come, I'm thinking, and the sooner we get to grips with it and beat it the better. So just tell me what happened from the time you left town this morning until the shooting with Rourke broke out.'

Jory nodded, taking a deep breath, and the prisoners listened stonily while he narrated the events that had befallen him. When he completed his account he fell silent, and listened to the sheriff's skilful questioning of the prisoners. But no revelations turned up, for all the men denied having anything to do with causing trouble. One by one they claimed that they were ordinary cowhands working under Rourke for Ben Sharkey.

'Okay, so we'll have Ben Sharkey in here and get him talking,' Conway said. 'You've had a hard day, Chuck, so you stick around town now. Brad can take over watching Jory's back. I'll ride out to Bar S and bring Sharkey into town. We'll get to the bottom of this, don't you worry. This is the first time we got something to work on. That Bar S rider you killed along with Rourke rode in there early, and Burnett set out for your place, Jory. I don't doubt that some of these men are lying, and I'll crack their stories before I'm done, you can bet. But right now there's little else we can do. We'll throw these prisoners in the jail and let them sweat it out a little, and I'll be very interested to hear what Ben Sharkey's got to say about all this.'

'I figure I can tell you what his story will be,' Jory said, smiling thinly. 'But you go ahead and talk to him, Sheriff. And you can forget about having your other deputy tail me around town. I won't be heading back to Broken J until morning. I got one or two things to do around town.'

'Okay, but we'll be watching out for you, although you've proved that you're more than able to take care of yourself.' Conway smiled grimly. 'I think we're going to see the end of this trouble before long. I'm also following other lines and angles that ain't connected with Ben Sharkey.'

The sheriff motioned for Reed to lock the prisoners in cells, and Jory stared into the little sheriff's hard face as he considered.

'Sheriff, all day I've been plagued with a hunch that someone else has got a hand in this somewhere. Sharkey is getting all the blame, and I don't doubt that he is trying to grab what he can, but it's a big woodpile, and there could be more than one skunk in it.'

'That's what I think!'.Conway nodded slowly as he met Jory's level gaze. 'You've got your wits about you, and no mistake, if you've worked that angle out since your arrival. It took me a long time to get around to it.'

'Have you got any suspects?' Jory demanded.

Conway smiled slowly, shaking his head. 'I'm afraid I can't talk about that right now. Knowing you for the man of action that you are I think you'd go straight in and blow the whole thing up like it was a barrel of gunpowder. Nope. You go back to Broken J and keep out of sight for a spell. Leave this to me and my deputies. If I need any gun help then I'll send for you and your boys. But in the meantime the one thing you can do, and carefully, if possible, is check your ranch accounts.'

'The accounts!' Jory frowned.

'Yeah! Your uncle has been dead more than six months. In that time there's been no one to handle the business like it should have been. Maybe there'll be a lead in that for us.'

Jory shook his head, his face lined with puzzlement. 'I spoke to Nick Marsh, the lawyer, and he said there were some things to be straightened out, but he handled the accounts while Craille ran the spread. But when I talked to the banker — Dillon — he said the business was in a bit of a mess. I think I'll go talk to Dillon and find out what he meant. I'll get some figures and see what they bring to light.'

'Yeah, and keep me informed, huh?' Conway held out his hand. 'And thanks for what you've done today, Jory! You took a big risk in walking in on Shank Rourke like you did. But it seems you brought matters to a head.'

'I didn't look on it as a risk,' Jory retorted harshly. 'I figure I can handle any three two-bit hardcases like Rourke.'

'There were more than three of them on the spread at the time,' Conway pointed out.

Jory nodded. He shook hands with the sheriff and left the office. The crowd of townsmen on the sidewalk threw a barrage of excited questions at him, but he shook his head and pushed through their ranks, swinging into the saddle of the bay and riding along the street towards the stable. Evening was drawing on, and the shadows from the westering sun were long across the street. A voice called his name and he turned his head to see Mortimer Dillon standing on the sidewalk in front of the bank. The banker had just emerged from the building. Jory swung his mount and rode in against the sidewalk.

'What's all the excitement about in front of the law office?' the banker demanded. 'I saw you coming out of there as I was locking up. Has there been some trouble?'

'Some,' Jory said, and dismounted to join Dillon on the sidewalk. He explained what had happened in terse tones, and saw shock and wonder appear in the man's narrowed eyes. 'But that's all beside the point,' Jory ended. 'I'm glad you called me. I'd like to have a talk with you. I figured to see you before I left town this morning, but after seeing Nick Marsh I figured a talk with you could wait. I'm sorry it's after business hours right now, but I've been too busy during the day to come and see you.'

'That's all right,' Dillon said. 'Don't worry about it. I'm always ready to do business, whether the bank is open or not. Won't you come home with me and share supper? We could talk over the meal. But tell me what's on your mind that won't wait.'

'You told me Saturday night when I deposited my money with you that the affairs of Broken J were in a mess. When I pressed the point you changed your description from mess to complicated. I'd like to know what you mean. Marsh told me early this morning that I had inherited a big ranch and a great deal of money.'

'We can't talk here on the street,' Dillon said, looking around, 'and I don't fancy going back into the bank at this time of the day. There are too many hardcases around for my peace of mind. Why don't you come home with me?'

'I got to stable my horse,' Jory said.

'Okay, I'll walk down to the stable with you. But let me assure you that when a banker talks of complications in regard to an account that doesn't mean trouble. Nick Marsh is a man of integrity. He's been handling the accounts of Broken J since your uncle died. He tried to locate you, knowing there was a nephew because of the will your uncle left. All I have to say at this stage is that with the rustling that's been going on in the county I didn't think it was in the best interests of the ranch to buy more stock to replace that which had been stolen because the rustlers were likely to strike again. But Marsh gave the go-ahead to Craille to restock on a large scale, and what I feared did happen. The rustlers struck again and a great deal of money had been lost.'

'Uhuh!' Jory nodded. His gaze swept around the street. 'Then I figure I better have a talk with Marsh before I talk to you. I guess you'll have to eat supper without my company. But I'll come to your office tomorrow and talk to you. I'd like to see exactly what state the Broken J account is in.'

'Sure. I'll have the account ready for your inspection by tomorrow morning.' Dillon nodded and touched his hat as Jory swung back into his saddle.

Jory rode on to the stable, dismounting outside and letting the bay drink at the trough. The stableman appeared, his limp most pronounced, as if his badly-set broken leg was giving him trouble. He took the horse, and waved aside Jory's offer of money.

'I didn't know who you were when you rode in on Saturday,' he said harshly. 'Now I got you pegged, and you can pay me monthly for taking care of your hoss here in town along with the other charges I make for supplying your spread with grain and feedstuffs.'

'You handle that business for Broken J, huh?' Jory demanded.

'Sure. Your spread has an account with me, same as with all the other businessmen in town,' came the steady reply. 'You don't figure I make a living from stabling hosses that come in and out of town, huh?'

'I never thought about it,' Jory said. 'Okay, if you don't want cash on the nail. Stick it on your monthly bill, but you better know that I got a good memory, and I'll know how many times in a month I leave the bay here.'

'I wouldn't take that off anyone but you,' the stableman said without a trace of humour. 'But seeing that you beat Lou Bragg to the draw and flattened Buster Pollard twice in a couple of days I guess you can talk just how you please to anyone, huh?'

'That's about the weight of it,' Jory said grimly. He left the bay and went back along the street, turning off into the eating house when he reached it, and he considered the new direction his thoughts were taking while he ate a meal.

Had there been some kind of double-dealing involving the lawyer and Shorty Craille? The question nagged at his mind while he chewed a good beefsteak. Nick Marsh might have figured that it would be easy to embezzle money from the Broken J after Silas Jory died. There seemed little likelihood that the absent nephew would show up, and perhaps

Marsh had not tried too hard to locate him! Jory shook his head slowly while he sipped his coffee. He was a good judge of men, and although Marsh had seemed to be a smooth operator who kept his emotions strictly under control, Shorty Craille had struck him as being an open-faced cowman with nothing but the best interests of Broken J at heart.

When he had finished his meal Jory left for Marsh's house, and now he found the street gloomy, with deep shadows piling up in the corners about him. He dropped both hands to the heavy guns on his hips and eased the weapons in their holsters. He felt like a cat trying to pick its way through a carpet of broken glass, and his reflexes were honed razor sharp after the trouble he'd had earlier. But he had to talk to Nick Marsh, and he was having difficulty trying to frame the questions he needed to ask. He had no wish to offend the lawyer if he were barking up the wrong tree, or to alert him if he had stumbled upon the truth.

There were three saddle horses standing at the white picket fence surrounding the lawyer's small garden, and as Jory moved closer he saw two men standing by the horses, one of them leaning against the fence. They were talking in harsh voices, but their words did not carry to Jory's ears. A third man was standing in the lighted doorway, talking to a woman that Jory recognised as Marsh's wife, and as he drew nearer, Jory saw the door close and the caller turn away. Then he was close enough to make out details, and a pang stabbed through him when he saw that the two men by the fence were Lou Bragg and Buster Pollard. The man coming from the lawyer's house was Ben Sharkey.

Jory halted, his hands down at his sides. Sharkey spotted him at about the same time and stopped in his tracks, remaining motionless. But Bragg and Pollard did not see him, and continued talking loudly.

'I'll catch that skunk unawares before I'm done,' Pollard was growling angrily. 'Twice he took me off balance. He ain't gonna make me a fool for the whole danged county to laugh at.'

'You talking about me, Pollard?' Jory called, and saw the big hardcase spin around.

'Lay off!' Ben Sharkey moved again, coming forward through the gateway. 'Jory, I've had about all the trouble I'm gonna take from you. I've been to see the lawyer to try and get the law to do something about you. Conway and his two deputies ain't about to give me any help. They figure I'm causing all the trouble around the county! Well I'm sick of this, and you better pull in your horns before there is trouble.'

'You've got a nerve!' Jory retorted thinly, primed for trouble. 'After everything that's happened today you got the gall to stand there and accuse me of doing the troublemaking. But I guess that's the only defence you do have, huh?'

'What's been happening today?' the Bar S rancher demanded raggedly in his usual insolent, arrogant tones.

'You been into the town yet?' Jory demanded. 'Have you talked to anyone around here?'

'Nope!' Sharkey chuckled harshly. 'There's nobody around here would go out of his way to talk to me.'

'I'll talk to you.' Jory kept his tones even. 'I'll walk across to the law office with you if you figure you got some kind of a complaint against me. The sheriff wants to talk to you, anyways.'

'I'm on my way to see him, but figured I better have the lawyer along,' Sharkey went on. 'I'm bringing a charge against you, Jory. Someone rode up to my place around noon today and emptied a rifle at the house. I didn't figure you for a back-shooter, but the tracks that gunman left led straight to your place.'

Jory took in the accusation, then chuckled harshly, and Sharkey started angrily, his shadowed face dark beneath the wide brim of his Stetson.

'I'm not laughing at you!' Jory said quickly. 'What happened to you happened at my place too, but I went a step farther than you in finding out who did it. You better go talk with Conway, Sharkey. I'm gonna have a talk with Marsh. I got more important business with him.'

'I'll see Conway, but I'm warning you that I can't be pushed any further, Jory. And you're wasting your time trying to see the lawyer. I just asked for him and got told that he left for Kemp's Ridge today. He won't be back inside of a week.'

Jory thinned his lips at the news, and stood motionless while Sharkey untied his horse and stepped up into the saddle. The Bar S rancher rode on along the street towards the law office, followed by his two hardcases, and after a moment's pause, Jory went along too. If Marsh had left town there was little he could do until the lawyer returned. In the meantime he needed to sort out the mystery of what had occurred during the day. If Sharkey was telling the truth and Bar S had been shot up the same as

Broken J then it was all the proof he needed that someone was trying to set the two outfits into action against one another. But trying to get evidence to back up that proof would be another matter, he knew.

Eight

Ed Conway was seated at his desk when Ben Sharkey, Bragg and Pollard walked in on him, and Jory, pausing by the big front window, peered into the office from the sidewalk before going on to the door. Pollard was about to slam the door when Jory stepped into the doorway, and the big hardcase scowled and moved away to the left. Jory entered and closed the door, moving to the right as Sharkey and Bragg glanced around at him.

'What's going on?' Conway demanded, getting to his feet. 'I was figuring on riding out to your place to talk to you, Sharkey. You've saved me a long trip.'

'Well I came in to talk to you,' Sharkey retorted. 'There's been a lot of talk around here about what I'm supposed to have done on the range. Now it's my turn. I got a complaint against Jory there. And you better do something about it.'

Jory listened while Sharkey gave a narration of the shooting-up at Bar S. It was almost exactly what had happened at Broken J, and Ed Conway's fleshy face registered surprise. He frowned when he threw a quick glance at Jory.

'Now wait a minute, Ben,' the sheriff said. He explained what had happened at Broken J and how Al Burnett had been killed.

Jory watched Sharkey's face while the lawman continued with the further events that had occurred. When Sharkey learned of Rourke's death he turned and stared at Jory, who was impassive and grim.

'What the hell!' the Bar S rancher growled. 'You figure I set my outfit against you?'

'One of your men rode out to the Jameson place early this morning and gave word to Rourke to send Burnett to Broken J,' Jory said. 'That much I learned.'

'Who was the man who rode to see Rourke?' Anger laced Sharkey's tones. 'I never gave any such order.'

'He's dead,' Conway said tightly. 'Jory had to kill him. It was Jed Elkins!'

'Elkins!' Sharkey swung around to stare at Buster Pollard. 'You're my range boss. What orders did you give Elkins for the day's work?'

'I sent him out to check the south line from Bitter Creek to Buffalo Ridge,' Pollard said in grating tones.

'But he rode to the Jameson place and told Rourke to send a man to shoot up the Broken J.' Conway spoke in heavy tones, and his dark eyes held a steely glint. 'I know that what happened at Broken J is fact because I had Chuck Reed trailing Jory all day. And Jory had Woody Arlen with him right until the time he rode into your place and braced Rourke.'

'You rode in there alone and braced my outfit?' Sharkey demanded, turning once more to look at Jory, and there was a glimmer of respect in the tough cattleman's hard features.

Jory nodded, making no comment. He wanted to hear what came out of this conversation, and the sheriff was asking all the right questions. But he was more concerned with attitudes and manner right now, and he fancied that Sharkey's shocked surprise was genuine, and came not from the fact that some more of his men had been killed but because there had been trouble which he did not order.

'I don't know what to make of this,' Sharkey said slowly, shaking his large head. 'I never gave any orders for my outfit to cause trouble.' He glared at Jory for a moment. 'And what about my place getting shot up? How'd you account for that?'

'I don't know a thing about it,' Jory replied.

'Well someone on the range knows a great deal about it,' Ed Conway said, 'and I'm gonna get to the bottom of it if it's the last thing I do. The way it looks right now, Sharkey, you've got some renegades working for you. They're playing a double game. They're drawing wages from you and playing their own deep game. I'm putting it like that because I got no proof that you're involved in this and I'm giving you the benefit of the doubt.'

'What the hell!' Rage spluttered through the big cattleman. 'I ain't gonna stand for anyone calling me crooked.'

'I just explained that I ain't accusing you,' Conway said quietly. 'But I'll tell you this much, Ben. After this I'm gonna hold you responsible for anything any of your riders try to pull. You got that? No matter what happens, if any of your men are involved then I'll come for you.'

'I came in here to make a complaint about someone shooting up my spread and wind up with a load of trouble I don't know about,' Sharkey snapped. 'What the hell is going on around here? Howcome I'm under suspicion?'

'Some of your outfit are involved,' Conway retorted. 'I got the whole crew you had at the Jameson place in jail, and they're gonna stay there until I've got at the truth.'

'Let me talk to'em,' Sharkey begged. 'I'll get the truth out of them!'

'No dice!' Conway shook his head. 'Now I'm telling you to pull in your horns, Ben. If there's any more trouble then you'll see the inside of this jail, and I don't mean maybe.'

'And what about the shooting that took place out at Bar S?' Sharkey demanded. 'What you gonna go about that?'

'I'll ride out there first thing in the morning and look around,' Conway promised.

'I can save you a trip.' Sharkey glanced at Jory again. 'I followed tracks, just like Jory said he did at his place, and you know what? Those tracks led onto Broken J. I didn't cross the line because I didn't want to be accused of trespass. I came here to get the law to act. This is the helluva note, Conway. You say you run the law good around here. Well you better get to work on this. I ain't gonna take much more, I can tell you.'

'What else have you taken?' Jory demanded.

Sharkey swung around. 'I run a big outfit, but that ain't stopped the rustlers hitting me!'

'You got any idea who's doing the rustling?' Conway asked.

Sharkey chuckled evilly, his eyes glinting. 'If I caught any thieving rustlers on my range I'd gun 'em down and bring them in like Jory did to my men at the Jameson place,' he growled.

'What about Rourke?' Conway's tones were gentle now. 'We know he was up to no good. Elkins carried a message to him this morning and Burnett rode out to shoot up Broken J.'

'I don't know about that, but I'm sure as hell gonna check on it,' Sharkey said. 'I'll go through my outfit with a comb, and if I find anyone's been drawing my pay and working against me I'll kill him.'

'You could have faked the shooting out at Bar S,' Jory said, 'just to make your side of it look good.'

'Why, damn your eyes!' Sharkey took a step towards Jory, who was grinning insolently. 'Howcome a stranger can come into this county and get better treatment from the law than me?'

'Maybe because none of my outfit are mixed up in this crookedness going on,' Jory retorted.

'Let's leave it be right there,' Conway cut in. 'I'm gonna dig into this, and I'll come up with the truth, you can bet. But in the meantime I'm charging you to keep the peace, Sharkey. I told you, if there's any more trouble involving your outfit then I'll come for you. Keep your men under control.'

'You tell Jory to do the same,' Sharkey countered. 'I'm as keen as anyone to stop this trouble.'

Jory let his gaze flicker to Pollard's heavy features, and he saw a tight grin on the big man's thick lips. Recalling what he had overheard Pollard saying to Bragg outside the lawyer's, Jory nodded slowly.

'I'm gonna have some more trouble with Pollard before this is done,' he said. 'He's the kind of man who can't take a beating. I don't care about that, but you better know, Pollard, that if you come at me again I won't be using my fists. Next time it'll be for keeps, with a gun. That goes for you, too, Bragg! If you got any ideas of getting at me you better be ready to die.'

'That's enough of that kind of talk,' Conway said sharply. 'Now you all better get out've here and let me settle down to think about this. It sure runs deep, but I'll get to the answers.'

'Make it quick,' Jory said, 'before somebody else gets killed.'

Sharkey scowled and turned to the door, which Pollard opened for him, and the Bar S rancher departed, followed by his two hardcases. Jory remained, watching the sheriffs intent face, and when Pollard banged the street door Conway relaxed a little and shook his head.

'This beats me,' the lawman admitted. 'We got proof that some of Sharkey's men are mixed up in this trouble, and all Sharkey has to do to stay clear is deny any knowledge of it.'

'He could be telling the truth,' Jory said.

'You think so?' Surprise edged Conway's tones.

'It's better to keep an open mind,' Jory retorted. 'It's possible that some of his men are running a racket on the side, without Sharkey's knowledge.'

'And it's more likely that it's happening on Sharkey's orders,' the sheriff said. 'I'm not forgetting the way Sharkey took over some of the smaller spreads on the range. He didn't exactly break the law, but he came mighty close to the line sometimes.'

Jory shook his head. He moved to the door. 'I don't know what to think,' he commented. 'I suppose all we can do is keep our eyes and ears open and wait for these hardcases to make some kind of a mistake.'

'Which they'll surely do! I just hope the breakthrough will come before anyone else is killed.'

'I'll see you tomorrow.' Jory stifled a yawn. 'I'll sleep on this and see what comes up in the morning.'

'Watch out for yourself,' Conway warned. 'There have been several attempts made on your life. Your luck can't last forever.'

'That's what I'm afraid of.' Jory nodded and opened the door. He went out to the darkened street and made his way to the hotel, where he took a room for the night...

Next morning the situation did not look any the less complicated, and Jory was on the street early. After breakfast he checked with the law office and learned that Conway had been unable to get any definite information from any of his prisoners.

'I'm riding out to Sharkey's place to check out his story about the shooting that occurred there yesterday,' Conway said. 'If you're going back to Broken J we can ride part of the way together. I'll have to take my deputy off your back because we're gonna have to be on our toes after this. I need all the help I can get.'

'I prefer not to have someone watching my back,' Jory said. 'There's nothing I can do around town until Nick Marsh returns. Then I want to go over the ranch accounts with him. But he's out of town for a week, so I heard.'

'He often makes trips out of town. He handles court cases for a couple of hundred miles around. Nick is a tricky cuss, I can tell you. He's managed to get some of my cases busted down in court. I know the accused were guilty in some of the cases he's won. But that is the way it goes.'

'I'll go saddle up,' Jory said. 'I'm setting a trap of my own to try and catch those rustlers. Craille told me that all his attempts to track the stolen stock have failed.'

'That's right. You got some wild country around your line.' Conway studied Jory's face for some moments. 'What you planning? I'd better know so I can judge if there's any way I can help.'

Jory told the sheriff about his plan to push a herd out from home range and have his crew take it in turns to watch for rustlers. Conway nodded slowly.

'It might work, and it's certainly worth a try,' he said. 'I can't spare a deputy to stake out with your outfit, but that is what's needed. The law should be represented.'

'Tell you what I'll do,' Jory said. 'If the rustlers take the bait I'll send a man into town to warn you. We'll hold back until you get out there.'

'Sounds good. I like the idea!' Conway nodded. 'Give me ten minutes and I'll be ready to ride with you. Ask the stableman to saddle my hoss for me, huh?'

Jory nodded. He went along the street, feeling the hot sun already burning down upon his broad shoulders. He did not relax his vigilance, aware that further attempts against his life might be made. But he figured the sheriff's straight-talking to Ben Sharkey might have put a curb upon the situation, and any respite would be welcome.

He was ready and waiting to ride by the time the sheriff's stocky figure made its appearance at the stable. Conway's horse was already saddled, and the lawman climbed into the hot leather, pausing to check his Winchester before nodding his assent to Jory. They rode out together, stirrup to stirrup, leaving town and hitting the open range, where they raised a canter and went north. For a time they travelled in silence, each lost in his thoughts, and then the sheriff spoke up.

'I've done an almighty lot of thinking since last night,' Conway mused, 'and I don't get part of this. Sharkey sure seemed surprised by the turn of events. I was watching him pretty closely when I hit him with the news of how you killed Rourke, and why. He didn't seem like a man who knew what was going on.'

'That's how it struck me,' Jory confessed. 'Sharkey has got kind of a bad name around the range, I guess, and I can understand why, judging by the way he busted into my room at the hotel last Saturday night. He's a man who's used to getting his own way, but that don't make him a thief and a grabber.'

'He bought out a lot of the smaller spreads around him, and he's chased off nesters and farmers,' Conway commented. 'But then so did your uncle, and he was as straight as a gun barrel. We got quite a mystery here, huh?'

'I'm a stranger on the range,' Jory said. 'But you know the men around here. You must have your suspicions.'

'I don't let that sort of thing enter into my caluculations.' The sheriff shook his head. 'I do check on certain men I figure might be involved, but I have to work on facts, and so far they've been very few and far between.'

'What about Woody Arlen?' Jory asked.

Conway looked into Jory's face for some moments before replying, and then the sheriff's tones were steady.

'I suspected Arlen for a long time,' he said at length. 'But I came to the conclusion that he's clean.'

'Why did you suspect him?'

'He was trying to buy up some of the spreads. I thought he'd caught grabbing fever. But I figured he was just trying to stay as strong as Sharkey to survive. Him and your uncle stood together, and so they didn't get much trouble. But when your uncle died and it looked like there was no one to claim Broken J, that's where the real trouble started.'

Jory nodded slowly, his gaze roaming their surroundings. 'I think I'll drop in and see Arlen on my way to Broken J,' he said. 'How'd I reach Box A from here?'

'We'll ride on a spell, and I'll show you the turn-off. It's a regular trail, so you can't miss the place.' Conway shifted his weight in his saddle.

They rode on, following the countours of the range, until they reached a slope where the trail divided. The sheriff pointed out a distant landmark, a broken ridge that was purple in the sunlight.

'See the break in that ridge?' he demanded. 'Head for that, and you'll find Box A sitting beneath that break. But watch your step out here now. If you've been watched then those men out to kill you will know you're alone.'

'I'm ready for them, and would welcome the chance to trade lead with them,' Jory retorted grimly. He patted the butt of his Winchester and took his leave of the lawman.

Alone, Jory pushed the bay into a steady lope, angling along the faint trail that led to Box A. He saw small bunches of cattle grazing in the distance, and wondered about the rustlers, half hoping that he could ride into the thick of them, but the range was silent and lonely, and apart from the grazing cattle there were no other signs of life.

He eventually came into sight of the Box A, and rode towards the gate. Entering the yard, he looked around as he let the bay trot towards the frame house. He liked the look of the headquarters. It was clean and neat, and there was a small flower garden in front of the porch which bespoke of a woman's touch. He also saw curtains at the windows, and a little smile touched his lips as he considered that his austere house could do with some trimming up to make it look more like home.

A man appeared in the doorway of the big barn, and there was a levelled rifle in his hands. Jory saw him as soon as he appeared, and the man called to him.

'Hold up there and declare yourself, mister! Who are you and what do you want around here?'

Jory halted the bay and sat easily in the saddle, his hands on the reins. He caught a flicker of movement from a small shed, half turned his head to take in the appearance of the second man who came forward with a rifle, and replied in strident tones.

'I'm Steve Jory from Broken J. I wanta talk to Woody Arlen. Is he here?'

'Not right now!' The man with the barn at his back shook his head. 'He rode out early with his daughter. I figure they went into town.'

'Didn't they tell you where they were headed?' Jory demanded.

'The boss ain't keen to tell the likes of us about his business,' came the swift reply. 'We just work here, that's all, and there's trouble on this range. You'll have to come back if you wanta see the boss.'

'They rode to town, you say!' Jory shook his head slowly. 'I just come from there and I didn't meet 'em on the way.'

'Mebbe they took the short cut! I didn't see'em ride out!' The guard waved the rifle he was holding. 'What's a matter? Don't you believe me?'

'Okay, so I'll come back!' Jory began to turn his mount, his keen gaze sweeping the yard. Then he hauled on his reins and stopped the bay in mid-stride, for he could see Arlen's horse in the corral. He looked again at the two men, who were converging upon him, rifles ready. 'How'd Arlen and his daughter travel to town?' he called.

'In their saddles, of course. You don't figure they set out to walk it, do you?'

'What horse did Arlen use?'

'His own, I expect. I didn't see him leave.' The guard doing all the talking began to lift his rifle again. 'What's it to you what horse he used?'

'Because Arlen's horse is in the corral over there,' Jory said thinly. 'What's going on here? There ain't no short cut to town. I just rode from there, and travelled in a straight line. You can't get a trail any shorter than that!'

Before he could catch his breath, Jory realised that he was in trouble. Both men were lifting the rifles, and he heard the ominous sounds of the weapons being cocked. Without pausing to think, he kicked his feet clear of his stirrups and hurled himself sideways out of the saddle. The bay started nervously, moving between him and the two men, and as Jory hit the dusty yard on his left shoulder the silence was shattered by the flat crack of a rifle. Dust spurted into his eyes, and he heard the bullet whine away in ricochet. He blinked rapidly, his right-hand sixgun leaping into his hand, and he was still wondering what was happening here at Arlen's ranch as he went into action. But this was a situation where he had to shoot first and ask questions afterwards, if he was still alive at the end of it.

Nine

The big .45 in Jory's right hand blasted and bucked as he aimed at the nearer of the two men. He could see a patch of red shirt as his bay cavorted clear, and there was a swarthy face behind the levelled rifle pointing at him. But a sixgun was easier to handle at close range, and Jory's speeding bullet struck the guard and sent him staggering. He rolled to the left as the second man cut loose, and felt a flashing pain along his right leg from the hip to the knee. If he had not moved he would have taken the 44-40 slug through the head. He thumbed off a second shot as his gun muzzle swung to the right and flickered upon the blue shirt of the second man.

Gunsmoke flew back into Jory's face. The gun kicked against the heel of his hand, and he rolled once more, moving to the left, for the bay had halted after a couple of dancing paces and Jory needed cover out there in the centre of the open yard. His slitted brown eyes took in the sight of the guard with the red shirt lying face down in the dust and unmoving. The other man was on his knees, swaying like a tree caught in a blue norther, but he was not out of it and his hands were frantically working the mechanism of the rifle.

'Throw it down if you wanta live!' Jory yelled, trying to take in his surroundings. He had no idea why these two should attack him. Arlen must have told his crew about the new owner of Broken J. But perhaps they were not members of the Box A outfit! The thought came to him as he covered the man, who ignored his warning and tried to bring his Winchester into action.

Jory tightened his compressed lips and fired again, the booming crash of the Colt tossing heavy echoes on the heels of the fading sounds already crossing the horizon. He saw the guard jerk backwards under the boring impact of his slug, and then the man was down in the dust and writhing convulsively. Jory rolled over once more in case there were other similarly-minded guards around, and came up on one knee. His right leg promptly refused to take his weight and he went down onto his face, twisting around to look at the offending limb. He saw blood on his thigh and sat up, peering around, blowing dust and gunsmoke away from his ready sixgun.

A figure was coming out of the house, and Jory saw a double-barrelled shotgun being lifted to cover him. The shade under the porch awning made it difficult for him to make out details, but he quickly saw that the newcomer was neither Woody Arlen himself nor his daughter Sue. As the shotgun was levelled, Jory thumbed back the hammer on his Colt.

'Don't try it,' he called, his ears singing from the shock of the shooting.

Again his warning was ignored, and Jory knew he could not afford to let the shotgun come into action against him. He thrust the Colt forward a fraction and fired. The man on the porch immediately flung down the fearsome weapon and jack-knifed to the dusty boards. He rolled off the porch and came to rest upon his back with outflung arms, and dust arose slowly around his lifeless body.

Jory looked around, ready for more trouble, but that seemed to be the end of it. He studied the front of the house, watching the windows closely, but there were no signs of life, and then he took in the rest of the buildings around the yard. There were no movements anywhere, except those made in the corral by the nervous horses. He holstered his gun and drew the left-hand weapon, then pushed himself to his feet, standing erect, his weight upon his left leg. He stared around once more, hair-triggered, ready to slip into lethal action at the first signs of trouble. But the echoes were fading now and an uneasy silence was settling over the ranch.

Why had these men attacked him without provocation? Jory's face was set in harsh lines. He took a tentative step with his right leg, pressed his foot into the dust, and found that he could use the limb. But sharp pains slashed through him and he gritted his teeth. He started for the porch, holding his gun in his left hand while the fingers of his right hand explored the gash in his thigh which had been cut by the 44-40 slug. The wound was painful, but seemed superficial, although it was bleeding a great deal, but he had no time for himself, and crossed the yard, followed by the bay. He checked both guards and found them dead, and kept going until he reached the man in front of the porch. A quick glance was sufficient to show him that here, too, death had struck in the form of his

.45 slug, and he mounted the porch steps with difficulty and went into the house through the open doorway.

'Arlen!' he called, and his voice echoed through the uneasy silence that followed the spate of shooting. 'Anyone at home?'

'In the kitchen!' The reply came from Sue Arlen, and Jory recognised fear and near-hysteria in the girl's tones.

He went forward instantly, gun ready, and thrust open the door leading into the kitchen. There he paused, for the girl was roped to a chair, and her pale face was filled with strain.

'What in hell is going on around here?' Jory demanded, going to her side. 'How many men are there on the place?'

'There are three of them here. Six came, but three rode off with my father during the night.' A tremor cut across the girl's tones.

'Where did they take him?' Jory holstered his gun. He began to untie the knots, and found that she had been cruelly tied. The ropes were cutting into her soft flesh.

'They were going to Sunset with him. He had to draw out of the bank what cash he's got there. I was being held hostage here to make sure he did like he was told.'

'What about your regular crew? Ain't there any of them around?'

'Pa sent four of them over to your place yesterday to stand by in case they were needed to tackle the rustlers. That left two. They must be in the bunkhouse. I haven't seen them around, and I heard these men talking. They said they'd dealt with our outfit.'

Jory loosened the ropes about the girl's lithe figure and moved away. 'I'll go check out your men,' he said. 'You better stay right here until I get back.'

She nodded, slumping limply in the chair, and Jory, mindful that his blood was flowing from the thigh wound, left the house by the back door and moved around until he reached the bunkhouse. He peered into the low building by a side window, his lips pulling tight when he saw two men stretched out. One was on the floor by the pot-bellied stove that heated the place during the winter and the other was crumpled on his face between two bunks. Jory went around to the door and entered, quickly ascertaining that both men were dead. They had been knifed.

Going back to the house, Jory found Sue on her feet, but still under the stress of her grim experience. Her pale face looked pinched and wan.

'My father!' she cried when Jory confronted her. 'They'll kill him.'

'Maybe not, if they get what they're after,' he replied. 'Are they coming back here?'

'Yes. They arranged to come back when they'd got the money.'

'Then I better get those dead men out of the yard,' he retorted. 'You stay here until I've cleaned up out there.'

'Our two men?' she asked, clutching at his arm.

'Both dead,' he retorted, and clenched his teeth at her cry of anguish.

'You're bleeding!' She had caught sight of the blood on his right thigh. 'I heard the shooting out there and wondered who had shown up. There was no way to warn you.'

'It doesn't matter now. I killed those three coyotes! Did you get a good look at them? Have you ever seen any of them before?'

She shook her head slowly, still dazed by what had occurred. Jory put his right foot upon a chair and examined his leg wound more closely, then removed his neckerchief and bound it around the split in his pants leg. He pulled it tightly around the wound, and when he tried the leg again he found it easier to move, although pains darted through the limb with every step.

'I'll go take care of those three outside,' he said. 'There are three others, you said. Okay, so we'll arrange a reception for them when they show up.'

'Save my father!' she pleaded, clutching at his shoulder. 'I heard the three who were left behind talking amongst themselves. I know they mean to kill us after they'd got what they came for.'

'We'll handle it,' he promised, and left the house.

Pausing on the porch, he looked around, trying to spot dust in the distance, but there were no riders approaching the ranch yet, and he bent over the first of the dead men, lifting the man and carrying him into the shelter of the barn. He quickly removed the other two, dumping them out of sight, then went back to the spots where they had lain and kicked dust over the blood stains that showed dully in the strong sunlight. He was breathing heavily when he went back into the house, and a glance at the position of the sun warned him that noon was upon them.

Sue Arlen had recovered some of her composure when he faced her again, and she smiled wanly in response to his enquiry about her feelings.

'It was horrible,' she said slowly. 'But if anyone can save my father, you can, Steve! Thank God it was you who showed up here.'

He nodded soberly. 'I figure your father and those other three should be returning any time now. I'd better turn my horse into the corral so they won't spot it.'

'How are you going to handle them? They'll shoot my father if they have the slightest suspicion that something is wrong.'

'Depends on which way they ride in,' he commented. 'I reckon to stay in the house. They may be cautious coming in, but they left three men here to handle any trouble that might come up.'

'Won't they expect to see one of those three outside on watch?'

'We'll have to take a chance on that. I want them to come right into the yard so I can take 'em on. You just stay out of sight and keep hoping it pans out the way we want it to.' Jory saw her nod, and she was trembling. Shock was showing plainly in her face. 'Why don't you make some coffee?' he suggested, knowing that if she were occupied with something then her mind would be eased.

She turned automatically and went to the stove, and Jory, holding a sixgun in his right hand, limped around the ground floor rooms, peering out through the windows to watch all approaches.

They drank coffee, and the morning slipped away imperceptibly. Jory did not relax his vigilance. But he was growing more concerned as the time passed. He never ceased prowling around, and finally spotted dust way out on the trail from town. He called the girl's attention to it, and she drew a shuddering breath as she narrowed her brown eyes and looked at the tell-tale cloud that drifted slowly on the breeze.

'It has to be them,' she said slowly, turning to look into Jory's hard-expressioned face. 'Please try to see that nothing happens to my father!'

'Okay. Now you better hunt up a corner and get down in it. There'll be some lead flying unless I miss my guess. I'll try to take 'em easy, but that'll depend on how they ride in. If they come together and pull up outside I might be able to get the drop on them. But if they're cautious then there could be trouble. If you can use a gun then get one and be ready for anything. If they get lucky and nail me you'll have to do some fighting for your Pa.'

She nodded slowly, her eyes showing that she was fighting off a sense of horror. She departed for her father's office, and returned carrying a 30-30 rifle and a box of shells.

'Take a look from the windows in the other rooms,' he warned, 'and stay out of sight. They might split up and come in from different directions. We don't wanta get caught on the hop. If you see anyone sneaking in don't yell. Come and tell me. I'll be here watching the yard.'

Again she nodded, and checked her rifle before leaving for a back room. Jory watched the dust clouds coming closer, and his nerves began to tighten, his reflexes sharpening. The silence on the ranch was heavy and oppressive. A heat haze danced on the far side of the yard, and he had to slit his eyes to peer through it. Soon he made out four riders just ahead of the rising dust, and a little sigh of hope came from him. Three badmen and Woody Arlen, and they were together. He watched them carefully, well out of sight of the window. He had opened the door a fraction, and remained ready to move out or fight from cover.

Eventually the riders reached the gateway, and reined up. Jory showed his teeth in a mirthless smile and shook his head slowly as he watched. This was where it could get tricky. If they split up he would have to go for the man covering Arlen, and that would give the others an edge he did not want them to have. But the three men with Arlen, who was easily recognisable, were not suspicious; merely cautious, and they came on under the ranch sign and started across the yard towards the house.

Jory saw that one of the three hardcases was slightly behind Arlen, and there was a sixgun in the man's hand. The other two were looking around alertly. One was watching the front of the house and the other kept turning his head to stare at their surroundings. They had no intention of being taken unawares.

When they were a dozen yards out from the porch the man covering Arlen snapped an order in rough tones, and they all reined up.

'Thomas, where in hell are you?' one of the men yelled. 'Mills, Timson! Come on out. I told you to keep watch around here.'

Jory set his teeth into his bottom lip, for the man covering the apprehensive Woody Arlen was partially concealed by the Box A rancher.

'Something's wrong here,' one of the other men growled, and his words carried clearly to Jory.

'Get down and go take a look in the house,' the man covering Arlen snapped. 'If the place ain't like we left it then I'm gonna kill this jigger.'

Jory watched one of the men swing out of his saddle. He lifted his sixgun, judging the difficult shot he would have to make if he was going to take out the threat to Arlen. The badman started for the porch, reaching for his holstered six-gun, and Jory knew the moment for action had come. The third man was twisting around in his saddle, watching the other buildings about the yard.

Crashing his gun muzzle through the pane of glass before him, Jory triggered a shot at the man covering Arlen. All he could see was the man's head above and beyond the Box A rancher, and it was a difficult shot. The sixgun bucked and blasted, and the silence fled once more under the bludgeoning crash of gunfire. Jory held his breath for a moment, watching intently, and he saw his target jerk backward as the bullet took him through the face. The shot caused the other two men to freeze instinctively, but Arlen acted with quick presence of mind. The rancher threw himself out of his saddle and went to ground.

Arlen's movement made the other mounted man spring back to life. Jory saw the man twist back in his saddle, then make a play for his holstered sixgun. The man coming towards the porch dropped into a crouch and made a fast draw. Jory shifted his point of aim, knowing he had to take out the other rider, for Arlen was defenceless on the ground and the gunman had every intention of shooting him. Thumbing a shot, Jory saw the second rider jerk under the whipping impact of a bullet. Then the third man was in action, and the window above Jory's head shattered and fell in upon him, spraying him with shards of glass. He ducked, thumbing back his hammer, and again he fired, this time dropping his muzzle to catch the third man.

Blood ran down Jory's forehead and seeped into his left eye. He blinked, shaking his head. There were darting pains in his face and he knew that the glass had cut him. But he concentrated upon the chore facing him and sent another shot at the mounted man, who was swaying in his saddle and trying to get his gun into action. The second bullet wiped the rider out of his saddle as if an invisible hand had thumped him.

The man on the ground was down on one knee, with blood showing on his left shoulder. The muzzle of his gun was steadying as he drew a bead upon Jory, who swung away from the window and hurled himself at the half-open door. Crashing the door open, he went out to the porch in a sprawling dive, just as the man's next shot went in through the window. Jory landed on his stomach and elbows, lifting his big gun quickly, covering the crouching man with a steady muzzle. The hammering detonations of the shooting were echoing away with seeming reluctance, and Jory clenched his teeth and shouted a grim warning.

'Throw down that gun or take the consequences!'

The gunman was covering the window, his gun muzzle angled away from Jory's position. Jory wanted a prisoner. He needed some answers to the questions in his mind. He waited, his trigger finger taut against the curved sliver of metal that was ready to set his big gun into more thundering action. Silence began to return, the echoes still grumbling away into the background. The gunman hesitated, staring death in the face. For an interminable moment he seemed ready to defy the odds stacked against him, but then he shrugged his right shoulder, opened his right hand, and let his sixgun fall into the dust.

Jory sighed with relief. Sweat was running down his face. He could feel it stinging in the tiny cuts he had collected from the broken window. He listened to the fading echoes of the shooting and watched Woody Arlen scrambling to his feet, dragging a gun from the holster of the nearest downed gunman. The Box A rancher checked both men down in the dust, then came forward grimly towards their prisoner.

'I'll get around to thanking you for showing up, Steve,' Arlen growled, reaching out and grasping the wounded hardcase. He jerked the man to his feet. 'Is Sue okay?'

'She's all right.' Jory could hear the girl's feet at his back, and he began to push himself up from the boards of the porch. 'Good thing for you folks that I decided to come calling today, huh?'

Arlen looked down at the two dead men, shaking his head in disbelief. His face was pale as he peered at Jory, and then the girl was emerging from the house, still carrying her rifle, and she passed Jory and hurled herself into her father's arms. Jory grinned, covering his wounded prisoner, watching the man carefully, and already the questions were beginning to rise up in his mind.

'Okay,' he said. 'Let's get down to business. How about tending the injuries? Then we can talk.'

'Did you take your money out of the bank, Pa?' Sue demanded.

'Sure I did.' Anger was beginning to seep into Aden's face. 'I wasn't gonna put your life in any worse danger than it already had. Those three hardcases who stayed behind. Where are they?'

'Stretched out in your barn,' Jory said. 'I had to kill them!'

Arlen came forward, careful not to step between Jory and their prisoner. The rancher shook his head in disbelief.

'I never knew a man like you, Steve,' he said. 'You cleaned up this crooked bunch without help. Hell, I didn't think anyone could handle such a chore.'

'They didn't either,' Jory retorted. 'Mebbe that's why I was able to beat them.'

'Stop talking, you two,' Sue Arlen said firmly. 'Steve, there's blood all over your face. You'd better come into the kitchen and let me take care of you.'

'I'm more interested in our prisoner,' Jory retorted, waving the girl away as she approached. 'Six hardcases showed up out of the night and terrorised you. They got money from you by holding Sue hostage. This is something new. We need to know more about it.'

Arlen turned to face their prisoner, who was sitting on the ground clutching his left shoulder. Blood was dribbling between his fingers and running down his sleeve.

'I'll get the truth out've him,' he said in savage tones. 'I took a lot of threats from these skunks all the way back from town. Just leave him to me.'

Jory lifted a hand to his face, cuffing away the blood that was drying around his left eye. His probing fingers discovered a long gash in his forehead, and there were numerous smaller cuts on his face. Sweat made them sting, and he shook his head as he tried to relieve the built-up pressure in his ears. He studied the hardcase, who was beginning to look scared, and figured that at last they had a chance of discovering exactly what was going on in the county. He could not accept that this latest outrage had no connection with the rustling and other trouble that had been occurring.

'Bring him into the house and we'll make him comfortable,' he said. 'Treating him rough ain't gonna help, Arlen.' He grinned as the gunman looked up at him. 'We'll save the rough stuff for later, if he proves harder than I think.'

'I got nothing to say,' the gunman snarled in sullen tones.

'You'll have time to think that over, and mebbe change your mind,' Arlen retorted. He jerked the man upright, disarmed him, and pushed him towards the house. 'I ain't happy taking the skunk in under my roof.'

Jory examined the man's shoulder wound and found that the bullet had passed right through a fleshy part just above the collar bone. Sue helped him bandage the wound after it had been cleansed, and then the girl fashioned a rough sling. The hardcase remained silent and sullen during their ministrations, and Arlen stood in the background, the six-gun in his hand a constant threat to the man's life.

'That'll do him,' Arlen said at length. 'Now you let Sue take a look at you, Steve, while I ask this skunk a few questions. If there's anything left of him when I get through we'll hand him over to the law.'

Jory sat down in the chair the gunman vacated and leaned back and closed his eyes while the girl bathed his face and examined the cuts he had received from the shattered window. He listened to Arlen's harsh voice asking questions of the hardcase, which the man would not answer. Arlen became angry, and threatened to pistol-whip the man, and Jory remained out of it until Sue had done what she could for him. Then he got to his feet, thanking the girl for her aid, but she smiled and shook her head. The colour had returned to her face now, and some of the shock had faded from her gaze.

'You're the one who should get all the thanks,' she said. 'I don't think we'll ever be able to repay you for what you've done here today.'

'We'll go into that later,' Jory said, smiling as he turned to face the prisoner. 'Let me ask a few questions. I got a feeling about this business.' He looked into the man's sullen face. 'There's nothing to stop us shooting you dead and saying that you was killed in the shoot-out! So you bear that in mind and think that you got nothing to lose but everything to gain. I want to know where you and the five men who came with you fit into the scheme that's going on around here.'

'We don't fit into nothing,' the man said, replying for the first time to anything that had been put to him.

'Six of you just showed up here with a scheme to make money, huh?' Jory shook his head slowly. 'I don't swallow that, mister. You're mixed up in the trouble that's hitting this range. Where have you and the other five come from?'

'That don't make no never mind,' came the sullen retort.

'Two cowpunchers have been murdered,' Jory went on easily. 'I guess your pards are the lucky ones, huh? They're dead. But you're gonna have to face a charge of murder, and that'll get your neck stretched.'

The man shook his head. 'I got nothing to say,' he snarled. 'I got taken fair and square so I'll stand for what I get.'

'And let others get clear away with it, huh?' Jory nodded. 'I don't call that acting very smart. You could save your neck by talking a little.'

'No dice!' The gunman refused to meet Jory's hard gaze.

'He's hoping that some more of his crooked pards will show up here and bust him out've our hands,' Woody Arlen said angrily.

'I guess the only thing we can do is hand him over to the law,' Jory commented. 'Conway will sort this out. In the meantime I can check on the tracks they left and see where they lead to. They had to come from someplace on the range, and the last time I followed tracks I got more than I figured on.'

'So did Shank Rourke,' Arlen said. 'But I'd like to go along with you, Steve. I missed out on all the fun last time.'

'But you had a front row seat in the showdown here,' Jory said. 'No, Woody. You've got to get this hombre into town. You'll make a stir when you ride in with those dead men roped to their saddles. So let's get to work. Saddle up horses and we'll prepare you for the trip to Sunset. Take Sue with you, and leave her in town where she'll be safe. I'll look at the tracks of the three horses outside that the gunmen rode, and try to pick up their sign around the spread. Then I'll head out.'

Arlen's expression showed that he was reluctant to follow Jory's advice, but there was no alternative for him, and Jory, limping a little, went out to the yard. His eyes narrowed as he looked at the two dead men sprawled in the dust, and for a moment he was motionless, wondering where it was all going to end. Then he went to the horses the men had been riding and studied the prints the animals had left upon the dry ground. He sighed heavily as he went to the corral for his bay, and he slid his Winchester into the saddle-boot before mounting. Then he rode out of the yard and began to circle the spread, eyes watching the ground intently, ignoring the tracks that led out through the gateway.

It didn't take him long to find what he was looking for. There were six separate sets of prints close together, clustered at a spot where the riders must have sat watching Arlen's place before moving in the night before. Jory drew a heavy breath as he stood up in his stirrups and stared down at the ranch below. He saw Arlen roping his prisoner to a saddle, and the five dead hardcases were already slung across leather and roped down.

Steeling himself for the effort that would be needed, Jory set out on the trail once more, following the tracks, which led off to the north and west, and he judged that they were making for his own place. He rode steadily, ready for trouble, and found that it was not long in coming. He was barely five miles from Box A when he heard the pounding of hooves coming towards him from the direction he was heading. Then four riders showed, galloping fast, and Jory halted and jerked his Winchester from its boot. No one rode that fast unless there was some kind of emergency troubling them, and he was only too aware of the fact. But he did not know if these men were friendly or otherwise, and could only assume they were hostile. He stepped down from his saddle and hunted cover, while the newcomers, spotting him, drew their guns and began to separate. Jory tightened his lips. He knew all the signs, and this did not look good for him.

Ten

The oncoming riders split up into two pairs and edged left and right to encircle the position Jory had taken. He watched them, waiting for hostilities to break out before cutting loose. But the men did not start shooting. They drew within range, then slowed, and came on carefully until they were within shouting distance.

'Declare yourself,' one of them called. 'Who in the hell are you, mister, and why you acting to spooky? You got some reason to be afraid of meeting anyone on this range?'

'I sure have,' Jory retorted. 'I'm Steve Jory of Broken J. Who are you?'

'Box A riders,' came the reply. 'You're on Box A range right now. We just left your place, if you are Jory! Shorty Craille figured we might be needed at your place. Rustlers are on the move. A big herd of your cattle is being pushed north-west.'

Jory got to his feet, lowering his rifle, but he remained alert as the four men came in, using the same brand of caution. Then he saw Box A branded on their mounts, and reached for the reins of the bay and slid his rifle into its boot. The four punchers dismounted and stood around him, and Jory explained the events that had taken place at their home ranch. They began to curse, and two of them immediately swung into their saddle and lit out for the Box A.

'We'll ride back with you,' one of the remaining pair said. 'I want to get in on the shooting. Nobody is gonna rough up my boss and get away with it.'

'I'm following tracks,' Jory pointed out. 'I wanta find the spot where those six hardcases came from. There's a mystery on this range that's got to be solved, and chasing rustlers ain't gonna bring us any nearer the truth, unless we can take 'em and know 'em for what they are.'

'Craille said they're a bunch of strangers,' the other cowpoke retorted. 'They moved in during the night and started pushing the herd out.'

'So many strangers on the range,' Jory mused. 'If Ben Sharkey was back of this, as most folks believe, then he'd be using his own crew.'

'Maybe not, if he didn't want anyone to recognise them,' came the thoughtful reply.

'Yeah, I already considered that fact.' Jory swung into his saddle. 'If you boys want to get into a fight then rejoin my outfit. Me, I'm gonna follow these tracks and see where they lead to.'

'We'll go back to your outfit. These tracks are veering away from your place.'

'Any idea where they might be heading?' Jory asked. 'What ranches lie in that direction?'

'A couple of small spreads that Sharkey took over. You got Sharkey all around you, except for Box A.'

'Yeah, so I recall!' Jory went on following the tracks while the two punchers headed back the way they had come. He wondered if he should make for the rustlers and take a hand in their capture. He could always come back to these tracks, and they might not be so important. But he could not shake the hunch that gripped him. He did not think Ben Sharkey would pay men to hold Sue Arlen hostage for money. He figured that Ben Sharkey was having troubles of his own, and someone was causing the trouble for both sides and blaming it on Sharkey.

The afternoon wore away and still the tracks led on. Jory wondered how his outfit were making out against the rustlers. He had given Craille orders to follow and not attack the thieves. They needed to discover exactly where the stolen stock was being taken and who handled it. He controlled his impatience, for it seemed that events were working around to providing some of the answers he sought.

Nightfall found him in rough country and probably on Sharkey's range. He came upon a narrow, winding river, and paused to let his horse drink. He could not follow tracks in the dark and knew he would have to make a dry camp until sun-up, and he led the bay into a stand of willows and knee-hobbled the animal. His wounds were throbbing painfully, and as he unrolled his soogans, Jory knew he would not get a good night's sleep. He left the camp area and moved up a slope, pausing from time to time to look around into the growing shadows. A thin crescent moon gleamed remotely from the clear sky and stars were beginning to sparkle. He heard the far-off cry of a coyote calling his troubles to the moon, and from another direction a second coyote added his plaintive howling to the ghostly echoes. Then an owl hooted, and Jory drew a long, shuddering breath as he topped the slope and found himself staring down into unknown blackness, from the centre of which an oblong of yellow light marked the presence of an unseen building.

Was that the spot the six men rode from? It was obviously another of Sharkey's recently acquired smaller ranches, and Jory wished he had brought a local man along with him to act as a guide. But he did not hesitate. He wanted to find out what was happening on the range, and the only way he could do it was by checking up on his neighbours, whoever they were.

He walked down the slope towards the light, moving slowly. He was tired, for it had been a hard, eventful day, and when he thought of his blankets back there in camp he needed a great deal of effort to keep going in his high-heeled riding boots. As he drew nearer the light, he saw a fainter glimmer of light coming from another spot close by, and guessed he had stumbled upon a ranch headquarters. He moved more cautiously, for if these people were involved in the trouble going on they would be on their guard.

Jory almost walked into a guard. Creeping silently forward and taking advantage of every bit of available cover, he reached the edge of the yard and made his way to the back of a tool-shed. Candlelight showed through the faulty chinking in the uncured pine logs, and when he peered through a crack in the wall, Jory saw a man standing inside the shed, a cigarette glowing redly from the centre of the black shadow that was his face. Ruddy features showed when the man drew upon the cigarette. Jory eased his guns in their holsters. But he could do nothing until he knew what the situation was.

The man suddenly straightened and moved to the door, crushing out the cigarette. Jory caught the tang of tobacco smoke, and eased back as the man came into the open. For a few moments the man was silhouetted as he hurried across to what proved to be a large cabin, and the yellow oblong of light that had caught Jory's attention in the first place was a large window beside the door of the cabin. Jory followed, moving silently in a half-circle, aiming to get in behind the cabin. He could see chinks of light showing now, from gaps between the logs forming the walls of the cabin, and there was still the fainter light issuing from another cabin to his right. Jory reached the side wall of the cabin and stopped to peak in between the logs.

There was a rough board table with a lantern standing upon it in the centre of the single room, with some roughly fashioned wooden chairs standing around it. The yellow glow of the lantern cast heavy shadows into the corners of the room, but showed plainly the faces of the three men seated around the table. They were playing cards, and two of them were drinking whisky. The door opened and the man Jory had seen in the tool-shed entered slowly, slamming the door.

'Can't see a blame thing out there!' the man in the doorway complained. 'It's darker'n the inside of a cow.'

'You can't see nothing from in here,' one of the men at the table rasped. He was a stoop-shouldered individual with a prominent chin that jutted pugnaciously as he looked up from his cards.

'Hell, there aint no one out there snooping around,' the other retorted. 'What we got to be worried about? Far as anyone is concerned we're just plain, old-fashioned cowhands holding a line shack for Sharkey.'

'If Sharkey rode into that yard with a score of his gunnies you'd find something to be worried about,' came the angry reply. 'Get to hell back outside. If you can't see nothing then keep your ears skinned. We got a big stake in this, so let's try to do the best we can.'

'The others should've got back by now with that dough from Box A,' another at the table said, and Jory tightened his lips and pressed closer to the wall, restraining his cautious breathing as he took in the words.

'They know what they're doing. But it sure beats rustling.' The stoop-shouldered man seemed to be the boss, and he chuckled harshly. 'You got to hand it to the boss. He figures out more ways of picking up easy dough than any man I ever come across.'

'Who'd ever figure a man like him for a crook, huh?' the third man at the table demanded of no one in particular.

'Sure is playing for big stakes. Everyone figuring that Sharkey is trying to grab all the range, and in the end we're gonna see it fall into the hands of the boss.' The stoopshouldered man chuckled again, then cut off his mirth and scowled at the guard. 'Go on, Jed, get to hell out there! We're all taking it in turns to watch. We can't take any chances.'

'There ain't nothing to worry over,' the guard replied, shaking his head. 'If Sharkey was making any kind of a move on the range we'd sure learn about it fast from Elkins or Pollard.'

Jory clenched his teeth at the mention of the names, and his dark eyes glinted in the lamplight coming through the wall. These men had not received the latest news from the range, that was evident, he told himself, and considered busting in on them to inform them of the latest development. But he thought of the other cabin and its occupants, and knew he would have to check up on this place before taking action. But there was information here for the gathering, and he remained motionless against the wall, listening intently, aware that he could learn more this way than by taking these tough men prisoner and trying to make them talk. But the guard departed, slamming the door, and the other three occupants of the cabin resumed their game, falling silent and limiting their talk to the game itself.

With his mind working over what little he had gained, Jory moved away from the cabin and started across open space to the other cabin. He saw the guard moving back to the tool-shed, and kept in the dense shadows to avoid silhouetting himself. When he reached the second cabin he found a convenient chink in the wall and peered inside, to see some bunks that were occupied by several men. Faint candlelight barely illuminated the interior, but Jory counted four men. He backed off, aware that the odds against him were too great. He left the ranch completely and walked back to his camp.

Now he knew where the six men had come from, and had gained the knowledge that Buster Pollard was working with these hardcases. It had come out that they had been involved in the rustling, but their boss had devised the method of taking a hostage to force Woody Arlen to draw his savings out of the bank. Who was the boss? And the rustlers actually running off some Broken J cattle right now! Who were they acting for? Jory shook his head. But he knew what he had to do now. He needed to get his hands on Pollard. The big bully could be made to talk.

He broke camp and mounted the bay, turning back the way he had come, working out in his mind what direction he needed to take to come upon his own place. He had also learned that this suspicion concerning Sharkey's innocence of all that was laid at his name had some foundation. Someone had been throwing the blame at the Bar S rancher, and some of Sharkey's own outfit were renegades.

Dawn was greying the sky and blanking out the stars when he eventually reached Broken J, and he held up on a slope as the sun tinged the eastern horizon, and stared down at the spread. Nothing moved down there, but he didn't doubt that at least one pair of sharp eyes was watching the surrounding shadows for trouble. He massaged his right leg where the bullet wound throbbed dully and considered all that had befallen him in the short time since his arrival. It didn't seem possible that all this range belonged to him and that he had walked into the middle of a big fight for it. He sighed heavily as he started down the slope, and the first rays of sunlight threw long shadows over the dusty ground as he reached the yard.

A voice challenged him from the shelter of the barn, and he reined up, giving his name. A figure appeared and came towards him, rifle in hand, but the weapon was not pointed at him.

'Glad to see you, Boss!' the guard greeted. 'How'd you make out? Chilvers and Rouse from Box A came back after meeting up with you and told us what happened to Arlen yesterday. Did you find out where them tracks led to?'

'Yeah! But that can wait. What's the news of the rustlers?'

'Shorty has got most of the crew with him trailing the herd, which is moving north-west like all the other herds we lost,' the guard reported. 'We sent a man into town to warn the law, and I expect one of the deputies at least will show up soon. That's all I can tell you right now.'

'How many men here on the spread?' Jory asked.

'Me and two others, just in case someone gets a nasty idea about causing trouble around here.'

'Okay, so remain on guard. I'll get me some breakfast, then move out. Perhaps you'll take care of my horse for me, and throw my saddle on another mount. The bay is tuckered out and deserves a rest. I'll use the black I brought in with me yesterday!' Jory's lips twisted a little as he thought of Hank Penner. He wished his old pard were alive and backing him now.

He dismounted and handed over his reins, limping a little as he moved towards the house. Then he paused and turned to the guard, who was leading the bay towards the corral. 'Say, what can you tell me about the two line shacks about twenty miles east of here, on a river? I assume they belong to Sharkey, seeing that he's got most of the range surrounding us.'

'Yeah!' The guard said, looking over his shoulder. 'They're the old Swanston place that Sharkey bought up. He keeps some tough gunnies around there to watch out for his herds on that grass.'

'You know any of those gunnies by sight?' Jory demanded.

'Nope. We never mix with that kind, and we avoid them in town when we can, although we don't run from 'em!'

'Okay!' Jory sighed heavily and went into the house. He walked through to the kitchen and started cooking some breakfast. He was tired, and knew that a few hours sleep would help him, but there were some important things to be done before he could think of himself. He fried eggs and bacon and made coffee, and had just sat down to eat when boots pounded in the front of the house. He looked up as the kitchen door was thrust open, and saw Brad Terrill peering in at him, his deputy badge glinting in the gloom.

'Howdy,' the deputy greeted. 'Just got in from town. The sheriff ain't got back from Sharkey's place. He rode out've town with you yesterday to check on Sharkey's story about the shoot-up that took place at Bar S. But when we got word about the rustlers trailing off your range Chuck Reed figured I should ride out here to see what's going on. What can you tell me?'

'I don't know much myself,' Jory retorted. 'Want some grub and coffee? If so, help yourself. All I know is that my outfit are trailing the rustlers to see where they're headed, and we should have some results soon.'

'You got a man who can show me where the rustlers are now?' Terrill asked.

'Sure. I figure there's gonna be one helluva battle when we do find out what we wanta know.'

'Which is?' Terrill prompted.

'What happens to the steers once they leave our range!' Jory gulped his coffee.

'You riding out after the rustlers?'

'Nope. I got me another chore to handle.'

'Mind telling me what could be more important to you than catching rustlers who have been robbing you blind?'

'There's nothing to tell, yet. But I'll keep the law informed of what's turning up.' Jory smiled. He ate his breakfast while the deputy poured himself some coffee and sat down opposite.

The guard came through from the front of the house, carrying his rifle. He paused in the inner doorway and grinned at Jory.

'The black is ready saddled and standing there at the rail in front of the porch, boss!' he reported.

'Thanks. Can you tell the deputy where the rustlers are at this time?'

'They were making for Buzzard Pass, the last I heard. I reckon there'll be a rider coming back soon with their position at dawn.'

'I'll make for Buzzard Pass then,' Terrill said, getting to his feet. 'Thanks for the coffee, Jory. Be seeing you, and watch out for your back when you go riding off the spread.'

Jory nodded. The deputy departed, and a moment later Jory heard the sound of departing hooves. He finished his breakfast and stood up, feeling less tired with a good meal under his belt. He went out to the porch and stood for a moment, looking around, taking in the scene that must have greeted his uncle's gaze for many years. Then he went to the black, checked the rifle in the saddleboot, and mounted. He motioned for the guard to join him, and reined up beside the man.

'If anyone wants to know, I'm riding over to Bar S,' he said.

'Bar S?' The guard's eyebrows shot up in surprise. 'Now you hold your hosses a bit, Boss,' he went on quickly. 'That don't sound like a good idea to me.'

'Mebbe not, but it's about the best thing I could do at this time.' Jory smiled grimly. 'There's one thing I need to know before I pull out.'

'What's that?' The guard's tones were filled with doubt, and his expression was one of anxiety and concern.

'Where is Sharkey's ranch headquarters situated?'

'North-east!' The guard swung around and pointed towards the house. 'See that big rise yonder? Make for that. It's to the north of the place you visited yesterday.'

'And opposite to the direction the rustled cattle take,' Jory mused. 'Will I find a trail up that way?'

'Sure. If you make for that rise you'll cut the main trail between town and Bar S. Turn left when you find the trail. But I wish you wouldn't ride into that rattler's nest alone, Boss.'

'Just remember I rode there,' Jory commented, and swung his horse around. He cantered around the house and headed for the big rise. It was not until he had left the ranch far behind that he realised he had not asked the guard how far it was to Sharkey's place.

The sun was high in the brassy sky when he finally hit the trail he had been told to look for, and he turned left along the broad ribbon of ruts that cut through the green slope looking as they came from nowhere and were heading back into the unknown. Two hours later he caught his first glimpse of the Bar S.

Sharkey's place was big, with plenty of space between the ranch buildings. Jory reined up and studied the peaceful scene. There was a wide creek near the house, and sunlight glinted upon the smooth surface. Trees grew around the far edge of the creek, and their shade looked black and foreboding from a distance. Nothing moved anywhere that Jory looked, and he drew a long breath and held it for a moment as he gigged the black forward and began his approach. He rode steadily, watchful, ready for trouble, skirting all likely ambush spots, but as he drew level with the mouth of a gully a rider kicked his mount into view, a rifle in his hands, and another man, afoot, appeared some twenty yards further on. Jory reined up under the threat of the weapons, and sat holding his reins, waiting for developments.

'Hell if it ain't Jory hisself!' the mounted man said. 'What you planning on doing now, mister?'

'I wanta talk to Sharkey!'

'Yeah? Well you ain't getting within a mile of the ranch. Them's our orders from the boss.'

'You paid us a visit yesterday,' the other man snarled. 'It'll take a week to fill in all the bullet holes you left.'

'I didn't shoot up the place, and if I was planning to do so I wouldn't have come riding up like this,' Jory said. 'I'm going in to see Sharkey, and that's flat.'

'What you got to see him about?'

'That's between him and me!' Jory kept his tones even. 'The fact that I'm alone should prove that I ain't primed for trouble.'

'Okay! But you take off your guns before you get within shooting range!'

'Nope.' Jory grinned. He gigged his mount and started on again, leaving the men standing, and for some moments his muscles were tensed in anticipation of a shot in the back. But nothing happened and he kept riding without turning to look bade. He had covered three hundred yards when a rifle cracked and flung a string of echoes across the range. It came from behind, but the bullet did not pass anywhere near Jory. He threw a quick look over his right shoulder and saw that one of the guards had fired his rifle skywards, obviously to warn the ranch of his approach, and Jory tightened his lips as he continued.

When he reached the yard he found a reception committee awaiting his arrival. Ben Sharkey was standing on the porch of the house, a Winchester in his hands. He was flanked by his inevitable bodyguards, Buster Pollard and Lou Bragg. None of the three seemed very pleased, and Jory smiled grimly as he rode steadily towards the porch, passing a bunk-house, which was on his right, where three gunmen were standing with ready sixguns, and a barn on the left, where two more men holding rifles were standing.

Ignoring the hired guns, Jory rode up to the porch and reined in. He sat his saddle casually, his hands steady on the reins, and looked into the scowling face of Ben Sharkey.

'What in hell do you want here, Jory?' the Bar S rancher demanded in rasping tones.

'Sounds just like a good taste of real old-fashioned western hospitality,' Jory countered, grinning. He let his gaze flicker to Buster Pollard, and saw hatred and evil desire showing in the big man's fleshy expression. Bragg was standing motionless, his right arm still in a sling, and Jory wondered if the gunman was in on the crookedness with Pollard.

'What the hell do you expect me to do, get out the whisky jug?' Sharkey demanded curtly. 'What's on your mind, Jory? What makes you figure you can ride in here and out again without getting hurt?'

'Maybe because I half believed you when you stood in the law office and said you was getting trouble like the rest of the range,' Jory said.

Sharkey's expression eased a little, although puzzlement came into his alert eyes.

'What the hell you getting at?' he demanded.

'You find any renegades in your outfit?' Jory countered.

'I can trust my life with any of the men on my payroll!' Ben Sharkey's thick lips twisted. 'What's on your mind?'

'What about the men you got out at the line shacks on Swanston's old spread?' Jory's gaze did not waver from Sharkey's big figure, but he could see both Bragg and Pollard out of the corners of his eyes, and Pollard tensed at the mention of Swanston's place.

'Who we got out there?' Sharkey half turned to look at Pollard.

'Four men,' Pollard growled. 'They're trustworthy.'

'What about the six men who rode out of those line shacks the night before last and hit Woody Arlen's place?' Jory explained what had happened to Arlen, and saw surprise and disbelief show on Sharkey's face. 'Three of those men were called Thomas, Timson and Mills,' he continued relentlessly. 'Ever heard of them before, Sharkey?'

'Never! But I don't expect you to believe that, Jory!'

'Maybe I do believe you,' Jory retorted. 'Maybe you've been fooled the same way a lot of folks around here have been taken in. Right now there's a gang of rustlers running off a big herd of my stock. They're pushing through Buzzard Pass about now.'

'And you've come here?' Sharkey demanded. 'What do you want, help to catch them thieves? They must be the same bunch that have been hitting my brand.'

'They're the same ones okay,' Jory said, nodding. 'But we don't need to go after them. My outfit is trailing them, and there's a deputy gone out to make sure the law is enforced. It looks like the beginning of the end for this bad bunch that's been causing all the trouble. But there is a man behind this who's got hisself buried deep under the wood-pile, and he's the one I'm trying to smoke out.'

'You figure it's me?' Sharkey rasped.

'I did at first, but I don't now. That's why I'm here, Sharkey. If I believed it was you I wouldn't have come in alone. But here I am, and I'm gonna tell you something that you don't know. There is a renegade in your outfit, maybe more, and it's time you knew about him.' Jory paused, knowing that he had taken a big chance in making this approach, and the only real weapon he had, apart from the guns on his hips, was bluff. He let his gaze shift slightly to focus upon Buster Pollard, who was looking tense and worried, and he nodded slowly. 'Yeah,' he drawled.

'You can look worried, Pollard! I got the deadwood on you! What you gonna do about it, huh?'

For a moment it seemed that the bluff would not succeed, for Pollard remained motionless, his eyes glittering. Then the big man uttered a curse and made a grab at his holstered sixgun. Jory reached for his holstered weapons, noting that Bragg, on the other side of the startled Bar S rancher, was also making a grim play with his left hand. Jory clenched his teeth. This was a situation that every gunslinger dreaded. It called for a two-handed draw and firing simultaneously at two different targets. If he missed with either shot he would be dead...

Eleven

It seemed that time stood still in that split second of action, and Jory could see that despite having to use his left hand, Lou Bragg was getting into the fight faster than Pollard. Jory was slightly faster with his right-hand gun, and as it cleared leather he swung the muzzle and cut loose at Bragg just as the gunnie got moving. The crash of the shot rocked the porch, and Bragg went slumping sideways against Sharkey. Jory had his left-hand gun coming clear by then, and saw that Pollard was also clearing the top of his holster and lifting his big .45. They fired almost together, gunsmoke pluming through the clean, bright air.

Jory felt a flashing pain in his left arm and his left-hand gun went spinning into the dust. He saw dust puff from the gay-coloured checks of Pollard's shirt, and the big range boss spun around clutching at his right shoulder with his left hand. He fell to the boards, losing his grip upon his gun, and lay writhing in agony.

Bragg was hard hit. He had bent forward under the impact of Jory's first shot, his three-quarters drawn gun sliding back into its holster. Bragg dropped to his knees, looking up at Jory as his life ran out of the gaping hole in the centre of his chest. As Jory returned his attention to the gunman, Bragg pitched forward silently upon his face and lay still.

Sharkey remained motionless, his eyes glaring, his face set in granite lines, and the rifle in his hands made no attempt to buy into the fight. Gunsmoke swirled across the porch. Jory clenched his teeth for a moment. His left arm felt as if it had been kicked by a mule, and the familiar numbing sensation that came with the heavy impact of a bullet wound was beginning to spread through the limb above the elbow. He looked at Sharkey.

'Pollard is our man,' he said grimly. 'I don't know about Bragg, but he bought into the fight. What about it, Sharkey? Are you mixed up in the trouble on the range or have these men been duping you with the rest of the folk around here?'

'If I was in with the crookedness I'd have worked this rifle when they cut loose,' Sharkey said jerkily, and now sweat was showing on his face.

'What about the rest of your crew? Whose side are they on?'

'You tell me! You seem to know more about this than I do!' Sharkey let his gaze swing past Jory to take in his men at the bunkhouse and barn.

'What are they doing?' Jory demanded. 'Why haven't they cut loose at me?'

'I guess Pollard never had any pards in my outfit. Nor Bragg neither.' Sharkey spoke gruffly. 'Okay, so you made this your play. You better go on with it, because I don't know what the hell this is all about. Hell, I never seen a gunhand like you before, Jory! I figured I was safe with Bragg and Pollard to guard me. But you took them both on and beat'em.'

'Bragg looks like he's dead, but Pollard is alive, so let's try to get something out've him. His name was mentioned by some of the men causing the trouble. Pollard and Elkins, and you already know that Elkins carried the word to Rourke about sending Burnett to shoot up my place. I guess that order originated from Pollard and not you, huh?'

'That's a fact,' Sharkey said. He put down his rifle and turned to Pollard, who was slumped against the front wall of the house, semi-conscious, his left hand clamped to the spreading bloodstain on his right shoulder. 'Come on, Buster! Snap out've it. You got some questions to answer, the hell if you ain't.'

Jory holstered his right-hand gun. He bent to pick up his second gun, and had to use his right hand to thrust it into his holster. When he looked at his left arm he found a bullet hole in his sleeve above the elbow. Blood was flowing from both sides of the arm and he knew the slug had gone clean through the flesh. He gritted his teeth against the pain and looked at Lou Bragg. As he had figured, the gunman was dead.

Sharkey hauled Pollard to his feet, holding the big man with one hand gripping Pollard's shirt. Jory stepped onto the porch and turned to look around the yard. He saw that the armed men were coming forward slowly, rifles ready, but none of them looked as if they contemplated shooting.

'What are you waiting around for?' Sharkey yelled. 'Benson, you take half a dozen men and ride over to the cabins on Swanston's place. You'll find some hardcases holed up there. Take 'em alive if you can, then head into town with them and hand 'em over to the sheriff.'

Jory heaved a long sigh of relief as the men turned and started for the corral. He gripped his left arm above the elbow with the fingers of his right, and turned his attention to Buster Pollard, who was sagging in Sharkey's powerful grip. Pollard looked out on his feet, but his eyelids were flickering, and despite the seriousness of the big renegade's wound, Jory figured the man was foxing a little. He reached out and slapped Pollard's face lightly, causing the man to jerk and open his eyes.

'What the hell!' Pollard spoke thickly, through his fleshy lips.

'I got just one question for you, Pollard!' Jory said grimly. 'Who's your boss?'

'Sharkey is,' Pollard said faintly, closing his eyes and slumping in Sharkey's grip.

'I mean the man who's running the crookedness with you,' Jory insisted.

'There ain't no one!' Pollard shook his head.

'You ain't gonna convince me that you're the boss,' Jory rasped. 'You don't have the brains for that. You better come clean. You might be able to help yourself. This crooked deal is all washed up right now. The men who were trying to get money out of Woody Arlen are dead and my outfit, along with the law, are trailing the rustlers. It'll all come out into the open now. Those hardcases at the Swanston place will be picked up, and I heard them mention your name in connection with a boss who's been running things.'

Pollard kept his eyes closed and shook his head. Sharkey took a tighter grip upon the big man and shook him fiercely.

'I bet I'll get it out've you,' he rasped. 'You've been making me look like a thief around here to my neighbours, Pollard, and all the time you've been telling me that it was my neighbours causing my trouble. Well I guess you know what I do to rustlers and renegades, huh? You've helped me string some of them up. So now it's your turn.'

Pollard opened his eyes. He was dazed, filled with the shock of his wound, but there was a glimmer of intelligence in his gaze. He looked into Sharkey's merciless features, then shifted his glance to Jory's intent face.

'You'll never pick him out in a hundred years,' he rasped. 'I got nothing to say.'

'I can tell you who I think it is,' Jory said easily.

Pollard's eyes widened, and his shock receded as he stared into Jory's grim features. Jory nodded slowly.

'I don't need you to tell me who it is, Pollard,' Jory said. 'I got my suspicions, and I'll prove it soon as I can get my hands on him. All I wanted you to do was confirm what I believe.'

'Who is it?' Sharkey demanded. 'Just let me get my hands on him.'

'Nick Marsh!' Jory watched Pollard's expressive face as he spoke. 'I figure he didn't expect Silas Jory's heir to show up, and he began to help himself to the ranch assets. When I showed up he knew he was in trouble, and I figure he brought in some of these strangers we've been seeing. He reckoned it would be easy to knock me off and lay the blame at your door, Sharkey.'

'That's what has been happening,' the big Bar S rancher said. He shook Pollard angrily. 'Is that the rights of it, you double-dealing skunk?'

'You think you know all the answers,' Pollard retorted. 'Well go ahead and prove it.'

Jory nodded slowly. 'Sharkey,' he said, 'the sheriff told me to check out my ranch accounts, so he must have suspected something like this. Conway was on his way out here yesterday when I left him. Did you see him?'

'No.' Sharkey shook his head. 'He didn't show up here. He said he was coming to check on the shooting that happened.'

'That's right!' Jory frowned. He clenched his teeth against the pain in his arm. 'I wonder what is going on around here. I saw Terrill at my place this morning before I rode here, and he said Conway hadn't gone back to town after setting out for this place.'

'Well he didn't show up here,' Sharkey said. 'Leastways, I didn't see him. What about you, Pollard?' He shook the semi-conscious man. 'Did you see the sheriff?'

Hoofs pounded and Jory swung round, to see some of Sharkey's outfit riding across the yard to obey the order to pick up the hardcases at Swanston's place. He shook his head slowly.

'Let's fix Pollard so he can ride and I'll take him into town and get someone to stick him in the jail,' he said.

'I'll ride with you,' Sharkey said. 'I wanta see the end of this. If that shyster Nick Marsh is involved then I wanta see him get what he deserves.'

They dragged Pollard to the bench on the porch and propped him on it. Sharkey fetched his medicine chest, and they applied some rough first-aid to Pollard's shoulder wound. Then the Bar S rancher attended to Jory's wound, and there was a glint in Sharkey's pale eyes when he gazed into Jory's face. He chuckled harshly.

'I wouldn't have believed it if someone had told me yesterday that we'd be here like this, helping each other,' Sharkey commented. 'That skunk in the woodpile you mentioned sure had us fighting the wrong shadows, huh?'

'Yeah, but I suspicioned something like this almost from the start.' Jory's eyes glittered as he considered. 'I guess they played this a little too smart for their own good.'

When they were ready to ride Pollard was thrust into the saddle of a horse, and Sharkey gave strict orders to the men he left behind on the ranch. Then he and Jory set out, leading Pollard's mount, and they headed for town. Jory relaxed a little, trying to ease his wounded left arm. They had a long ride ahead of them, and it was going to be uncomfortable, but Pollard was going to suffer worst of all.

They followed a faint trail, and by midmorning were well on their way. Then Jory spotted buzzards circling in the faultless blue sky a mile or so ahead, and brought the sight to Sharkey's notice.

'Hell, someone or something is down in the dust,' the rancher commented. 'Let's get on and find out what.'

They pushed on faster, despite Pollard's complaints about his wound, and when they rode over the crest of a hill they spotted a horse down on the ground in the middle distance. Jory rode ahead of Sharkey, his glittering eyes narrowed, and before he reached the spot where the horse was lying he had recognised it as the animal that Sheriff Conway rode the day before. Jory sprang out of his saddle, scaring off half a dozen buzzards that had been ripping the carcass with their vicious beaks. He took in the gory scene, his experienced gaze looking for tracks and signs to tell him what had occurred.

There were boot tracks in the dust, leading away from the dead horse in a wavering line, as if the man who had left them had been hurt in the incident that had killed the horse. There were also the tracks of another rider, and Jory dropped to one knee to check the prints of the horseman who had come up, inspected the scene, then rode away.

'What do you make of it?' Sharkey called. He had reined up some yards away to avoid spoiling any prints that might be around. 'That's Ed Conway's hoss, for sure!'

'Could have fallen and broken a leg, or stopped a bullet,' Jory said, swinging back into his saddle. 'Come on. Looks like Conway wasn't killed. His tracks head out that way.'

'Towards your place,' Sharkey said. 'He must've needed help real bad.'

They rode on as fast as possible, and had barely covered two miles when they spotted more buzzards circling in the sky, swooping down and showing interest in a particular spot. Jory tightened his lips and urged the black into a run, leaving Sharkey behind, who was handicapped by having to lead Pollard's horse. Jory expected to find the sheriff's body, but as he neared the spot where the buzzards flew he heard the rolling echoes of a shot, and kicked the black into greater effort. If it was Ed Conway then the lawman was still alive.

Another shot sounded, and Jory saw that whoever it was scaring off the buzzards was forted up in a gully. He rode up carefully, halting within yards of the rim of the gully, and called harshly.

'Hello, there! This is Steve Jory. Who's in there? Is it you sheriff?'

'Jory!' Conway's faint tones came in immediate reply. 'Hell, am I glad to hear you! I was making for your place.'

Jory dismounted and went forward, peering into the gully, and he saw Conway stretched out on his back, a gun in his hand. The sheriff had blood on his shirt front which had oozed from a bullet hole, and Jory was puzzled as he went down to the lawman's side.

'What happened, Sheriff?' he demanded. 'We spotted your horse a couple miles back.'

Conway sank back as Jory reached him, and lost consciousness, his will-power fading with help at hand. Ben Sharkey swung out of his saddle, his boots thumping the hard ground, and the Bar S rancher came hurrying to Jory's side.

'Is he dead?' Sharkey demanded.

'Not yet, but he's in bad shape,' Jory replied, opening the sheriff's shirt. 'You got a canteen on your saddle?'

'I got better than that,' Sharkey replied with a grin. 'I got a bottle of whisky in my saddlebag. I'll get it.'

'And water,' Jory said. 'He must have been out here since yesterday.'

Between them they worked on the unconscious lawman, and after some minutes, when Conway had been forced to swallow some of the whisky, the sheriff's eyes flickered open. He groaned and reached out to grasp Jory's right hand.

'Hear me out,' he said hoarsely. 'You listen good, Sharkey. It concerns you as well as Jory, and you'll both need to get this as evidence.'

'Take it easy, Sheriff,' Jory warned.

'No time. I'm done for.' Conway shook his head. 'Just listen, will you? Nick Marsh is the man you want, Jory. He's been milking your ranch dry. He didn't figure you'd ever turn up. I got mixed up in it when I went to Marsh for back taxes on Broken J after your uncle died. Like a fool I fell in with Marsh to get what we could from the spread. It was easy to lay all the blame at Sharkey's door, him being the way he is. But when you showed up, Jory, I knew we couldn't get away with it any longer, but Marsh was in too deep to get out. He's met a lot of badmen in his time, defending some of them in the courts, and he brought in some gunnies. You and Sharkey had that run-in soon as you showed up, and that made it easy for Marsh to make it look that the pair of you was heading for a final showdown. With Pollard on Marsh's side Sharkey couldn't win nohow.'

Conway suddenly slumped, and as Jory checked the lawman, his big hands steady and gentle, he looked into Sharkey's face.

'It's all coming out now, huh?' he demanded.

'And then some!' Sharkey shook his head. 'I can't believe it though. Do you figure he's out've his head?'

'He's giving it to us straight,' Jory retorted. 'He's dying!'

'Pour some more whisky into him,' Sharkey said harshly. 'We wanta get all we can out've him. How'd he come to be shot? Who done for him?'

Jory lifted the sheriff's head and Sharkey pushed the whisky bottle against the lawman's teeth. Conway gulped and opened his eyes.

'Who shot you, Ed?' Sharkey demanded.

'Marsh! He was gonna plug you, Ben, and I had to put the blame on you, Jory. It looked like you had to be put out of the way legal, if possible, the way you kept beating all the traps Marsh set for you. But I wanted out of the game. I knew we couldn't get away with it. Marsh let it out that he was going to Kemp's Ridge for a week, but he didn't head out there. He came to knock off Sharkey.'

'So you quarrelled with Marsh about the killing and he shot you, is that it?' Jory demanded.

'Yeah! He took me by surprise, but he didn't kill me like he figured.' Conway grinned slightly, his teeth stained with blood. 'You go get him, Jory, and fix him good. He's planning on getting clean away. I told him your outfit was trailing his rustlers, and when I said I had to throw in with you to save my own skin he pulled a hide-out gun and let me have it in the chest. But mebbe you're too late now! He shot me yesterday! He's had almost a whole day to clear up his business in town and pull out.'

Jory pushed himself to his feet, his face set in harsh lines. 'Don't worry about that, Sheriff,' he said thinly. 'I'll get Marsh if it's the last thing I do, no matter where he runs to. But what about my outfit? Marsh got any men on my payroll?'

'Nope. He didn't need any. But you're wasting time.' Conway slumped a little. 'Go nail that snake, Jory. Take my law star with you. I disgraced it, but if you can stop Marsh for me it'll even up matters a little.'

Jory took the sheriff's star and dropped it into his pocket.

He turned to leave the gully, and Sharkey called to him.

'Hey, what about me?' the Bar S rancher demanded. 'I want in on the action.'

'You've got Pollard to bring in, and you better do what you can for Conway. I'll ride on ahead in case Marsh is still in town. My arrival started this showdown, and I figure I'll be there to see the end of it!'

'Don't underestimate Marsh,' Conway muttered, 'and watch out for his hideout gun.'

Jory scrambled out of the gully and threw himself into the black's saddle. He spurred the big horse and went on along the trail, leaving a semi-conscious Buster Pollard staring after him with glazed eyes. Sharkey climbed out of the gully, leaving a dead sheriff at his back, and the big rancher cursed angrily as he climbed into his saddle and set out to try and catch the fast-moving Jory. But he was handicapped by the horse he was leading, and he vowed that if he missed the action in town he would have the satisfaction of watching Buster Pollard hang when his time came.

By the time he sighted Sunset, darkness was creeping in across the range to envelop the town, and bright splashes of lights from saloons and stores warned Jory that he might be too late to catch Nick Marsh. He was feeling the strain of the past days, and rode along the main street at an easy pace, making for the law office. Dismounting, he left the tired black at the hitchrail and crossed the sidewalk. When he tried the door of the office he found it locked, and a sigh escaped him as he wondered where Chuck Reed could be. He needed to inform the law of the developments that had taken place, and it would be up to Reed to arrest Marsh.

He went on to the hotel, passing Marsh's house, where a light was showing in a ground floor room, and then riding by Marsh's office, which was in total darkness. He slid out of his saddle in front of the hotel and reeled across the sidewalk, almost falling through the doorway. His left arm was throbbing painfully and he knew he had to get some medical attention before the wound turned bad. A hand reached out to touch him as he straightened on the threshold, and he was surprised to see Sue Arlen's anxious face peering at him.

'Steve, you've been hurt again!' the girl declared.

'Sue!' He clutched at her shoulder with his right hand. 'Where is your Pa? Have you seen Chuck Reed around?'

'Reed rode out with a posse as soon as we came into town and reported what had happened out at our place. A big clean-up is going on right now. By tomorrow all the trouble on the range will be over.'

'Nick Marsh! Have you seen him around?' Jory kept his voice steady, but he was tense and strained inside.

'I saw him this afternoon. He was on the street in front of the bank, talking to Mortimer Dillon. Is anything wrong, Steve?'

'Not now, especially if Marsh is still in town.'

'His wife and daughter left on the evening stage. It pulled out two hours ago.'

'And there's a light in Marsh's house!' The tiredness fell away from Jory and he straightened his weary shoulders. 'Where's your Pa, Sue?'

'In one of the saloons, I think. He said he needed a drink.'

'Well I can't look for him. He wanted to be in on the showdown, and I figure I might need a witness. But I must get to Marsh. You stay put here, Sue, and don't leave the place.'

He turned, ignoring the girl's further questions, and went out to the darkness of the sidewalk. He started to the left for Marsh's house, but when he reached the batwings of the big saloon he paused and let his dark, narrowed gaze sweep the interior. His eyes glinted when he saw Mortimer Dillon sitting in on a poker game at a nearby table. Pushing through the batwings with his right shoulder, he went to the banker's side, and Dillon looked up as Jory's tall shadow fell across him.

'Steve! Hell, you look like you've had a rough time of it. Are you all right?' Dillon started to his feet.

'I'm okay,' Jory spoke stiffly through his thin lips. 'You spoke to Marsh this afternoon. I figured he was out of town for a week!'

'Had to come back for some vital papers,' Dillon retorted. 'He also drew a considerable sum of money from his bank account.'

'Did he leave town again?'

'I don't know his plans, but his wife and daughter left on the coach earlier.' Dillon shrugged. 'I don't know what's going on, but you ought to see Marsh as soon as you can and get your accounts straightened out.'

'I plan to make that the next chore I handle,' Jory said, and turned away.

He left the saloon and went on along the sidewalk, seeing the lighted window in Marsh's house, and the oblong of yellow brilliance attracted him as a candle attracts a moth. He stole across the garden, his right hand down by the butt of his holstered gun. When he tried the front door he found it was locked, and he hammered upon the thick panels with his fists. The sounds echoed away into the night, but there was no reply, and when he went to the lighted window and tried to get a glimpse inside the room he found that heavy drapes blocked off his vision. He tightened his lips, then went back to the door and lifted his right foot, lunging at the door with his boot. His weight crashed the lock and the door flew inwards while he blundered forward off balance and stumbled across the threshold.

A gun exploded from inside the house, the bullet fanning Jory's cheek. He answered it mechanically, without conscious thought of drawing his gun. A shadow moved in the blackness of the interior and an orange streak lanced at Jory again, illuminating briefly the crouched figure in the background. Jory ducked, throwing himself to the right, and took his silhouetted figure out of the doorway. He held his fire, waiting for the echoes to fade before calling vibrantly.

'Marsh I got you dead to rights,' he said urgently. 'I came across Ed Conway out on the range, and he wasn't dead.'

The sound of a door slamming somewhere in the back of the house warned Jory that he was alone, and he blundered to his feet and went forward through unfamiliar surroundings. He fumbled for a door that led into a kitchen, and a gun crashed from the open outer door that gave access to the back lots. There was a splat as the slug struck the doorpost by Jory's head, and he thumbed off an instinctive reply at the gun flash which showed. He went forward determinedly, and caught a glimpse of a figure dashing along the rear of the buildings fronting the street, trying to keep within their protective shadows.

Jory's gun muzzle lifted and roared, jerking as the heavy slug was tossed through the night. He blinked his eyes against the flash and ran after the moving figure. He saw a bag clutched in Marsh's left hand. The lawyer seemed to be making for the stable. But Jory clenched his teeth. There was not a chance that Marsh could get away, he told himself grimly. The lawyer had left it too late.

Marsh did not fire again, but twice more Jory caught a glimpse of the lawyer's fleeting figure, and he increased his stride, his tiredness and aches and pains forgotten in the thrill of the chase. The big livery barn loomed up in the background, and Jory slowed imperceptibly, aware that his boots were making a lot of noise on the hard ground. A gun flash winked from the dense shadows surrounding the barn, and he sent two quick shots at it, spacing them a couple of inches apart. He kept moving forward, intent upon the final showdown, and came up against the open rear door to the barn. He eased through the doorway, then froze in surprise, for the blazing lantern suspended from a nail in a post showed him Nick Marsh standing at bay, a bulging leather bag in his left hand, a gun in his right.

Jory halted, his .45 lined up on the lawyer's sleek body. He saw the desperate expression on Marsh's face.

'No need for talk,' Jory said breathlessly. 'This is the end of the trail, Marsh. I know all about it. You got a choice. Throw down your gun and take your chance in court, or try to kill me. You been trying hard enough to have me put out of the way.'

'I got no choice,' Marsh said thinly. His face was covered with a sheen of sweat. 'You said you found the sheriff! But if I kill you now no one will know about me.'

'Wrong!' Jory shook his head, a grim smile on his lips. 'I was with Ben Sharkey when I found the sheriff. Sharkey knows about you.'

Marsh's gun moved slightly then, and Jory knew the moment had come. An intangible message was flashed from his brain to his gunhand and his trigger finger jerked convulsively. He saw Marsh's gun buck as it spurted smoke and flame, and a double clap of gun thunder shook the barn as Jory's Colt joined in almost simultaneously.

An invisible giant fist blasted a bolt of burning lightning through Jory's chest and slammed him back and away from Marsh, his brain seeming to numb under the crushing impact. His gun hand faltered and he felt himself falling, his sense of balance gone. He tried to halt the sickening movement but found he could do nothing about it, and hit the ground heavily, his staring eyes upon Marsh's heavy figure. He saw the lawyer huddling over, dead on his feet with a bullet through the heart, and then Jory's head struck something hard and his senses darted into a tunnel that rapidly grew darker and darker, until there was nothing left at all except blessed release from the roaring and thundering echoes...

The next thing he knew was something shimmering through the blackness, and for a moment his vision cleared and he saw figures about him. But only one fully materialised and he recognised Sue Arlen. The girl was on her knees beside him, his head pillowed in her lap. He saw concern and relief mingled in her lovely features.

'Lay still, Steve!' she said. 'They've sent for the doctor. 'You've been shot through the chest, but Pa says it won't kill you. You've got some broken ribs and you're losing a lot of blood.'

'I'll survive,' he muttered stiffly, 'if you'll nurse me.'

She pressed a cool hand against his fevered brow, and he saw a smile touch her lips.

'That's a promise,' she said softly.

Jory nodded and closed his eyes. It was a promise all right, and there were other promises in the background that he had not even begun to think about yet. All he was aware of, as he slipped back into senselessness, was that he had survived the shooting, and it looked as if he could now follow Hank Penner's dying advice. He would quit the gun trail and settle down to a more peaceful way of living. There was a readymade life here for him in Bowie County.

Wild Men

One

The bullet struck hard rock with a frightening thud, then screamed away across the range in shrill protest. Steve Blaine gulped in surprise and reined up, throwing a quick glance around to see who was shooting at him. His blue eyes narrowed when he spotted three horsemen heading up a slope and making for him. He dropped a hand to his gun holstered on his right hip, but did not draw the weapon. He had recognised Zeke Coppard, owner of the Circle Z Ranch, leading the other two. Anger surged upwards inside him as he waited for the cowman and two of his hired hands to arrive.

"What the hell are you up to?" Blaine demanded as the trio came within earshot. "Are you trying to start a range war? Don't you know it's dangerous to start throwing lead around? Someone is likely to throw it right back at you."

"Simmer down, Blaine," growled Zeke Coppard, his dark eyes glittering with anger. "Sit still and take your hand off that gun or you'll maybe wish you'd never settled in this part of the country."

"I've had about all I can take from you," Steve snapped, eyeing the two gunmen with the rancher.

They had halted at Coppard's side and were moving apart in case trouble flared. The one on the left was Frank Trory, a sandy-haired man with sharp features and a fast gun. Steve did not know the other, but quickly summed him up as a hard-case. He threw his gaze back at the watchful Coppard. "What are you doing on our range?" he demanded.

"Your range?" the rancher snarled. "I ran my cows on this grass before you were born."

"And now you can't do that any more," Steve told him. "Me and my pa bought this land, and you can keep off it, Coppard."

"You should show some respect for your elders," cut in Frank Trory, his pale eyes glistening.

"What do you want here?" Steve repeated to Coppard, ignoring the gunman completely.

"I lost three good saddle horses this morning," the rancher snapped. "And we followed their prints clear across your line."

"So?" Steve straightened his big frame in the saddle, his eyes hardening. "Are you saying that we steal horses too? We don't bar folk from our range. If anyone stole your horse flesh and headed this way then they kept right on going. You're at liberty to take a look around, Coppard, but don't come here shouting accusations, and don't ever throw lead at me again on my own range."

Frank Trory chuckled, and Steve gazed angrily at the gunman. He was tempted to draw his Colt and show these hard-cases just what a newcomer could do, but he fought down the urge. Trory had a big reputation. There was no sense asking for trouble and getting killed. His father would never get over the shock. Steve gathered up his reins.

"Where is your old man?" Coppard demanded. "I want to talk to him. Maybe I'll get more sense out of him."

"You know where our house is, "Steve retorted. "But the next time you want to cross our range, Coppard, you'd better ride up to the house first and ask permission."

"Damn you, you young cub," the rancher grated. "I've a good mind to get down out of my saddle and teach you some manners."

"The fault lies with you, not me, "Steve replied tightly. "You're full of spite because two strangers came in here and bought some of the best grazing land in the county out from under you. You used this land for years, Coppard, but it was never yours, and me and my father have got legal right to it, so don't come growling around here. This is our land and you've get to accept it."

The old rancher's face was tight with anger, his dark eyes Hashing. Frank Trory had lost his grin. He sat hard-faced and taut, with his gun-hand resting on his hip just above the black butt of his notorious .45.

"Do you want me to teach him a lesson, Boss?" he demanded.

"You may get a surprise," Steve told him. "Don't push your luck, mister, on my range."

Coppard wheeled his horse away. Then he reined in and glared back over his shoulder. Steve grinned at the older man, feeling his anger grow cold as he realised that he was pushing for a fight. He relaxed instantly and turned the head of his horse and rode slowly up the slope, trembling a little. He glanced back once and saw the three riders heading back for the Circle Z.

There was a lot of truth in what he had said, he reflected. Zeke Coppard was still angry at having lost his best range when Steve and his father Heck had moved into the country. The Circle Z had no title to what was now the Double B Ranch, and Steve could understand Coppard's anger at the oversight which had robbed him of valuable water as well as good grazing land. For the first six months after they had moved into the Double B, Steve and his father had been primed for trouble from the Circle Z, but Tom Griffin, sheriff of nearby Buffalo Grove, had made it clear to everyone that he would stand no nonsense from any source, and the fact that there had been no trouble was a tribute to Griffin's reputation as a tough lawman.

Steve rode home slowly and swung down into the dusty yard. He looked around for his father but could not see the older man. He left his horse at the hitch rail he had put up in front of the house and thrust open the front door.

"Pa," he called, "are you here?"

"Sure, son," came the husky reply. "Come on in." Steve entered the house and walked through to the kitchen. He shouldered open the door, then halted in surprise. Three rough-faced men were with his father, and all four were tense and angry looking.

"What's going on here?" Steve asked, dropping his right hand to the butt of his gun. "Have you got some trouble, pa?"

"No, Steve," Heck Blaine said. "These are three old friends who have just dropped by to see me."

"They must be old, "Steve retorted. "I can't remember ever seeing them."

"I know them from way back," Heck Blaine responded, and Steve's eyes narrowed. He knew his father well, and realised that something was bothering the older man.

"Suppose you tell me what's on your mind," Steve snapped. He was still feeling sore at the way Coppard had spoken to him. "They don't look like any friends of yours."

"Watch your tongue, youngster," one of the men growled. He was a bitter-faced man in his middle forties, with penetrating dark eyes and a rugged face.

"It's easy to see that he's Heck Blaine's son," said another, whose fat body shook as he laughed. A blond moustache braced a thick upper lip, and the straggly ends of it hung over the fleshy mouth. "Better not rile him, Milt. He may be as fast with that gun as Heck used to be."

"What do you mean, used to be?" Heck Blaine demanded. He was an older model of Steve, with a big frame, blond hair and light blue eyes. "I can still draw a fast gun," he announced.

"You've been arguing about something," Steve accused. "I reckon it must be something in the air hereabouts. I just met Zeke Coppard, and he was riled up about losing three horses. He wanted to take a look around here for them. I nearly called him out."

The fat man laughed in a high pitched tone. "Would Coppard be the owner of the ranch just west of here?" he asked.

"That's right." Steve spoke sharply. "What about it?"

"That's where we stopped and changed horses, that's all."

"Do you mean to say you rode into the Circle Z and took three horses?" Steve demanded.

"We left three in their places," said the bitter-faced man called Milt. "Do you call that stealing?"

"It doesn't matter what I call it," Steve snapped. "But Zeke Coppard had two gunmen with him, and they were calling it stealing." He glanced at his silent father. "What kind of friends are these, pa?"

"You mean to tell us your pa ain't never told you about the Wild Men?" demanded the third man, a mean-faced broad-shouldered man of around forty-five.

"The Wild Men! Why sure I've heard about them, but what would my pa know about them?"

"You should ask him," retorted the fat man, and laughed in his irritating high tone.

"What's going on, pa?" Steve demanded. "What the hell has got into everyone today?"

"These men are old friends of mine, like I said," Heck Blaine said softly, but his blues eyes were fierce. "I guess I never did get around to telling you, using all my time to make you grow up good and honest and clean like you should, but I was the leader of the gang called The Wild Men. We robbed and stole from here to the Texas border. It was when your ma died that I gave up the wild life and collected you to bring you up. I ain't seen any of these men in twenty years."

Steve leaned back against the wall, his face pale with shock. He stared at his father. The three outlaws watched him, grinning.

"That's knocked some of the iron out of you," the fat man said. "You didn't know your pappy was a crook, huh?"

"What was the trouble, Heck?" demanded the man called Milt. "Was you ashamed of your youth?"

"What do you want now?" Steve demanded.

"We just looked in to see how an old pard was making out." said the mean-faced man.

"You'd been arguing about something when I walked in," Steve said slowly. "Better tell me what it was all about."

"It's none of your damned business," Milt said. "You'd better watch your tongue, youngster. It could get you into real bad trouble."

"This is Scrap Pierce," Heck Blaine said quickly, pointing to the fat man. "This one is Milt Dolan, and the other is Ike Brewster."

"And there isn't a state in the country where they aren't wanted by the law, I suppose." Steve said bitterly. "What is it you men want from my father? He left your kind of life twenty years ago. Why have you come here?"

"We figured he could help us a little." said Milt Dolan, his bitter brown eyes sharp under dark, beetling brows. "There was a code among us wild men. No matter where we rode, we always helped one another."

"You plan to commit a robbery in this county, I suppose, and want my father to help you, is that it?" Steve gazed at them, his right hand tense, his blue eyes cold and glistening.

"That's about the weight of it," Scrap Pierce said softly. "What are you aiming to do about it, kid?"

Steve opened the door stepped aside.

"There's the way out," he said harshly. "Better take it. We've got enough trouble building up around us here without men like you showing up to complicate matters. Get out and don't show your faces around here again."

"Do you let your kid give the orders?" Milt Dolan demanded of Heck Blaine.

"Steve puts in most of the work around here," Blaine said. "We've always worked in together, and he gives the orders if he thinks he's right, and I do the same."

"So you figure he's right in kicking out old friends, huh?" asked Ike Brewster. He was a massive, bullying type of man, and Steve studied him with shrewd eyes as the man moved towards his father.

"It ain't what he figures but what I say," Steve snapped. "Like I said, you'd better get moving or there'll be trouble."

"You ain't short on cold nerve," Scrap Pierce said lightly. "Seems to me you've got more than your share of the Heck Blaine we knew. Come on, fellers, let's get moving. We'll live a lot longer if we don't overstay our welcome."

The other two looked as if they might argue about the wisdom of Pierce's words, but the fat man walked out through the back door and kept going to where they had tied their horses out of sight. Dolan and Brewster stood for a moment, eyes hot with intention, but they hesitated too long, and Steve knew the danger moment had passed. He stood still until they had spun with jingling spurs and departed. Then he slammed the door on them and turned to confront his father.

"You sure were asking for trouble with them fellers, Steve," Heck Blaine reproved. "I never taught you to do a thing like that. What's got into you, son?"

"It was Zeke Coppard, I guess," Steve retorted. "I've had a belly-full of his shouting. Anyone would think that we stole this range off him." He paused as a thought struck him. "I suppose the money we used to pay for it was stolen?"

"It was," his father said. "Listen, Steve. I'm real sorry you had to learn about my past like you just did. You know I've always done my best for you, son, and I didn't think it was necessary to let on about me. I've always taught you to be honest, and maybe you would have thought the opposite to what you do now if you'd known about me. I've been an out and out bad man, but I've reformed, and I think I've done a good job on you."

"I ain't gonna hold that against you," Steve said tightly. "I'm thinking about those stolen horses your friends are riding. We'll be in real trouble if Zeke Coppard tracks them here. He as good as accused us of stealing them anyway."

"We don't have to worry about the likes of Coppard," his father said. "It's Scrap Pierce I'm thinking about. He's got a real loose mouth, or did have twenty years ago, and I sure bet he ain't changed none. He'd likely start some bar-room tales about me around here on account of how you just threw him out."

"He seemed eager to go," Steve said uneasily. He studied his father's wrinkled face. "Can they do anything to you in this country, pa?"

"Do you mean if the sheriff found out who I am?" Heck Blaine's eyes narrowed. "I reckon just about every sheriff in the land would like to get his hands on me, son. I did some terrible bad things in my time."

"But that was all such a long time ago, pa. I was so young I didn't know anything about it."

"True, but that won't make any difference." The older man's voice dropped slightly. "I sure am sorry, Steve."

"Why should you be? You sure made a good job of reforming, didn't you? Anyway, what you did before you came back and took me out of that orphanage after mom died ain't none of my business, pa."

"I'm glad you look at it like that, Steve. I figure I've done my best by you, boy."

"I've got no complaints." Steve tilted his head to one side and screwed up his face as he listened to something outside.

"What is it, son?" his father demanded. "I don't hear so good nowadays."

"Riders coming," Steve said, his voice hardening. "It could be Coppard and his two gunnies."

"Well you stay in here and keep quiet. I'll go out and have a talk with them. You'll only get riled up and start shouting, and if Frank Trory is along then it may lead to something else."

Steve followed his father through to the front of the house and stood behind the half-opened front door after his father had left. He peered through the crack of the door and saw Zeke Coppard sitting his horse in the yard. Frank Trory was with the rancher.

"Howdy, Coppard, what can I do for you?" Heck Blaine asked.

"We followed the tracks of three of my stolen horses across your range, and they passed close to your house, Blaine."

"So if they passed the house what do you want me to do about it?" the ex-outlaw asked quietly. "Do you figure that I stole your houses?"

"No. We'll find out who took them. We're gonna trail them clear across the state line if we have to. I've got another matter I want to raise with you.'

"Spit it out then," Heck Blaine said. "I don't hanker on standing around in this hot sun. What's on your mind?"

"I'd like to buy you out." Coppard sat erect in his saddle and gazed around the range he had always taken for granted. He lifted a hand when Heck Blaine started to speak. "Now hear me out before you turn me down. I'm gonna offer you a fair price, but you'll only get this one chance to accept. If you say no then I'll use other methods to get you off this grass."

"You know what my answer is, without me telling you." Heck said. "This is my son's place as much as mine. I heard him say that you know how he feels about you, so I needn't consult him. No, Coppard, this place ain't for sale to you or anyone."

"Then you're gonna find yourself in a lot of trouble. I've always had this grass, and it took a lot of swallowing for me to come over here and offer to buy you out. Well, I've done my best to prevent trouble, but I'm telling you, Blaine, that I'm gonna get this range back."

"All you'll get is a bullet in the belly," Steve called, stepping out of the house. "We've got the law on our side, Coppard, and you ain't forgot what Sheriff Griffin said. You can forget that this range ever belonged to you. It's ours by legal right, and there's nothing you can do about it. Now turn around and ride out of here. We've got enough to do working the place without having you at the door every two or three days, whining about what you had or should have."

Zeke Coppard reined his horse back a few furious steps. The Circle Z owner's face had whitened under its weather-beaten exterior. Frank Trory remained perfectly still in his saddle, and the gunman's face was impassive. Steve watched the man, could see eagerness flashing in Trory's eyes.

"By hell, Blaine, I don't know how I can control myself," Coppard said. "I came over here bent backwards to avoid trouble, and you and your son ain't got savvy enough to realise it."

"I can see through you all right," Heck Blaine said. "But you don't seem to grasp the facts, Coppard. We're here on our range and we're gonna stay come hell or high water." He smiled thinly and a glitter sparkled in his blue eyes. "I reckon you're making a big mistake if you think we can be frightened out. And before you start threatening to use violence you'd better be sure that you're ready to dodge lead yourself."

"Are you threatening now?" Trory demanded.

"No." Heck Blaine shook his head. "I'm just promising. All I've got to say is if you come around here again trying to get my son and me out then you'll be damned sorry. We don't scare easy, we Blaines, and we can take care of ourselves. So don't come pushing your luck."

"Well, boss?" Trory demanded. "Are you gonna take that kind of talk from this shoe-string outfit?"

"You'd better cool off, Trory," Steve advised, "or someone is gonna get hurt."

"That's the idea," the gunman retorted, grinning. "If you fancy your chance you can pull that gun you're wearing."

"Lay off, Frank," Coppard said. "I'm not ready to start trouble yet. I'm gonna give these two knot-heads time to think over what I've said. I'll be back to see you in a couple of days, Blaine, and you'd better have more sense when I come. Now if you've got no objection, me and my men will follow those tracks left by my horses."

"You've got my permission to check on those tracks," Heck Blaine said grimly.

"But don't come back to this door again, Coppard, if you're figuring on continuing this talk. The answer is no, and will always be no. Now take off and leave men to do their work."

Steve and his father stood watchful until Coppard and his two men had ridden away. When the trio were lost to sight beyond the barn, following the tracks of the horses stolen by the three outlaws, Heck Blaine turned to his son.

"Listen, Steve, I know how you feel about this, but I'm gonna try and talk some sense into you. You know as well as I do that Coppard means to try and get his hands on this place. I reckon I know my way around any kind of man, and I can sure see the signs on Coppard. Maybe we should sell up and get out. It'll be better than staying on and fighting, for that's what it'll come to." He lifted a hand as he saw anger flaring in Steve's cold blue eyes. "Now hold your horses a moment, son, and try to see reason. I know you're set to stay and fight if it comes to that, but listen good. I can't afford to get into any trouble. Twenty years ain't a long time when it comes to folk and their memories. If I start helling around again someone is gonna remember that I was one of the Wild Men, and that tough sheriff they've got around here will come out one day and take me. Now what do you say? Shall we call it a day and sell out? We can settle down somewhere else easy enough."

"No, pa," Steve's voice was low pitched and vibrant. "I can see your reasoning, but there's something inside me that won't let me back down."

"I know just what you mean," Heck said slowly. "I guess you're only a chip off the old block. I really was a hard case at your age." He sighed. "I escaped the punishment of the law, and I've been happy about that for a long time, but I reckon there is a higher justice than man's and it looks like I'll stand trial yet, and it'll come about through you, the only person I care about in this world."

"Don't talk like that." Steve said angrily. "We don't have to quit, and there's no reason why we should have to fight. We've got a legal right to this place, and so it's up to that tough sheriff you mentioned to see that we ain't bothered. I'm gonna ride into town and have a word with Tom Griffin. I reckon he should know the facts of this before any trouble starts. Are you gonna ride with me. Pa?"

"No, Son. You know I don't like showing my face to too many folk. You never knew the real reason, but what you've learned today should make you realise why I've always been shy of company."

"Okay, Pa." Steve hitched up his sagging gunbelt. "You stay here and look after the place. I'll ride into Buffalo Grove and see what I can do to put a stop to Coppard's plans. But if the law won't or can't do anything about that old wind bag then I'll take a gun to him myself."

"Zeke Goppard ain't no wind bag, Steve," Heck Blaine said softly, "and that's what I'm afraid of."

Two

Scrap Pierce reined up on a ridge and twisted in his saddle to stare back at the Blaine place. There was fury on his fleshy face, and he turned his pale eyes to his two crooked companions, looking at Dolan's bitter face and the mean features of Ike Brewster.

"Well, what do you make of that, huh?" He jerked a thumb back at the small ranch. "Our old pard has got mighty uppity in the last twenty years. He doesn't want anything to do with us now he's a cattle baron."

"We don't need him." Dolan growled. "I said all along that Heck wouldn't come in with us. He's been living too soft for too long. We can do the job ourselves, and it'll mean only a three-way split."

"I don't like it," Brewster said, deftly rolling a cigarette one-handed and lighting up. "Tom Griffin is a tough lawman, and this country ain't too hot for a quick getaway. You know Dakota as well as I do, and I'd be a lot happier if we were nearer to the Kansas border."

"You must be getting old, Ike," Pierce retorted. "We could hit that bank in Buffalo Grove and be out of the country before anyone is the wiser."

"It can't be done like the old days," Milt Dolan retorted. "They've got the telegraph now, and more organisation. They don't have to chase outlaws any more. They can wire ahead and have posses close all the likely trails."

"I figure that the least Heck could have done was let us use his place to lie up in." Brewster said.

"There'd have been trouble for sure with his youngster." Dolan commented.

"Yeah, he surely is like his father used to be. Pity Heck didn't bring his boy up in the old ways. We could have done with him this trip."

"The way he was carrying that gun. I'd say Heck hadn't neglected his son's education any," Pierce observed. "And that young feller was all for drawing against the three of us back there." He shook his head wisely. "I wouldn't want to tangle with him, no sir."

"Do you reckon they'll keep quiet that we're in the country?" questioned Brewster. "If word gets to the law that we plan on raiding the bank in Buffalo Grove then they could have a gun trap waiting for us."

"Heck wouldn't open his mouth about anything," Pierce said.

"I wasn't thinking about Heck," Brewster retorted. "But that son of his didn't take kindly to us. Maybe it would be a good idea if we laid up for a bit and watched the place. We can tell if anyone is riding to town."

"And if someone does?" Dolan demanded.

"We'll stop him and shut his mouth." Brewster grinned. "I take back all I ever said about Heck Blaine. Thinking back. I seem to recall that he was an ornery cuss at times. He always had a mind of his own and wouldn't pull with the crowd. If he didn't feel like doing a job then he wouldn't. He was always that kind of a man."

"He was good enough to do just as he pleased," Fat Scrap Pierce said, "We got along okay. But suppose we forget Heck now and start making a few plans? When are we going to hit that bank in Buffalo Grove?"

"We haven't decided for certain whether we're going to," said Dolan. He got down from his horse and stretched. "I don't know about operating in Tom Griffin's county. I ain't forgot what he did to Bill Warner and his gang. He sure took care of all of them."

"We got to take a few chances." Pierce said heavily, flinging himself to the ground, and he almost pulled his horse off balance as his weight shifted in the saddle. "I reckon the sheriff would die as quickly as anyone else if he stopped a slug."

"I ain't arguing about that," Dolan snapped. "But who's gonna put a bullet in him, and what's he gonna do while you're fixing to bore him?"

"We only picked this county because we found out that Heck lived here." Brewster said. "So if you're scared of Tom Griffin why don't we drift south again and find some place that'll be quieter?"

"They've never had a robbery in Buffalo Grove," Pierce said. He dropped to his knees and shaded his eyes as he stared back at the Blaine place. "We've got the chance of making it their first one, and they won't know what's hit them. Hey, take a look down there." He pointed a thick finger at three riders who had appeared from around the barn of the Blaine place.

"They're following tracks." sand Dolan, making for his horse.

"Our tracks," Brewster said. "Must be the Coppard feller, who owns them horses. They sure got good tracking eyes."

"We don't want any trouble from them," Pierce said. "We'd better split up until after we've thrown them off our trail."

"I say we stick together." Brewster said, grinning. He eased the weight of the big gun off his hip. "Unless you figure that we shouldn't do the bank in Buffalo Grove. In that case I reckon it would be smart of hightail it right out of the country. What are we going to do?"

"We'll take the bank in Buffalo Grove," Pierce said irritably. "We rode all this long way up here, didn't we? There's more than one way of robbing a bank, you know. We don't have to walk in there in broad daylight and stick them up. We can go in after dark and blow the safes open."

"I don't like the sound of that either." Brewster said. "No, Scrap, if we're gonna do it, we'll ride down there and look the place over, pick our time, then go in and raid it."

"I'll go along with that." Dolan said, his dark eyes watching the slowly moving figures below. "But what about those guys? They're gonna come up with us sooner or later. Why don't we lay for them and give them a fright when they get in range?"

"If it is that Coppard guy then we'll rouse up the whole county by shooting him." Pierce said patiently. "Let's put some distance between us and them. We'll head away from Buffalo Grove to lay them a false trail. It looks like there's a lot of hard ground to the north. We'll lose them up there."

They mounted and rode on, pushing their stolen horses at a fast pace. Pierce knew where Buffalo Grove lay, and headed away from the town. Long hours passed, and they never sighted the three riders trailing them. By nightfall they were riding in the foothills south of Buffalo Grove, and halted to make camp on the edge of a high cliff on the rocky slopes.

"This will do us." Pierce said, thankfully dismounting and stretching. "Buffalo Grove is about six miles north. We'll hide up here for a couple of days, while we take it in turns to go down into the town and take a look around. We've got to find out when the place is quietest, and which will be the best way to get out of town after we've got what we want. I've got a good idea in the back of my mind, and I'll think some more on it before we make a move."

"I hope it ain't anything like the idea we tried in Denver County" Brewster said sourly. "The law nearly got me that time."

"Let's make camp and get some grub cooking." said Dolan. "I'll ride into town for a drink and a look around."

"Why can't we all go together?" Brewster asked. "I don't like all this playing around. I say we should get in there, do the job and then get out."

"That's the way to get caught." Pierce said. "You know we've got to do it my way, Ike, so cut out the wrangling about it. If we all ride in there together someone is bound to spot us, and we are known almost everywhere. No, we've got to play it smart and do like I say. That way we'll get out of it with our saddle bags bulging. Okay, Milt, so you want to ride in tonight. Do that, and keep your eyes open. Find out if the sheriff is in town, and if he's likely to be out of it at any time. If we can hit them while he's away on business we'll have that much better chance of making it."

They sat around the small camp fire, situated where it couldn't be seen, and ate the poor food that Pierce prepared. They drank coffee and relaxed.

"I'm moving out now." Dolan said at length. He drew his gun and pointed the weapon at the fire while he checked it. "I'll have me a good look around, Scrap."

"Do that. Tomorrow night Ike can go, and the night after, I'll ride in."

"What's the idea of that?" Brewster demanded. "Damn me, Scrap, I'm getting tired of your fancy plans. Why don't we just ride in there tomorrow and hit the bank? In three days we can be back in Kansas and spending some of that dough."

"Yeah, and we could be dead or in jail in Buffalo Grove. Let's get something straight before we start." Pierce gazed at them with harsh expression. His pale eyes were filled with flickering firelight. "Do we work the job my way or do I quit?"

"You shouldn't oughta ask a question like that." Dolan said. "I wouldn't do any job unless you organised it, Scrap."

"What about you, Ike?" Pierce studied the hard face of Brewster. "Are you going along with what I say?"

"Yeah," the big outlaw mumbled. "Dang it, Scrap, you do like to drag everything out and examine it."

"Yeah, and you should be glad that I do," the fat outlaw retorted. "I've saved our necks more than once with my care in preparation. Okay, now listen. We each of us is going to ride into Buffalo Grove on different nights to take a good look around. Then we're going to sit around here and tell each other what we saw. That way nothing will be overlooked. We'll know all the details and we'll know just how to do the job. I told you I've got an idea up my sleeve. Well, I can use it to get the sheriff out of the town when we're ready to make our move. If we play our cards right we'll make this the easiest job we've ever done."

"What do we do when we get inside the bank?" Brewster asked.

"We'll handle it like we always do." Pierce retorted. "You'll watch the door, Ike, and me and Milt will take the dough. No need to go into the details over that. We've done it too many times before."

They laughed. Dolan got up and left the fire, shivering as the cold mountain breeze struck him. He saddled his horse and mounted, then rode close to the fire. Scrap Pierce gazed up at him.

"Do you reckon you can find your way back here, Milt?" he demanded. "It'll be tricky in the dark. We've got to do it like this because I don't want anyone to see us in this county before the raid."

"Yeah. I'll be back before sun up," Dolan said confidently. "So long."

He turned his horse and rode away, and Pierce watched him until a boulder hid both horse and rider from sight. Then the fat outlaw heaved himself to his feet and went for his blanket roll. He spread the blanket close to the fire and lay down. It was cold up here among the peaks. He lay looking up at the coldly glittering stars, and slowly drifted into sleep. Ike Brewster snored in his blanket on the other side of the fire.

Milt Dolan rode carefully through the darkness, letting his horse find its own way down out of the high country. He grinned when he saw the lights of the town, and found the trail and rode into Buffalo Grove. Dolan had been an outlaw ever since he had been old enough to lift a gun. He was crooked right through, and high thoughts followed a dishonest course in his head. He had spent all his adult life in the company of men like Brewster and Pierce, and was callous and brutal when the occasion demanded it.

He rode along the wide main street, his dark eyes watching for the stable, and he found the livery barn and rode into the big yard. He left his horse and headed for a saloon, and sighed with relief when he stood at a bar and lifted a beer to his lips. He thought of his two crooked pards out there in the rocks, and smiled. He was about through with Pierce and Brewster. Pierce was a know-all and Brewster was one of the meanest killers he had ever met. He had been thinking for some time about getting away from them, and had already decided in his scheming mind that if this job here in Buffalo Grove went according to plan he would cut and run from the other two after they had split the money.

Having satisfied his thirst, Dolan shouldered his way out of the lively saloon and went along the dark sidewalk in search of the bank.

The bank was an old building that was failing the test of time. Plaster was falling off the outside walls. The paint was chipped and peeling, but there was nothing wrong with the massive front door and the great iron-barred windows. They would resist any effort made to force them, he thought, and discarded the idea that they could force an entry and blow open the safes. It looked like this would have to be an old-fashioned hold-up.

Dolan stood in the shadows opposite the bank and studied the building. The wide main street terminated some two hundred yards away on the right, extending clear through the little town. On the left the prairie began a block away. So it seemed they would have to leave town by riding out to the left. That meant heading north, when Dolan wanted to go south, but he did not worry about that. They could always circle, if they got clear of town.

The bank stood in the centre of a row of business establishments, and there was a narrow alley on each side of it. Dolan was pleased to see them, for they could leave their horses in one of the alleys until they were ready to ride out. If there was a side door in the bank then so much the better. They would be able to leave by it and make a clean getaway.

Dolan crossed the street and entered one of the dark alleys beside the bank. He kept close to the wall of the building, moving silently like a shadow, and peered in through a window. He saw a long counter with a wire grille occupying the entire length of the bank. The door was on the left, and at the other end of the counter was a railed-off open office, containing a desk and two chairs. There were two places behind the grille where cashiers worked.

He moved away, satisfied that they would have no trouble inside the bank while the job was in progress. One man could cover the interior while the other two grabbed and sacked the money. He went into the alley, looking for a side door and smiled grimly when he saw one almost at the rear of the bank. It would be ideal. If they could come out through here after the raid they wouldn't have to risk stopping lead from the main street if the alarm was suddenly raised.

Dolan went back to the main street and walked along the sidewalk. He saw the sheriff's office, and broke his stride as he noted the features of the place. But he was pleased to see that a hundred yards separated the law office from the bank. He went on again, and re-entered the saloon. He drank two more beers and a whisky, then bought a bottle of liquor, thinking of Pierce and Brewster up in the rocks. He left the saloon and walked steadily of the stable.

A tingling sensation warned him of impending danger as he reached the livery barn, and he paused on the threshold with his hand on his gun and his eyes studying the interior. He had lived long enough on the dodge from the law to know that a man developed some sixth sense after living with danger, and he had never disregarded the uneasy feelings that sent icy tremors down his spine and made his hair lift on his neck. But he could see nothing unnatural inside the stable, and stepped cautiously to the stall where he had left his horse and began to saddle the animal.

"Hold it right there." a harsh voice at his back after he had lifted the saddle to the animal. "Don't turn round yet. There are three of us and you're covered. Put up your hands."

Dolan lifted his hands instantly, and stood very still. Footsteps scraped behind him, then a hand lifted his Colt out of its holster on his right hip. He tightened his lips, and his breath escaped slowly through his nostrils in a long sigh.

"Now turn around," the same voice commanded. "Do it slow or you'll stop lead."

Dolan spun around and faced three men. All three held guns that were lined up on him, and the outlaw was relieved when he saw that none of them was carrying a law badge. He eyed the hard-faced oldish man standing slightly in front of the other two.

"What's this?" he demanded. "Are you robbers?"

"Stand still and shut up," said Zeke Coppard. "Is that your hoss, mister?"

"It's the one I'm using," Dolan said, glancing at the animal and seeing the Circle Z brand on it. It came to him then who these three were, remembering the trio who had ridden out of Blaine's place that morning. "A feller held me up south of here this afternoon and made me swap horses with him."

"Did you report that to the sheriff?"

"No. I figured that fair exchange was no robbery. This look like a good horse to me."

"Yeah, it is," Coppard said thinly. "It's my horse, mister, one of three stolen from me yesterday or dawn today."

"I see. So that makes me a horse out. You'll want it back, I figure."

"You figure right, and you can tell your story to the sheriff now. Come on. Out of the door and along the street, and don't try anything stupid or you'll stop a slug with your spine."

Dolan shrugged his shoulders, he was not a tall man, and only slenderly built. He walked out of the stable and crossed the yard. Coppard and his two men followed closely. They reached the sheriff's office, and Dolan pushed open the door and entered. He heard the door slam shut at his back. He looked at the man seated at the desk in front of him, noting the sheriff's star on the narrow chest. So this was the famous Sheriff Tom Griffin, he thought.

Griffin was a tall, thin man of about fifty years. He had been a lawman for thirty-odd years, and knew every trick in the book. He stood up now, squinting at his visitors, and his lips pulled tight when he saw Coppard and two Circle Z gunhands behind a stranger whose holster was empty.

"What's been going on, Zeke?" he demanded, staring at the rancher's set face. "Are you still on the war path?"

"What do you mean, still on the war path?" Coppard demanded. "You ain't had no trouble from me."

"Not yet," Griffin replied, his long, thin face crinkling like old leather as he grimaced. "But I've had Steve Blaine in here, and he's been complaining about your behaviour. I figure it's about time you pulled in your horns, Zeke. You know the Blaines have a legal right to that land, and you'll only make yourself a heap of trouble by pushing them. The way young Blaine spoke, he'll be smoking lead at you if you bother them again. So take a tip from me and stay away from there."

"You don't have to tell me anything, sheriff," Coppard said, scowling. "Just do your job and save me the agony of a sermon. I had three good horses stolen last night, and when I rode into town a short time ago I found one of them tied up in the stall in the livery barn. This guy came in and started saddling it. He reckons some feller held him up this afternoon and made him swap horses. You can believe that it you like, but I don't. What are you going to be about it, or should I handle it?"

"And just how would you handle it?" the sheriff demanded.

"I'd take him out and string him up," Coppard boomed. "That's the only way to handle thieves."

"Well you just simmer down and I'll handle this. There'll never be any law in this country while responsible men like you stick to the old ways. The frontier days are over, and the sooner some of you old-timers realize that the better for all concerned." The sheriff looked at Dolan. "What's your name, mister?"

"Milt Dolan."

"Where are you from?"

"Came up from Kansas. I'm looking for a riding job."

"You stood more of a chance of a job of that kind down in Kansas, I shouldn't wonder." Griffin's eyes were steady as they regarded Dolan. "Now tell me about this man who held you up. What did he look like?"

"I reckon he was about forty years old, tall and thin. He had a long face and dark eyes that told me he meant real business. Said that he was in a hurry and that his horse was nearly done. I reckoned it wasn't no good arguing with his gun, and the horse he left me was a good one. So I let it go. He took my horse and I got his."

"Only it wasn't his," Coppard said savagely. "It's mine, and I'm missing two more just like it."

"Stay out of this, Zeke," the sheriff ordered. "Which way did that feller head when he left you?"

"North. He came this way."

"You're lying, mister," Coppard snarled. "If he stole my horse this morning, the animal wouldn't be on its last legs. I say you're making this up."

"If he stole a horse then he'd want to get rid of it."

Dolan shrugged his shoulders. "He didn't want to tell me it was stolen, I guess, so he said the animal was done. I didn't find it so when I got on it, but the feller was gone by then, so I couldn't argue with him."

"Yeah, well I ain't satisfied," the rancher said angrily. "I'm gonna bring a charge of horse stealing against you."

"Don't bother, Zeke," Tom Griffin said. "There ain't no evidence against this feller. The judge would have to turn him loose."

"So that's the kind of law we get from this department." Coppard cursed. "I'll be real glad when the next election comes up. I'll vote for anyone who stands up against you, Griffin."

"Yeah, you do that, Zeke, and remember to keep the peace out on your range. If you keep aggravating your neighbours you're gonna wind up with a hole in your head. I've got enough trouble now without you starting a range war or something. So knock it off and keep your hands off what don't belong to you."

"By God, I've taken about all I can stand in this county," Coppard raged. He slammed Dolan's gun down on the desk. "I catch me a horse thief and you're gonna turn him loose. Okay, I can see how the game is going." He looked at Dolan, who eyed him serenely. "You'd better get out of this country if you want to stay healthy. If I catch you around after tonight I'll have you strung up higher than a kite." He swung round and stamped to the door. His two men followed closely. Jerking open the street door, Coppard paused and faced the sheriff. "I'm not satisfied with the way you're handling things. I'm going to have a word or two to say to men in higher positions. You'll hear more about this.

"You've taken Steve Blaine's word against me, and you warned me against starting trouble. Well, what you want to do is ride the range a bit more and watch your county. You'll see more from the back of a horse than from this office. The Blaines have been up to some shady tricks, and I only want to catch them at it and they'll stop lead."

"Now hold your horses a moment, Zeke," Griffin snapped. "If you've been getting trouble from your neighbours then make a proper complaint and I'll look into it."

Coppard shook his head and departed, slamming the door at his back, and Frank Trory glanced at the sheriff and grinned. Then he opened the door and went out after his boss, followed by his companion. Griffin sighed and sat down at the desk. He looked up at Dolan.

"You better get yourself another horse, mister, then get the hell out of this country. Zeke Coppard may sound like a big mouth, but I can assure you that he keeps his word, whatever he says. Pick up your gun and get."

"Where the hell do I get a horse from?" Dolan demanded. He was thinking of the six miles between the town and his camp, where Pierce and Brewster would be snoring their heads off right now. "I can't afford another meal, let alone a horse."

"I'm sorry I can't help you." Griffin said. "Coppard will take that horse of his, and you want to think yourself lucky he didn't string you up, if you stole the horse or not. You can sell your saddle and other gear and take the stage out."

"Yeah, and thanks." Dolan picked up his gun and slid it back into its holster. He turned for the door and left the office. On the sidewalk he paused and gazed around the street. He sighed heavily. It would be a long walk back to the camp. He dared not steal a horse because the sheriff would think of him immediately such a theft was reported, and would probably start a search that would make a bank robbery impossible.

There was only one thing for it, he thought angrily. He would have to walk the six miles to the camp, and that would be quite a chore. Like all westerners, Milt Dolan hadn't walked six miles in the last twenty years.

Three

Zeke Coppard led Trory and the other gunman back to the stable. The rancher was angry, and showed it in his harsh voice and jerky, vicious movements. He began saddling his horse, and Trory stood with folded arms and watched his boss, his black hat pushed back to reveal sandy-coloured hair.

"Ain't we gonna stay in town tonight?" Trory demanded. "What are you gonna do, Boss?"

"What the hell do you suppose?" Coppard swung round and stalked angrily out of the stall. "There's gonna be a lot of trouble in this county. I'm getting back that range from the Blaines. I pay you high wages, Frank, to take care of my interests, so what are you standing there for and complaining about riding out to night? We're gonna hit the Double B and make them two jug-heads sorry they ever saw the sky over this county."

"That's what I figured you'd try and do," Trory retorted. He unfolded his arms and stood with legs braced apart. "And you know the first thing that'll happen, don't you? Griffin will come out to the Circle Z with a posse and take us all in. What's wrong with you, Boss? You know better then to go off half-cocked. All right, so you want to get that range back. Well it can be done. I ain't afraid of a good fight, and that's what we'll get from the Blaines. The old man and his son look like they can handle trouble. I've been around long enough to recognize the signs. Both them Blaines carry themselves like gun-handlers. I reckon the old man must have done some lead slinging in his time, and he's taught his son all the tricks. So we'll have to go easy around them. If you want them bumped off you've only got to say the word and it'll be done, but that way you'll tell the sheriff that you are responsible."

"For God's sake stop beating around the bush," Coppard snarled impatiently. "What the hell are you trying to say?"

"The quickest way to get the Blaines off that range is for the sheriff to arrest and jug them." Trory grinned craftily. "The next best way would be for a dozen of us to catch them Blaines rustling Circle Z stock. Then we could shoot them or string them up, and Griffin couldn't do a thing about it."

"Yeah, but it so happens that neither of them Blaines will touch a hair of my beef, let alone steal a herd." Coppard leaned against a post and stared at his top gunhand. "What are you planning, Frank?"

"Two or three of the men could cut your fence and drive some of your beef on the Blaine's land. They can be penned up in a canyon somewhere, and tomorrow a party of us could trail the stolen herd and find them. That should be good enough to give them two Blaines five years each in jail."

"Frank, I think you've got something there." Coppard's face lost its anger, but his eyes narrowed. "We'll have to kill them two, I'm thinking. It wouldn't be safe to bring in Griffin until we've finished them off."

"We can leave them dead and our herd on their range. There'll be tracks leading off the Circle Z." Trory smiled broadly. "It's a good set-up, Boss."

"Well let's get on with it, then." Coppard went back to his horse and finished saddling. He waited for Trory and his other gun-slammer to prepare their mounts. "What are we gonna do about them other two stolen horses?" he demanded.

"Forget them for the time being," Trory told him. "This other business is more important than a couple of horses. From what that Dolan guy said, if he's to be believed, the three men who stole our horse flesh must have split up. It would be a helluva job to track them down."

"You're right, but I don't like losing out to stealers," Coppard said harshly.

"You've got no room to talk," Trory retorted. "You're about to steal something yourself."

"That ain't stealing," the rancher grated, "and if you want to stay on working for me then don't ever use that word on me again. That range the Blaines have got is mine. It's always been mine. All I'm doing is taking it back."

They rode out and headed south. Coppard travelled in silence, his mind filled with thoughts of the Blaines and what he would do to them. He was a hard man who had always got what he wanted. The Circle Z was a big ranch in the county, one of the biggest, and Zeke Coppard had built it up from nothing. The fact that Heck and Steve Blaine had bought the range they now called Double B was of no consequence to Coppard. He had used the range for years, and the ruins of three nester cabins testified to his resolve to keep it under his own brand. But that violence had occurred before Sheriff Tom Griffin had taken over the dispensation of local law. With Griffin in the lawman's saddle, Coppard realized the need for caution.

Coppard was unmarried, and all his life was focused down to his ranch. Circle Z! It was his kingdom and represented his own personality. His riders were hard and merciless. They worked hard and played hard, but not in Buffalo Grove since Griffin had taken over. Now Circle Z riders rode out to Bear Canyon, where miners lived and worked, some fifteen miles north-west of Circle Z. The law there was a tough miner who did not object to drunkenness and brawling in the one dusty street the little town possessed.

Frank Trory was content to ride in silence through the night. He was a fast gunman who had learned his grim trade in every state west of the Mississippi. He had killed a dozen men, give or take one or two. He had never troubled to keep tally. Some of his victims had been shot in the back, for Trory was not an ethical killer. He killed the best way he could. He liked to study a victim before he killed, and if a man seemed too fast with a gun then he would collect a slug in the back. It was the result that counted with Frank Trory, not the method.

His mind was busy now as he rode along through the dark night, trying to weave a plot that would completely ensnare the Blaines. He would have been content to lay an ambush for father and son, but realized that he would have to leave the country immediately afterwards, and he liked it here in South Dakota. Every other state was too dangerous for him.

The fact that Coppard was determined to get the Blaines off the range, even to the extent of going directly against the law, did not surprise Trory. The rancher was a fighter, and most of his trouble lay in the fact that he would not accept Blaine's claim to the Double B as being legal.

They rode along for some time in complete silence, each busy with his thoughts, and the third man had worked long enough for the Circle Z to know Coppard for what he was.

When they reached the ranch, Coppard dismounted stiffly and stomped on to the wide porch. Then he turned and faced Trory, who remained in his saddle. They gazed at each other in the shadows.

"Get the horses put away, Frank," Coppard directed. "Saddle fresh mounts and turn out half a dozen of the men. I'll ride with you and make sure the job is done properly. It'll take us until dawn to get done."

"Right, Boss." Trory wheeled away, leaving the other man to bring the horse they had taken back from Dolan. He rode to the bunk house, swung out of his saddle, and entered the long building. He shook several men awake and told them to get dressed and saddle up. Then he went across to his own small cabin and hunted up a bottle of whisky. He took several pulls from the bottle before going out to saddle up a fresh horse.

Coppard was impatiently pacing the porch when Trory returned to the house to tell him that they were ready to move out. Coppard grunted and went to his fresh mount. He gritted his teeth a little as he climbed into creaking leather, and his bleak eyes narrowed as he stared at Trory.

"Let's get moving then," he snapped. "I want one of the crew to be riding for the sheriff by dawn."

"We'd better take some of our herd from the east pasture," Trory said. "I've sent five of the men on to start gathering. Where do you figure we should hit Blaine's wire?"

"On the other side of the ridge, north of their house. They won't hear anything then. But what about tracks? When we get Griffin out he'll take his time looking around. We'll have to lay some false tracks for him to find."

"I'll take care of that while you get the men to push the steers on to Double B range. Head them for that gulch west of the big creek."

"I know where to head them," Coppard said irritably. "I had that range long enough, didn't I?"

"It was your own damn fault for losing it." Trory snapped back. "I'll take a man with me and make some tracks around the Blaine place."

"Better go easy around there. We don't want a slip up." Coppard stared grimly at his top gunman. "I'm only going to try this once, and if it fails I'll do it my way."

"And you'll land us all in jail," Trory said thinly. "But don't worry. My way will work."

"I hope so. I'm getting too old for this kind of life." Coppard twisted in his saddle as they left the yard. "It wouldn't be so bad it I could rely on my crew," he complained. "But I have to come on out and supervise everything."

"The boys ain't as bad as that," Trory objected. "There's no need for you to come with us now. We can handle everything."

"I want to know what's going on in case anything goes astray." Coppard set his horse into a run, eyeing the dark figures of their horsemen ahead. "Now listen to me, Frank. When this is over and the Blaines have gone I want you to settle on their place. I'll pay you well, but the Double B will be mine. Have you got that?"

"Sure thing, Boss." Trory grinned to himself. He had worked for Coppard for a long time, and now it looked as if his waiting tactics were about to pay off. If he kept his wits he would come out of this with a lot more than he started with.

They reached the bedded-down herd on the range adjoining the Double B, and Coppard sat his horse and watched his men get to work. Two riders approached Blaine's wire, and soon breached the obstacle. The rest of the cowboys roused up the herd and headed it for the gap in the wire. Trory appeared out of the darkness on Coppard's left and reined in beside his boss.

"There they go," the gunman said. "We'll keep them moving fast, and they should be penned up by dawn. Now I'll take one of the fellers with me and start laying those false tracks. Are you going on with the herd?"

"No. I'm heading back to bed," Coppard said. "Tell the men here that they will draw an extra ten dollars each for tonight's work. Report back to me as soon as you've got the herd planted and a man on the way to town for the sheriff. Me and you will then ride over to Blaine's place and demand an explanation. If I've got young Blaine figured right he'll make a play for his gun soon as I call his old man a rustler. You'd better be ready for him, Frank, and drop him good. Do you figure you can take him?"

"It'll be too bad for both of us if I can't," the gunman said softly. He smiled as he wheeled his mount away. "You don't have to worry about the Blaines, Boss. I'll take them both."

"Just make sure you do." Coppard sat his horse and watched the herd spill through the gap torn in the wire fence that separated Circle Z from

Double B. He grinned. There was more than one way to dry a hide. Maybe Frank Trory had some sense after all. He watched the gunman follow the two hundred steers on to Blaine range, then nodded in satisfaction and pulled the head of his horse around. He rode slowly back to his house, and there was exultation in his heart.

Trory followed the herd across Blaine range and saw to it that the Circle Z steers were securely penned in the natural corral west of the big creek that made Blaine's range the best in the territory. He sent the rest of the crew back to the Circle Z and, with one man, rode for Blaine's house. He had a chore to do, and it he did it right then both Blaines would be in serious trouble with the law.

It was almost dawn when Trory rode back through the breached wire fence and moved on swiftly to Coppard's house. He slid tiredly out of the saddle, leaving the horse standing in the yard, and was surprised to find the rancher up and dressed. Coppard met him at the door, having heard his pounding arrival.

"Well?" Coppard demanded.

"It went off just like we planned." Trory leaned against the door post. "Now I suppose we make another move."

"That's right." Coppard came out to the porch and stood for a moment to look at the sun coming up. Then he turned his tired eyes to his gunman. "We're gonna take a ride over the Blaine place and demand an explanation. Better round up some more of the men and have them trail the herd to where you penned it. We'll handle the Blaines, and kill them if they want to fight."

"Maybe we should wait for Griffin to show up," Trory said. "It would go down a lot better if the law handles it from here on in. You've got to tread carefully, Boss."

"I want it done my way," Coppard snapped. "What's got into you. Frank? Are you scared of tangling with them Blaines? If you are then you can pick up your time and drift out of the country."

"I don't even have to answer that," Trory retorted. He wiped his dry lips with a dusty sleeve. "I'm trying to save you a lot of trouble, Boss." He shrugged resignedly. "But if you're set on making trouble for yourself then go ahead. If you want to hit the Blaines yourself then let's get at it, and you'll see if I'm afraid of them or not."

"Get me a horse saddled,' Coppard said, and his dark eyes were glittering. "You'd better bring along one other man. We may need a good witness."

"All you'll need are a couple of men to dig graves," Trory said heavily. "I suppose you want the rest of the men out today tearing down the fence that Blaine put up?"

"No. I'm hanging fire on that. I don't want Griffin getting any ideas about me. I'm thinking of giving Blaine another chance of selling out to me. I can tell him I won't press charges of rustling against him if he does."

"Do that and you're putting him wise to the whole plan," Trory snapped. "You've got to play the part of the honest, angry rancher who's just lost two hundred head of cows, and don't expect to get them back."

"Yeah. I'll try that first," Coppard decided. "Am I supposed to know where these steers have been penned up?"

"No." Trory shook his head emphatically. "But you can say you've sent men to track them down."

"Right. Get the fresh horses and let's be riding over there."

"I still say we should wait for the sheriff."

"Let me think about it." Coppard went back into the house, and emerged again when Trory showed up with his horse.

"We'll take Hank along with us," Trory said. "He's mighty handy with a gun."

"How long ago did you send a rider for the sheriff?" Coppard demanded.

"He should be in town by now. We'll likely get to the Double B about the same time as the sheriff, and if you play it like that, Boss, you'll be picking up the pot in this game."

"I said I'd think about it," the rancher snapped. He mounted and set off across the yard at a gallop.

Trory considered his feelings as he followed Coppard out to the Blaine place. He watched the small spread very closely from the instant of spotting it, and saw no movement about the place. He loosened his Colt in its holster, and glanced at the gunman he had brought along.

"Don't make a move unless they do, Hank," he instructed. "We don't want to lay ourselves open to a murder charge."

Hank grinned, and Coppard swung in his saddle to face them. "Let's do this right," he said. "No mistakes. If they do try and start something, then cut them down without mercy. If the sheriff takes them in and they only get a couple of years, it'll mean that they'll come back at us sometime in the future. I want this finished today, here and now."

"Leave it lie, Boss," Trory said. "We'll take care of it."

They entered the yard of the Double B and rode up to the house. Trory held his horse in a little behind Coppard, and his pale eyes probed around the yard for sign of either Blaine.

"Hey, Blaine," Coppard yelled hoarsely. "It ain't no use you hiding away. I want to talk to you. Come on out into the open where I can see you, and bring that thieving son of yours out too."

The door of the house opened and Heck Blaine emerged into the bright sunlight. He stepped down into the dust from the porch and stood erect before them.

"What's on your mind now, Coppard?" he demanded.

"You've got a nerve to stand there and ask me that," Coppard snarled. "Yesterday I lost three horses, and today I find two hundred head of cattle gone to blazes. All you can say is what's on my mind. Well, I'll tell you, Blaine. You are. I figure that you and your son are trying to establish yourselves at my expense."

"You're talking through your hat, Coppard. We don't know a thing about stolen horses or cows."

"Where's your boy?"

"Out riding. He found some strange tracks near the house, and went to check up. There's some funny business going on around here, and we're going to get to the bottom of it."

"You ain't gonna do nothing," Coppard said. "We got you dead to rights, Blaine. That fence you put up on my boundary has been torn down, and my cattle passed through it. Their tracks lead right across your range, and I've send some men to trail them. I figure that you and your son will have a lot of explaining to do. I've sent for the sheriff. We'll hear what he's got to say about this."

"Are you calling me a rustler?" Heck Blaine demanded.

"That's about the weight of it," Trory said, grinning wolfishly and leaning to the left in his saddle. His right hand rested on the butt of his gun, and his pale eyes were fixed upon the man facing them. "You're a damned sneaking, thieving four-flusher, and I'm gonna cut you down as soon as you make a play for that gun you're wearing."

Coppard glanced in surprise at his top gunhand. This was exactly what Trory had advised him not to do, but he realised that his gunman was going to try and take advantage of the fact that Steve Blaine was not on the place. It would be easier for them to get these Blaines separately, and it came to him then that if one or the other died now it would add to the appearance of their guilt.

"Kill him, Frank," he snapped. "There's only one thing we can do with a rustler."

Heck Blaine fell back a step, his wrinkled face grave and unrelenting. His right hand dropped to his side and hung lifelessly. But his blue eyes were full of fire, and a grin slowly formed on his lips.

"So that's the way of it, huh?" he asked easily.

"You're gonna try and take me while my son is away. Let me tell you this, Coppard. You're making a big mistake if you think you can get us off this range like this. I've seen this sort of thing happen before. Okay, so make your play. I've lived long enough to know when the game is going. There's gonna be no backing out of this. You're the sort to keep pushing until you've killed someone or stopped a slug yourself. So who's it gonna be, one or all of you?

"Are you prepared to face up to the three of us?" Trory asked in surprise. He could feel tension seeping into his chest, and a knot of apprehension was gathering in his throat. It was always like this when he prepared to fight, and he knew that it would never be any different.

"I'll take you all on," Blaine said. He was smiling tightly. "I don't want you to go away from here disappointed. I could tell by the way you rode in that you are hunting trouble. Well, if you think I'll be a push-over then you'd better get started."

"I'll take him," Hank said thickly. "I can handle him, Frank."

"Well he's all yours," Trory said, smiling coldly. But he did not take his eyes off Heck Blaine, and was ready to draw his gun the instant a movement from the rancher signified the opening of action.

"I'm your man," Hank said, and slapped his holster.

Heck Blaine drew his gun swiftly, and the grin on his lips widened when he saw that it was Frank Trory who was drawing. He levelled his big Colt before Trory could clear leather, and squeezed his trigger when the gunman had lifted his sixgun. The crash of the gun made Coppard flinch, and the big rancher was fully occupied with trying to control his suddenly prancing mount. But his wide eyes saw Frank Trory reel in his saddle, and he grabbed at his own weapon as his top gunhand fell heavily to the ground.

The smile fled from Hank's face, and horror filled him when he realised that he could not lift his own gun in time to beat this old man. He lifted his hands quickly in token of surrender, and glanced sideways at the shocked Zeke Coppard. The big rancher had half-drawn his Colt, and sat frozen now, his eyes wide with fear.

"Finish it." Blaine said grimly. "It's your play, Coppard, so make an end to it."

"This isn't the time," Coppard said grimly. He thrust his gun deeper into leather and lifted his hands clear. His eyes flickered to the motionless body of Frank Trory.

"You needn't check him over," Blaine said. "He's dead all right. He made the same mistake you did, Coppard. He figured that I was a pushover. Well, he never lived to learn the difference. But you've got a chance. You'd better get out of here now and keep on your own side of the fence. And you can take Trory's carcass with you."

"This ain't the end of it." Coppard snarled. "I've got it figured that you lifted my cows, Blaine, and I'll have the law take care of you."

"You do that. Get the sheriff out here and I'll talk to him. But don't ever come back trying to raise hell, Coppard, or you'll wind up like your no-good gunhand there."

Coppard sat his horse with his brain frozen in shock. He watched Hank dismount and lift Trory's body up out of the dust. The gunman threw the corpse across a nervous horse and roped it there. Blaine stood with levelled gun until they turned to ride out of the yard. He didn't expect any more trouble after what he had done to Frank Trory.

He stood for a long time, watching the dust drifting back from the hooves of the departing riders. He felt no pity as he eyed the body of Trory jolting on the saddle that he had sat coming in. Trory had been a killer, and had taken one chance too many. Blaine understood that perfectly. He had ridden similar trails in his younger days. Trory had under-estimated him, and paid for the mistake with his life.

When Coppard and his other man had gone, Blaine holstered his gun and stood gazing across the yard. He knew that this was not the end of the affair. Coppard would not be satisfied until he had gotten himself killed. For himself, Blaine did not care. He had lived most of his life just the way he had wanted it. There was only one care in him right now, and that was for his son Steve. He wondered where the young hot-head had gone. He didn't want all the trouble that was surely brewing. Steve was a good youngster, and deserved a chance. Heck Blaine wondered how to act for the best. What could he do to give Steve the opportunities he had missed?

Four

Steve Blaine reined in and squinted his eyes against the glare of the brassy sun. He had followed tracks through rough country to the north and east of the house, and felt uncomfortably certain that they were no ordinary prints of riders passing over the range. He remembered seeing other tracks around the house, and had seen prints leading into the yard before turning away to make the trail he was now following.

It had crossed his mind that his father's old saddle pards might be responsible for the tracks. Perhaps two of them had ridden in to contact his father, but he was not sure of that because the older man hadn't said anything when Steve decided to ride out on the trail.

There was a lot happening below the surface that Steve could only guess at. He believed that the three outlaws had come to the Double B in the first place for aid. They were probably planning a raid locally and wanted a hideout. He smiled grimly. He had told them plainly that they couldn't use the Double B. He hoped he had seen the last of them. He did not want anything happening to his father.

He urged on his mount again, and smiled grimly when he thought of his father being the leader of the Wild Men. He had heard something about that particular group of outlaws, and hadn't yet recovered from the shock of learning about his father to consider what he really felt about it.

He breasted a rise and reined in to gaze down at the shimmering expanse of water in the big creek. As he studied the area, noting that the tracks he had been following led straight down that way, he spotted a movement in the mouth of the gulch to his left, and swung his horse in that direction. He clenched his teeth when he saw six riders emerging from the gulch, and eased his gun in its holster when they came up fast towards him.

As they drew nearer he recognised three of them as Circle Z riders, and his features hardened as he wondered when they were doing on Blaine range. He sat easily in his saddle and waited.

The six men reined up just below the crest, and their leader was carrying a rifle across his saddlehorn. Steve dropped his gunhand to his thigh.

"What are you doing on our range?" he demanded.

"We've just found our stolen herd," the Circle Z man said. "It was penned up in that gulch. Tracks lead plain to it all the way from our range. I reckon you've got a lot of explaining to do, Blaine."

"We don't know anything about it." Steve snapped. "Yesterday it was three horses stolen from the Circle Z. What does Coppard pay you cowboys for?"

"You'll find out from the boss pretty quickly if you had anything to do with stealing that herd." the Circle Z cowboy said angrily. "Your fence was down and the herd was driven clean through. Maybe you ought to ride with us to the Circle Z and have a talk with Coppard. He was madder than a wet hen at dawn when he got word about this."

"If this is as you say then the sheriff is the man to take action," Steve said. "I wouldn't advise you to try and take me anywhere I don't want to go. I don't like the sound of all this. Someone was snooping around our place last night. You can see the tracks. I've been following them."

"That's just what we're doing. They lead from the gulch in this direction."

"No one at our place made them," Steve said firmly. "I'd like to come up with the men who made them."

"We've sent a man for the sheriff. You'd better wait here until he shows up."

"And if I won't?" Steve demanded.

"We'll keep you here," he was told.

"Well, I'm going to ride into the gulch and take a look around," Steve said, "This is our range, and I've got a right to know what's going on."

"We all know what's going on," the Circle Z man said thinly.

"Then you'd better tell me," Steve commanded. "And if you say that I've been rustling I'll cut you down."

"Maybe you should sing a bit smaller than you are doing." he was told. "There are six of us, and we don't take kindly to rustlers. If you ain't careful you'll find yourself under a tree a rope around your neck."

"I'll kill at least three of you before you stop me." Steve said. "If you think killing me is worth those odds then get to it. If you ain't gonna do anything about it then get out of my way. If your herd is in that gulch like you say it is then I'll go and see the sheriff myself. I want to get to the bottom of this."

"We'll string along with you," he was told, and he urged his horse forward between them as they scattered left and right out of his way.

There were close to two hundred head of good cattle penned up in the gulch, and Steve sat his horse and looked at the seething mass. His keen eyes studied the ground, but the original tracks of the rustlers had been obliterated by Coppard's riders. Steve turned on the silent cowboys, his face stiff and his eyes hard like chips of blue granite.

"So you figure that me and my pa are responsible for this, huh?" he demanded, and chuckled harshly. "Well, Coppard would have to do better then this to get us off our range. What kind of fools does he think we are? Now you fellers had better drive this stuff back to where it came from, and don't let me catch you on Double B range again."

"I surely admire your nerve," the rider whom Zeke Coppard had left in charge of his cowboys said. "But you can't bulldog your way out of this, Blaine. Coppard said for us to wait here until the sheriff shows up."

"Where is Coppard?"

"Him and Trory went to your place to pick up you and your father. Now don't give us any trouble of it'll go worse for you. Just sit tight and wait for the sheriff."

"Here he comes now," one of the other riders remarked, and Steve swung his horse to see the sheriff riding up the long slope from the creek. There was another rider with the lawman.

Tom Griffin reined in and studied the penned up cattle. Then he turned his keen gaze upon Steve. He straightened his long frame and sighed deeply.

"What's this all about?" he demanded.

"You tell me," Steve retorted.

"I'll tell you what happened this morning," Coppard's man said. "We got word that this herd had been busted off the Circle Z, and we trailed it here. Coppard sent Judd there into town after you, Sheriff. We started for the Blaine place because a lot a tracks led in that direction, and we found this Blaine riding towards the gulch."

"I found strange tracks around the house at dawn," Steve said. "Someone has been riding the range all night, judging by the signs. I followed the tracks in this direction."

"Where's Coppard?" Griffin demanded.

"He went on to our place." There was a sharpness in Steve's voice that betrayed his apprehension. "I just hope he hasn't gone raising hell, that's all. If he's set Trory on to my father I'll do some smoking on my own account."

"Well, we'd better get back to your place and check up," the sheriff decided. "You ride with me, Steve, and you others had better start driving this stock back to Circle Z."

Steve set his mount into a run and the sheriff was hard pushed to keep up. The old lawman glanced back over his shoulder and was relieved to see the Circle Z cowhands getting the stolen herd moving.

"What's really been going on, Steve?" Griffin demanded. "Who do you figure stole that herd and planted it on your range?"

"Someone tried to make trouble for us." Steve was thoughtful for a moment. "There's only one man we can't call friend in this country, and that's Zeke Coppard. I've got a notion that Coppard has done this himself to put us in wrong with the law, sheriff. But you surely realise that if me and pa had a notion to steal any Circle Z stock we wouldn'd pen it up on our own range."

"It ain't what I think, Steve," Griffin said worriedly. "The stock was found on Double B. That puts everything in a bad light."

"It puts me in a bad frame of mind," Steve said flatly. "I'm more than tired of Coppard and his troublemaking. You'll have to do something about him, Sheriff, before I take the law into my own hands. I'm convinced that this is an attempt on his part to put you against us."

"If that was Coppard's intention then he wouldn't have sent a man for me. He would have brought his riders to your place and strung up you and your father."

"Maybe that's what's happened," Steve said harshly. "Frank Trory wasn't with those riders back there. Maybe Coppard and Trory went to my place to get me and pa."

"Is your father there alone?"

"Yeah. Let's make fast tracks. I don't like the smell of this whole deal."

They rode at a gallop, and the sheriff was certain in his own mind that neither Blaine was responsible for the cattle raid, and he wondered if there could be any truth in Steve's allegation that Coppard had planted the cattle himself to discredit the Double B. He hadn't been informed by other ranchers that rustlers had been operating in the county.

"Do you know that Coppard lost three good horses a couple of days ago?" the sheriff asked.

"Yeah. He came over and raised hell about it. Did just about everything but accuse us openly of stealing them. Has he told you that we're guilty?"

"No. He caught a guy with one of them and brought him in. It was just after you left me yesterday. Fellow by the name of Dolan. He said some stranger had held him up at gun point and forced him to swap horses."

Steve smiled. So his father's old friends had run into trouble. He had hoped they'd left the county. He didn't want complications arising from that source. Zeke Coppard was proving more then troublesome on his own.

"What happened to Dolan?" he asked.

"I turned him loose," the sheriff said. "There was no evidence against him. But it means that there are some strangers in the county. I'll have to do some riding around and try to pick up sign. It looks to me that trouble is brewing, and I want to put a stop to it before it goes any further."

"Maybe it's gone too far now." Steve said. "Coppard is playing a deep game. He's threatened to get us off this range, and he ain't particular about his methods. He as much as said that he'd use force to get us off it we didn't sell out to him."

They rode on until they sighted the little house that Steve and his father had built. Steve pounded into the yard and sprang out of his saddle before the horse could stop. He ran across to the door and thrust it open.

"Pa," he yelled, "are you there?"

"Over here, Steve," come the reply, and both Steve and the sheriff swung around to see Heck Blaine emerging from the barn. "What's the trouble? Anything wrong? You both came in here pretty fast."

"I was worried about you," Steve said. "Has Coppard been here?"

"Yeah." Heck Blaine's blue eyes remained on the sheriff. "I'm glad you're along. You'll get a mighty different tale from Coppard, I figure, so it's as well that you hear my side of the story before you get to him."

Steve listened with growing astonishment as his father related the trouble he had handled when Frank Trory died. He glanced at the big gun strapped to his father's right side, and looked down at its twin around his own waist. When the older man had finished, Steve stepped up beside him and slapped his shoulder.

"Good for you, Pa." he said with a grin. "But I wish I'd been here to see it. I bet Coppard don't feel so happy now. So you killed Frank Trory. Well, he's no loss to this community."

"This is more serious than I thought, Tom Griffin said worriedly. "I'll take a statement from you, Heck, and then I'll hear what Coppard has to say about it."

"You can't take any action against my father," Steve retorted. "He was on home range, and Frank Trory was a gunman." He chuckled again. "But it's just what should have happened. I bet it set Coppard back on his heels."

"It may not stop there," Griffin warned. "He's not a man who'd see reason, and after he gets over the shock you gave him this morning he may come back here with his crew and try some frontier law."

"We'll be ready for him if he does," Steve said. "We've had more than enough trouble from Coppard. If you're riding on to his place, Sheriff, you can tell him from me that it he shows his face around here again he'll get a bullet. There's a limit to what we'll take, and this business has pushed us up to the line."

"Don't make my job any harder," Griffin said. "If you haven't done anything against Coppard yet then my advice to you is don't ever start. I'll get this sorted out, and you'll come out of it a lot easier if you keep quiet."

"We'll go along with that, Sheriff," Heck Blaine said. "Don't mind Steve. I'll keep him on a tight rein. But you'll have to do something about Coppard before he starts something else. It was a mighty close thing this morning. There were three of them here, and Coppard almost lifted his gun. I'm lucky aren't three corpses in my yard."

You're damned lucky you ain't dead yourself," Griffin said. "Well, I'd better be riding out. I'm heading for the Circle Z. Maybe you'd better come along with me, Heck, and hear how Coppard tells his side of it."

"We'll both ride with you, Sheriff," Steve said. "Let's get to the bottom of it now. This whole thing could develop into a range war."

"I'll get my horse," Heck Blaine said. He hitched up his sagging gunbelt and went back into the barn.

"Well if that don't beat all," Steve said reflectively. "My father can sure handle a gun if he took Frank Trory like that."

"Do you doubt his story?" Griffin asked.

"Hell, no!" Steve glared angrily at the smiling lawman. "My father wouldn't draw a gun on any man unless it was a matter of life or death."

"It was surely a matter of death with Trory up against him," Griffin remarked.

Heck Blaine came up on his horse and they set off together. They rode fast and in silence, and when they struck the fence marking the boundary between the two spreads, they turned right and followed it until they came to the spot where it had been cut. The sheriff ordered Steve and his father to remain in their saddles while he got down and walked around to check up on the numerous tracks. When he came back to them he was shaking his head.

"There's a lot of sign, but it's all mussed up," he told them. "I can't read much out of it." He swung into his saddle. "Let's get on to the Circle Z house."

When they sighted the big ranch with its sprawling buildings, Sheriff Griffin reined in. He glanced at the harsh faces of both Blaines.

"Don't let us have any trouble here," he told them. "I don't want more than I can handle, so whatever Coppard says, keep your hands off your guns."

"You won't have any trouble from us," Heck Blaine said. "I never touch a gun unless I have to. But you'd better watch Coppard close in case he tries anything." He broke off and chuckled harshly. "But I don't think he'll make another play for his gun. I sure taught him a thing or two this morning."

They rode into the massive yard in front of the house. The sheriff went through the dust and reined up at the rail at one end of the long porch. He stepped down carefully into the dust and waited for both Blaines to join him. They mounted the four steps to the porch and the sheriff knocked on the door. They stood looking around the yard while awaiting a reply.

There was no sign of life around the spread. Silence was heavy over the buildings, and Griffin grabbed the handle of the door and thrust it open.

"Zeke, are you home?" he called, and his voice echoed eerily.

"Maybe they circled our place, then headed for town," Steve said. "We didn't think to look for tracks, did we."

"I'll take a look around," Griffin said. "You two wait here for me." He stepped into the house and they heard his heavy boots sounding all over the building. When he emerged again there was a worried frown on his rugged face. "Coppard ain't here. I reckon he must have done what you said." He sighed heavily. "It's my fault. I should have looked for tracks. I can see now that it was the obvious thing Coppard would have done."

"He might have circled to that gulch where you found the cattle," Heck Blaine said. "He knew his men were there."

"Well, it almost a direct ride from here to the gulch and town," Griffin said. "I reckon I'd better get started. I suppose you two will be back home?"

"That's if you don't want us to ride in with you," Heck Blaine said. "We've got a lot of work to catch up on. If you do want me, Sheriff, you know where to find me.

"Yeah, I surely do. But I don't think you'll have any more trouble now. Maybe you've taught Coppard a lesson. He certainly needed one."

They went back to their horses and mounted. They moved together until they reached the breach in the fence. Then the sheriff set off along the tracks left by the stolen herd, and Steve and his father set their mounts towards home. Steve twisted once or twice in his saddle and watched the lawman riding away.

"He's a good man, Pa," he observed, when Griffin had finally vanished over a ridge. "You could have been in a lot of trouble with any other kind of lawman."

"We ain't out of the wood yet, Son," Heck Blaine said softly. "Zeke Coppard ain't the man to take what I did lying down. I reckon we can prepare ourselves for visitors. What do you say about selling out and moving? Maybe it's too late now to do so, but we could try."

"You know what I feel about that, Pa." Steve sighed and eased his body in the saddle. "I don't figure we've got any reason to run. If Coppard wants trouble then he'll surely get it off us. We're ready for him, and maybe if he does come and gets a bloody nose it'll simmer him down some."

"I don't see it like that, Steve, but if that's how you want to take it then I'll go along with it. But you know what it means, don't you? We've both got to sleep with a gun in our hands. If they come for us we've got to fight it out, and we can't expect any quarter when the shooting starts. We won't get any help, either, because Coppard will see to it that the sheriff is nowhere around when he starts in on us."

"Let them all come," Steve said hotly. "This is our range and we are going to keep it. I've taken more than I ever thought I could because I figured that Coppard was only trying to scare us out. But now I know he means business I'll know what to do about him when he comes around again."

Heck Blaine did not reply. He did not argue with his son because he knew that Steve was his own flesh and blood, and he could not forget his own early years. Twenty years ago he wouldn't have taken this. He would have gone out into the open with a blazing six-gun, and he would have kept his land from all challengers. He was older and wiser now, but the love he felt for Steve outweighed his wisdom. Since leaving outlawry he had doted upon his son, and the youngster had grown to manhood under his guidance. Steve Blaine was his father's life.

The old man studied his son's harsh face, and a small nerve twitched in his weather-beaten cheek. He didn't care so much about the Double B. But if anything happened to Steve in this coming fight then no amount of range would ever make up for the loss. He resolved then and there to hit Zeke Coppard hard at the first opportunity. If the rancher wanted trouble he would get it, but upon Heck Blaine's own terms. The ex-outlaw hadn't lost the cunning and cold nerve that had made his gang feared out here in the west. He was still the same man although he had grown older and lived soft for two decades.

Five

Milt Dolan was foot-sore and weary when he reached the silent camp where Scrap Pierce and Ike Brewster lay snoring in their blankets beside a low fire. He limped to the fire and threw on an armful of wood that one of the outlaws had gathered. Then he sat down on a rock and pulled off his boots. He sat massaging his feet, gazing into the fire, and the flames were reflected in his eyes. When Pierce stirred, then sat up, Dolan turned his head and glanced at his pard.

"You've been a hell of a while," Pierce complained. He grinned. "What did you do, walk back from town?"

"Yeah, I did," Dolan growled, and saw the smile fade from Pierce's thick lips as he narrated the incidents that had befallen him.

"We sure slipped up there," Pierce commented when Dolan had finished. "It's a damned good job you thought up that alibi, Milt, or you'd be in jail right now. What are we gonna do about getting you another horse? Where's your saddle?"

"I left it in town," Dolan grunted. "You didn't think I was going to carry that six miles, did you?"

"No." Pierce got out of his blankets and came to the fire. He squatted down opposite Dolan, and gazed across the leaping flames at his pard. "It won't be safe for us to ride in on those Circle Z nags," he mused almost to himself. "Maybe we can trade them in somewhere for others."

"Not a hope," Dolan said. "That brand the animals are carrying will be known for miles around. We ain't got time to ride out of the county for fresh broncs. We should have brought an extra mount apiece, anyway. This is hard country on a horse, and if we do have to run for it then we'll be hard put to get clear. I don't like this at all, Scrap. Everything seems to be going wrong. We'll maybe walk into trouble when we hit that bank. Let's use our sense and pull stakes to get out of this country. We can always pick up easy dough down in Kansas."

"No," Pierce said obstinately. He picked up a twig and thrust it into the flames. "We're here now and we'll hit Buffalo Grove. We can't make a move until you've got another horse, so I'll ride out tomorrow and try to pick one up. We needn't worry about getting caught for stolen horse flesh because from now on we're only riding at night."

"What about the day of the raid?" Dolan demanded. "We'll have to ride into town when it's light. It'll be just our luck to get caught as we come out of the bank."

"It'll go off all right," Pierce persisted. "We're old hands at this sort of thing, so quick belly-aching about failure. Maybe we'll make a good haul this time so we can lay off for a month or two. There are only three of us to split the dough."

Dolan thought about that. He studied Scrap Pierce's fleshy face across the fire, and the thought suddenly struck him that he had ridden with Pierce and Brewster for quite long enough. If there was a good haul from the bank then the dough wouldn't be split three ways. Dolan smiled at the thought. He wished he had thought of it before. When they got clear of the county after the raid he would shoot down both his pards and make off with all the money. He wouldn't have to do another job as long as he lived. He figured that maybe Heck Blaine had got the right idea when he gave up owl-hooting. He was almost happy as he turned into his blankets for a couple of hours sleep.

Ike Brewster kicked him awake just after dawn, and Dolan, deathly tired after his long walk, cursed Brewster loudly. He turned over on his other side and went back to sleep. There was nothing else for them to do. Pierce was going riding today, and Dolan hoped that the fat outlaw would return with a horse for him. He didn't even stir for breakfast when Brewster called him.

"Leave him lie, Ike," Pierce directed. "He had to walk back here from town last night. I'm going out today to try and pick up a horse for him. We can't make a move until Milt is mounted again."

"The same thing will happen to us if we show our faces during daylight," Brewster said sourly. "We were fools to swap horses like that, Scrap. We've got the county half roused up against us before we think of hitting their bank."

"I'll ride back and see Heck Blaine," Pierce said. "I reckon Heck will be able to let us have a horse."

"You'll have to be careful around that son of his," Brewster warned. "He sounded real salty, and we don't want any more trouble around this county than we can help. Let's get this job done fast and then pull out.

I've got a bad feeling, and my hunches have never been wrong. You know I haven't liked the idea of working up here."

"You and Milt must be getting old," Pierce said with a chuckle. "I don't get those hunches. We've worked together for a long time and we know each other. We know we can rely on each other if we ever get in trouble, so why the worry now?"

"It ain't that, Scrap," Brewster said uneasily. "It must be the country. We're a long way north. We haven't worked this far north before."

"The dough's the same where ever we get it from," Pierce said. He went to his horse and swung into the saddle. "Don't move around here, Ike." He gazed down at his crooked side kick. "There's no telling if that Goppard feller is still out looking for his horses. We don't want to fall in with him. From what Milt said about him, he's a real tough guy."

"We'll still be here when you get back," Brewster said.

Scrap Pierce touched spurs to his mount and rode out of the camp. He headed south and kept an alert eye on his surroundings as he rode. He breathed a sigh of relief when he reached flat range. It was in his mind that both his pards were becoming too much weight on him. He had always thought for them since Heck Blaine gave up the business, and lately, both Dolan and Brewster had turned sour. Perhaps they had been in the business too long. Pierce grinned at that. He knew they could never give it up. They made plenty of money, but it always went just as easily.

He envied Heck Blaine for having made the break with crime. But Blaine hadn't gotten completely away with it yet. Pierce wouldn't forget that his former gang boss had refused to come across with some aid when requested. To the fat outlaw that was something far worse than killing a bank cashier during a raid. So Heck Blaine had found a way out! Now he was too high and mighty to stretch out a hand to his old friends.

For a long time Pierce rode with his senses dulled by thought. He was startled to hear approaching hooves in front of him, and looked up swiftly to see three horses bearing down upon him. In the split second it took his mind to regain its full alertness he noticed that one of the horses was carrying a corpse.

Pierce reined in and dropped a hand to his gun. The two men in front of him had reined up, and the younger of the two was already holding a gun. Pierce tightened his lips and took his hand away from his own weapon.

"You're riding one of my horses," shouted Zeke Coppard, riding forward, lifting his six-gun as he reached Pierce. "What have you got to say about it?" For a moment Scrap Pierce was at a loss for words. He cursed himself for not remaining alert. Thinking about the others had betrayed him into danger. He moistened his dry lips. He could recognise Coppard from the description Dolan had given him.

"I left a good horse in place of this one," Pierce said. "You can't call that stealing. Anyway, I was on my way back to your place to pick up my own mount. A good-hearted rancher wouldn't get upset about this if his horse wasn't hard ridden. Take a look at this animal. There ain't a bead of sweat on it. I ain't the kind of man to go tearing around the countryside."

"Who were the two men with you when you made the swap?" Coppard demanded.

"We parted after we left your place," Pierce said.

"When they come back this way they'll call in at your ranch and trade back them animals they took. We were hard pushed at the time, or we'd have waited for dawn and asked you to make a deal."

"Are you running from the law?" Coppard demanded. He glanced back at the carcass of Frank Trory. He was a good man short now, and would need fast guns to finish off the Blaines.

"No. We were after a man who did us a great wrong." Pierce smiled inwardly. "When we lost his tracks we split up and searched around. I lost my way, and was heading back to your place right now."

"Well, maybe, you've left that a bit too late," Coppard said. He was still shaken by the death of his top gunhand. "I'm Zeke Coppard, owner of the Circle Z ranch, and I make my own laws regarding my stock and ranch. I've always hanged thieves, whether they took horses or cattle. If you know any prayers then you'd better polish them up."

"Don't do anything hasty," Pierce said quickly. "I've always found that a man who acts in haste usually makes a bad mistake."

"I'll make no mistake about you," Coppard snarled. "Keep your gun on him, Hank."

"It looks like you've had some trouble," Pierce said, glancing at the body draped across the saddle. "I reckon maybe we could do a deal. I heard hereabouts that you are having a lot of trouble with a smaller rancher called Blaine. I figure you've just had a run-in with him and come off second best. Well, maybe I can just help you to get rid of Heck Blaine, and without a lot of gunplay."

"Do you know Blaine?" Goppard demanded.

"I sure do. What about a deal?"

"What kind of a deal, and what do I get out of it?" Coppard was suspicious but ready to grasp at anything that would help him to evict the Blaines.

"I'll give you the means of removing Heck Blaine if you'll forget this business, and throw in an extra horse."

"What do you want an extra horse for?"

"That information ain't part of the deal." Pierce grinned. "You'll be getting off cheap if you get Blaine's range for the price of a couple of horses."

"You've got something on Blaine from way back, is that it?" Coppard demanded. "Damn me, I figured he was too fast with a gun for an honest man. Is he wanted by the law?"

"You make a deal with me and I'll tell you what you want to know."

"I'll go along with you," Coppard decided. "What do you know?"

"Not so fast," Pierce retorted. "Tell your man to put away his gun. I never was a man to take unnecessary risks. You give me two horses; the one I'm riding and another, and write me out a bill of sale for them so I don't get pulled in for stealing, and then I'll tell you what you want to know. You'll figure it's worth twice as much when I set you straight."

"All right." Coppard glanced at his gunman. "Put away that iron, Hank." He waited until the man had complied. "Now ride on to Buffalo Grove with that corpse and I'll go back to the ranch. I don't figure Griffin to be in town now, anyway. I sent a man in earlier to fetch him. So you stay in town, Hank, until I show up."

The gunman nodded and took the lead rope of Frank Trory's horse. Scrap Pierce waited until he was alone with Coppard, then grinned at the rancher.

"I reckon you and me speak the same language, Coppard," he said. "It's a pity I'm just passing through the country. Maybe we could do each other some good."

"I don't want no truck with thieves," Coppard said thinly. "You just keep to this bargain we've made, then leave the country. If I set eyes on you after today I'll string you up from the nearest tree."

"There are rules to my business that no one ever breaks," Scrap Pierce said. "I'll keep my word to you, but I ain't so sure about you."

"You'll just have to take a chance." Coppard smiled harshly. "I'm only interested in one thing, and that's getting my range back."

"That should be an easy thing to do, if it is your range." Pierce said. "I know Heck Blaine pretty good, and he ain't the man to sit down on someone else's ground and try to hold it."

"It's my range all right. I've used it for years."

"How far are you prepared to go to get it back?"

"As far as I have to. You saw that corpse. It was Frank Trory, my best gun. Heck Blaine shot him out of the saddle so fast I never saw him draw."

"Blaine was always the fastest gun," Pierce said. "I never yet seen one faster. So he hasn't lost any of his speed, and I reckon his son has inherited some of it."

"Have you spoken to Blaine recently?"

"Yeah. I called on him a couple of days ago. You won't never scare them two out there. I know Heck Blaine better than I knew my own father. You've got to kill him, and that'll be difficult, or you can do it easy on what information I give you. It's lucky for you, Coppard, that we bumped into each other today."

"You're the lucky one," the rancher growled. "If I wasn't set on getting back that range, I would have strung you up."

"I'd hate to know you when you're in a bad temper," Pierce said with a grin. "How far is it to your place?"

"A couple of hours. We're on Double B range now. I've got to watch out for the Blaines. I don't want any more trouble unless it's on my terms."

"That's the only way to handle it," Pierce agreed.

They rode on, skirting the Double B ranch, and Coppard paused and toyed with the idea of using his rifle on Steve Blaine, whom he spotted in the distance. But Scrap Pierce talked him out of the intention, and they continued. It was past noon when they rode into the Circle Z yard. An old man with grey hair and wizened features came running out of the bunkhouse. He grabbed Coppard's reins and held the horse when the rancher dismounted.

"The sheriff was out here some time ago," the old man reported, "and them two Blanies were with him."

"What did they want?" Coppard demanded.

"I didn't try to find out. I stayed hid until they rode out."

"Yeah, that was probably the right thing to do. I reckon Griffin learned about Trory's death. Well, I give Heck Blaine best on that. Now what about our deal? What did you say your name was?" He glanced at the watchful Pierce.

"I didn't give the name." Pierce grinned. "You needn't know anything about me. But first you get another horse saddled up and ready for travel, and make out a receipt for it and the one I'm riding. Then I'll give you the means of removing Heck Blaine. It'll still leave the son, but I figure that if you want that range bad enough you'll find a way of getting him out there."

"I'll attend to the details," Goppard said gruffly. "Seth, go saddle up one of them hosses in the small corral. Bring it here. Come on into the house, stranger, and we'll make this deal."

Pierce followed Coppard into the house. He took the drink that was poured for him, and sat down on a very comfortable chair.

"Nice place you've got here," he remarked.

"It suits me," Coppard retorted. He want to his desk and quickly made out a receipt, which he passed to Pierce. The outlaw studied the paper at great length, then folded it and put it in a pocket. The old man came in and paused in the doorway.

"The hoss is ready outside," he said.

"Now what's this you've got on Heck Blaine?" Coppard demanded.

"Not yet," Pierce said. "Mount up again and ride with me out of range of this place. I'm a mighty cautious man, Coppard, and I never trusted another guy in my life. If I had done I would have been killed a long time ago."

Coppard cursed, but moved quickly to the door. Pierce followed closely, and they remounted, and Pierce took the lead rope of the extra horse. They headed out of the yard and Pierce rode back the way they had come.

"I thought you were heading south," Coppard observed.

"I was. I wanted another horse. Now I've got him I'm going back to where I came from."

They rode on until Pierce judged himself to be safe from interference from Circle Z riders if Coppard wanted to double-cross him. He reined up and stuck a forefinger and thumb into a breast pocket. Coppard eyed the dirty square of paper that the outlaw produced. He watched Pierce unfold the paper, and immediately recognised it as a wanted dodger. Pierce passed it over and sat waiting for the rancher's comment.

Coppard scanned the faded print. There was a brownish reproduction of a young man's face. He could see immediately that it was a picture of Heck Blaine. The writing on the paper informed him that the sheriff of Mason County, Kansas, wanted Mike Slade, dead or alive, for robbery and hold-up. A reward of two thousand dollars was offered.

"This is all of twenty years old." Coppard lifted his gaze to Pierce's harsh face.

"That don't make no difference. They're still looking for Mike Slade, alias Heck Blaine. He was the leader of The Wild Men."

"You're joking." Coppard's eyes widened in surprise.

"Well, you can believe that if you like, but contact Mason County in Kansas and they'll have a special deputy up here faster than you can whistle. I'm telling you that Heck Blaine is Mike Slade, the leader of The Wild Men."

"I reckon you've got a deal, mister," Coppard said. "Can I have this dodger?"

"It's yours. It goes with the information. Show that to your local sheriff and he'll haul Blaine into jail. You'll even collect the two thousand dollars reward on Blaine. You've made yourself a good deal."

"I'll get some men together and go pick up Blaine myself." Coppard swung his horse around and headed back to his ranch. He glanced over his shoulder. "I'm a man of my word," he called. "Them two horses is yours now. But if I catch you on my range after today I'll have you hung. Better keep going north, though if you do come south, you'd better give my range a miss."

"I'm heading out of the country, Coppard," Pierce said. "I ain't ever coming back to these parts." He grinned and stood up in his stirrups. "Better watch out for Blaine if you try and take him. His bite is poison." Coppard did not reply, but headed fast for his ranch. Scrap Pierce sat his horse for a moment, shaking his head slowly as he thought about Heck Blaine. They had been good pards in the old days. He sighed deeply and clicked his tongue to encourage the horses. He rode quickly away from the Circle Z.

When he passed through the breach in Blaine's wire, Scrap Pierce hesitated, then turned his mount towards the Double B ranch house. He rode fast, knowing that Coppard would not be far behind with his crew. Pierce was already regretting his action. If Blaine found out how he had sold up the river, then the ex-outlaw might do some talking himself, and that would put paid to the bank raid planned against Buffalo Grove.

Heck Blaine was leaning on a rail by the small corral when Pierce rode in. The outlaw did not dismount, and the older man looked up at his former pard.

"I didn't figure you'd still be in the country" Blaine said.

"I ain't got yet what I came after." Pierce grinned. "I've never missed out yet, Heck. But I've dropped by to give you a warning. I just came by the Coppard place, and Coppard has just got an old wanted dodger with your face on it. I reckon you know the one I mean. Your name was Mike Slade in those days."

"You're joking, Scrap," Blaine said, his face paling. He came upright and dropped a hand to his gun.

"I wouldn't dream of making such a joke," Pierce said. "I swear to God, Heck, that Coppard is gathering some men to come and take you. If he doesn't kill you in the attempt, he'll run you into town and have you locked up."

"How would Coppard get to know about me?" Blaine's eyes were cold, and they seemed to bore right through Pierce. The fat outlaw shifted his weight in the saddle, and leather protested. "Where did he get that dodger from, Scrap?"

"Why ask me?" Pierce pouted his fleshy lips. "Heck, you ain't suspecting me of spilling the beans about you, are you?"

"I'd be greatly surprised if you did, Scrap, but I've heard of such things happening. How do you come to be riding through Circle Z, and keeping two of Coppard's horses?"

"Listen, Heck, if I'd told Coppard about you, do you think I'd ride in here and tell you so?" Pierce leaned forward in his saddle. "You knew me well enough in the old days, Heck. I never put the deadwood on a man, not for any reason."

Blaine gazed into the distance, looking for sign of Coppard and riders. He glanced around at the ranch buildings, and a sigh escaped him. He turned his brooding eyes back to Scrap Pierce.

"Scrap, if you are responsible for taking all this away from me, I'll kill you. It ain't so much for myself as for my son. I'll have to ride out now, before Coppard comes, and what'll the boy do alone?"

"It's a tough break after all these years," Scrap Pierce said. "What are you gonna do, Heck?" He ran the tip of his tongue around his dry lips. "You could do worse than ride with me and the boys again."

"I've got a feeling that you've done this just to get me out with you, Scrap." Blaine breathed harshly, his lips twisted, betraying the agony he was feeling inside. "I left the outlaw trail twenty years ago to take care of my son, and I aim to keep on doing that. I can't run now while Coppard is out to take this place. I know Steve, and I guess I wouldn't blame him if he lifted a gun in order to stay here. I'd do the same, and mighty quick."

"But you can't stay here, Heck," Pierce protested. "Coppard will be showing up mighty soon, and in the mood he's in, you won't be able to argue with him. If you don't want to join the gang again, then c'mon up into the hills and use the hideout."

"I'll have to do something." Blaine stared again in the direction of Circle Z, looking for the first black dots that would signify the approach of trouble. "Wait here for me and I'll have a word with my boy." He glanced towards the barn, then again at the range before scuffing disconsolately through the dust to where Steve was working.

Scrap Pierce felt a sudden pang of regret. But it was too late for remorse. He had done the deed, and nothing could stop the ensuing events.

Six

Steve straightened his back when his father entered the barn. He grinned at the older man, then sobered when he saw his father's expression. He came forward, wiping sweat from his forehead.

"What's eating you, Pa?" he demanded. "Something's troubling you, and that's for sure."

"I just got some bad news, Steve. Scrap Pierce rode in with word that Zeke Coppard has learned about my past, and he's heading this way with some of his men. He'll kill me or take me into town."

Steve dropped a hand to his gun and drew the big weapon. He checked its loads, then slid the gun back into leather. He looked up at his father, and there was blue ice in his narrowed eyes.

"No one is going to take you anywhere, Pa. If they do, it'll be over my dead body."

"They'll kill you if they have to, Steve," Blaine said bitterly. "That's why I'm running. I'm all washed up around here. You can hang on if you can. I'll stay up in the hills to see how you make out. If you do get in deep with Coppard, I'll come smoking my Colt, and that'll clear the air."

"You can't run, Pa," Steve said, grasping his father's arm, but the older man tore himself free.

"No, Steve, there ain't time for arguments. Coppard will come dusting into this yard at any time, and I don't want to see you lying in the dust. I'm getting out, and that's my final word."

"Who spoke out about you, Pa? Who else knew about you in this country?"

"Anyone could have found out." Heck Blaine said. He sighed. "I don't suppose I can complain. I've had a good run. I've got away with it for a long time. But I've always known this good life would one day come to an end. Well, the time has come, and I've got to be riding, Son. I ain't leaving the country, Steve. I'll be around to see you."

"Do you figure it was your three crooked pards who told on you?" Steve persisted.

"I've got my own ideas on that, but it ain't no good saying. Get me a horse saddled, Steve, and I'll throw some grub together in a sack. I've got to get moving. I don't fancy starting a jail sentence at my time of life."

Steve picked up his father's saddle and went out into the sunlight Heck Blaine hurried into the house. When Steve saw the silent Scrap Pierce sitting his horse over by the corral he hurried through the dust, and paused at the fat outlaw's stirrup.

"If I thought you had anything to do with Coppard finding out about my pa," he said, "I'd pull you out of that saddle and kill you with my bare hands."

"Hell, I'm doing your father a favour," Pierce said, gazing worriedly a the skyline. "If Coppard knew I'd dropped in here, he'd come hunting me. I want your father to get out of here before those cowboys show up."

"Do you think he should ride with you?"

"He will if he's got any sense," Pierce said. "Me and the others sure know how to take care of ourselves out there in the open. Your father was one of us a long time ago, but he's lived soft for a number of years,. Maybe that old life will come hard to him now."

"He's not going back to the old life," Steve said. "He going to hide out until I've sold this place. Then we'll clear out of the country and find somewhere else to live."

"That would be the wise thing to do" Pierce said.

"It's the only thing we can do," Steve said harshly. He entered the corral and caught his father's horse. By the time the animal was ready for travel, Heck Blaine was coming across the yard with a bulging sack of supplies under an arm.

"Steve, I'm real sorry I've got to run off like this," the older man said. "The last two days must have been a great strain on you. I should have told you all about my early days."

"Forget it, Pa," Steve said huskily. "Like I said, what you did before you came for me is none of my business. What you've done for me since more than makes up for your wrong-doing. You'd better get moving before Coppard shows up. If he does come out here shouting off that big mouth of his, I'll cut him down to size."

"Promise me that you'll leave your gun holstered unless someone tries to harm you, Steve". Heck faced his son and put a hand on Steve's shoulder. "It's a long step to take, crossing from the law's side to the outlaw trail, Son. One angry shot can do it. Promise me that you won't do anything foolish. Then I can ride away easy."

"You've got my promise, Pa." Steve gazed across the flat range. "Look, there's dust in the air, and it's heading this way. You'd better ride now. If Coppard is coming here I'll try to stall him. How will you keep in touch, Pa?"

"I'll come down here and see you. They won't be watching for me all the time. Just watch your temper, Steve."

Steve grasped his father's hand. A lump constricted his throat. He watched with dimmed gaze while his father swung slowly into his saddle and turned his horse away. It couldn't be possible that the old man was on the run again. He glanced angrily at the nearing dust cloud, then transferred his anxious eyes back to his father's straight figure. Heck Blaine turned once and waved, and Steve returned the gesture. He swallowed hard on the lump that seemed to be choking him.

Fifteen minutes later Zeke Coppard and five men came pounding into the yard. Steve stepped down off the porch and the red-faced rancher reined in and held his mount on a tight rein. Coppard's slitted eyes swept around the yard, probing in every direction.

"Where's your father?" he snarled.

"I can handle Double B business as well as my father," Steve snapped. "What do you want, Coppard?"

"Get down from your horses and search the place," Coppard ordered his men. "If Heck Blaine resists you then kill him."

Steve slapped leather as the cowboys began dismounting. His Colt came into his hand and lined up on Zeke Coppard. The rancher choked on his rage.

"Get back on them horses or Coppard takes a slug through his thick head," Steve grated. He pulled back the hammer of the long-barrelled weapon, and his knuckle whitened as he put pressure on the trigger. "Now perhaps you'll be good enough to tell me what this is all about, before I start shooting."

"I'll tell you," Coppard raged. "Your father is a notorious outlaw, and I'm gonna see that he gets what he deserves."

"Since when have you worn a law badge?" Steve demanded.

"It's every honest man's duty to turn in a criminal."

"Especially if he owns land that you want," Steve retorted, smiling tightly. "Well, Coppard, you won't find my father here. He rode out to town a couple of hours ago. You're looking into the mouth of hell right now. Can you give me a couple of reasons why I shouldn't blast you? You've caused us nothing but trouble these last few days. Damn you, you land grabbing bully! If you keep pushing like you do you'll draw more than you bargained for. Now turn those horses around and get to hell out of here. I'm telling you just one more time. If I see hide or hair of you on this ranch again I'll shoot you down like I would a rattlesnake. Now get moving. Ride out."

Coppard's scrawny cheeks puffed out with rage. The colour of his face darkened and his eyes narrowed to pin points of hatred. For a moment Steve thought the old rancher was going to make a play for his gun despite the menace of his own levelled weapon. But Coppard controlled his emotions and drew a shuddering breath.

"By hell, youngster, I'll come back and settle with you when I've caught your old man." Coppard pulled around the head of his horse, causing the animal to rear sharply. He curbed the beast with hands and spurs, and shouted at his men as he thundered out of the yard.

Steve watched them go, and anger was burning fiercely in his breast. He lowered his gun when the riders drew out of range, then holstered the weapon. For a moment he stood undecided, then went to prepare his horse for travel. He locked the house when he was ready to leave and went slowly to his horse.

He swung into his saddle and set out at a fast clip on the trail of Coppard and his men. The rancher was heading for Buffalo Grove, and Steve could imagine what kind of a tale the sheriff would hear. He decided to see Griffin himself and lay his cards on the table. The sheriff was a fair-minded man, and he would be able to say what could be done about Heck Blaine.

Steve rode for an hour before running into trouble. He was heading for a wide stand of timber when a bullet hummed past his head. He saw the puff of smoke that marked the position of the gunman, and pulled his horse aside and headed for a depression in the range. A second rifle opened up at him and he heard slugs whine all around. He dived out of leather and hit the ground hard, rolling over and over in a desperate effort to reach cover. Dust spurted up under the rapid impact of striking lead, and a thrashing pain stabbed through his left leg as he rolled down a slope and out of view of the ambushers.

He clawed at the slope with tensed fingers to halt his progress, and forced himself upright. A quick glance at his leg showed a trickle of blood issuing from a hole in the flesh just above the knee. He slapped a hand to his holster, and cursed angrily when he found the gun missing. The ground shook then under sudden pounding hooves, and he guessed that the ambushers were coming for a look at him.

His desperate eyes saw the glint of sunlight on the barrel of his Colt lying some distance above his head, and he lunged up the slope and grabbed the weapon. He clenched his teeth against the pain in his leg and climbed the rest of the way to the top of the slope.

Two riders were hammering through the dust towards him. Steve thumbed back his hammer. He crouched a little to minimise his own target area, and waited for a good shot. A flash marked the first shot from the nearer of the two riders, and dust spurted beside Steve's position. He ignored the shot. His eyes were narrowed as he waited. Both riders began shooting fast, and Steve lifted his gun and threw a reply at the nearer. He fired coolly, and watched the result of the shot. The horseman jerked as the slug hit him, but hunched low in his saddle and kept coming, emptying his gun in the hope of scoring a lucky hit. Steve fired again. The riders were only forty yards away and closing distance fast. He knew that he would die if he lost his head, and forced his mind to remain clear. His father's instruction in the art of gun fighting was plain in his mind and actions.

The muzzle of his gun followed the movement of the nearer rider, and his ears were almost completely shut to the noise of the shooting directed at him. He fired as the blade of the foresight moved ahead of the rider to allow for the man's speed, then he fired again. The bullet struck the man in the chest, and his body thumped into the long grass.

The second rider kept throwing lead, and Steve felt pain in his left hand. He glanced down quickly and saw a great splotch of blood covering the back of his left hand. He moistened his dry lips, and weakness filtered into him when he saw small slivers of white bone protruding starkly through the spurting blood. Another bullet threw dust into his eyes, and he pushed himself backwards on his elbows as fear sprang into his mind.

The second rider was almost upon him. Horse and man looked frighteningly large and menacing from Steve's position. Steve lifted his gun almost instinctively, following his father's advice, which had been drilled into him on countless days of instruction. He fired, and cursed as the horse screamed at the impact of driving lead. The animal came down in the dust, rolling and thrashing, and the rider hit the ground on his feet and came running forward towards Steve, gun blazing and lead seeking Steve's cringing flesh.

Steve thrust his gun out to arm's length and fired again. He saw dust spurt up from the dark shirt of the man, and blood began spreading rapidly through the dry fabric. The man threw down his gun and bent at the waist. His face went into the dirt and his legs were still moving, trying to run. He came forward on his face several yards before finishing on his knees with his features buried in the long grass.

Steve stayed where he was for long moments while he tried to break the paralysing hold of shock. The echoes of the shooting had died away, but his ears still sang from the noise. He stared at the blood pouring out of his smashed hand, and sickness stirred inside him. He dropped his gun and grabbed his left wrist with his right hand, squeezing frantically in an attempt to stop the bleeding, but he was unsuccessful, and wondered how much blood he could afford to lose without endangering his life. His hands trembled uncontrollably as he watched the bright red fluid streaming out of the wound.

He pulled his neckerchief loose and clumsily wrapped it around his hand. When he tried to get to his feet he fell sideways as his left leg gave way beneath him. He rolled down a slope and finished up in a cloud of dust at the bottom. Coughing and choking, he crawled away from the dust and tried to get to his feet. At the third attempt, with his teeth snapped tightly together against the pain that filled him, he stood up and staggered back up the slope. On the crest, he fell to his knees, still holding his left wrist with his right hand.

Both fallen riders lay as he had dropped them. Steve clenched his left hand, groaning at the pain as broken bones grated, and he thrust the hand under his chin to hold it still. He picked up his gun and reloaded awkwardly with his one good hand. Then he went forward to check on the men he had shot.

There was a roaring sound in his ears which threatened to overwhelm him with every step. He could sense the blackness hovering inside his brain, waiting to sweep in on him when shock struck. He gazed incuriously at the first body, and didn't need a second glance to tell him the man was dead.

He had never killed a man before, and studied the careless position of the carcass while ice gathered in his brain and his stomach heaved. He gulped at the bitter taste in his mouth, and could feel a trembling inside which threatened to burst uncontrollably into every limb. He felt that he wanted to run away, but thrust aside the panic that tried to betray him and went over to the second man. He stared at the second corpse and wonder filled him. He had killed two men and they had all the breaks. He concentrated his wavering thoughts upon his father, and strength flowed back into him. These two men had been with Zeke Coppard a short time ago. Steve clenched his teeth until his jaws ached. So the old rancher had ordered the shooting to start.

He went back to his horse and had to pull himself into the saddle by grasping the horn with his right hand. He mounted from the right side, thrusting his right toe into the stirrup. The horse ribbed a bit at the unusual event, and he calmed it with a few words. For a moment he sat and stared at the carnage he had wrought. The he rode to where the surviving horse stood with trailing reins and gathered the animal. He led it as he rode on to town.

There was a little knot of riders gathered outside the law office when Steve rode along the street. The pain in his hand and leg was almost unbearable, but the iron will inside him held weakness at bay. His hard blue eyes searched the riders for a glimpse of Zeke Coppard. He reined up when he saw the rancher, and the expression that crossed the old man's face when he saw Steve was enough to tell Steve that the two men who had tried for him had done so on Coppard's orders.

"Coppard," Steve called, and there was a sudden silence in front of the law office. Sheriff Griffin emerged from the office and stood in the doorway, a watchful expression coming to his rugged features. "I've just killed two men who ambushed me about five miles out between here and my place." Steve pulled on the reins of his horse and then sent the animal he was leading towards the mounted rancher. "Here's one of the horses they rode. It's carrying your brand. Those two men were with you when you left my place. I figure you set them on to me. Well, here I am. Now you can do your own fighting. I've had a belly full of you. Lift your gun and we'll settle this now."

Zeke Coppard sat unmoving on his horse. One of his riders dropped a hand to his gun, and Steve slapped leather and half lifted his weapon. His eyes were wide and blazing, filled with agony and shock, and his teeth were barred in a snarl as he waited for someone, anyone, to start the shooting.

"Hold it," Sheriff Griffin shouted, coming forward to the edge of the sidewalk. "There's to be no shooting in town. Steve, you look like you need the doctor urgently. Get your hand off that gun and dismount. Come into the office and I'll send someone for the doctor."

"I don't need a doctor. I need to do some skunk-killing. Coppard figures he's a big man in this country. He thinks he can ignore the law and do just what he pleases. Well, he's gone as far as he can with me. If he won't fight, then I'm making a charge against him. He had his men wait for me just now, and they sure enough tried to kill me."

"What about this, Zeke?" Griffin demanded sharply. "I've warned you often enough about causing trouble. What have you got to say for yourself? Did you order two of your men to ambush Steve?"

There was silence amongst the dozen or so men sitting their mounts outside the jail. Zeke Coppard moved uncomfortably in his saddle.

What kind of a man do you think I am?" he growled angrily. "Do you think I'd deliberately order two men to kill another in cold blood? Damn you, Blaine, for even suggesting that I did. I sent those two men back to the ranch. What they did after I left them ain't none of my business."

Steve smiled thinly. He leaned his right elbow on the saddle horn and rested his weight upon it.

"I figured that was what you'd say, Coppard," he rasped. "Well, you've got two dead men, and when you check on that fight out there, Sheriff, you'll find that they fired at least a dozen shots at me. I've stopped two of theirs. I reckon you should lock up Zeke Coppard. He's a menace to the community. He's worse than a wild animal."

"We're on our way to ride down your father, Blaine," Coppard shouted. "Everyone knows what he is now. We'll bring him in dead."

"You'll have a job to do that," Steve said with a grim smile. "I'd just like to see you try it. You seem to think that you'll get your hands on the

Double B if you turn my father in. Well, you'll never get away with it. I'm not an outlaw and I'm in possession, and, Coppard, this is the last time I'll tell you. If you come on to Double B grass again and I see you, I'll drop you. That goes for any of your riders, too. Sheriff, I want to talk with you."

He slid out of the saddle, and almost collapsed as his weight fell on his wounded leg. Griffin came down into the dust and grabbed him, then helped him onto the sidewalk and into the office.

"Sit down there," the sheriff said kindly. He helped Steve into a seat. "Let me take a look at those wounds, son."

"Don't touch my hand, Sheriff," Steve said faintly. "It's a real mess. My leg ain't so bad. The slug bored through the flesh. But I want to talk to you about my father. What are you going to do about him?"

"Coppard has given me information about him being an outlaw," Griffin said gravely, "and I've seen the wanted poster. It's an old one, I admit. But I'd be failing in my duty if I didn't try and bring him in. I've already sent a wire to the sheriff who put out the poster; at least, it's gone to that law department. I figure that wanted notice came out more than twenty years ago. Has your father been living honest all that time?"

"He has, and would have continued so if Coppard hadn't started all this trouble. Sheriff, you'd better lock up that old man before I kill him. I'll do just that if my father dies or goes to jail because of him."

"Don't make threats, Steve, in case anything happens to Coppard and you ain't to blame. You won't help anyone by using your gun, least of all your father. If I bring him in and he goes before the judge, he may get off lightly on account of his good living these past twenty years. I can't promise you it would happen, but it very well might. As things are, if Coppard is going all out to get rid of you and your father, then jail might be the safest place for Heck Blaine."

"What are you going to do about Coppard? It's certain that he sent those two riders to get me."

"I can't do anything without proof. It's unfortunate that you killed both those men. Maybe we could have got some talk out of one of them. I don't suppose any of the other three who rode in with Coppard will have anything to say. You'd better stay here for as bit, Steve, and I'll send the doctor in to you. Tell me, though, did you know your pa was Mike Slade the Wild Man?" "Not until a couple of days ago," Steve replied bitterly. "Three of his old pards dropped by. I figure they were trying to talk him into something, but he wouldn't have anything to do with them."

"Three old pards, huh? Coppard said he lost three horses. Could be a tie-up there somewhere. Can you describe them three? Wait a minute and I'll send one of my deputies for the doctor." He crossed to the door and opened it, shouting to one of the riders waiting impatiently in the street. When he came back to Steve his eyes were alive with excitement.

"I know one of them well enough to describe," Steve said. "He rode into our place this morning just before Coppard showed up, and told my father that Coppard had found out about his past. My father rode off with him." Steve gave the sheriff a description of Scrap Pierce.

"Well, he ain't the man Coppard brought in here and accused of stealing that horse."

"What was that man like?"

"Small fellar, bitter-looking and hard-faced. Looked like a long rider, but I let him go. He spun some yarn about being held up and having his horse taken from him. The robber left him with a Circle Z animal. He walked out of town the other night and I haven't seen him since."

"This Scrap Pierce was leading an extra horse," Steve said quickly. "It and the one he was riding were both carrying the Circle Z brand."

"Just a minute." Griffin went back to the street and called to Zeke Coppard. The rancher entered the office with great reluctance. "Zeke, what kind of a trade did you make for that horse an old outlaw got off you?"

"What the hell are you talking about?" Coppard blustered, and Griffin smiled thinly when he saw a spark of fear in the rancher's eyes.

"I'm talking about the horse you gave to a fat man named Scrap Pierce. I think you gave it to him in return for the information against Heck Blaine."

"It doesn't matter how I got word about Blaine," Coppard protested. "He's an outlaw and I've told the town about him. What are you going to do about him?"

"I'm going out to try and pick him up," Griffin said. "But I want to have the whole picture of what happened. I think you did a deal with Pierce. He gave you information which you hoped would help you remove Heck Blaine. You gave Pierce a horse. I could charge you, Zeke, for helping a wanted outlaw. I've heard about Pierce, and he's wanted all right. Did you know that he rode into the Double B after he left you? He warned Heck Blaine that you knew about him." "The dirty double-crosser," Coppard exclaimed furiously. "So him and that one I took the hoss back from are in cahoots. I'll rouse my entire crew out to find them." He paused and laughed harshly. "So Heck Blaine has gone back to his kind, huh? Well, it'll be easy to run them all down together."

"I ought to gut-shoot you," Steve said tensely. "You can pull just about every dirty trick in the book and get away with it."

He pushed himself to his feet, but sprawled sideways as his leg gave way beneath him. His smashed left hand hit the sheriffs desk, and he cried out at the agony released in the limb. His face struck the floor and he lay still, washed by surging pain. Darkness swooped in upon him and his pain receded with his senses. He was unconscious when the sheriff bent over him.

Seven

Heck Blaine was a silent, thoughtful man as he rode across the empty range north of his ranch. He kept glancing at Scrap Pierce, who maintained his own silence with a sullen manner.

"You've got something on your mind, Scrap," Blaine said eventually. "And I reckon I know what it is. You told Zeke Coppard about me, didn't you?"

"Honest to God I didn't, Heck," the outlaw returned. "Do you think I'd turn in an old friend?"

"How is it that you've got two horses from Coppard? I know that old man well; I ought to, he's been coming round my door nearly every day since me and Steve took over the Double B. I've never met a more persistent cuss in my life."

"I bought them two nags, Heck. Look, I wouldn't have come to warn you like I did, would I, if I'd turned you in? You've hurt my feelings by thinking I'd do such a thing."

"You're forgetting that I know you." Blaine lapsed into silence again. He was thinking of his son, wondering how Steve would make out against the scheming Zeke Coppard. He had no fears that Steve could not handle himself in any trouble that might arise, but he was afraid that Coppard would try some underhand trick that would take the boy unawares.

When they reached the outlaw camp both Brewster and Dolan came out of hiding holding levelled guns. Dolan pulled a wry face when he saw Blaine, but Ike Brewster grinned broadly.

"So you've thrown in with us," he said. "I always knew you were a clever man, Heck. You've realised that you can make more with us than you can nursing cows."

"Let's get one thing straight," Blaine said quietly. "I'm on the run from the law, or I shall be when Coppard gets to the sheriff. But I'm not going back into the old business. I finished with that a long time ago, and I vowed then that I'd never pull another crooked job. I haven't gone back on that word in twenty years."

"You had no need to," Pierce said. "But now it's different. The law will start looking for you again and you've got to go on the dodge. You've got to live. There's only one way out and that's the old game."

"I'm a bit too old for all that helling around," Blaine said harshly. "I've got a good ranch down there, and a hell of a good son running it."

"You'd better forget all that," Brewster said. "If the local law is on to you then you'll never be able to go back. They'll grab you if you do, and with the crimes you've committed you'll never come out of a cell again in this world."

"Ike is right," Pierce said. "Listen, Heck, we're going to do the bank in Buffalo Grove any day now, then we're clearing out of this country. You can throw in with us and take over bossing the outfit again. We can always get some good men to form a larger gang, like we had in the old days. What do you say?"

"No, and don't ask me again, Scrap." Blaine's blue eyes glittered angrily. "I'm an honest man now. I wouldn't steal a dime if I was starving. I'm through with that business."

"So what are you going to do?" Dolan sat down on a rock and drew his Colt. He stripped the weapon down and began to clean it. "Are you going to wander around this country for the rest of your life, running back to the ranch every night to see your boy? That spread will be so thick with deputies you won't be able to step out of your saddle without standing on one."

"I'll lie low around here until the heat wears off," Blaine said. "If I know Griffin he won't look too hard for me. He knows what kind of man I am and what I've been trying to do for Steve."

"That don't make no difference," Brewster said. "He's a lawman, and a pretty hot one, so I've heard, and he'll come out of town with a posse and search under every rock in the country." He glanced at Pierce. "What about us, Scrap? We'd have to find a better hidey hole than this one."

"I'm thinking that this has come as a blessing." Pierce said with a grin. He glanced at Blaine. "It's hard luck on you, pard, but it'll do us a bit of good. We'll cut you in on this deal. If that sheriff take all the men out of town in a posse it'll leave the place wide open for us. Maybe we can work something out, Heck. You don't have to come into town with us to do the job because you'll be too easy to recognise. But if you was to cause some trouble out on the range, like shooting Zeke Coppard, to draw the posse, you'll make our job that much easier, and you'll qualify for a cut."

"That's a good idea," Ike Brewster said, his brown eyes gleaming. "Especially the bit about knocking off that Coppard guy. He's the one causing your son all the trouble. Well, you're an outlaw again, so you can bump him off and save your boy a lot of grief."

Heck Blaine listened to their coarse voices, and his mind teemed with conflicting thought. He knew inside that what they were saying was true. He would never be able to go back to the ranch. He was trying to fool himself into believing that after a week or two the hue and cry for him would fade and he would be able to return to the Double B. But in his heart he knew it would never be so. He was an outlaw, and had always been one. For twenty years he had kidded himself that he had given up hell raising, but it wasn't so. He had known all along that some day he would be caught.

Now it had happened and he was back where he had stood twenty years ago when he fetched his son out of an orphanage. It had taken him years to get out of the habit of looking over his shoulder or starting at a sudden footstep at his back. He had always been ready to shoot first and ask questions afterwards. The passing years had taken the edge from his alertness and he had begun to feel and think like an honest man. But he was an outlaw who had robbed and killed.

He knew that he should really be thankful that Steve was now at an age where he could take care of himself. He had taught the boy everything he needed to help him along in this harsh country. Perhaps that was what fate had intended he should do. Now Steve was able to take care of himself, fate had stepped back into his life and yanked him out of his comfort and peace and thrown him back into the hell that had been his young years. Even his old friends had come back to him.

He glanced at the three men with whom he had ridden. Sight of them took him back a long time. They were all that much older, like himself, he thought, but time had not erased or changed their manner. Scrap Pierce still grinned all the time as if he couldn't forget a funny joke, and Milt Dolan was still the bitter-faced man of twenty years ago. Ike Brewster was still the vicious gunman who had ridden the twisted trails with the notorious Mike Slade, and Brewster looked as if he was still ready to shoot down anyone who got in his way.

When he accepted the fact that he could never go back to the Double B as the honest man he had been, Blaine felt a little more settled. He sat down on a rock and thought over the situation. The years hadn't changed his brain. He could still think as quickly as ever, and he soon saw that, at the expense of his own life and liberty, he could make sure that no one ever bothered Steve and the Double B. He even smiled a little as he realised that he had only to shoot down Zeke Coppard to rid his son of all trouble.

His features turned grim when he realised that he should have challenged the scheming rancher, then killed him. If he had done that, no one would know now about Mike Slade.

Scrap Pierce approached him. Pierce was still not sure that Blaine would not suddenly explode into action and shoot him down like a dog He knew that Blaine realised who had told Coppard about his past. Pierce shivered. He realised exactly what he had done to the ex-outlaw, He had taken away his peaceful existence and parted him from his son.

"What do you want, Scrap?" Blaine demanded.

"We're only about six miles from Buffalo Grove here," the outlaw explained. We've figured that we oughta find a better place to lie up in until we're ready to make our raid. Milt went into town last night, and I'm riding in tonight to have a look around. When Ike has been in the night after, we will be ready to make our play"

"I don't want to know any of the details," Blaine said.

"Are you going to ride along with us?"

"I don't think so." Blaine studied Pierce's fleshy face and saw apprehension in the man's furtive eyes. He fought down the urge to draw his gun and blast the life out of this two-timer. Scrap Pierce had condemned him to a outlaw's life again. "You go your way, Scrap, and I'll go mine. You aim to leave the country after you've hit the bank. Well, I ain't leaving until I've settled with Zeke Coppard."

"If you'll ride with us we'll consider helping you to take care of Coppard and his crew. You've got nothing to lose, and your boy will gain from it. It's the only way you can help him now. If you don't take care of it then he will, I'm sure, judging by the way he handled me and the others when we dropped in on you a couple of days ago. If he downs Coppard he'll maybe find himself in jail. But if we kill that old coot, well, one more killing won't matter to fellers like us."

"When are you hitting the bank?"

"If you throw in with us we won't have to delay," Pierce said. "You know the town better than any of us. You could take over and run the business. If the sheriff and his posse are out of town tomorrow about noon we can go in there and really clear up the dough. What do you say?"

"No, Scrap." Blaine shook his head. "I've lived like an honest man for twenty years, and I can't just toss aside the principles I learned when I taught them to my boy. I'll be letting him down if I turned back to crime. I hope you're satisfied with what you've done. You sold me out to Coppard for a horse, didn't you?" He laughed bitterly. "Damn you, Scrap, you could have picked up half a dozen re-mounts from me for nothing."

"I didn't want no trouble from your boy," Pierce said. "He's fast with a gun and quick on the temper, I shouldn't wonder. I'm real sorry, Heck, that it happened like it did."

"Yeah, but not as sorry as me. But you needn't worry about me. It's my boy you'll have to watch out for if he hears from Coppard how they got on to me."

"I never thought of that," Pierce said. "But we'll be clear of this county in a day or two. We'll give you a share of the dough we pick up, Heck. It'll help you and your boy."

"I don't want any, Scrap. Just ride off and leave me, will you?"

"Sure, Heck. Best of luck." Pierce turned away, then paused. "Do you figure this Coppard guy has got into town yet and told the law about you? If he hasn't then maybe we can intercept him and kill him. That'll make everything right for what's happened."

"Forget it, Scrap. I'll take care of my own trouble. You just leave me alone to wipe it all out."

"We're riding out then. So long, Heck."

Blaine lifted his eyes and watched his three old pards ride out. He was tempted to call them and tell them he would go along with their plans. He knew that he could never resume his happy life with Steve. That was a thing of the past. He also knew that if he stayed around here he would finish up dead or in jail. But he stifled his impulse and waited until the three outlaws had gone before standing up and pacing to and fro.

At first he could formulate no plan of action. His brain teemed with conflicting thought, but the shock that lay inside him had taken his ability to plan, and his thoughts ran round in circles. He knew that he could not leave the country until Steve was settled. That meant some kind of action had to be taken against Coppard, and his eyes hardened as he thought about the interfering rancher.

The urge to kill Coppard grew in his mind, strengthened by the knowledge that he would do anything to protect his son.

He went to his horse and climbed sorrowfully into the saddle. He paused then and wondered which way he should ride. He knew that he had to be careful because a posse would be out looking for him. He could not yet fully grasp the fact that he would have to leave this county, his son and everything he loved, and because of that he would not commit himself to hasty action against Zeke Coppard. If he rode down and killed the rancher he would irrevocably sever all his claims to lawful life. He would become a killer and would have to keep running until they caught him or he died.

He glanced around at the rough, silent country, feeling that even the hills and the rocks were hostile to him now. He had long ago lost the feeling of being hunted which had been ever present during his notorious career as Mike Slade, but it had returned to him now as strongly as if it had never been absent.

He urged his mount into action and headed towards Buffalo Grove. Until he was sure of pursuit he would not make a move in any direction. Perhaps it would be safer for him if he stayed close to town. It was obvious that the sheriff would come out with a posse, and they would probably search farther afield before looking around the town. No doubt they would put a deputy or two out at his place in the hope that he would return, but he had no intention of visiting his son again unless it became imperative.

When he came in sight of the town he off-saddled his mount. His life would depend upon the animal's fitness and condition if the posse got on his tail and chased him. He left the animal in cover and dropped down out of sight, taking up a position from which he could see the town and most of the approaches to it.

While he lay quiet his brain began to revive from the shock Scrap Pierce had given him that morning. He drew a shuddering breath when he realised the gravity of his position. Long experience told him that he should mount up and get as far away from this country as possible, but he wouldn't even consider leaving until he had at least seen his son once more. Perhaps Sheriff Griffin would be aware of that, but Blaine did not care if the lawman set a trap. He would see Steve again, and he would do what he could about Zeke Coppard.

When a group of riders emerged from the cluster of buildings that boasted the name Buffalo Grove, a hard smile played around Blaine's bitter lips. So word had got out. Now everyone knew that Heck Blaine was Mike Slade, the notorious leader of The Wild Men. Blaine shook his head sadly when he thought of all the trouble he had taken to make Mike Slade disappear. He had read in some papers that Mike Slade had died, and had been secretly pleased with his efforts to erase his crooked past. But now the twenty-year gulf between his colourful past and his hard-earned respectability was as if it had never been.

Half-forgotten memories of the rough life of an outlaw came flitting back into his mind, and he disliked the prospects. He was twenty years older, and the score of easy years had made him soft. He was not fitted now to sleeping out in the open in all weathers. His bones would ache at contact with the hard ground, and he had no inclination to fight it out with all and sundry who fancied the bounty money on his head.

He watched the riders split into two parties and begin their search. One group rode west and began to circle. The other rode straight along the trail that led to the Double B and eventually to Coppard's place. He could guess that Griffin would search his county by sections, and hope rose in his bitter heart when he realised it would be no difficult task to evade the lawmen.

It was mid-afternoon, a glance at the sun told him. He studied the group of riders who passed directly beneath his lofty position, but could not see Coppard among them. He recognised Griffin leading the party, and his jaws ached as he clenched his teeth. The sheer helplessness of his position came home to him with harsh impact, and he closed his eyes and clenched his hands in anguish.

There was no animosity in him against Scrap Pierce for what the outlaw had done. He had none to blame for his predicament but himself. He had been an outlaw, and he would have to take any punishment that caught up with him. But it was hard, after all these years, when he had settled down with his son and was living an honest and useful life, to have to uproot himself and go back to the old trails.

When the bout of self-recrimination was gone he got up and went to his horse. He took his blankets from behind his saddle and spread them out. He figured that he had one friend in town who might overlook his past, and that was Doc Cantwell. Perhaps he could leave word for Steve with the doctor. He lay down and slept until darkness, finding the habit of sleeping despite the pressures of mind and body still in his system.

When he awoke he gazed up at the starry sky and tried to find some simple solutions to his problems. The right thing to do was ride into town and surrender himself to the law. He thought back over the acts of lawlessness he had perpetrated, and shook his head sadly. He would draw fifteen years from even the most lenient and sympathetic Judge. His hopes were cold in his heart as he saddled up and rode the short distance to town.

He left his horse well-hidden and went on foot the rest of the way to the doctor's house. He slunk through the shadows like a wolf, and paused in darkness at the side of the building. Dare he reveal himself to the doctor and hope to find help? But he had already decided to do so. He had to get word to Steve, and he knew it would be foolhardy to visit the ranch.

He sighed resignedly. He had always believed in fate, and now accepted this latest development in his life as being inevitable. He lifted his gun and spun the chamber. Well, if he had to go back to the old life, he had better start thinking like an outlaw again or he would wind up in jail before he got moving. He had to retrieve all his half-forgotten experiences. He had to turn his mind into a calculating power to size up every circumstance. He had to recapture his old cunning to keep that one step necessary ahead of the law.

He stepped on to the doctor's wide porch and tapped gently on the door. His nerves were jumping while he waited for a reply. When the door was opened and a shaft of light bathed him, he stepped quickly aside into the surrounding shadows.

"Heck Blaine," Doc Cantwell gasped. "What in blazes are you doing here? Don't you know that the sheriff has taken just about every man in town out with a posse to hunt you down? I thought you'd be riding for the border right now."

"And so I should be, Doc," Blaine said harshly. "But I want to get word to my boy. I figure I can count on you as a friend, whatever the rest of the town thinks of me."

"Come on in, Heck," Cantwell said, moving his tall, thin frame back out of the doorway. "Hurry it up before someone sees you."

Blaine stepped into the house, and felt easier when the doctor had shut and locked the door. He held out a hand to the older man, who grasped it and shook it warmly.

"Heck, it doesn't matter to me what you've been. I've known you for fifteen years, and I've never had reason to complain about you. Lots of men were wild and lawless after the war, and lots of them settled down when they were given the chance. Your best bet is to surrender yourself to the law. You know that, don't you?"

"Yeah, Doc," Blaine sighed. "But I figure that I'd draw fifteen years in the pen, and I can't face that. I deserve it, I know, but I'm too old to start a sentence. I'll never see the outside again. I've decided to do what I can for my boy, then I'm drifting out of the country. It's a hard thing I've got to do, but I intend stopping Zeke Coppard from bothering the Double B any more."

"No, Heck, you can't do that. Leave Coppard to the Sheriff. Griffin will handle him. If you kill him you'll be hunted down, and they won't let up until they've got you. But if you can get out of the country right now, why, I'll bet that Griffin won't look far for you, and if he does and can't find you, I don't figure he'll inform the rest of the country about you. I heard him talking to Steve in here a short time ago, and from what I gathered he ain't too keen on picking you up. He's got to make a show for Coppard's benefit. But he's really gone out to try and pick up them three outlaws who stopped by your place the other day."

"Steve was here today?" Blaine demanded. "There wasn't anything wrong with him?"

"Haven't you heard?" A shadow crossed the doctor's face. He explained how Steve had come riding into town with a bullet-smashed hand and a bored leg. While he narrated the story he saw anger and hatred build up in Blaine's hard eyes. The doctor sighed. "Don't do what you're planning, Heck, for Steve's sake as well as your own. You'll die for it, but think of your boy. He'll have to go on living here. It'll be hard enough for him as it is, with everyone knowing that he's the son of Mike Slade. But he'll never survive if you murdered Zeke Coppard."

'I'm not going to murder Coppard," Blaine growled. "I'm going to find him and call him out."

"Duels are illegal in this county," the doctor reminded. "You'll never get away with it, Heck."

"I don't care," Blaine declared. "My life is nearly over, anyway. I'm getting tired of all this fuss. If I die making Steve's life easier then I'll be satisfied. Did Coppard ride in today? I guess he must have done, but has he left? He wasn't with the posse. I saw them ride out."

"Griffin wouldn't let him ride along," the doctor reported. "The sheriff told him to stay in town until he got back from this man-hunt."

"Then I'll go look him up. He's been pushing his luck a lot lately. Well, this time he's over-played his hand. I'll go take care of him. If it wasn't for him there'd be none of this trouble now. That old fool couldn't grasp the fact that we bought that land he used. He told me he'd do anything to get his hands on it again. I'll go and handle him."

He turned for the door, but paused with his hand on the latch.

"Where's Steve now, Doc?"

"He's got a room at the hotel. I expect that's where Coppard is staying. So I wouldn't go over there and cause any trouble if I were you. If anything happens to Coppard, his men may kill Steve as a reprisal. Have you thought about that?"

"I think the Circle Z would go to pieces if Zeke Coppard died. I'll remove any threat that hangs over my son. We didn't ask for this trouble, Doc. All I ever wanted was peace. But Coppard sure pushed his nose in deep."

"That fat outlaw named Scrap Pierce is the man who told Coppard about you," the doctor said.

"Yeah, I know." Blaine opened the door, He stepped out into the darkness of the porch, and was for a moment outlined in the light issuing from the house. He saw the orange flash of a gunshot wink at him from across the wide street, and his age-old reflexes had him diving for the ground before he realised exactly what was happening. His gun jumped into his hand with astonishing speed as he hit the dirt, and he sent two shots crashing through the night almost immediately after a slug had breathed upon him.

A heavy thud behind him made him whirl to look at the doorway, and horror filled him when he saw the doctor laying slackly half out on the porch. The man had stopped the slug meant for him.

There was a harsh voice shouting across the street, and Blaine recognised Zeke Coppard's hate-filled tone. The rancher had hit the doctor. Blaine got to his feet, and Coppard's gun crashed again, but he ignored the flying lead and stepped over to his friend. He dropped to one knee, his smoking gun forgotten in his right hand, and he looked up at movement inside the doctor's house. His wide eyes saw the doctor's wife appear and come towards him. She halted when she saw the gun in his hand, and her hands went up to her mouth.

Blaine whirled away and stepped down off the porch. He stalked across the road towards the spot where Coppard still stood firing at him. He did not heed the flying lead. A stab of pain pierced him somewhere in the body, but he did not falter. He got half way across the street before he sent hot lead towards the scheming rancher.

The crashing echoes of the shots raged through the town, summoning all those men who had not ridden out with the posse. Coppard's loud voice was still raising the alarm, and shots from the rancher's gun punctuated his hoarse voice. Boots began pounding the sidewalks as men came to find the cause of the disturbance.

Blaine emptied his gun at Coppard, aiming for the rancher's shadowy figure, but Coppard had experienced enough of the ex-outlaw's gun prowess when Frank Trory died. He faded into the darkness and fled up an alley. He had seen Blaine enter the doctor's house and decided to ambush him when he left. Now that he had failed, he wanted to disassociate himself from the incident. He had seen the doctor go down to his first bullet, and grinned exultantly as he ran along the dark back lots.

Heck Blaine was a wanted outlaw. So Blaine had shot the doctor. Coppard was already wondering where he could get hold of his men. He wanted two of them to act as witnesses. With two of them to swear that they had seen Blaine deliberately shoot down the doctor, who had tried to apprehend the outlaw, it would be a certainty that Blaine would swing when they caught him. That would suit Zeke Coppard very well. With Heck Blaine safely taken care of it would be an easy mater to deal with his son Steve.

Eight

Steve Blaine lay on his bed in the hotel room. He was not asleep, for the nagging pain in his hand and leg prevented him. When the shots blared out he started up nervously, and cursed at the fresh agonies released inside him. He gritted his teeth and forced himself up off the bed, wondering at the shooting, and, hearing more shots, he tried to buckle his gunbelt around his waist. The thought struck him that it could be to do with his father, and he limped to the door of the room and let himself out. He knew he was taking a risk, for it was obvious that Zeke Coppard would make another bid to kill him. He knew that the rancher had been barred from riding with the posse, and that fact might give the unscrupulous man the chance he wanted.

Out on the sidewalk, Steve leaned against a post and looked around at the scurrying men who were converging on the street down by the doctor's house. He began to walk that way, and long before he reached the crowd he had heard the news that was shouted around the town. The doctor was dead on his porch, and the doctor's wife had seen Heck Blaine, with smoking gun, bending over the dead man. The outlaw had made off as soon as he had been seen.

Several men gave voice to the fact that they had recognised Heck Blaine, and swore that they had seen the man hurry across the street, shooting as he went, but vanished into the darkness on the far side. Men with lanterns immediately crossed the street and began a search. Steve halted in the shadows, at a loss for action. He could not believe that his father had shot down the doctor. There must be some other explanation, he though dazedly.

Zeke Coppard appeared in the centre of the crowd. Steve moved in close to hear what the rancher was saying to the deeply interested townsmen.

"I saw it all," Coppard was saying. He had heard that the doctor's wife saw Heck Blaine bending over the dead man, and that the woman supposed the outlaw was responsible for her husband's death. He decided that the widow's testimony would be better than the words of any two of his men, and decided to back up the theory. "I saw Heck Blaine come out of the doctor's house. He stood on the porch with the doctor, and I heard their voices from across the street, so I figured they were arguing. Then there was a shot and the doctor fell. I opened up on Blaine immediately, and he turned his gun on me. He came straight across the street at me, and I took off and pulled out. I didn't forget that he killed Frank Trory. He's a menace to the community, and I reckon you oughta do something about him. The sheriff has gone chasing off all around the countryside, and he ain't doing any good. Here's what I'll do, men. I'll give five hundred dollars to the man who kills Heck Blaine tonight."

There was a ripple of excitement through the crowd, and men began running away to fetch guns and lanterns. Steve eased out of the shadows, and his harsh voice stopped them and brought sudden silence to them.

"I'll kill anyone who lifts a gun against my father," he shouted. "He's not responsible for the doctor's death. I'd swear to that. If Zeke Coppard is mixed up in it anywhere then it's a certainty that my father is innocent."

"Do you hear that, men?" Coppard snapped. "That's the son of a killer talking. He's just like his old man. What are you gonna do about it? This is your town. Are you going to let a couple of outlaws come in here and play up hell with the county? The doctor was a good friend to everyone in this town. Old Doc Cantwell! He's helped all of us at some time or other. Now he's dead, shot down on his own doorstep by a ruthless killer without mercy. That killer is still in town, men. Seek him out and we'll give him some old-fashioned justice. My offer of five hundred bucks to the man who gets him still stands despite the threats you have heard. Now go out and get him."

"You'd better wait until the sheriff gets back," Steve shouted. "I'm no outlaw, and my father hasn't done anything to be ashamed of in the last twenty years. He gave up the wild life a long time ago, and I know he'd never go back to it. This is all some trick by Zeke Coppard to get us off the Double B. Don't listen to him. If you do anything hasty tonight you'll have to reckon with the sheriff when he comes back."

"Shut his lying mouth for him," Coppard yelled. "He's holding you here with his talk while his old man is getting away. What about the doctor? Doesn't his years of service to all of you count for anything?"

"Get back to your hotel room, Blaine," someone shouted. "Or we'll give you what your father will get when we catch him."

The crowd split up then, hurrying away into the shadows, and Steve stood frozen on the sidewalk, cradling his smashed hand in the crook of his right arm. Gunshots split the silence and he cursed and began running in the direction of the sound. When he reached an alley he heard more shooting, and his heart almost stopped beating. Then he realised that the shooting was being done by some of the drunks in town, who were opening up at every shadow.

Steve went down an alley. He knew that he'd have to find his father before any man of the town did. He hoped and prayed that the old man had got clear of town. If he was still around then there wouldn't be any chance for him if he was taken while the sheriff was away.

A footstep sounded at his back and he turned swiftly, dropping a hand to his gun. A dark shadow loomed up, and Steve stepped back into blackness.

"Is that you, Steve?" came a hoarse whisper.

"Yes," he replied eagerly. "Is that you, pa?"

A long tongue of orange flame reached out for him, and by its momentary brightness, Steve recognised one of Coppard's riders. He heard the bullet strike the wall at his side, and his own Colt came up and he fired swiftly without a thought. As darkness swooped back to blot out the flashes, he heard the thud of a falling body. He was astounded to hear Coppard's excited voice from only a few yards away.

"Blaine is over here. He's just got one of my men. Come on, you townsmen. Now we can trap the murdering crook and finish him off."

Steve's blood ran cold. He could see through Coppard's plan. His father would be taken care of by the law for murdering the doctor. But Steve himself had committed no crime, and it would be a tragedy if Steve were killed by mistake in the darkness of an alley by a crowd of men who thought they had trapped an outlaw.

Steve tried to run, but the wound in his leg was painful, and the limb had stiffened. He knew his only chance was to reach the hotel and get under cover. If the townsmen did not press after him, he was certain that Coppard would. Murder could be done in town this night and none would be able to point an accusing finger in any direction.

A gun flamed behind him and a string of shots reached for him. He crouched and listened to the whining lead passing by. He had holstered his own gun, and did not intend using it again. The chances were that in this darkness he might well kill a townsman, and that would put him in as much trouble as his father. He intended that Zeke Coppard would have no chance of reclaiming the Double B as his own range.

When the shots were fading he got up and went on. He cursed himself for having left the lighted main street. Coppard must have been watching him all the time, hoping he would do something like this, and the rancher hadn't missed out on the opportunity.

A cold rage laid hold of Steve and he began to tremble. He lifted his gun and turned to wait for his pursuers to come up with him. He didn't care whom he killed so long as he got Zeke Coppard. The rancher was responsible for all the trouble that had befallen the Double B.

The fact that Coppard had done just as he pleased with no redress from the law infuriated Steve. His own father, who had preached tolerance and peace, was now branded an outlaw after spending twenty quiet years forgetting about his lurid past. There was a big hurt inside Steve, and he clenched his teeth and waited. He had taken enough. Now it was his turn to hand it out, and he meant to do just that.

"Steve." He spun quickly at the voice, and his gun hand lifted. He had been caught once already by that trick. He pulled back the hammer as a figure materialised at his side. "Don't shoot, son, it's me, your pa"

"Pa!" There was relief in Steve's voice. He lowered his gun and holstered the weapon. With his uninjured hand he grabbed at his father. "Pa, tell me what's been going on. Did you kill the doctor?"

"Did I hell!" Heck Blaine's voice was almost unrecognisable with bitterness. "Zeke Coppard did that. He fired at me as I came out of the doctor's house, and his bullet missed me and hit the doc."

"They're saying you did the killing," Steve said hopelessly, "and we'll never be able to prove otherwise, pa."

"That's true, son. I'm finished in these parts. I'll have to pull out. You'll have to go it alone from hereon in, Steve."

"I won't stay, Pa. I'll sell out and we can go somewhere else."

"No. Don't do that." Heck Blaine's voice was thick with despair. "The same thing would happen elsewhere. Look at this business. Twenty years I have hidden the identity of Mike Slade, but it's come out now, and I'll likely lose my life through this. How are you feeling, son? The Doc told me what happened today. I'm real glad you've handled everything. But are you hurt bad?"

"My left hand is smashed up bad, Pa, and I've got a hole in my leg just above the knee. But otherwise I'm okay. I killed two of them. I'm damn glad you showed me how to use a gun. Zeke Coppard got more than he bargained for when he started on us. You've got to get out of here, though. The townsmen are roused up about you, and they'll hang you before the sheriff gets back."

"That's Coppard's idea, son. But they haven't got me yet. I'm going to kill Coppard. Then you'll be able to settle down in peace and have the chance you deserve. I don't see why you should have to suffer for my sins."

"They'll kill you, pa." Steve leaned back against a wall and closed his eyes. His head ached and his mind spun with the shock of these fast-moving events. "If you won't run then I'll stay with you."

"Don't make it hard for me, Steve," the older man pleaded. "It's got to be like this. I've always kidded myself that it wouldn't be, but now I can see that it couldn't end up any other way. I'm an outlaw."

"Not to me, pa," Steve said bitterly. "Not to me." Heck Blaine put a gentle hand on his son's shoulder. His ears were strained for sound of anyone approaching. He felt tears prickle his eyes as he studied the faint outline of his son.

"Steve, I guess I've been wrong all these years," he said thoughtfully. "I can see now I should have left you in that orphanage. You would have grown up knowing nothing about me. You would have made your way. But look what I've done to you. I've brought you up right, sure, because I figured you'd get more breaks than I ever had. But right now, when you're on your feet and going well, this came along and hit you right between the eyes. It's done you a lot of harm, son. I just hope it won't hit you too hard. Now I'll tell you what I want you to do. Go to your hotel and stay in your room until morning. I'll do what I have to, and if I can get away from town after this then I'll do so. When the sun comes up tomorrow, all your troubles will be over."

"Pa, I'll give them a hunt through the town while you get away," Steve said quickly. "I won't listen to any other reasoning. You're my father, and I won't stand by and watch them take you. I don't care what you say or what argument you use. You're my father and I'm sticking with you."

Heck Blaine swallowed the lump that rose in his throat. He sighed deeply as he let his breath go slowly.

"Steve, my life is nearly over. I've had a good one, and I'm mighty tired of all the shouting and the shooting. Zeke Coppard has asked for what he's got coming. But you're lessening my chances of getting away by keeping me here. You can hear that shooting as well as me. The whole town is out looking for me. Let me get on and do what I mean to."

"What will you do if you kill Coppard and get away?"

"I'll find myself a job somewhere miles away. I aim to live out my life in peaceful fashion. You'll be set up at the Double B."

"Pa, you keep talking about that ranch as if it meant everything in the world. Against you, it doesn't count. You're my father, and I want you. I ain't settling for the Double B or anything else. Let me sell out to Coppard and we'll both drift. That's the only sensible thing to do."

"I ain't gonna take you along with me, Steve." Heck Blaine spoke softly. "I'm repeating myself now. You'll have to learn to get along without me. I've realised that today, and already accepted it. You've got to do the same. The old days of you and me and the ranch are finished. Face up to it, son, and you'll be able to live after this is all done and the smoke has blown away."

"I refuse to, pa. This is all Zeke Coppard's fault. If it wasn't for him none of this would have happened. And those three friends of yours. Well, they'll get a hot reception when they start their games around here. I've told the sheriff about them."

"You did?" the older man was aghast. "You shouldn't have done that. It ain't right to give evidence against a man when what he is doing ain't none of your concern."

"Do you still think like that, pa, after all you've taught me about right and wrong?" Steve was surprised. "Of course it's my duty as an honest, law-abiding man to report criminals to the law. I've done that, and it's the main reason why the sheriff has ridden out with a posse. He's not really hunting you, pa. He knows what you've tried to do, and he said he respects you for what you have done. Let me sell out and we'll go away together. There's no need for shooting and killing."

"You're too late for that suggestion, son. You're forgetting that the doctor has been murdered. His wife saw me bending over him with a smoking gun in my hand. You've heard Coppard say that he saw me shoot the doc. With my past I ain't got no chance at all. I'm done for, and you'll see that as soon as the sheriff gets back and learns what happened. You saw those townsmen tonight. What sort of a chance do you think I'd get with any twelve of them on a jury?"

"Go hide out in the hills until I've sold up," Steve pleaded. "It'll only take a couple of days. I'm certain that Coppard will come across with a fair price."

"Not him. If you approach him with an offer he'll know you're half-way licked, and there's a lot of wolf in Coppard. He'll turn you down and take the place away from you for nothing."

They both heard the noisy approach of someone at the top of the alley. An empty can clattered under an unsteady foot, and a harsh voice cursed vociferously.

"Come on, pa," Steve commanded, grabbing at his father's arm. "Let's try and make it across the back lots. Where did you leave your horse? You're getting out of here."

Heck Blaine knew it wasn't the time for argument. He followed his son through the darkness, and they left the alley and moved swiftly but quietly across the open ground behind the buildings fronting the street. A gun blasted through the alley they had left, and the slug whined perilously close to Steve's head. Heck pulled him down, and they crouched and stared around at the shadows. A gun fired repeatedly until it was empty, and when the raucous echoes faded they could hear a harsh voice shouting and calling.

Heck took the lead and grasped his son's right wrist as they hurried through the darkness. He had holstered his gun, knowing that the worse thing he could do was fire a shot. The whole town would converge upon the spot the instant he split the darkness with gun flame.

"He didn't see us," Steve gasped, pulling his father to a halt. "He's doing like everyone else. He's firing a shot and shouting that he saw something in the hope of flushing you out."

"I'm too long in the tooth to fall for something like that," his father replied. "I'll tell you what I'll do, Steve. I'll ride out of here now, and you can go back to your room. Stay out of sight until the sheriff returns.

These men are in a bad mood right now, especially as they wasted a lot of time and energy to get me and failed. If they lay their hands on you there's no telling what they might do. Go on. We'll part here. You go your way and I'll go mine. I'll drop in on you at the ranch in a couple of days time."

"Will you promise to do that, pa?" Steve demanded.

"I said I would and I will. Go on now. You're only making it more difficult for me."

"I can't do it, pa," Steve said desperately. "No matter what you say, I can't turn my back on you and go off, knowing that you'll probably be dead come morning."

"No, son, it won't be like that. I'll get out of here. For God's sake do as I ask."

"All right." Steve gripped his father's hand tightly. "Have it your way, pa. I know you can more than look out for yourself."

"Yeah. I've done a good job of that for the both of us for a long time. Steve, don't think too badly of me for what I was. I was only one of many. We were the product of an era. We saw the end of one way of life and the start of another. That Civil War was hell. Some of us were forced by it to turn away from the law. But that's the way history is made. Now you always remember what I've told you. Never draw your gun unless you're gonna kill someone, and don't ever think about killing unless it's to save your own life."

Before Steve could reply he felt his father's hand on his shoulder. Then the older man was gone. Steve made as if to follow, but something held him back, and he waited alone in the darkness, with desolation filling his heart.

Zeke Coppard was to blame for all the trouble, he thought, and the rancher would be the cause of his father's death, he knew, for Heck Blaine would not leave this country until he had killed the crooked rancher. With that thought in mind, Steve turned for the main street. If he got to Coppard first and did the shooting then there would be no need for his father to risk his life.

Nine

Scrap Pierce was satisfied with the new hideout he had picked for the gang. They were not far from town, and the secluded spot was unapproachable by riders who hoped for surprise. They had circled the town, following the lie of the land, leaving behind good grass and passing into a belt of sun-bleached rock. They saw the two groups of riders emerge from Buffalo Grove, and Pierce grinned.

"We should have been ready to hit the bank today," he observed. "Look at the posse out for Heck Blaine."

"Scrap, you've pulled some hard tricks in the time I've known you," one of the others said, "but this one, turning an old pard over to the law, is about the lowest yet."

"I felt real mean doing it," Pierce said with a chuckle. "I figured that Heck Blaine had a break due, but not from us. I guess he'll keep that posse jumping from rock to rock for a couple or three days, and that should be long enough for us. I'll ride down there into town tonight and take a good look around. Ike, I reckon you'll have to forgo that pleasure. We will do that job tomorrow, while half the town is out in the saddle."

"I can see just what the lawman is going to do," Dolan said. "He'll look over Heck's place, then get down to study tracks. I don't figure he thinks Heck will come in this direction at all. After we hit that bank, Scrap, we'll drift north until we're clear of the country. I reckon it's a cinch everyone will think we've run for the Kanas border after the job."

"Yeah, you've got the rights of it." Ike Brewster grinned. "I'm damned glad Heck Blaine didn't want to trail along with us. What did he say he was going to do?"

"He didn't." Pierce twisted in his saddle, grunting as he moved his bulk. "I think maybe I could have used him to greater advantage, too. But there wasn't time to work out details. You know, I figure that if that guy Zeke Coppard was killed, everyone would think Heck did it on account of the trouble between them two. I wonder if we can do something about that. The whole county would start looking if a murder broke. Buffalo Grove would empty of good men, and we'd have a clear field."

"How would you get to Coppard now?" Dolan asked. "It's a long way back to his place, and we ain't got the time to spare."

"I figure it like this," Pierce said, warming to the task of plotting. "Coppard will ride into town and tell the whole world about Heck Blaine. We know he's already done that because we saw the posse come out. Now if Coppard has stayed in town it will be an easy matter for us to find him."

"Do you plan on the three of us riding into town now?" Brewster demanded. "It will be risky, us riding horses branded Circle Z."

"No. I'm going into town tonight." Pierce's eyes were filled with speculation. "I reckon I can handle old man Coppard. Anyway, I'll take a look around. If he ain't in town then I'll think of something else. But, whatever happens, we want the sheriff and a posse out on the range when we hit that bank in town."

They settled in their new hideout and waited for the sun to go down. They ate a sparse meal in the fading light, and then Pierce prepared to ride out.

"I hope you'll have more luck than I found," Dolan said.

"I ain't riding openly into town," Pierce said. "I'll leave my horse out in the brush and walk in the last couple of hundred yards. Well, I'll be seeing you two. Be good while I'm gone."

There was a deep silence pressing down on the land when Pierce rode out of his camp. He travelled cautiously, aware that men would be abroad in the darkness, listening and watching for Heck Blaine. He did not want to run into any law party with a Circle Z horse between his legs.

Buffalo Grove was just a cluster of faint lights when he first spotted the town, and he rode in closer before dismounting and looking for a place to leave his horse. He left the trail and tied the animal in thick brush. Then he walked on into town.

He spent a long time looking at the bank, then crossed the street and entered one of the alleys beside it just as Dolan had done. He peered through a dusty window and studied the interior of the bank. A plan for the robbery was knitting together in his crooked brain, and he went back to the main street and headed for a saloon. He had one hand on the batwing when the first shot crashed out, and in the split second that he spun to get a glimpse of the gun flash, Doc Cantwell died.

Pierce faded into the shadows at the side of the saloon and watched the vicious flashes of the shooting between Coppard and Heck Blaine. He heard Coppard's voice but could not identify it. When all the townsmen who hadn't ridden with the posse came out to the street, he went on into the saloon. He waited until some of the more serious drinkers, having learned the cause of the disturbance, returned to their pleasures, and grinned when he heard what had happened out there on the street.

The townsmen were shocked and angry about the death of the doctor, and he could hear pistol shots as some of the more venturesome tried to flush out the outlaw Heck Blaine. Pierce listened to a couple of men discussing the incidents, and heard the word lynchlaw mentioned more than once. He hoped it would not come to that. He wanted Heck Blaine to make a run for it. That way, the whole town would be out come dawn, looking for the mean killer.

Shooting continued sporadically for an hour or more, but no one caught up with Heck Blaine. The outlaw had vanished into the night. Pierce was well pleased. He finished his whisky and made for the batwings, and almost bumped into Zeke Coppard as the rancher entered the saloon. Coppard was with a couple of his men, and the man's eyes glittered when they found Pierce's face.

Pierce stepped aside for the rancher to pass him, but Coppard put out a hand and grasped the outlaw's shoulder. Pierce dropped a hand to his gun, and the rancher smiled harshly.

"Don't try that, mister," he said. "I want to talk to you. Come on over to a corner table where we won't be overheard." He glanced at one of his men. "Get a bottle of Redeye and four glasses," he commanded.

Pierce felt his stomach muscles tense. His eyes narrowed, and he studied Coppard's pale face for a moment. The he shrugged. He had always played his cards as they came to hand. He would do so now, and perhaps he could make his own plan safer by using Coppard. He turned obediently and made for a corner table. He sat where he could watch the saloon, and the rancher slid into the seat next to him. The two gunmen sat down, and one of them poured whisky into four glasses.

"That deal we made worked out fine," Coppard said. "It was worth a couple of horses to me. I guess you heard that Heck Blaine is wanted for murdering the doctor. He'll never get away from that one."

"Very convenient for you," Pierce said shrewdly, and saw a shadow cross the rancher's harsh face. "What do you want with me?"

"Steve Blaine is in town and he's still in the saddle at the Double B. I'm wondering what you're doing in this country, mister, and I figure I have a job that you will be pleased to handle."

"You'd like me to kill Steve Blaine." Pierce's eyes were bright and watchful.

"You're quick on the uptake," Coppard said. "You've got enough gunhands on your payroll to take care of an easy chore like that," Pierce observed. "They'd do a job like that for a lot less than I'd take."

"I want me and my men to be here right in the public eye when it happens." Coppard said. "I'll give you two thousand dollars."

"That's a lot of money," Pierce said. "Is Steve Blaine's death worth that much to you?"

"Just about. That's my offer. I think I've got your measure, mister, and I reckon you won't bicker about the price. So what about it?"

"Well, I always like to handle the real McCoy," the outlaw said. "If you had two thousand green backs on you to put in my paw, then I'd ride out of here in an hour and your man would be dead. I could do that job for you tonight and that would be the end of it."

"Steve Blaine is in town right now, and he's hurt," Coppard said ruthlessly. "But I don't have two thousand dollars in cash on me right now. Will you take a bank draft?"

"I don't know about that. I could do that job for you tonight and you could stop payment of that draft tomorrow. And what about the bank? Someone there might wonder why you would pay me two thousand bucks." Even as he spoke, Pierce was already deciding that he would not do it. The two thousand dollars that Coppard planned to pay him would come out of the bank tomorrow when they robbed it. He didn't have to take any extra risks like killing the son of an old pard to get that money. But Pierce did not like the look of Zeke Coppard. He could tell by the rancher's face that the man was pushing all out to achieve his own ends, and nothing would stop him now, except an bullet, and that was exactly what he was going to get before the sun rose again. Pierce could guess what would happen to him if he refused point blank to work with Coppard. So he grinned. "I've had some experience in these matters," he said, and saw Coppard smile bleakly.

"I knew it," the rancher said. "I could see the sign on you as large as day."

"Okay, you draw that two thousand dollars out of the bank tomorrow and have it ready for me when I call to see you," Pierce said. "I figure it'll be easier for me to get young Blaine out at his place, where he'll be alone. It'll be too risky to drop him here in town with everyone hotted up about the doctor's death. Does that suit you?"

"It'll have to," Coppard snarled. "Where do I see you again and when?"

"Make it at eleven tomorrow morning on the north trail out of town. I'll take the money and ride straight on to the Blaine place."

"I'll trust you to do the job once you've got the money," Coppard said. "If you don't, I'll send out my entire crew to hunt you down and kill you. Do you understand that?"

"I sure do," Pierce said. He intended hitting the bank at ten, and by eleven he and his pards should be helling it far to the north of town. But before he left Buffalo Grove he meant to do Steve Blaine a favour. He would kill this scheming rancher, and that act would make up in part for the damage he had done to young Blaine's life for turning in his father.

"All right. Eleven tomorrow morning on the trail north of town." Coppard's eyes glittered. "You were on your way out as I came in. Make it out of here now. The less we are seen together the better I shall like it."

Pierce drained his glass and set it down. He arose and passed quickly out of the saloon. Outside in the darkness, he paused and peered in through a window, studying Coppard for a long time. Then he crossed the street and stood leaning against a post outside the saloon. He wanted to get Coppard when the man left, and he was hopeful that when the rancher died his murder will also be blamed on Heck Blaine.

A furtive movement in the shadows to his left attracted Pierce's eyes. He had been standing motionless for more than fifteen minutes, and knew that if he didn't move he would not be spotted by whoever was slinking through the darkness. He heard a board squeak under a hesitant foot, and let his eyes slide around as far as they would. He dared not move his head for fear of revealing his presence and position. He saw a figure emerge from the shadows and stand watching the batwings of the saloon. A thrill passed through him when he recognised the figure of Heck Blaine. The ex-outlaw was standing only feet away.

"Heck," Pierce hissed through tense lips. He saw Blaine stiffen, and heard the rasp of steel against leather as the man pulled his gun. "Don't shoot. It's me, Scrap Pierce."

Heck Blaine uttered a smothered curse and came swiftly to Pierce's side. Pierce wondered at Blaine's state of mind after killing the doctor, and realised that he had made a bad mistake in attracting the killer's attention. Blaine might now be cursing the man who had exposed him, and another killing wouldn't bother him.

"What the devil are you doing here, Scrap?" Blaine demanded thinly. "I didn't see you. Who are you waiting for?"

"The same man you are, I'll bet." Pierce said. He thought he had better go along with Blaine. The man wouldn't kill him if he thought Pierce was trying to help his son. "Zeke Coppard is in that saloon, and I'm waiting here for him to come out. I feel that I owe you something for what I did, so I'm gonna kill Coppard. That way, your son will have no more trouble."

"That's damned white of you, Scrap," Blaine said, and Pierce heaved a silent sigh of relief. "But I want that pleasure for myself. I'm gonna take care of Coppard when he steps out of the saloon."

Pierce was well pleased to hear that. Everyone was trying to make things easier for him. He half-wished that Dolan and Brewster would offer to ride in here tomorrow and do the bank job alone.

"You're taking a big chance, Heck," he said. "The town is aroused now. There's a couple of posses out looking for you. I spotted them this afternoon."

"They're after you as well as me," Blaine told him. "But I'm not worried about myself. I'll give what's left of my life to make sure my son gets a good chance."

"What do you mean, they're out after me?" Pierce demanded.

"The sheriff knows that you and the other two are in the country, and he's got a good idea why. If I were in your shoes, Scrap, I'd pull up my stakes and get the hell out of here."

"We're taking that bank tomorrow," Pierce said obstinately, "and nothing is going to stop me. Why don't you throw in with us, Heck? We could pull the job tomorrow, and drop on Zeke Coppard on the way out of the country. It'll be easier to get him out at his place. If you fire a shot here in the street you'll never make it to your horse."

"You were fixing to gun him down from here," Blaine accused. "Have you got tired of living, Scrap?"

"You don't know the half of it," Pierce said. "I bumped into Coppard as I was leaving the saloon, and he had a talk with me. I can read sign on a man better than most, Heck, and I could see that Coppard will die trying to get what he wants."

"He'll do that right enough."

"Yeah, but the point is this. They'll hang you for killing the Doc. That's taken care of you. But it'll still leave your son. Coppard offered me two thousand bucks to kill your boy. I accepted because I figured he'd turn a gun on me if I refused. That's why I'm waiting here for him. I want to make sure he dies. He could give me and the others a bad time tomorrow. He's like a mad wolf. I don't want him loose in the country when I'm running for it."

"Where have you left your horse, Scrap?"

"Out of town a couple of hundred yards. It's too far away for a quick getaway."

"Mine is out there too. I'll make a deal with you, Scrap. I'll come in with you on the bank job. But you help me get Coppard. There are a couple of gunmen with him, and I ain't as young or as foolhardy as I used to be. I ain't afraid of dying, but I don't want to go until I've made sure of Coppard. If he's willing to pay you to kill Steve then he really means trouble, and I've got to stop him."

"It's a deal, Heck." Pierce turned and thrust out his hand. "I've been feeling real mean about the way things have turned out for you. Maybe I'll get the chance now to help make up for it. How do you want to take Coppard?"

"I figure to walk into the saloon on him right now."

"In front of half the town?" Pierce was astounded. "How do you figure your half of the bargain? They'll cut you to pieces before you more than step through the doorway. Let's do it right, Heck, and we'll both live longer. Wait until he comes out of there and we'll find out which room he's got at the hotel. We'll take him there. No need to use a gun. I've got my old blade inside my right boot, where it's been for the last thirty years. I'll open up Zeke Coppard slicker than a doctor could do it."

"We'll go along with that," Blaine decided. "But I don't want any trouble at the hotel. My boy is there, and he's had a bad day."

"No one will know we're around." Pierce said. "Listen, you stay here and I'll go into the hotel and book myself a room. I'll get Coppard's room number, and maybe we can be in there waiting for him to show up. That'll give him a shock."

"I'll stay here until you get back," Blaine promised.

"Well, don't cut loose at him if he shows up before I get back," Pierce said. "Use your head, Heck. You always did in the old days."

"Yeah," Blaine muttered. "The old days. You know, Scrap, I sometimes wish I'd stopped lead in those days. At the time I was supposed to be lucky, the way it all avoided me. But now I ain't so sure. It would have saved a lot of trouble for my boy if I'd died before he was old enough to know me."

"Don't think like that, Heck. You've got your own life to live, and so has your son. He'll make out. I figured when I saw him that he could take care of himself. With Coppard out of the way he'll be able to settle down. Likely he'll meet some nice girl who will make him a fine wife."

"I'd like to think that he would," Blaine said morosely. "By God, he'll get all the chances if I have my way. Damm it, Scrap, I'm going across there now and blast Coppard clear into hell. What the devil am I standing around for? I ain't got one hope in hell of ever getting back to my place like an honest man. The longer I live the worse chances my boy will have of making a go of it. Coppard's got to die, and I'll do it like I ought to. I never did skulk around in the darkness."

"Don't do it, Heck," Pierce said desperately. "You'll rouse out the whole town, and we'll all be in trouble. Play it smart and everything will go right."

"For you it will." Blaine said. "But I don't want to go along on that bank job. I'm an honest man now, Scrap. I made a vow twenty years ago that I'd never do another crooked thing in my life. So far I've lived up to that, and I ain't gonna break my word now. It would be like letting Steve down. You go ahead with what you plan, Scrap, and I'll take care of my own affairs."

"Heck, it won't gonna work out like that," Pierce retorted. "You've got to play it smart. If you go into that saloon and start raising hell it will be all up with you."

"Do you aim to stop me?" There was a dangerous tone to Blaine's voice. Pierce recognised the warning and made haste to placate the outlaw.

"Hell, no, Heck. I've told you that I'll go along with you. If that's the way you want to play it then okay, I'll go along with you."

Heck Blaine stepped down into the street. He paused with his boots in dust, his blue eyes fastened on the batwings of the saloon. Scrap Pierce felt desperation seep into his heart. If Blaine got himself killed now, so the town knew about it, then the sheriff and the posse would be back in town tomorrow, and that would put paid to the bank job.

Pierce stepped heavily into the dust beside his old pard, and the fingers of his right hand closed around the handle of the big-bladed knife nestling inside his right boot. He lifted the fearsome weapon, and, with a sudden vicious movement, sent the blade plunging deeply into Heck Blaine's back.

Blaine gasped in shock and pain, and went up on his toes as if to avoid the cold steel. Pierce grasped the outlaw's gunhand as Blaine instinctively grabbed at the butt of his notorious .45. He twisted the knife sharply and dragged it out wickedly, slashing and cutting flesh and vitals. Blaine choked and dropped to his knees. He remained in an attitude of prayer for a moment, then toppled sideways and pushed his face into the dust.

Pierce stared down at the motionless figure, then glanced quickly around the gloomy street. The town was deserted. He bent and wiped the blood from the long blade on the shirt of his victim. He sheathed the weapon, then bent and grasped the body by the shoulders, dragging Blaine around to the end of the sidewalk and thrusting the body into the narrow space between the ground and the boards. With luck, he thought, the corpse wouldn't be discovered for at least a couple of days, and that would give him and his men time to get out of the country.

"I'm sorry, Heck," he muttered as he straightened. "But you forgot how to play it smart. I'll get Coppard for you, though. His last hour has come."

He stepped away from the sidewalk and went along the street to the hotel. He paused under a flickering lantern and checked his hands and clothes for blood. He was clean. He went into the hotel and rented a room for the night, and when he signed the register he saw Zeke

Coppard's signature above his own. He made a note of Coppard's room number, took his own key, and went up to the room. He did not intend staying all night, but before he left he meant that Zeke Coppard should feel the point of his vicious knife.

He sat in his room with the lamp out and the door ajar. Several men came along the corridor and passed his room, and he studied them through the crack in the door. When Coppard came along he waited until the rancher had opened the door to his room, then slipped out of his own room and went swiftly along the corridor. He reached the rancher as Coppard stepped into his room.

Thrusting open the door that was closing in his face, fat Scrap Pierce sprang like a wolf upon Zeke Coppard. His big knife was in his hand, and the fine point slid into Coppard's belly easily and cleanly. Zeke Coppard opened his mouth to scream at the agony which seared through him. Pierce slapped a heavy hand across the rancher's mouth. He stabbed repeatedly, viciously, mercilessly, and Zeke Coppard wilted with each murderous stroke. The rancher died silently.

Scrap Pierce straightened and turned to thrust the door shut. He wiped his blade clean on Coppard's shirt, and, after putting the gleaming knife back into its sheath, he dropped to one knee beside the body. He rapidly searched the rancher, transferring all valuables to his own pockets. Then he left the room and the hotel. He went quickly out of town to find his horse. Tomorrow they would rob the bank, then quit the county.

Ten

The dimmed beam of a lamp filtered through a crack in the sidewalk and touched Heck Blaine's eyes. The light seemed to pierce the blackness that enveloped the badly injured ex-outlaw, and he came slowly back to consciousness. When he opened his eyes the light of the lantern dazzled him. He twisted his head from side to side, and, when he tried to move, a thousand barbs of agony burst loose in his back. He lay for a long time trying to remember what had happened. Then it slowly came back to him.

So Scrap Pierce had double-crossed him again! The knowledge that every man's hand was against him was bitter in his mind. He lifted a wavering hand and clutched the sidewalk above his head, and it slowly came to him that Pierce had left him for dead. He tried to ease himself out of the black space, but the pain was almost too much for him. He was weak from loss of blood, and when he lifted his arms they felt heavy and strange.

Pierce had thrust him feet first into the space, and this fact alone enabled him to get into the air again. He reached out beyond his head and his weakening fingers hooked on the end of the sidewalk. He lay for some moments, marshalling what strength he had, and then pulled his head and shoulders from under the smooth, boot-worn planking. The pain that filled his lower body at the effort made him groan. There was a roaring sound in his ears, and blackness clouded his brain and threatened to overwhelm him. He fought it silently with his teeth clenched and bared.

He checked the area of his wound with expert fingers, and was thankful that Pierce's knife blade had struck him a little high. It was only an inch, but it meant the difference between a few more hours of life and the instant death that Pierce had aimed for.

By degrees, Blaine crawled out of the blackness under the sidewalk. He lay on his face at the side of the street and dust clogged his nostrils as he breathed. He tried to get to his feet, but the mortal wound in his back just below the lower ribs in the left side, had taken most of his strength.

He knew that he was dying, and desperation was slowly building up inside him. There was so many things he wanted to do before he kicked off But the only thing that mattered was Steve's future. He would die gladly if he knew that his son would be all right.

The urgency of his thoughts made him summon up his last strength. He tried to ignore the pain that was spreading in stifling waves through him, radiating from the wound. He got to his knees and hauled himself upright by grasping the post of an awning that hung over the sidewalk. His hands gripped the woodwork, trembling as he used his strength. Then his legs gave way and he dropped on to the sidewalk. He managed to sit on the edge of the boards, and leaned his pain-filled back against the post. His chin sunk to his chest and he drew breath with great difficulty through his slack mouth.

Footsteps coming along the sidewalk aroused him and he lifted his head and spotted a dark figure moving towards him. When the man drew level, Blaine spoke in a croaking whisper.

"Help me, mister. I've been knifed."

The stranger uttered a surprised oath, and paused. It was evident that he feared some kind of trick that would end up with him being robbed. But he must have seen the blood that covered Blaine for he stepped off the sidewalk and bent over the dying man.

"Who did that to you?" he demanded in a voice that was high-pitched with shock.

"Never mind that," Blaine said faintly. My son is over at the hotel. Steve Blaine. Fetch him, will you? But make it fast. I don't reckon I've got much time left."

"You're Heck Blaine, the man who killed the doctor." The townsman turned and ran quickly back along the sidewalk.

Blaine listened to the receding boots. He wished Zeke Goppard would be the first to hear the news and come running. It would be a fitting end to die along with that scheming rancher.

The minutes passed slowly, and Blaine felt his strength and life ebbing. The pain did not seem so harsh now, and he realised that numbness was seeping into him. His legs had already lost all feeling. They were probably dead. He slid sideways and his back left the support of the post. He felt the dust of the street come up and cover his face. He coughed chokingly, and struggled to twist upon his back.

Boots were pounding the boards, and he could faintly hear excited voices shouting, but everything seemed to be a long way off. Then he sensed that someone was bending over him, and looked up and spoke his son's name. He caught the glitter of a bright object on the chest of the man bending over him.

"Sheriff Griffin?" he asked.

"No. This is Deputy Wells. Who did this to you, Blaine?"

"Scrap Pierce, an old friend," Blaine said weakly. "Where's my son?"

"He's coming. Hang on a bit. Are you hurt bad?"

"I'm cashing in, I reckon. Don't try to move me. I ain't got long. But I want to talk to my boy."

"He's coming," the deputy repeated. "I've sent for him. But tell me why you killed the Doc, Blaine. I thought he was a friend of yours."

"He was a good friend," Blaine muttered. "Zeke Coppard killed him. Coppard threw a shot at me as I was leaving the doctor's place, and he hit the Doc. Watch Coppard, Deputy, for he's out to kill my boy."

A crowd quickly gathered, and the deputy glanced around at the peering faces that surrounded him. He knew by experience that death was settling upon Heck Blaine, and he looked eagerly for sign of the outlaw's son. Then he spotted Steve trying to force a passage through the crowd, and stood up, shouting authoritatively, urging the townsmen to stand back.

Steve came to his father's side. He tried to drop to one knee beside the stricken man, but the wound in his left leg prevented him from doing so. He flopped down into the dust and propped himself on one elbow. Someone came up with a lantern and stood over him, holding the light so that the rays fell upon his father's face.

"Pa," Steve cried, "who did this to you?" He glanced at the deputy who squatted at his side. "Get a doctor."

"The doctor is dead, remember?" the lawman retorted. He repeated Heck Blaine's words concerning the shooting of Doctor Cantwell.

"That's right, and it's the truth," Steve said. He looked at his father's ashen face. "Pa, speak to me," he cried. "I want to know who did this."

"He mentioned a name," the deputy told him. "Scrap Pierce. I don't know him. He must be a stranger around here."

"I know who he is," Steve said grimly. "He's one of those three outlaws the sheriff wants to talk with."

"So they're in town. I wonder what trouble they're planning."

Steve bent low over his father. He saw the older man's eyes flicker open. Heck Blaine opened his mouth to speak, but nothing issued from between his thin lips. There was a harsh rattling sound in his throat. His eyes rolled horribly, then his pain-racked body slumped back into the dust. Steve remained in his cramped position, aware of the intense silence that clung to the town. His eyes suddenly misted with tears. His father was dead. It came home to him then that he was all alone in the world. He had to make his own way now.

"What about that story he gave me?" The Deputy looked worriedly at Steve. "Do you figure he was telling the truth about the doctor's death?"

"There's only one way to find out," Steve said harshly. "Ask Zeke Coppard." He got awkwardly to his feet. "If you don't arrest Coppard on some charge or other I'm going to kill him. If he hadn't tried to get us off the Double B in the first place none of this would have happened. My father would be alive and so would the doctor."

"Let's get your father's body under cover," the deputy said. "Then I'll come with you to talk with Coppard. That old man has run things too long around here."

When Heck Blaine's body had been removed to the undertaker's, Steve went with the deputy back to the hotel. They ascertained from the clerk on duty at the reception desk the number of Zeke Coppard's room, and ascended the stairs silently. The deputy tapped at Coppard's door, and when there was no reply and several minutes had faded by, the lawman grasped the handle of the door and turned it. The door opened at his touch and swung wide. They both saw the sprawled figure and the blood that had spread over the cold body and stained the bare boards of the room.

"Looks like that knifeman has been busy tonight." the deputy said, straightening from a quick examination of Coppard. He sighed deeply. "Well, Coppard ain't going to bother you again, Blaine."

"I've got Scrap Pierce to thank for this," Steve muttered. "I'll do it before I kill him."

"How do you know that Pierce did it? Just because your father died from a knife wound doesn't make this murder the work of the same man." The deputy thought for a moment. "I reckon you could have done this, Blaine. You had reason enough to see Coppard dead, and you are staying in the hotel."

"Yeah, that's right," Steve agreed. "I could have done it. But I didn't know Coppard was staying in the hotel, and if I had wanted to kill him I would have done it before today. I would have used a gun, too."

"Yeah, I guess it would be too much of a coincidence to have two murders in one night, both committed with a knife and done by different killers, but I wonder why Pierce killed Coppard?"

"If you really want to find out then you'd better get to Pierce before I do," Steve said grimly. "Most of the trouble started the day those three outlaws rode in."

"That's right. I heard the sheriff say that Pierce told Coppard about your father. It's a tough break for an outlaw who has managed to evade the law for twenty years. I reckon your father was telling the truth about the doctor's death. He knew he was dying, and he wouldn't have gone with anything on his conscience."

"Well, Coppard's escaped me," Steve said. "But those three outlaws are still in the country, and they're here for some devilment. I'll be riding in the morning to pick up their trail. If I come up with them I'll try and bring them in. If they want to make a fight of it then we'll see how it goes."

"You're in no fit state to go after three tough outlaws," the deputy said hastily. "You'll only get yourself killed, Blaine. Better wait until the sheriff comes back. I'll send a man out at dawn to contact him and inform him of what's taken place here. If you want to ride along in a posse then you're welcome, but riding out on your own, with a wounded arm and leg, is another matter. I won't let you do it."

"I don't see how you can stop me," Steve said. "I sure don't advise you to try. By the time you get around to catching those outlaws, I'll have the job done."

"Or we'll find your body ready for burial," the deputy retorted.

"I don't care about that. I'm going to find the man who killed my father."

"You can't do anything until the morning. If I were you, I'd try and get some sleep."

"Do you think I'll be able to close my eyes?" Steve demanded. "My father has just been killed. I'll never sleep again until I've dealt with his killer." Steve studied the inert form of Zeke Coppard. He smiled cynically. "Well, if ever a man asked for what he got, Coppard did. He should be mighty satisfied now."

The deputy picked up the key of the door, which Coppard had dropped the instant Pierce's knife had touched him. He stepped aside for Steve to leave, then locked the door.

"I'd better leave everything just as it is for the sheriff to see," he said. "Look me up first thing in the morning, Blaine, and I'll let you know if any new developments have occurred."

"I'll check with you," Steve promised. "But I'll be riding out at dawn."

"Where will you head for? Have you any idea where the outlaws may be hiding?"

"No. But I know they're in the country, and that's good enough for me. I'll find them. They didn't come up this way for nothing, and they haven't done yet what they came for. I'll get them."

"Yeah, well maybe I ought to keep my eyes open around here in case they're planning to rob the bank or something."

"You'd better do that," Steve told him. He went slowly along the corridor to his own room and entered. He sank down thankfully on the bed and lay on his right side, his face hard and his eyes filled with hatred. His whole world had come to an end. It had taken only three or four short days to wreck the twenty years his father had spent trying to repair the damage of his actions during his wild youth had caused. He thought of his father, who had always been a kindly, patient man, and felt bereft and lonely. He felt that he would never be able to return to the Double B.

Dawn found him gaunt-faced. There was pain in his leg and hand, and he thought of the doctor, now dead, who had told him only a few short hours before to rest up, and visit him during this morning. Well, perhaps he would see the doctor again soon, but it would not be in this world.

He got up off the bed and stretched cautiously. Pain rippled through his stiff muscles. He cursed his wounds. He didn't feel at all like taking to the trail. He knew he wouldn't have much chance against three tough outlaws in his present condition, but the agony that was in him would not admit the impossibility of his intention. He was going out as soon as he had eaten, and he wouldn't give up the trail until the man who had killed his father was dead.

He limped out of the hotel and went along to the small eating house down past the bank, and as he passed the bank he studied the great windows. He wondered if Pierce and the other two were after the money in there.

Breakfast put him in better humour and gave him fresh strength. He asked for a packet of sandwiches, and paid with a silver dollar. The he went along to the stable for his horse. The livery man helped him to saddle up, and he had great difficulty climbing into his saddle when the animal was ready for travel. When he was finally in leather, his left leg ached intolerably, filling him with frustration and impatience.

After he had ridden out of town he reined in and stared round, his lips compressed into a thin line. Where the hell did he start looking? How could he hope to track down three men who were expert in covering their tracks? He saw a dust cloud approaching from the south, the direction of the Double B, and sat his horse in the middle of the trail and waited for the riders to materialise.

Sheriff Griffin rode out of the dust, a tired-faced old man who had spent eighteen hours in the saddle. He was dusty and ready for bed. He reined in beside the silent, hard-faced Steve, and studied the younger man for a moment before speaking.

"I'm sorry to hear about what happened last night, Steve," he said at length. "Wells sent a rider out to find me, and we met a couple of hours ago. I don't know what to make of this yet, but I'll find out exactly what did happen. I suppose you're looking for those three outlaws."

"That's right, although I'm interested in only one of them; Pierce."

"Which way are you planning to ride?"

"I don't know. I was just looking around and wondering where to start."

"I can save you a lot of trouble," Griffin said wearily. "I know it's no use me trying to talk you out of it, so go ahead and get yourself killed, if you have to. You needn't look south, east or west of Buffalo Grove. We never saw sign of them. I was heading north until I got Wells' message a short time ago. We found some tracks around your place that pointed north, but I'll have to ride into town and sort out that mess before taking a look in that direction."

"Okay, so I'll ride north," Steve said. "Thanks, Sheriff. If I do come up with those three, I'll bring them in; dead or alive."

"This country is full of optimists," Griffin said harshly. "Just take it easy, Steve. The Circle Z ain't got an owner now, and that'll give me a lot of extra work. I'd hate for the same thing to happen to your Double B. Why not ride back into town with me? I'll be sending out a posse under my deputy. You can ride with him."

"No thanks, Sheriff, I prefer to ride alone. I've got a lot of thinking to do, as well as hunting."

"You'd better keep your eyes and mind on what you're doing," Griffin warned. A man who knifes two men in one evening ain't the kind to fool around with."

"I'll take care of it." Steve reined about. "I'll be seeing you, Sheriff," he called back over his shoulder and set in his spurs. He suppressed a groan as pain flashed through him at the sudden movement of his horse. He left the posse standing and headed on a detour of Buffalo Grove, gazing up at the hills to the north. Some-where in that direction was the man who had killed his father, a man his father had once called a friend.

He glanced back and saw the sheriff leading his tired men into town. Then he turned his face north and kept looking in that direction. Perhaps the man he sought was watching him from concealment. Steve felt a muscle twitch in his hard face. He hoped that was the case. He wanted Scrap Pierce to see him and come out of hiding to meet him. The fat outlaw would find that the son of Heck Blaine alias Mike Slade was good enough to take care of the man who had killed the leader of The Wild Men.

Eleven

It was two hours past midnight when Scrap Pierce rode into the camp north of Buffalo Grove. He dismounted wearily and attended to his horse. Then he walked to the low fire in a cluster of rocks and threw an armful of wood upon it. He roused out the sleeping Dolan and Brewster.

"Come on, you two," he called, stirring each man in turn with the toe of his boot. "You'd be a couple of dead outlaws if I'd been that sheriff and his posse coming in here. Don't you want to hear the news I've got?"

Both Dolan and Brewster grumbled as they sat up in their blankets. Pierce picked up the coffee pot and emptied it. He put fresh water on to boil and squatted beside the fire, his pale eyes wide and expressionless as he gazed into the leaping flames. He caressed his long moustache.

"Well, what the hell's happened in town?" Brewster demanded, "You didn't wake me up just so I could sit and look at you, did you? What are you so pleased about, Scrap?"

"Everything," the fat outlaw said. He gave them a graphic account of what had happened in town. The other two joined him at the fire. They studied his intent face and brooding eyes, astounded by what his terse voice revealed. "So we rob the bank tomorrow, boys."

"You killed Heck Blaine, huh?" Dolan said. "I don't like that, Pierce."

"So?" Pierce turned his eyes upon Dolan. His face turned vicious. "Was Blaine a particular friend of yours, Milt? Would you rather I let him walk into the saloon and ruin all my plans?" He snarled like an animal. "I told Blaine that I would help him take care of Coppard, and I did just that after I killed Heck, but he didn't want it like that."

"Why did you have to kill him?" Brewster demanded. "I don't see how Heck killing Coppard would affect our plans at all."

"You don't huh?" Pierce growled. "Well, I know now why I'm the boss of this outfit. It's because I know well enough how much trouble we'd have on our hands tomorrow if Blaine had gone ahead. Don't you realise that half the menfolk in that town are out looking for Blaine? If he had got himself killed in that saloon the sheriff would be back in Buffalo Grove before we are ready to hit the bank, and so would a score of men with guns. I had to stop Blaine quick, and using my knife was the only way I could do it. Tell me what either of you would have done."

There was no reply from the two outlaws. Pierce studied their hard faces for a moment. A great irritation was beginning to well up inside him. But he controlled it.

"Look, tomorrow we're going to hit that bank and ride off with enough dough to keep us in luxury for a long time to come. If you don't want to go along with this then say so now and I'll find myself another gang. This bank in town has never been raided. It'll be a push-over. I wouldn't let Heck Blaine come between me and that money, even though he was an old friend. Now have you got anything else to say about it before we start making plans?"

"How can you be sure that Blaine's body will be found where you put it?" Dolan asked.

"I don't think it will be found for a week or two," Pierce replied. "None but the kids ever go under the sidewalks, and the kids are afraid to play under there because of snakes. I think it's a safe bet to say we'll have a clear day tomorrow."

"Yeah, and it'll be handy to have that posse out of town," Brewster mused. "There's a good score of riders with that sheriff. Okay, so it's a pity you had to bump Heck Blaine. But what's done is done, and it'll probably work out for the best. Just so long as Blaine's boy don't find that you killed his old man. I wouldn't want him on my tail. I reckon Heck taught him a thing or two about gun-fighting, and there wasn't a man in our bunch in the old days who could ever shade Heck Blaine."

"I heard in town that Steve Blaine killed two of Coppard's men," Pierce said heavily. "They were laying in wait for him, too. He's a good hand with a gun, but we don't need to worry about him. No one knows that I knifed his old man. No one knows about me in that town. So let's get down to cases about the raid. What I've got planned will knock you cold. What do you think of this for a bank raid?"

He began to talk rapidly, and the other two listened intently.

"I don't know about that," Dolan said soberly when Pierce had finished. "I think it's a bit risky. I like the idea, but what about the horses? They've got to be handy for the getaway, and you can't leave them in an alley from before dawn till the bank folk show up."

"Okay, so we leave one of you outside with the horses," Pierce snapped. "You, Ike. You can wait out of town with our nags, and at a certain time you ride into the alley beside the bank and we come out of the side door. We'll get away with it." He slapped his thigh. "Damn me if I don't like it better than anything we've ever done."

"It might work at that," Brewster said. "It'll be a whole lot better than riding into town in broad daylight with the Circle Z brand showing plain on our horses. But I figure Milt should stay outside with the nags. I ain't been into Buffalo Grove, remember?"

"Yeah, that's right. Okay. You go in with me, Ike, and Milt can come in later with the horses."

"You'll have to get your timing right," Dolan said. "We ain't been to town to find out what time the bank opens. How will I know when to come in?"

"The bank will open at nine-thirty," Pierce said. "That much I have learned. You've got a watch, Milt. Come into that alley at about nine forty-five. We'll come out of that side door like two bats out of hell."

"I'll be there waiting for you," Dolan said. "Do you figure you can bust into that place without rousing half the town?"

"Yeah. I checked the windows in that alley, and one of them will yield to a little persuasion by my knife." He grinned and patted the slender weapon that had ended two lives only hours before. "That banker will get the shock of his life when he walks into his place and finds us waiting."

"There are a lot of windows in the bank." Dolan observed. "Most of them don't have shades. Anyone can look in and see you."

"We've got to run some risks," Brewster said. "Why should you worry about that, Milt? It'll be me and Scrap inside."

"It'll go off all right," Pierce promised. "So long as there's no shooting to arouse the town. We'll be out of there in no time at all, and we'll be lost in this rough country before anyone can raise the alarm."

"We'll have to start out now." Brewster said. He turned away and began rolling his blankets.

"I noticed that the shades on the windows facing the street were all drawn." Pierce remarked. "The only risk will be from someone walking along the alley, and I don't think there'll be much risk from that. It's gonna be easy, boys."

"They broke camp quickly and expertly, and mounted up and rode out. They headed south through the darkness and rode alertly until Pierce reached a spot where he had left his horse the previous evening.

"We'll leave you here, Milt," he said to Dolan when they had dismounted and squatted together for a last talk. "Make sure your watch is wound up. We don't want to have to hang around inside the bank. I reckon you'd best get there in that alley dead on half-nine. The staff will arrive before then because they open the door for business right on the dot. It'll only take us a couple of minutes to pick up what we want."

"Right," Dolan said. "You can forget about the horses now. I'll have them in the alley outside that side door at half-nine. I sure hope you'll be ready to ride by then."

"Don't use the street at all when you come in," Pierce warned. "Someone is sure to spot the brands on the horses."

"I'll ride in over the back lots," Dolan said.

"Well, that's it then," Pierce showed his teeth in a faint grin. "Come on, Ike, we've got some walking to do. See you at half-nine, Milt."

Brewster hurried to keep up with Pierce as they walked the last two hundred yards to town. They went cautiously into Buffalo Grove, moving through the silent shadows until they reached the alley at the side of the bank. Pierce took the lead and paused beside the window he had tested the previous evening. Its catch was loose, and Brewster lifted his knife from its sheath and soon prised the window open. Brewster climbed in through the window, and then went to open the side door from the inside. Pierce could not get his great bulk through the window, and was relieved when Brewster opened the side door. He grinned as he entered the darkened bank. This was going to be too easy.

Once inside the building, Pierce quickly checked around, and he was still grinning when he got back to Brewster.

"Ike, we're never going to get another job as easy as this one," he exulted. "We'll squat down over there by the door and wait for the staff to show up. We'll grab them as they come in, and as soon as the guy with the keys comes in we'll start helping ourselves to the dough. Come on, let's try and make ourselves comfortable. We've got a long wait."

They settled down to wait for dawn.

Milt Dolan felt his nerves tighten as day-break came. He was safe enough in the brush with the horses, but he knew that if anything went wrong in town he would ride into trouble as soon as he entered the alley at the side of the bank. He had the feeling that something was amiss, and couldn't lose it. He tried to shrug it off as nerves, but knew that he was too old a hand at this business to be suffering from tension. That would only become apparent when he rode into town.

He had never liked the idea of hitting the bank in Buffalo Grove, especially after Heck Blaine had pulled out of Pierce's plans. They had all counted on Blaine helping them and none of them had suspected that their old boss would refuse the offer of some easy money. But Blaine's desire to remain honest had shaken Dolan's confidence. It had always been in the back of his mind that if Blaine didn't lead the job then it was bound to go wrong.

The sun came up and he glanced at his watch. There was still three more hours to pass before he could saddle up and ride down to Buffalo Grove. He stood up and stretched, then sat down again. He knew the dangers of too much movement in a place like this. He began to long for the time when he could get astride his horse. For the next two hours he sat and stared at the surrounding ground, watching alertly for sign of passers-by. It would need only one curious pair of eyes to see him to ruin the whole operation. Once, when his horse suddenly whickered, he stood up and gazed carefully around, suspecting that someone was near, but he saw nothing suspicious and sat down again.

Steve heard Dolan's horse, and immediately leaned forward in his saddle and clamped a hand over the nostrils of his own mount. He had headed directly for the high ground north of Buffalo Grove and chance had taken him within twenty-five yards of the brush-filled depression where Milt Dolan crouched with three horses for company He moved gently away from the spot where he had heard the horse, and dismounted awkwardly. He tied his horse and then lifted his gun to check the weapon. He drew a deep breath and began to move slowly back towards where he figured the horse he had heard was standing.

It took him a long time to get into a position from which he could see Milt Dolan, and he recognised the outlaw immediately. He saw the three horses with Dolan, and wondered what had become of the other two riders. He crawled in closer to the unsuspecting outlaw.

He dared not jump Dolan in case Pierce and the other man were around. He waited, and noted every movement that the outlaw made.

When Dolan began to cast impatient and anxious glances at the watch he kept lifting out of a breast pocket, Steve felt excitement filter through him. He knew that the three outlaw pards of his father had come into the country for some lawless operation, and it was clearly about to take place. Pierce and the third outlaw were not around. That meant they were in position somewhere, and Dolan was guarding their horses.

Several times, Steve felt the urge to jump Dolan, but still he waited. He did not know if the other two had arranged to come back to the spot, and if they had, he did not want to spoil his chances of catching all of them by acting prematurely. He waited until Dolan suddenly got to his feet and began saddling up the three horses.

Steve sighed. His horse was some distance away, and he could not hope to reach it and return mounted in time to follow the outlaw. But he waited to see the direction in which Dolan headed, and was surprised to find the outlaw riding towards town, leading the other two animals. Dolan did not travel fast, and was in fact riding leisurely. Steve began to limp forward, keeping to cover as best he could, and he followed Dolan the two hundred yards to town. When the outlaw rode into the alley on the far side of the bank, Steve understood what was happening. So the bank was the gang's objective. Two of the outlaws were inside right now, and Dolan had timed his arrival to coincide with the others' departure with the stolen money.

Steve hurried as best he could across the rough back lots of the buildings fronting the street. He crossed the mouth of the alley on the nearer side of the bank, and lifted his Colt and thumbed back the hammer of the weapon. He flattened himself against the back wall of the building and took a cautious peep into the farther alley. He saw Dolan sitting his horse outside the alley door of the bank, and the outlaw was glancing nervously at his watch.

Steve stepped into the alley with his gun levelled at the outlaw. Dolan was only a dozen yards away. He sensed Steve's presence immediately, and looked up quickly, his hands dropping to his hip.

"Don't do that if you want to go on living," Steve called. "Just lift that gun out slowly and drop it." He waited until the outlaw had obeyed. "That's better. I take it that the other two are inside conducting some sort of crooked business. Climb down out of that saddle, mister."

"Why don't you get out of this?" Dolan demanded. "It ain't none of your business.

"Scrap Pierce is my business," Steve said tightly, "and, being an honest man, bank robbery is my business, especially as I've got some dough in there. Grab those horses and lead them out here. You can play this right and live. If you try anything, I'll cut you down, and you know what a shot will do now, don't you?"

Dolan grabbed at the reins of the three horses and brought the animals to the mouth of the alley. He kept glancing nervously at the side door of the bank, expecting Pierce and Brewster to show at any moment. He knew there would be shooting the instant Pierce appeared, and he was between the door of the bank and Steve Blaine.

"Let me mount up and ride out of here," Dolan pleaded. "I'll keep going south. I never was in favour of robbing this bank.

"Shut up and get down on your belly with your hands out in front of you. I'll be standing behind you when the others show, and if you try anything I'll split your spine with a .45 slug."

"I felt badly about your pa getting killed," Dolan said. "Pierce shouldn't have done that."

"You're right," Steve said. "Now get down on your face and stay there." He grinned. "It'll be the safest place when your two pards emerge from the bank."

Steve threw a quick glance at the side door, and in that instant Dolan kicked up some dirt with the toe of his boot. Earth and dust flew up into Steve's face and he fell back a step. Dolan closed the distance between them with a desperate leap, his hands reaching out for Steve, who dropped to his knees instantly, and the outlaw blundered over the top of him. One of Dolan's knees caught Steve's wounded hand, and he groaned aloud at the agony released in the limb by the blow. He rolled over and came up on his right elbow, his big Colt lining up instantly on the fast moving Dolan.

The outlaw was coming in again with uplifted foot. Steve squeezed his trigger and saw dust spurt up from Dolan's pants just below the waist line. The outlaw screamed thinly through the crash of the shot, and fell limply like a sack of potatoes being dumped from the back of a wagon. He lay writhing on the ground, both hands pressed to his stomach.

Steve twisted around, holding himself off the ground with his wounded hand, and agony was spreading through the limb at the rough usage. He watched the side door of the bank, and saw it begin to open. He recognised instantly the man who thrust out his head to take a quick look around the alley. It wasn't the man he wanted, but Ike Brewster. Steve sent a shot at Brewster, who ducked back into the bank.

"C'mon out, Pierce." Steve yelled. "You can't stay in there. The shots will rouse the town. The sheriff and the posse moved back in this morning. The whole place will be swarming in a minute. Your horses are out here. Dolan is dead. There's only me between you and your getaway, and I want you, Pierce, for killing my father."

"Don't be a fool, Blaine," came Pierce's reply. "I killed Zeke Coppard for you. I got that rancher off your back."

"That's a chore I wanted to do myself," Steve replied. "Now what are you going to do? The sheriff and the rest of the townsmen will be on their way here right now."

Two figures appeared in the alley from the side entrance of the bank, and both began throwing lead at Steve. He ignored their shots, although slugs cut up the ground about him. He lifted his gun and centred the weapon upon the big brass belt buckle that adorned Scrap Pierce's massive stomach. He fired once, and saw Pierce jerk under the impact of the speeding slug. But the outlaw didn't stop. He kept coming at full pelt, and his gun threw a string of angry slugs at Steve.

Steve's second shot smashed Pierce's gunhand, and the fat outlaw staggered and weaved from side to side as his strength seeped out of the hole in his belly. He dropped suddenly to his knees, and Ike Brewster swerved wildly to avoid stumbling over the massive body of his pard.

Brewster came on, firing a Colt with his left hand. A big canvas sack was gripped tightly in his right hand. Steve squinted his eyes against the gunsmoke that swirled about him. He thrust the muzzle of his gun forward as Brewster came up. Their guns exploded together, and flame lanced from hot gun barrels and death belched forth. Steve felt his hat whirl from his head, and then a red hot iron seemed to burn his back from neck to waist.

But Brewster pulled up short as if he had run into an invisible wall. He dropped the sack of stolen money, yet his gun came up once more to point its black mouth at Steve, who snapped off a shot that sent echoes hammering after the other raucous sounds of battle. Brewster fell sideways and banged his head against the wall of the bank. He slid down the wall and lay in a threshing heap.

Scrap Pierce was lying in the centre of the alley, and his gun was wavering in an almost nerveless hand. Steve felt panic rise in him as he realised that he could
not stop the fat outlaw's shot. He thrust his gun towards Pierce and squeezed the trigger desperately. The weapon clicked harmlessly on empty chambers. Pierce laughed hoarsely.

"This is it, Blaine," he growled. "It'll all finish here in this alley. The Wild Men are done for after all these years, and it had to be the son of Heck Blaine who did it. Well, goodbye, sucker. I'm going straight to hell, but I'm taking you with me. Your old man will be there already, waiting for us."

A gun crashed and the light died out of Pierce's eyes. Steve watched the gross outlaw. He saw the man try with all his dying resolve to pull the trigger of his gun. But Pierce was dead, and his weapon fell uselessly away. His fat face plumped down into the dust and his hand shook a little. Then he relaxed, and Steve could hear his last breath hissing out through his slack mouth.

Sheriff Griffin came grimly pacing along the alley. The lawman was holding a levelled Colt that was dribbling smoke from its black muzzle. He paused at the side of Scrap Pierce and studied the bitter scene.

"Well, you said you'd get them," he said simply. "But the next time you take on odds like that you'd better pack two guns. Have you stopped any more lead, son?"

"Just a burn along the back, by the feel of it," Steve said weakly. "Will you give me a hand up, Sheriff?"

"You can have anything you want in this town, Steve," the lawman said, and Steve smiled.

"There's nothing I want," he said. "Nothing that you could give me. Maybe yesterday wouldn't have been too late." He groaned as the sheriff pulled him gently to his feet. "All I want now is some peace. That's all my pa ever wanted."

"Well, he's got that," Griffin said. "I figure that he'll be a happy man, where ever he's gone. He had a son he was proud of, and he sure did a fine job of bringing you up, boy."

Steve looked down at the three dead outlaws, the four sacks of stolen money that lay discarded now in the dust. He handed his gun to the sheriff, and started along the alley on trembling legs. When he reached the street he had to push his way through a crowd of excited, curious townsmen, and he couldn't hear what they were shouting. He began walking out of town, heading for where he had left his horse, and he thought of the Double B, silent and empty now his father had gone.

He would have to go on for he was alive, he told himself. He would have to swallow his grief and work the spread just as he had helped his father to do. But the place wouldn't be silent and empty. His father still lived in every blade of grass on the range, in every corner of the house they had built together. His father wasn't dead while he lived inside the mind of his son, and so long as that son followed the teachings of the father.

Steve reached his horse and swung painfully into the saddle. He heaved a great sigh of relief as he turned the head of the animal for home. He would never be alone so long as he could remember the voice of his father and hear the older man's words in his head. He smiled as he thought of all the work he would have to do to build up the Double B as he and his father had planned, but there were tears in his eyes and an ache in his heart as he turned his back on the town.

Coyote Breed

One

"Freeze, Mister, or you're a dead man," the harsh voice snapped, and Chet Boardman reined in and lifted his hands. "Sit mighty still," the voice went on, "or you'll start that long trip to hell."

Boardman tightened his lips and let his breath go slowly. He had known there was someone in the area for he had smelled woodsmoke a long way back. But he had not counted on running into the outlaws so soon. He sat his black horse without movement, knowing that the threat was not an idle one. He heard movement behind him, and tensed, his brown eyes narrowed against the glare of the sun almost directly overhead.

"Get out of that saddle, Mister, and do it slow. Wait. Chuck your gun first."

Boardman lifted his bone-handled .45 and dropped it into the dust. Then he climbed slowly from his saddle and stood beside the nervous horse, a tall, sharp-featured man of thirty years, dark-faced and brown-eyed, his range clothes dusty and travel-stained. He turned slowly and looked at the grim figure that was moving towards him with levelled Colt.

The stranger was of medium build, dressed in similar dusty clothes, but it was the man's face that held Boardman's attention. He had never seen such coldness in human eyes, so much hatred lining a face, as now confronted him. He sighed as he realised that he had found the outlaws much quicker than he could have hoped for.

"Don't move," the stranger warned harshly. "You just blink twice and you'll draw a slug. Where are the rest of them?"

"The rest of who?" Boardman demanded.

"The Coyotes. I want the Coyotes."

Boardman had heard plenty about the gang of outlaws calling themselves the Coyotes. He knew that a killer named Luke Harper bossed the dozen or so coldblooded killers and robbers. He knew that the sheriffs of a score of counties wanted the gang, and had tried more than once to capture it. But Harper had the instinct and cunning of a predatory animal, and so far all efforts to trap the Coyotes had failed. The gang had shot its vicious way through a number of ambushes, and they never pulled a raid without leaving someone dead or wounded behind them. All this he had learned, but he did not know where the gang was. Some said there was a hideout in the bleak hills north of Burnt Hill, and that was where Boardman was headed.

"I've heard of the Coyotes," he replied steadily. "Who hasn't? But I sure don't know where they are. Are you a robber? Are you after my dough? I'm afraid I'm nearly broke."

"I'm after those killers, and I've got you pegged as one of them," the man retorted. "I got to make a start somewhere, and you're the likely candidate for my first slug."

"Hold your horses," Boardman said quickly. "If you're not an outlaw then you ain't got a quarrel with me. I'm Chet Boardman, a cowboy, and I'm heading for the town of Burnt Hill. I don't know any outlaws."

"I got them spotted yesterday," the man said, "and I'm damned sure that one of them looked like you."

"What have they done to you?" Boardman demanded.

"Done?" The man laughed harshly, his eyes glittering. It came to Boardman that he was a little mad. Perhaps the sun had touched him. "My name is Jed Marsden, Mister, and I own a little ranch south of Mason's Crossing. Them outlaws dropped by my place two weeks ago, and stayed the night. When they rode out next morning my wife and boy were dead. That's why I want to meet up with them."

"But you can't hope to take on the whole gang!" Boardman said.

"Can't I?" Marsden grinned, showing yellowed teeth. He looked to be around forty, but Boardman was not fooled by the mask of grief. Marsden could be ten years younger, or even more. "I don't give a damn if I die when I catch up with them. I ain't got nothing to live for now. I just want to take as many of them Coyotes as I can." He laughed again, in a high-pitched, peculiar manner that had a trace of madness in it. "Whoever named those killers sure called them right. Coyotes! By God, I'll stomp them all before I get through."

"I'm sorry I can't help you," Boardman said. "I'm a stranger in this country. I'm only passing through. I sure wish you luck though. Something should be done about that gang."

"Do you mean by the law?" Marsden chuckled harshly. "That sure is a big joke. When I rode into town at Mason's Crossing the sheriff shoved me in jail. That's a laugh, ain't it? All I did was make ready to come after those outlaws. But they didn't think I could handle it. They jugged me."

"How did you get free?" Boardman decided to humour the man. He could see that grief had pushed Marsden way over the brink from sanity.'

"I cracked the skull of the jailer." Marsden laughed long and furiously. "That showed them I wasn't playing around." He narrowed his eyes as a sudden thought struck him. "Say, you ain't a lawman sent to fetch me in for that, are you?"

"No." Boardman shook his head. "I told you, I'm a cowboy. I figure on seeing Burnt Hill, then finding myself a riding job."

"Then you'd better pick up your gun and get the hell out of here," Marsden told him. "I ain't in the mood for company. You get to hell and gone, and don't let on to anyone that I'm around. I want that gang, and, by God, I'll bring them all into the nearest town when I get through with them."

"I hope you manage it," Boardman told him, picking up his gun. He holstered the weapon and climbed back into his saddle. "I'm mighty sorry to hear about your family, Marsden."

"Get out of here," the man snarled.

Boardman nodded and spurred his horse, tensing his muscles as he left the grieving man standing. He expected a shot in the back, but nothing happened, and he breathed easier when his horse carried him through a cluster of rocks and there was cover between him and the menacing gun.

The incident had shaken him, and he shook his head in wonder as he recalled Marsden's tense face, the haunted expression around the eyes. He wouldn't want to be in the boots of any member of the gang. Jed Marsden would die trying to get them.

As he rode, Boardman wondered if Marsden's presence would complicate his own dangerous chore. He had lied to the man. He wanted to find the Coyotes, and for a very good reason. He was a Texas Ranger, and he had been assigned the job of tracking down the gang's hide-out and laying a trail for a posse to capture the outlaws.

He wiped sweat from his forehead as he continued. Jed Marsden had scared him. Never had he seen such grim determination in a man. Marsden was more than ready to die so long as he could take some of his family's killers with him. The man was a danger to any unwary traveller who took him wrong.

This was bad country for a man and a horse, he figured. There was plenty of rock and little water in this area. There was desert and death in this south-western corner of Texas. The Coyotes had raised hell throughout the country, and had come to terrorise half the state. The law had been struck badly, and all efforts to track and capture the gang had failed. Wherever they moved, the Coyotes killed and plundered with impunity. They seemed to be getting stronger as the law lost out against them. Other outlaws and bad men had been pushing into the county to try and join up with the gang, and there were many lonely campfires on the back trails as the owl hoots drifted, attracted by the success of the gang.

Boardman knew the risk he was taking. He had been well briefed before riding out of the Ranger barracks at Austin. Five Rangers had lost their lives trying to get the information he was now seeking. The Coyotes were tough and brutal, and life was cheap in this country where every man carried a gun at his hip to settle his arguments. But Boardman was not concerned with the risks. He took things in his stride. He had been given a job to do, and he would carry it out until he succeeded or died.

He rode for the rest of the day, following a faint trail that he knew led to Burnt Hill. He had heard about that town. There were more saloons and gambling dens than other buildings, and a man could always judge the degree of lawlessness in a country by the number of such places. He had heard it said that in Burnt Hill everything goes, and he wondered how the sheriff of the county managed to stay alive. It was probably because the lawman took the middle course. He didn't bother the outlaws and they didn't bother him.

As night drew on he began to look for a likely camp site. He judged that he would reach Burnt Hill about dusk the next evening, and from what he'd heard there were almost as many sympathisers for the Coyotes in the town as there were members of the gang.

He halted before full darkness dropped upon him, and lit a small fire in a crevice under a large rock. He settled his horse, attending to its wants before thinking of himself. Then he put a pan on his fire and half-cooked some beans and boiled some coffee. By the time night was settled around him he was unrolling his blanket and his fire was out. He didn't sleep immediately. His mind was filled with conjecture, and he thought of Jed Marsden on the trail behind him. Something had to be done about these outlaws, and that was no idle thought. Women and children were not safe while the Coyotes rode at large.

He had been told to try and join up with the Coyotes, and he knew the risks involved. If there should be one outlaw who had come into contact with him in the past then his goose would be cooked before he got started. Then again, if he managed to pass himself off as an outlaw he would find it difficult, after learning all he could about the gang, to get away in order to pass on his information. That sort of thing had been tried before, and he knew that good men had died trying it.

The gang, as he knew it, consisted of about a score of men, all of them killers and robbers. There were about half a dozen better-known outlaws riding with Luke Harper, and they were in the nature of minor bosses of the gang. At times some of them actually led the gang on a raid. He ran through some of their names in his mind, having seen what pictures there were available at headquarters. The names conjured up a brutal scene in his head. The value of the rewards lumped upon the various heads ran into something like $150,000, and more than one bounty hunter had moved in with the intention of helping himself to some easy money. But there was nothing easy about trying to collect on any of the Coyotes.

A scraping sound aroused Boardman, and he reached quickly for his gun, which was in its holster beside his head. He peered around, and there was enough light from the stars to let him see the outline of the rocks around him.

"Don't lift that gun, Mister," a soft voice warned him. "Sit up slowly and lift your hands where we can see them."

For a moment Boardman thought that Jed Marsden had stumbled upon him again. Then he saw three figures moving, and they closed in on him menacingly. He sat up and lifted his hands, saying nothing.

"What's your name?" he was asked, and gave it, adding his destination. "What's your business?"

"I'm a cowpuncher," he replied.

"Get up, and stand easy. Don't try anything."

He got to his feet, and the men closed in around him. He saw a fourth come forward, and they all peered at his face, trying to see his features.

"I don't know him," one of them said.

The others said the same, and there was a short silence.

"Who are you?" Boardman asked. "I'm only an out-of-work cowpuncher. I ain't got more than a couple of dollars on me, if that's what you're after."

"We've been told to watch out for a lone rider," one of them said. "There ain't many men roaming this part of the country. I guess you must be the man we want."

"I don't know you," Boardman said.

"We don't know you," came the harsh retort. "You ain't a cowhand, though. More likely you own a ranch south of Mason's Crossing."

"Let's get out of here, Pete," one of the others said.

"No," the big man replied, his face unseen in the night. "We were told to get a lone rider, and we have got him. Link, you're the knife artist. Get to work on him. You heard what the boss said. He's got to be discouraged. He's been following the boys for the last two weeks."

"Not me," Boardman said tightly. "I came through Wilsonburg last week. You can check it if you like."

"We're sure to," came the harsh reply. "It's only a week's ride to Wilsonburg. And you'll wait here for us to come back, too, huh?"

"Maybe we'd better let him go," one of the others said. "If we kill him he might be missed, and you know we don't want any trouble so close to Burnt Hill."

"We ain't gonna kill him," Pete said. "If I recollect rightly, the boss said to discourage him. You know what to do, Link. You're part Indian, ain't you? Your red brothers sure knew a thing or two about using a knife." Boardman gritted his teeth as one of the men approached him. He was grabbed by two of the others and thrown to the ground. He struggled, but was helpless in their grip. The third man dropped across his legs and pinned them down. The fourth knelt beside him, his face black and unseen. Boardman tried to struggle, but he was as helpless as a hog-tied calf. He saw the cold glitter of starlight on a long blade in the kneeling man's hand.

"Lay off me," he gasped. "I don't know you guys. I ain't the man you want."

"Knife him, Link," came the grim order, and the steel blade descended slowly.

Boardman tensed his muscles. He thought the blade was stabbing for his stomach, but it changed direction suddenly and plunged into his right wrist. The agony of the blow seemed to explode in the limb. Boardman yelled at the top of his voice. He struggled, and managed to break free. They threw themselves upon him and he was once more pinned down.

"Now one through the hand," he heard a rough voice command, and struggled again.

But they were too much for him. He was stretched out, and merciless fingers dragged open his right hand. He felt hard rock under his knuckles as they turned the hand palm upwards. The long blade stabbed again, and he felt the fire of the stroke riot through his hand. The palm was pierced through its centre, and he tried to suppress his bubbling cry of agony. His senses reeled under the shock, and he heard a throbbing fill his ears, blotting out the harsh voices. Pain such as he had never known filled his hand and arm, and he rose almost to his feet despite their restraining hands.

Then a heavy fist sledged against his jaw and he blacked out. The pain receded with his senses, and he slumped inertly upon his blanket. He did not see the dark figures fade away. He lay as dead, and blood poured from the deep wounds in his wrist and hand.

The fiery pain in the limb dragged him back to his senses, and probably saved his life, for he would surely have bled to death had he not recovered. He groaned and writhed in the darkness, then got unsteadily to his feet. He looked around, gripping his wrist with his trembling left hand. The pain was intolerable, and he rocked to and fro, staring at the dark stains of his blood. He gritted his teeth and pulled off his neckerchief, wrapping it around hand and wrist to cover the wounds. He knotted it tightly, then removed the thong from the bottom of his holster and tied it around his upper arm, pulling it tight with his teeth in an attempt to stop the bleeding. His whole arm was pulsating with agony, and he had to bite his bottom lip to prevent an outcry.

He left his blankets and moved to his horse, intent upon saddling up and riding. He had to get to a doctor before he bled to death. He forced himself to saddle up, groaning each time he had to use the right arm, and his thoughts and mind were filled with the hazy blankness of wild pain.

He felt a little easier when he was astride his black. He eased his right hand inside the front of his shirt, trying to keep the hand higher than the elbow, and the pain became worse as the horse started forward, jolting him in the saddle. He could feel blood trickling down inside his shirt, sticky and cold, and congealing on his clammy flesh. He tried to keep to the trail, but had no idea of his direction after leaving the camp site.

All he could do was keep the horse moving, and he rocked in the saddle as the pain increased. He loosened the thong around his arm, and felt pins and needles in the forearm.

He never could remember how long he rode that night. Everything was a blur to his rioting senses. The pain in his arm and hand almost drove him insane, and he couldn't collect his scattered thoughts. He forgot all about the men who had done this to him, and concentrated upon staying in his uneasy saddle. He let his knotted reins lay on the neck of his mount, and the animal moved in its own direction, unguided.

Boardman slid from his saddle when the animal halted suddenly, and landed heavily in the dust. The raw, ragged pain in his arm was almost unbearable. He had never known agony like it. He heard someone moving just outside the circle of his awareness, and tried to get up. Then a strong hand grasped his shoulder, and he groaned and his injured hand dragged against the rocks. He passed out, and all pain fled.

The sun in his eyes awakened him, and he groaned as the pain returned to his hand. He lay for a moment with his eyes closed tightly against the brilliance of the new day, and his thoughts came back. He recalled the terrible incident in the night, and could hear the harsh voices of the men who had taken him. Then a shadow fell across his face and he opened his eyes. He saw a tall figure standing over him, and lifted his eyes to a rugged face. The man dropped to one knee beside him.

"Howdy," he greeted. "You stumbled into my camp last night, and a good thing for you. You'd have bled to death, likely, judging by the wounds you've got. But I've patched you up good enough to last until we get to Burnt Hill. My name is Frank Quinn. I'm a rancher. I own the Big Q ranch south of here."

"I'm Chet Boardman, cowpuncher. I was heading for Burnt Hill." Boardman explained to the rancher what had happened, and watched the man's face harden when he mentioned the outlaws. Quinn was a thin man, but tall, and his greying hair was short and bristling. His brown eyes were shrewd, and he stared at Boardman for a long time.

"You say they told you they was waiting for someone?" he said. "Well, likely you saved me from some trouble. I've had a brush or two with them thieving guys, and I proved too good for them more than once. I run a tough crew. I did hear that the Coyotes intended having a go at me."

"I met another man yesterday," Boardman said. He explained his meeting with Jed Marsden. "I figured at the time that they were after him. He's gonna make bad trouble for any of that gang when he comes up with them."

"Maybe so, but I reckon it's me they were after," Quinn said. "If that is the case then I owe you something. You ain't gonna use your right hand for a month or more. I don't figure you'll ever hold a gun with it again."

"I can use my left hand just as well, if not better," Boardman said through his clenched teeth. "I've got a spare gun and a left-hand holster in my saddlebag." He sat up, and the smell of fresh coffee wafted across his nostrils. "I could sure do with some of that," he remarked.

"It's ready," the rancher replied, putting a gnarled hand under Boardman's left armpit and helping him to his feet. "I let you lay as long as I could."

Boardman reeled forward a couple of tentative steps, blinking in the strong light. He saw two other men hunched over by a small fire, and they got to their feet and came towards him.

"Two of my men," Quinn said. "You've found out that it ain't wise to travel alone in this country. This is Hank Parfitt and that's Bill Newman."

"Howdy," Boardman said. He liked what he saw when he studied the two men. They were tough-looking and capable. Parfitt was not so tall, but built like a bull. He carried a gun on his left hip. Both men greeted him, but they were watchful, and he noticed that their eyes were never still. They kept glancing over their shoulders, a sure sign of the gunman, and their hands never moved far from the flared butts holstered at their waists.

"Sit down and eat," Quinn said. He dropped onto a flat rock beside Boardman and scooped some beans and bacon out of a sizzling pan, ladling the food on to a tin plate. He placed it on Boardman's knees, and passed over a fork. "You'll have to get used to using your left hand," he observed. "Coffee?"

"Please," Boardman said. He ate with relish, wincing at the darting pangs of agony in his right hand. He stared at the thick bandaging around his right wrist, and glanced down at his heavily blood-stained shirt. He drank some of the scalding black coffee that the rancher poured for him, and some of the faintness in his stomach receded. When he had finished the meal he got unsteadily to his feet.

"I don't know how to thank you for what you've done," he said, and Quinn held up his hand.

"Don't say another word. If you're looking for a job in this country then you can ride for me. I can always do with another good man."

"With this?" Boardman held up his bandaged hand. "I ain't gonna be much use to anyone for a long time."

"We ought to get to town as soon as we can," the rancher warned. His two men were already breaking camp. "I did what I could for you, but you'll lose the arm if gangrene sets in. The sooner the Doc in town sees you the easier I'll feel. Now don't you worry about a thing. I still say you got what was meant for me. I'll take care of you until you're fit to ride."

"That's good of you." Boardman felt like telling the rancher about himself, but he knew his life depended upon the secret of his identity. If word got out to the wrong men then he would be in bad trouble. He already knew that the Coyotes had a lot of friends in this country. "I'll make it up to you somehow," he said.

"Forget about it." Quinn chuckled. "You better strip off that shirt. I've got a spare one in my saddlebag. It'll be a tight fit by the looks of your shoulders. I ain't so wide myself. But it'll do you until we hit town."

Boardman's horse was saddled for him, and he changed his bloodstained shirt. He took his left-hand gun and belt from his saddlebag and buckled it around his waist, hurting his right hand as he did so. He was glad that he could use a gun equally well with either hand. If he had been unable to he would have had to return to Austin, and someone else would have been sent in his place. But he had no intention of giving up this assignment. Something had to be done about the kind of men riding with the outlaws.

They started riding, and Boardman looked around at the rough country about him. His spirits began to sink. How could he hope to find the gang's hideout? It would take an army years to cover every possible location in this area. He sighed heavily.

"Is that arm bothering you?" Quinn demanded. He was at Boardman's side, and there was genuine concern in his brown eyes.

"It's giving me hell," Boardman admitted. "I never knew a cut could give so much deep pain. It ain't so bad now as it was last night. Holy Cow! I thought I would have died from the pain."

"You've got my sympathies," Quinn said. "I've never seen such brutal work, except for what the redskins did. You've got a stab wound clean through the wrist; there's a wound either side, and another through the palm. I don't figure you've got any broken bones, but it's a bad mess."

"Indians," Boardman mused. He suddenly recalled that the man who had used the knife had been named by the apparent leader of the party who had attacked him. "Say, the knifeman was called Link. He must be Link Loman, one of Harper's henchmen. He's a quarter Indian, they say."

"You know about this gang?" Quinn demanded.

"Yeah." Boardman threw a quick glance at the rancher, and saw nothing but brightness in his brown eyes. "Say, you don't think that I'm one of that gang, do you? That I might have fallen out with them?"

"No, son," the older man said softly, "I found your papers on you last night. I know who you are. I can appreciate that you want to keep your identity a secret. Well, I'm telling you that I'll help you all I can. This country is hamstrung by the outlaw gang. If you do get a lead on them, then call for my crew. I've got plenty of gunhands on my payroll, and we're all itching for the chance to shoot some of the hell out of them outlaws."

"Thanks," Boardman said. "I'm in your debt, Mr Quinn."

Parfitt and Newman were riding several yards ahead, and they reined up suddenly, slapping leather and drawing their guns. Boardman glanced ahead and saw a horseman blocking their trail. He dropped his hand to his gun, holding his right across his chest. Then he recognised the newcomer as Jed Marsden, and saw the drawn gun in the man's hand.

"Don't shoot," he yelled, as sunlight flickered on moving steel. "There ain't no outlaws here."

They rode slowly towards the motionless horseman, who stared at them with wild brown eyes. Boardman thought the man was about to fire on them regardless, but he seemed to recognise Boardman, and lowered his gun.

"This is Jed Marsden, who I told you about," Boardman said. "This is Frank Quinn, a local rancher, Marsden."

"I found a blanket-roll back that way," Marsden said thinly. "It looks like you found yourself some trouble last night, Mister. Were they some of the Coyotes?"

"They were," Boardman admitted. He lifted his right hand. "You can expect something like this yourself if they catch up with you, Marsden."

"They won't get that close to me," the rancher snarled. He was obviously half demented by grief. "I wish I'd been in your boots last night."

"It was probably you they were after," Boardman said. "But I wouldn't wish this upon anyone else."

"Are you gonna try and get even with them?" Marsden demanded.

"No. The next time it will likely be more than my hand," Boardman told him.

"You wouldn't think like that if it had been your wife and kid got killed," Marsden said. "Here's your blanket-roll." He passed it over, and Quinn took it and fastened it behind Boardman's saddle for him. "I'd better get riding. I ain't gonna come up with them Coyotes sitting here."

"We're riding into Burnt Hill," Quinn said. "You're welcome to go along with us if you're so minded."

"I ain't coming into town until I need some stores. I've got enough to keep me going for a couple of weeks. I want to catch up with them outlaws."

Marsden reined away and rode fast across the rocks. Boardman watched him through narrowed eyes. He didn't think that Jed Marsden had any kind of a chance of coming out of this alive. But perhaps that would be a blessing, for the man was badly cut up about his dead family. There was silence until Marsden had vanished, then Quinn shook his head.

"That's a good man going there," he observed. "Those outlaws had better look out when he gets up with them. By the looks of him a bullet won't stop him."

"They'll kill him," Boardman said slowly. "He won't come through it. I've got a feeling, too, that he doesn't want to."

"That's about the weight of it," Quinn said sadly. "Come on, let's get back to town."

They rode fast along the rocky trail.

Two

The town of Burnt Hill was a sprawling collection of drab buildings. There were three streets, wide and rutted, covered in inches of dust that quickly turned to mud in the rains. The biggest building in the town was Boyd's Hotel, a massive place that was three storeys high. The number of saloons was greater than the rest of the buildings put together.

It was mid-afternoon when Boardman rode in with his new-found friend, and Quinn led the way immediately to the doctor's house. Boardman was all in when he reeled out of his saddle, and the rancher helped him through the dust and into the house, calling over his shoulder to his two men to put up their horses at the livery barn.

There ensued a period of intense pain when the doctor attended to Boardman's injuries, and Boardman gritted his teeth and bore the ministrations stoically. Quinn produced a hip-flask of good whisky and handed it over, and Boardman gulped the liquor, sitting slumped in a chair while the doctor operated on his wrist and hand.

"Well, that should take care of it," the doctor said after what seemed an interminable time. "You'd better come and see me every day until it heals. If you get gangrene in those wounds you'll lose the arm or die. You met up with Link Loman of the Coyotes, huh?"

"Yeah, who told you?" Boardman demanded.

"I don't need no telling, son. Those two wounds are Loman's brand. I've attended to a dozen men in the past couple of years who have carried wounds like them. It's Loman's favourite trick. Stab a man in the gun hand and he can't come back at you too quickly."

"I'd like to meet up with Loman some day," Boardman said through his clenched teeth. "He should have done the same to my left hand, because I'm a two-gun man."

"But you weren't wearing your left-hand gun," the doctor observed. "Lucky for you that you didn't or you should have had both hands bandaged now."

"Yeah," Frank Quinn said slowly. "I've heard about Link Loman, now you come to mention it. Well, I reckon it's about time something was done about these Coyotes."

"You ain't kidding." The doctor finished bandaging Boardman's hand. "Does that feel any easier now, son?"

"Sure thing, Doc," Boardman replied. "Thanks."

"I'll take care of the bill," Quinn said. "I've got the feeling that those outlaws were watching for me last night. I know they've had men watching my spread for some time, since I had that run-in with them. They're out to get me."

"I wouldn't want to be in your boots," the doctor said. "We had some trouble in town yesterday. A coach was held up at Chokeberry Creek. The cause of most of the trouble around here nowadays is that everything is blamed on the Coyotes, but I reckon they don't do half they get blamed for. The sheriff has given up riding out after them now. He just files the reports and goes for a drink. I don't blame him, either. He's ridden a thousand miles around this town and never found a single clue. It's enough to get a saint down."

"I'm on my way to have a talk with Wendell right now," Quinn said harshly. "If he's willing to take out just one more posse then I'll throw the whole of my crew into the search. I reckon we've got to make a big stand against these outlaws. They're running the entire country. If we don't soon put up some resistance then we'll be run out of the country, and that will be the end in this area. The outlaws will take over, and even the army wouldn't beat them."

"An army couldn't find them," the doctor said. He sighed. "I shouldn't grumble, I suppose. I get more than my share of the living. I must be the best businessman in town, but it's a trade that I could do without. I reckon I've handled more gunshot cases than any three army surgeons during the war."

Quinn moved to the door, and Boardman got up and followed him.

"I'll be in to see you in the morning," Boardman said, and was thankful that he was on his way out instead of just coming in. His hand was throbbing madly, and he twisted it in the sling the doctor had made for him.

"You just take good care of it, son," the doctor warned him. "Keep it in that sling. If you keep the wrist above the elbow it won't hurt so much."

"Thanks." Boardman closed the door and followed Quinn out to the street. They walked along a crowded sidewalk, and Boardman looked around, taking in all the details. There was a wagonload of timber lying overturned, and three horses out of a four-horse team were down in the dust, kicking and threshing. A stagecoach was pulled up further along the street, and one of the lead horses was lying in the dust behind the coach. It was obvious what had happened. There was a group of angry men standing in the street, shouting and all talking at once, and Boardman spotted a law star on the chest of a huge man before Quinn pointed out the sheriff.

"That's Sam Wendell," the rancher said. "Better wait until he's finished here before we go talk to him. Let's go get ourselves a drink. I reckon you can do with one, huh?"

"You can say that again," Boardman retorted. He followed Quinn into the nearest saloon, and they procured drinks. Boardman glanced around, studying the several faces in the saloon. They were all rugged, features burned almost black by the sun, and he told himself that somewhere in this town there were contacts for the Coyotes. He would have to be very careful what he said or did. He had been told that Luke Harper had a very efficient spy service.

Men started drifting in from the street scene, and they were talking about what had happened. Quinn walked to the door and peered out over the batwings. He yelled at the sheriff, and moments later the lawman shouldered his way through the swing doors and came towards the bar.

Sam Wendell stood six feet four inches in his socks, and he was a man of immense girth. He had pale grey eyes, and a drooping moustache concealed the generous lines of his upper lip. He listened to Frank Quinn, then lifted his gaze to look at Boardman.

"Do you want to make a complaint about Link Loman, Boardman?" he boomed. "I'd better warn you though that I've got nearly a score of complaints on my desk against him. I ain't been able to catch him in a couple of years, nor any of his crooked pards." He glanced back at Quinn. "Did you hear that they stopped another coach? Chokeberry Creek this time. I rode out and looked around, but there's nothing I can do about it. I've got four deputies, and we can't raise a thing."

"I've come in to tell you that if you'll start another posse out to look for those crooks," Quinn said, "I'll throw in my crew. They're yours for as long as you need them. But something's got to be done about the outlaws."

"I agree," the sheriff said in a great, booming voice. "But can you tell me where to start looking, Frank? If you could do that then I wouldn't need your crew. I'd take out a posse that could handle the job."

"There's a man we met on the trail," Quinn said, and told Wendell about Jed Marsden. "He ain't wasting any time. I reckon he'll find that hideout if anyone can."

"Then we'll never see him again," the sheriff asserted. "There's been a lot of men thought they could find that hideout and come back for a posse. I'm still waiting for them. I sent in some deputies myself, and they ain't never reported back. Even the Texas Rangers have given it up as a dead loss. They've had nearly half a dozen Rangers killed trying to track down the Coyotes. The last one came through here about six weeks ago. I ain't seen any more since. If the Rangers are beaten then what can you expect me to do?"

Quinn bought the sheriff a drink, glancing at Boardman and smiling. Boardman nodded slowly. He had no illusions about this job. He guessed that every stranger was noted upon arrival, and most likely the details were forwarded to the outlaws.

"Come across to my office, Boardman," Wendell said, setting down his glass. "I could show you some wanted dodgers on some of this gang, and perhaps you might recognise a few faces."

"I didn't get a good look at them," Boardman said. "It was dark, and they jumped me too quickly. But I'd like to see your pictures. I want to know some of the faces in case I come up with them again."

"You're carrying Link Loman's brand," the lawman said. "I see you're wearing your gun on the left. Can you use it well enough?"

"As fast as the right," Boardman told him. "I was a two-gun man, but recently I've got into the habit of wearing just one gun."

They left the saloon and went across to the law office. There was a deputy seated at the desk, and he grinned knowingly when he saw the bandage on Boardman's right limb. He jerked open a drawer and lifted out a sheaf of papers. Scanning through them, he picked one out and passed it across.

"Link Loman," he said simply.

Loman looked part Indian. He was dark-featured, and his black hair was straight as an Indian's. Boardman stared into the picture's dark eyes and could almost feel the baleful intensity that must have been directed at the photographer when the shot was taken.

"I reckon I'll know him again when I see him," he remarked.

"When you see him?" Wendell demanded. "Boardman, you want to pray that you'll never set eyes on him again. What he did to you last night he does to every man who crosses his trail. But that's the first time. If he ever comes up with you again you'll be so scarred your own mother won't know you."

"He won't get that close the second time," Boardman said grimly, thinking of Jed Marsden.

"What are you doing in this part of the country?" Wendell asked.

"He's working for me now," Quinn said. "He was heading for this area, intending to find work."

"You won't be riding for a long time, not with that hand," the sheriff said.

"It'll heal." Boardman picked up the other pictures as the deputy passed them across, and found himself regarding other harsh, brutal faces belonging to some more of the outlaw gang. He read the description under the face of one named Pete Merrill, and recalled that the name Pete had been used the previous evening. Most of the other faces he had seen back at Ranger headquarters. He handed them back, shaking his head. "I've never seen a harder bunch," he commented.

"You want to pray that you don't see any of them in the flesh," Wendell told him, laughing harshly. "They're all about as bad as Loman."

"Let's go over to the hotel and get ourselves a couple of rooms," Quinn said. "I plan to stay over a couple of days at least. I'll take you around and introduce you to some of the folks, Boardman. If you plan to stay in the country then you'd better start getting to know everyone."

"I'll see you around, Sheriff," Boardman said as he followed the rancher out to the street, and the lawman lifted a big hand to him.

Boyd's Hotel was a huge building that boasted fifty rooms. Boardman let the rancher handle their business, and they went up to a couple of rooms on the top floor. Boardman walked to the window of his room and stared down at the broiling street. Quinn dropped down onto the bed and stared at Boardman.

"It ain't none of my concern, Boardman, I know, but I'm wondering how you plan to handle this business of hunting up the Coyotes. I reckon you must know your job, but you heard what Wendell said back there in his office. There's been a whole parcel of lawmen killed trying to find that hideout. Have you got a plan?"

"Not yet," Boardman admitted. "What few ideas I had have been knocked out of my mind by this." He held up his bandaged hand. "I'll have to get around town and keep my ears open. If I can pick up any information then I'll start in on the job."

"I might be able to help you there," Quinn said. "I've heard a lot of talk around the country, and there's no smoke without fire, as you likely know. There's a trading-post some twelve miles to the north, and I have heard it said that the Coyotes use the place as a clearinghouse. They dump loot there that they want to sell, and pick up supplies and information. The owner is a rough-looking guy. He's got only one eye. Had the right one taken out on the point of a greaser's knife about ten years back. He used to peddle whisky and guns to the Indians in the old days."

"What's his name?"

"Scar Calhoun. You'll have to meet him. Maybe if you made it worth his while he might open up and tell you a thing or two. But make no mistake, son. As soon as you start asking questions about the Coyotes around here, you're gonna be marked. They'll be watching you."

"I've got a good reason for trying to find Link Loman," Boardman said. "I owe him something for this." He held up his right hand for a moment. The whole limb was throbbing powerfully, and the pain of the wound was reaching up past his elbow.

"Maybe you won't have to try and find him," Quinn went on. "If he gets to hear that you're asking after him then he'll drop on to you one dark night in a back alley somewhere. It's happened before."

"Yeah. Well, I've got to make a start sometime, Quinn. I think I'll get cleaned up and then take a look around town. I might be able to learn something. You'd be surprised what you can pick up when you're trying."

"Okay. But hear me out before you get started. I'll spread the word that you're working for me. You can start when that hand has healed up. That should give you plenty of time to look around. But if you do find something I want you to cut me and my boys into it. I've got something to repay those Coyotes for, and I'll be obliged and pleased if you'll give me the chance."

"Sure thing. If I do manage to learn anything then I'm gonna need all the help I can get. I should let the sheriff know who I really am, but I've been warned against it. You heard Wendell say that nearly half a dozen Rangers have been killed trying to get something on the gang. Well, in each case the sheriff was warned in advance that a Ranger was on his way."

"And you figure there might be a leak in the law office?"

"It looks that way." Boardman's brown eyes hardened. "I hope to find out before this is finished."

"I wish you luck," Quinn told him, "but I've got a feeling this job is too big for any one man."

"I'll tell you more about that later," Boardman retorted.

"Yeah, but don't forget what I told you. My crew is at your disposal. Any time you want them just let me know. They are men you can rely on, and they'll back you all the way." Quinn got to his feet and made for the door. "I'm gonna have a sleep before supper. If you like I'll show you around town later. There's a lot to see, and I'll be able to introduce you to a few men who might have some undercover dealings with the outlaws."

"Thanks, I'll see you later then." Boardman waited for the rancher to leave the room, then dropped on to the bed. He nursed his right hand as he stared up at the ceiling and let his thoughts drift. This was surely going to be the toughest chore he had ever undertaken. Not only was there the gang to contend with but an army of spies and informants who would soon pass the word that a stranger was in Burnt Hill and asking questions.

He figured that he had better let it become known that he was interested in meeting Link Loman for revenge. Then folk wouldn't be so curious or surprised when he started making enquiries. For most of them it would seem natural that a man should want to meet up with the brute who had maimed him. He had to make a start somewhere, and that seemed the only way to do it. If Loman heard about him and came along to meet him then he would have to take his chance. He would have to see some of these outlaws through gunsmoke before it was finished, and the sooner he got started on the job the sooner it would finish.

His hand troubled him greatly, and he let his mind rove over the incident. He heard again the hoarse, callous voices, saw in his mind the flash of the long blade as it stabbed down at his flesh, and his stomach muscles knotted as he relived the agony. Sweat broke out on his forehead, and he wiped it away with his left hand. Fear was cold and hard in his belly, and he gritted his teeth and closed his eyes. Was he losing his nerve? He wondered about that. Then he thought of Jed Marsden, and shook his head. He wished he could have done something for that man.

But perhaps Marsden would find the Coyotes! It would take a lot to stop the bereaved rancher. Yet Boardman could see nothing but death for the man. He let his mind work over all that he knew and had been told about the gang. His eyes narrowed and his lips compressed as he realised exactly what he was up against.

He drifted into sleep despite the pain in his hand, and opened his eyes when Frank Quinn touched the handle of his door. He found the room gloomy, for the sun had gone, and he yawned and stretched, wincing as the movement stirred his hand and set the fiery pangs of agony loose.

"Looks like I wasn't the only one," Quinn said good-naturedly. He struck a match and came forward to light the lamp standing on the small table. "How's your hand feeling now, Boardman?"

"A little easier. But it's gonna be a long job, I'm thinking." Boardman pulled his gun and checked it, easing it back into the left-hand holster. He wasn't worried about having to use the left hand. He was naturally suited to drawing a gun with either hand, but he would have to put in some practice to sharpen up his reflexes.

"I reckon we can go down and get ourselves a bite of supper. Then we'll take in the sights of Burnt Hill. You can always reckon on there being a dozen gunfights a night. There's always enough noise around here to raise the dead. No wonder Wendell doesn't ride out to look for these outlaws. There's always more than enough around here to keep him occupied."

"But the Coyotes have a monopoly on the crime in this country, don't they?"

"You can be sure of it," Quinn said, shaking his head. "The trouble is, a lot of the Coyotes ain't got a price on their heads. They ain't known to anyone except Luke Harper, and they can come and go just as they please in this town."

Boardman considered that as he followed the rancher down to the big dining-room, and he was thoughtful through the meal. Afterwards they went along to the biggest saloon in town, called The Cartwheel, and, bellying up to the long bar, they found Quinn's two cowhands, Parfitt and Newman, standing there. Quinn bought the beer, and Boardman stood glancing around. The bar must have been all of thirty feet long, he told himself, and there were more than thirty small tables dotting the floor-space. At the far end of the saloon was a wide stage, festooned with glittering curtains, and it was obvious by the noise of the men at the tables that some sort of entertainment was expected.

"Frederick Moss owns all of this," Quinn said to Boardman, who nodded. "I'll introduce you later to Moss. I reckon he's in the know about a lot of things. He might be able to tell you something, especially if you put a bit of pressure on him. But watch out for him. He's got some tough characters on his payroll, and if he doesn't like your face then you'll wind up in some alley with a knife in your short ribs."

Boardman drank his beer, his eyes studying the scene before him. There were a lot of tough characters in this town, he thought, and wondered how he would ever manage to handle this chore. But he knew that he could only do his best. If that was not good enough then he would die, and someone else would come and take his place. He smiled as he considered what had already happened. He had better get it fixed into his mind that he was really up against it, and he knew that he would have to shoot first and ask questions afterwards if he were to have any chance of succeeding. He wondered if he should put it about that he would be willing to join up with the outlaws. That course had been suggested to him back at Ranger headquarters, but they had given him a free hand to work as he pleased.

The curtains covering the stage were suddenly opened to the accompaniment of a chorus of yells and catcalls. A piano and a violin began to play, and a girl dressed in a shimmering blue gown appeared and began to sing. There was near silence, and Boardman turned to the bar and ordered a round of drinks. When the singer went off, four dancing girls appeared, and the mood changed. The girls finished their spot and came down to mingle with the customers, and another girl appeared to sing. She had a good voice, and sang old frontier favourites.

Boardman stared at the girl, frowning as he figured that her face was familiar. He hoped he didn't know her, or, more to the point, that she didn't know him. It would be bad luck to meet someone around here who knew that he was a Ranger. He watched her for several moments, but she was too far away for him to see her features clearly. Then she came down off the stage and threaded her way among the tables, singing as she moved, and a thrill of horror struck Boardman as she closed on him.

Josie Whalen, he thought, staring hard at the girl. He had figured she looked familiar. Well, he hadn't seen her in five, maybe six years, but there was no mistaking her face. He recalled the last time he had seen her, in a courthouse at Austin. She had drawn two years in prison for being concerned with a robbery, and Boardman had collected the evidence against her.

She came along the saloon, pausing to sing snatches of her songs, and Boardman turned back to the bar and lifted his glass to his lips. But she paused behind him, singing, and she was so close that he could smell her perfume. He raised his eyes to the mirror behind the bar, and met hers. He saw by the expression that crossed her face that she had recognised him. Then she was gone. She finished her song quickly and hurried back down the saloon.

"She's a pretty girl," Quinn said, reaching for his beer.

"Yeah," Boardman told him. "I knew her about five years ago. I busted a crime wave and she was in it. She drew two years in prison for her part."

"Hell!" Quinn set down his glass. "Did she recognise you, do you think?"

"She saw me in the mirror. I think she knows me."

"What are you gonna do? Will it pay you to have a word with her?"

"No. I'll try and keep out of her way. I'd better get out of here now, just in case she tells someone about me."

"She's a good friend of the sheriff's," Quinn said. "I reckon she's in the right job to be able to help you, son. I don't want to tell you how to run your business. It's your life at stake if you make a mistake. But maybe you could make a friend out of her."

Boardman rubbed his chin and thought hard. "She definitely recognised me," he said. He sighed. "I don't know if she's still up to her old tricks. She might even be working in with the gang. You know what they say about birds of a feather."

"You've got me around, and my two men, if you should need any help," Quinn offered. "You ain't on your own. I reckon I'd better start sounding out some of the honest folk in this town. All they need is a leader and they'll start hunting down the outlaws. The sheriff ain't the man they need, but if you can get anything on this gang of outlaws then maybe you can raise up enough feeling to get a posse to follow you."

"That's what I intend doing," Boardman said. "Now I'm getting out of here."

He turned from the bar and found the houseman standing at his back.

"Is your name Boardman?" the man demanded.

"That's right."

"Josie Whalen recognised you just now, and says she's an old friend of yours. She'd like to talk to you. Follow me and I'll take you to her dressing-room."

Quinn stiffened at the bar, and Boardman threw the rancher a quick glance.

"Wait for me here," he said. "I shouldn't be more than a couple of minutes."

"Sure thing," the oldster replied, throwing a glance at his two men. "We'll be waiting for you."

Boardman nodded and followed the houseman along the bar. They passed through a doorway set in the wall beside the curtain screening the stage, and Boardman followed the man along a curving corridor. There were many doors opening off the corridor, and most of them were ajar. Glancing into the rooms as he passed by, Boardman saw that they were all occupied by showgirls. The houseman paused at the last door but one and rapped sharply on the panel, and Boardman heard a girl's voice call out an invitation to enter. The houseman grinned at him and turned away, and Boardman seized the handle of the door and opened it. He walked in and stood on the threshold, staring at Josie Whalen, his eyes narrowed and calculating, his mind jerked back into the past.

"Close the door," she snapped, and he did so. She was wearing a gown now, working on her face in front of a mirror, and her lips were thin as she caught his eyes in the glass.

Boardman advanced to her stool and stood staring into the mirror, holding her gaze. He was remembering that he had loved her once, and could still feel a faint trickling of emotion as he studied her.

Her face showed no welcome. There was no softness either. Her dark eyes were bright, wide and hard. Her hair was shoulder-length, glinting redly in the glare of the lamp. She lowered her eyes and picked up a brush from the table and started brushing her hair. Boardman was content to study her.

He had spent a long time five years ago, running down her associates. He had fallen in love with her, but had never been sure that she loved him. She had worked in a dance hall then, and had got information for a local gang from the men who had come to dance with her. It had all come out at the trial, and Boardman could remember her words when he had at last confronted her with his identity and accusations. She had promised to get back at him somehow, somewhere, for using her as he had done. He didn't get around to telling her that he really loved her. She had drawn two years for her part in the crime, and he had gone on to other assignments. They had never met again.

"I knew I would see you again someday," she said suddenly, and there was hatred in her voice. "What are you doing in this part of the country? Are you looking for some poor sap of a girl you can soft-talk into helping you?"

"I left the Rangers a couple of years ago," he lied. "I'm just an ordinary cowpoke, looking for work."

"My heart bleeds for you," she snapped. "So you've come down in the world. I thought for a moment, when I saw you out there, that you'd come to Burnt Hill to get the Coyotes."

"No, I've finished with that kind of a life," he told her. "And I hope you've finished your old living."

Her face hardened, and she got up from the seat. Her eyes dropped to his bandaged hand, and noted that he was wearing his gun on his left hip.

"So you've found some trouble already in this country. Word gets around fast in Burnt Hill. I didn't know it was you who found it. So you want a job, huh? Well, maybe I can help you, Chet."

"You wouldn't help me if I was dying," he retorted. "I can see it in your eyes, Josie. So you haven't forgotten the old days! I really loved you, you know, but I had a job to do."

"Sure." She smiled wickedly. "You loved me all right. Pity I ever believed you." Her eyes narrowed "Maybe I ought to get back at you for what you did to me." Before he could reply there was a knock at the door, and she called out an invitation. The door opened quickly and a big man walked into the room. He stood on the threshold, staring hard at Boardman, who studied him with narrowing eyes. The face was familiar, and he wondered if this was another from his past. Could it be a man from Josie's old gang? Then it came to him. He had seen this man's face on a dodger in the sheriff's office a short time ago. He had also seen it on a similar paper back in Austin. It was Pete Merrill, one of the Coyotes, and Merrill had been with Link Loman last night, when the half-breed had stabbed Boardman's gun hand!

Three

"Hi, Josie," the big, red-headed outlaw greeted. "I just looked in to tell you I'll be seeing something of you later." He paused and looked at Boardman. "Who's this? I ain't seen him around before. You ain't thinking of two-timing your old pard, are you?"

"This is Chet Boardman, Pete," the girl said, smiling at Boardman. "You must remember him. I've told you about him. He's the guy that got me that two years I spent in prison."

"A Texas Ranger!" the outlaw pushed the door shut with his heel and stiffened. There was no mistaking the menace that spread slowly through him.

"He was a Texas Ranger," Josie said. "Just simmer down, Pete. I don't want blood all over the floor around here. He's just an ordinary cowhand now, looking for a riding job. He called in to pay his respects to an old friend."

"Once a lawman always a lawman," Merrill snarled. "You better get out of Burnt Hill, Mister, or I'll get one of my pards to look you up."

"You already did that," Boardman said through his teeth. He lifted his right hand, showing the bandage. "Last night!"

"Are you that guy?" Merrill grinned, but did not relax. "So you got to town okay, huh? I figured you might bleed to death on the trail. I also figured that you wouldn't be fool enough to show up around here."

"Maybe that should be the other way around," Boardman snapped.

"I'm among friends here," Merrill said, creasing his fleshy face into a wide grin. "That's more than you can say, Boardman."

"That's so. Where's Loman?"

"You ain't still wanting to see him, are you? Can you use your gun on the left?"

"Try pulling yours and find out," Boardman invited, and saw hardness brighten in Merrill's eyes. "I'm gonna teach that Indian to be more careful when I meet up with him again."

"I'll tell him what you called him," the outlaw replied, grinning again. "I'd hate to mention in front of Josie what he did to the last guy who called him that to his face."

"I'll tell him. You just warn him from me," Boardman said. "I wasn't the man you were looking for last night."

"I don't think Loman will worry too much about that. Maybe I should take you to him, huh?"

"I'll come up with him," Boardman promised. "I'm sticking around in this county." He waved his right hand. "I don't take this off any man."

"Regular tough guy, huh?" Merrill sneered. "I've a mind to take your scalp back for Loman."

"You're welcome to try." Boardman wanted to give this man the opinion that he was as tough as any outlaw in the gang. If he was to get anywhere with this job he had to break the ice. This was as good a way as any. It was also the most dangerous.

"I'll leave you to Loman. Since you're so anxious to meet up with him I'll pass the word. He'll come looking you up. Now I got to be going. I hope for your sake that you've forgotten that you were once a lawman. If you go running to the sheriff here with tales I'll get to know about it before Wendell can make a move, and I'll put out your light. See you later, Josie."

"Okay, big-boy," the girl replied. Merrill backed out of the room and closed the door quickly. Boardman let his breath go slowly. He felt the girl's eyes on his face, and glanced down at her.

"What kind of a town is this?" he demanded. "Do they let crooks like him come and go as they please?"

"The Coyotes are a powerful gang," she said. "If you are still a Ranger and you've come here to try and trap them then you're a bigger fool than I thought. I hope you are doing just that, because they'll catch you if you are, and I'll be able to watch you squirm when Loman starts in to cut you to pieces. You always were a tough guy, Chet, but you've bitten off too much of a mouthful this trip."

"I'll kill Loman when I get the chance," he replied. "As for the rest of the gang, well, I gave up law work a couple of years ago, and I ain't doing anything that I don't get paid for. I'm after a riding job, and I think I've got one. I'll leave everything else to the lawmen who get paid for it."

"So you've actually got some sense." She laughed harshly. "But if you have got the sense you were born with you'll jump on your horse tonight and get out of this country."

"I'm set on staying, and I hope for your sake that you aren't running with the gang, Josie. I'd hate to see you go down for another term."

"This is a different set-up," she told him. "The Coyotes are stronger than the law. You'd better remember that. If anything happens to Loman you'll have every outlaw in the country out after you."

"I'm scared." He started for the door. "See you around sometime. Watch your step."

"Don't bother to call here. If I want to see you I'll send for you."

"That's mighty kind of you," he retorted, and left the room.

But his eyes were hard as he went back to the bar. He couldn't believe that she was not back working with the gang. He reasoned that she would never change, and hoped that she had swallowed his talk about having finished with the law. If she didn't fall for it then he was in bad trouble, and if he didn't take her advice and get out then he would be dead in a very short time. Thought of Pete Merrill showing up in town as if he had every right to be here made him realise just how secure the outlaws were in this part of the country. He hadn't believed them back at headquarters when they told him about this, and recalling Merrill's words about knowing if he went running to the sheriff warned him that there was a leak in the local law office. No wonder the five previous Rangers sent here had soon died. Perhaps it was the sheriff himself in league with the outlaws! He clenched his teeth, determined more than ever to do something about this blight that was lying on the country.

"Well, how did you make out?" Quinn demanded when he returned to the bar. He pushed another beer in front of Boardman.

"I don't know yet," he replied, and told the rancher what had occurred.

"We'd better get over to warn the sheriff," Quinn snapped, straightening, and Boardman grasped his arm.

"Not so fast. That's not the way to handle it. Someone in the sheriff's office is in contact with the gang, and I'm not gonna tip off my hand. I plan to hang around here until Loman shows up. If I kill him maybe I'll get somewhere."

"You'll surely do that," Quinn agreed. "You'll head straight for Boot Hill. That gang ain't no pushover, you know."

"That's right. That's why I'm holding my horses." Boardman let his gaze shift around the saloon. He sighed. "There must be half a dozen men in here right now who know where that hideout is. I ain't gonna find it by showing my hand. That will only draw me a bullet. I've got to play it smart, and somehow I can't help thinking that I ought to try and renew my old acquaintance with Josie. It'll be hard going at first. She's almost ready to throw a slug into my back herself. But I think I can handle her. She's mighty friendly with Pete Merrill, and he's a big gun in the gang. Maybe I should let it become known that I was thrown out of the Rangers for dishonesty. I might be able to worm my way into the gang."

"Rather you than me," Quinn told him. "There must be forty outlaws riding with Luke Harper. You'd die quicker than the flame of a snuffed-out candle if they ever got wise to you."

"I'm trying not to think of that," Boardman confessed. "I came into this country to try and pave the way to the end of the Coyotes, and this is the only way I can do it."

"I take my hat off to you, son," Quinn said. "I'll surely be ready to back you up any time you get on to something."

"I'm afraid this is one of those chores where a man has to work alone," Boardman reflected. "I prefer it that way, too. If anything goes wrong it'll mean I die. I don't want other men depending on me. I'm just groping in the dark, and it'll be like that until the outlaws make another move."

"Here comes Frederick Moss," Quinn observed. "He's making for us. Likely he's just got word that you were back there with Josie. There ain't much can happen in the whole county that he don't get to know about. I reckon you could do worse than try to make friends with him."

"I'll play it as it comes," Boardman said. He studied the man who came towards him with a smile on his fleshy face.

Moss was well dressed in black broadcloth. There was a pleasant expression on his face, and his pale blue eyes were filled with brightness. Moss was nearing forty, Boardman guessed, and the saloon owner still retained that elusive quality of youth. He was tall and broad, and his fair hair was slicked down, parted in the middle and brushed meticulously back. There wasn't a hair out of place. Reflected light glittered from the stone of a ring on one of his thick fingers. He came easily to where

Boardman was standing, and paused in front of him, although his eyes were on Quinn's weathered features.

"Howdy, Quinn, glad to see you in. Is this a friend of yours?" Moss's tone was smooth. Boardman got the feeling that Moss tried to convey an atmosphere of goodwill, tried to present a cordial manner, but didn't quite succeed. Perhaps for nine out of ten men it was good enough, but to Boardman, accustomed to looking deeper than the surface, there was an artificial front that could be seen through. He received the impression that for all his attempted smoothness, Frederick Moss was a rough, tough hardcase under it all.

"I met him on the trail last night, Frederick," Quinn said. "But I guess you already heard about that, huh?"

"Yeah, I got the word." Moss grinned disarmingly, and his blue eyes lifted to Boardman's tense face. He smiled reassuringly, and set himself on his widely parted feet. For a moment Boardman thought the man was going to take a swing at him, but Moss lifted a hand and signalled to the waiting bartender. He ordered beer all round, and didn't take his eyes off Boardman's face. "I also heard that you're an old-time friend of Josie's," he said. "I'd like to have a talk with you, Boardman."

"Anytime," Boardman replied.

"No time like the present." It seemed that Moss's pale blue eyes took on a glint that did not come from the glare of the many lamps.

"That's okay by me. In your office?"

"I'll lead the way." Moss turned and went back the way he had come, and Boardman caught Quinn's eye as he followed. The rancher gave him an almost imperceptible nod, and Boardman felt a little easier as he passed along the saloon. He had some chance of survival while the tough rancher and his two men were waiting for him, but he realised with a shiver that when Quinn went back to his ranch there would be no one and nothing to cover his back.

Moss's office was luxuriously furnished, and Boardman sank deep into a padded chair when he sat down. The saloon owner went to his desk and poured whisky into two glasses, then came back across the office and handed one to Boardman.

"I heard about your trouble last night out on the trail," Moss began. "I've since heard that you've threatened to kill Link Loman for doing it. Now I reckon it's a natural thing to want vengeance for an injury like that, but I better warn you that you'll wind up dead before this time tomorrow if Loman comes into town looking for you."

"I reckon I could about hold my own in a fair fight," Boardman responded.

"Who said it would be a fair fight?" Moss smiled. "I guess you've heard something about the Coyotes, huh?"

"More than enough to convince me that something should be done about them."

"That's the lawman in you talking. It's a very dangerous attitude for a young man. You should have left that attitude back in Austin, with your star."

"I don't doubt that. But you haven't called me in here just to warn me about my behaviour. And if you're worried about the Coyotes getting me then I've got you summed up wrong."

Moss stared at him for a moment, and it seemed to Boardman's watchful eye that the saloon owner's poise slipped a little. Then the smile returned, and the pale eyes were serene and friendly again. But the voice was sharp.

"You're right. You're a stranger to me, so why should I concern myself about your fate? You came off bad against the outlaws last night, and any young man who can handle a gun reasonably well would want to have a shot at the man who maimed him. But I'm interested in you because you knew Josie several years ago."

"If you spoke to Josie about me then you'll have found out that she hates me worse than a polecat," Boardman said. "I sent her down for two years, and she was under the impression that I played on her emotions in order to get at the gang she was working with."

"That's about the weight of it, Boardman. But I'm curious about the past. Josie talked about you some since she's been here with me, and I reckon that many women taken as she was wouldn't have breathed the name of the man who had betrayed her. I think Josie is still in love with you."

"That's a laugh." Boardman did not change expression, for he knew that Moss was watching him closely for reactions. "If I showed Josie my back she'd stick a knife in it." He drank some of the whisky. "But what's so interesting about that?"

"I'm in love with Josie, and one day I'm gonna marry her. I've waited some time now for her to get around to accepting me. I want you to know that I won't stand for you coming into this country and busting things up for me."

"I'm just a cowpoke looking for work," Boardman said. "I've got myself fixed up, thanks to Frank Quinn. I'm not interested in Josie or the past, or the Coyotes. If I do meet up with Loman then I'll kill him, but that's as far as it goes. Does that satisfy you?"

"I'm a man of intense emotions, Boardman. I don't want you around here, even if you promise to stay out of Burnt Hill. I have a lot of influence in this country, more than most people suspect. I'm not being nasty about this, but I'm telling you straight and plain. It would be wiser for you to leave this part of Texas."

"I've got to make a stake before I can pull out," Boardman retorted.

"I'll give you a hundred dollars."

"I'm a mighty independent man. I couldn't accept money from a stranger."

"Then I'm sorry for you, Boardman. If you stick around here someone might get the idea that you're in the way. You'll wind up on Boot Hill."

"I'm also an obstinate man," Boardman said smoothly. "And I don't take kindly to threats. I'll tell you just one more time that Josie means nothing to me. I don't want to see her again, and I'm damned sure that she's of the same mind. If she stood near me in the saloon it would be to poison my beer. I guess that takes care of that, huh?"

"Not quite," Moss said, getting to his feet and taking the glass from Boardman's hand. He went to his desk and set down the glasses. When he returned his eyes were hard and intent. His face was filled with deadly intention, the façade gone for the first time since Boardman had met him. Now he could glimpse the real man in Frederick Moss, and he didn't like what he saw. "I'll tell you just once, Boardman. Get out of town, and don't even stop to water your horse until you're out of the county."

Boardman got to his feet and moved to the door. He turned when he reached it, his hand on the handle. He smiled thinly, then shook his head.

"You know, Moss, I've got the feeling that we would have got on much better if you'd laid all your cards on the table. But you're lying through your teeth, and you've made me curious about the whole thing. I reckon I'll stick around, and you can tell that to your friends. I'm in this county to make some dough and I'm gonna do it."

He jerked open the door and a houseman nearly fell into the office. Boardman side-stepped the staggering figure and departed. When he got back to the bar he found that Quinn and his two men had gone.

Pausing to glance around, Boardman saw Josie down at the far end of the saloon. The girl was looking at him, and he reached up and touched the brim of his hat. Then he turned for the door and left the saloon.

As soon as he stepped into the shadows on the sidewalk he got the icy feeling that all was not well. He pushed his back to the wall and surveyed the stretch of darkness. There were lighted lamps at intervals along the street, but they did nothing to dissipate the darkness. They formed pools of yellow light, and made observation harder than if they were not there. His eyes were baffled by the alternating extremes, and Boardman sharpened his ears, knowing that he would have to rely more upon them than sight.

He let his mind touch the situation, and quickly realised that either Pete Merrill or Frederick Moss could have arranged for someone to wait for him out here. He had been outlined in the doorway as he emerged, and now he could be under the alert gaze of some hired killer. But what really touched him was the absence of Quinn and the two cowboys. Was Quinn mixed up in this somewhere? He grinned at the thought. He had told the rancher that he was a lawman. He knew that the outlaws were really well organised in this country, but had they run over men like Quinn?

Boardman began to edge for a corner. There were a narrow alley each side of the saloon, he had noted, but coldness filled him when he figured that an ambusher might be waiting in one of them. His spurs tinkled, and he stopped moving immediately. He didn't like this. He thought of Link Loman, of the knife that had wounded him, and his nerves tightened. He had to take a grip on himself before he could move again. It wouldn't do to let his thoughts scare him. He would have to face out the hours of darkness, for it was then that they would likely come from him.

Why was it a known outlaw like Pete Merrill could come and go as he pleased in this town? Merrill had said, although not directly, that he had a friend in the law office. Was that friend the sheriff himself? The outlaw had told Josie that he would see her again later. Did that mean Josie was back at her old tricks?

Boardman reached the corner and eased himself into the alley mouth. Something poked him in the back, and he stiffened. It was the muzzle of a gun, and there was something lethal in its hardness.

'Okay, Chet, I recognise you,' a soft voice hissed in his ear, and he recognised Quinn's voice. He turned to face the old rancher, and Quinn pressed him against the wall. 'A houseman came and told me that you were leaving the saloon by the side door. When we got out here and didn't find you I figured that it was a gun-trap, but I ain't seen nothing yet."

"They want to get me alone," Boardman said.

"What did Moss have to talk about?"

Boardman told the rancher, and tried to guess what was behind Moss's attitude. Was it as Moss had said? Did the saloon owner love Josie so much that he couldn't bear to see an old friend of hers around? He couldn't believe that. Moss wasn't the kind of man to buy off opposition. What was happening now was Moss's usual way of handling trouble.

"Parfitt and Newman are across the street, Chet," the rancher said softly. "I don't like the look of this. They must suspect that you are still a Ranger. They won't let you get away. I think the only thing you can do is ride out with me. I'm leaving in the morning. We'll head for my ranch, and then I'll have you escorted out of the country. Your usefulness is gone. You're a marked man."

"It seems that way," Boardman admitted. He narrowed his eyes and studied the dark patterns. There was plenty of light from the star-crowded sky, now his eyes had become accustomed to the gloom, and he could even make out the shape of one of Quinn's men standing on the other side of the street. He saw nothing else suspicious. He moved his right hand slowly, wincing at a sudden twinge of pain. "I've made a real mess of this job," he mused. "My hand is busted. Josie recognised me. I've been warned off by Moss. I don't get the half of it, Quinn. How can a bad man like Pete Merrill wander around town as he does?"

"It'll need more than my local knowledge to answer that," Quinn replied. "Come on, we'd better get back to the hotel. I shan't be happy until you're locked in your room, and don't open the door until dawn. We'd better get out of town as soon as we can."

"I can't leave," Boardman said stubbornly. "I've got to stick this out. I came here to do a job, and I knew before I arrived that I would likely stop lead before it was over. Five Rangers have already been killed. I'm the last effort before the whole country is taken over. Martial law will be declared if I fail. But the trouble with that is the outlaws will drift if things become tough. We don't want that to happen. We want to catch them."

"I admire your nerve," Quinn said gruffly. "I'll stay on in town another day and see what I can do to help. I should be able to get some of the local men to back you up."

"I reckon something will break before tomorrow is over," Boardman said. "What do you think of the sheriff? Is he straight? Is he the contact man for the outlaws? They'd surely try and get him into their pockets. Or is it one of his deputies?"

"No one can tell what's in a man's mind, or what he's really like," Quinn said slowly. "Personally I'd stake my life on Wendell's honesty, but I've been wrong before. You'll never know the answer to that one until it's proved either way."

"I'm in the dark and alone," Boardman said. "I know you've offered to help, and I'm grateful, but you must see that at first I've got to work alone, if they don't kill me. If they see I'm running around with men backing me they're gonna realise that I am still a Ranger. It's a one-man job, and I'm elected."

"So what are you going to do?"

"Nothing right now. I don't think it's my move. I've got to wait for events to develop. If Loman shows up I'm gonna have to fight him. If I die then it doesn't matter, but if I beat him I'm gonna have to find out where Frederick Moss fits into this, and Josie." His heart seemed to lurch when he spoke her name, and he realised that he still had a lot of feeling for her. But now there was no hope. He would have to arrest her with the others, if he got the chance. She was bad, and there could be no excuses for her. She'd had more than one chance of turning over a new leaf, but it had never been her intention to go straight. "Come on," he said, suddenly sickened. "I think it's time for bed."

Quinn led the way out of the alley and they went quickly along the sidewalk to Boyd's Hotel. Glancing back once, Boardman saw the two cowhands moving along behind, and he was thankful that someone was covering his back. He went straight up the stairs to his room, and Quinn escorted him to his door.

"Lock it behind you," the rancher directed, "and don't open it to anyone until the sun shows."

"Sure, and thanks." Boardman went into the room and closed the door, turning the key in the lock. He crossed to the window and drew the heavy curtains before striking a match and lighting the lamp. Then he lounged back on the bed, placing his injured right hand across his chest. He lay gazing up at the ceiling, trying to piece together those small items which he had already picked up. But he didn't like the set-up. Outlaws were wandering around the town after dark as if they had nothing to fear from the law. Josie was involved, and so was Frederick Moss. Moss had already intimated that he was more powerful than most folk thought. Did that mean a tie-in with the Coyotes?

He lay thinking until he dozed into sleep, but his brain refused him rest. His hand and wrist were hurting like hell, and he kept holding up the limb, which seemed to lessen the intense throbbing. He wondered if the wounds were turning gangrene. Surely the pain should be dying by now! He sighed and sat up, and a slight movement at the door attracted his eyes. He frowned when he saw a white slip of paper moving under the door. It was flicked from the outside, and came several inches into the room.

For a moment Boardman stared at it. He couldn't hear the sound of footsteps outside. Then he stood up and moved noiselessly to the door and bent and picked up the paper. It was a single sheet of notepaper, folded once, and there was a short message scribbled in spidery handwriting. It was unsigned. The message intimated that the writer had some information that would be of value to him, and it would be divulged if he were to leave his room now and head for the bank. If he stood in the alley on the north side of the bank he would be met.

So it had come quicker than he'd hoped! He read the note again, staring with narrowed eyes, and his heart slowly increased its beating until he had to breathe deeply to compose himself. It was so obviously a trap that he just had to go and hope to beat the play. He checked his gun, flexing the fingers of his left hand and wishing that both hands were able to hold weapons. Would it be Link Loman waiting in the darkness for him, holding that cruel, glittering blade? Or had Frederick Moss decided to finish him off?

Boardman placed the position of the bank in his mind, and recalled the alley at its side. He eased his Colt in its holster and blew out the lamp. He stood for a moment in the darkness of the room, then remembered his spurs and removed them, making it an awkward task with his left hand. He opened the door gently and peered into the passage. It was deserted, and he slipped out of the room, pausing only to lock the door. He went the opposite way along the passage and found the back stairs, wondering if the writer of the note would expect him to make such a move.

He had to believe that they would expect him to try and cover his approach. He knew that he was in their hands by doing so, but he could not bring himself to walk boldly out the front door and along to the bank. If he was going to die then he wanted to take at least one of these bad men along with him.

There was complete darkness outside the back of the hotel, and he stood for several minutes in the shadows, waiting for his eyes to become accustomed to it. He found that he was breathing deeply through his mouth, and realised that he was stiff with tension. This was the toughest assignment he'd ever tried to handle.

When he moved off he walked deliberately, knowing that he was likely heading into a gun-trap. But he had to follow every lead that came his way. Yet he was puzzled that someone should know he was interested in the situation around here. He was, on the face of it, only a no-account stranger, and that fact alone prompted him to believe that this was a trap.

He counted off the alleys as he passed them, glad that his training stood him in good stead. He had automatically studied this town when he first arrived, and thought that he could find his way around now without too much trouble. He paused when he reached the alley beside the bank, and flattened himself against the wall of the building. Now his gun was in his hand, and he bated his breath, his eyes flickering around. When he moved it was very slowly and silently. Yet he believed that he was already under observation by the person who had sent the note. If it was a gun-trap then the killers would already be closing in.

There was a breeze blowing along the alley, fanning his face, cooling the sweat on his forehead, and he shivered. He had looked for excitement when he first joined the Rangers but figured now that he'd had more than his fair share. He walked into a pile of crates, and the top one fell from the stack and hit him on the head. The impact drove him to his knees, and he stayed down, teeth clenched against the pain in his hand, which had been struck. He cursed under his breath, knowing that he had betrayed his position, and now there was nothing for it but to stay where he was and wait for the next move. He was almost shocked when a woman's voice spoke to him from the other side of the crates.

"Is that you, Boardman?" she demanded.

Four

Boardman regained his feet quickly. He flattened himself against the wall, the fallen crate somewhere at his feet. He caught sight of a faint movement, and levelled his gun. The next instant a woman's soft body was pressed against him, and the muzzle of his Colt was boring her stomach.

"For God's sake don't make any more noise," she whispered harshly. "They'll kill me if they find out about this. And you can put away that gun in case it goes off. It's not a trap. I'm alone."

"Who are you? I don't know you. What could you tell me that I'd find valuable?"

"We have a mutual friend," she replied. "Listen, I'm taking a big risk coming here. If I should be missed then I'll die. They don't take any chances, and everyone is watched around here. I've got to warn you that they'll try for you tomorrow. If you've got any sense you'll saddle up right now and get out of the country. But I've been told that that's the last thing you'll do. Don't go to the sheriff. There's someone in his office working with the outlaws."

There was the sound of an uncertain foot in the darkness at the street end of the alley, and the woman thrust herself into Boardman's arms, trembling with fear. They remained in close embrace, and Boardman could smell her perfume. He had thought at the first instant that this was Josie, but he could just make out the shape of her head and knew it wasn't Josie.

They stood motionless, listening to someone coming along the alley, and Boardman drew his gun again. He peered around the crates, and spotted movement, slowly picking out the shape of a man. The woman pressed herself closer to him, and he could hear her quickened breathing, felt the fast beating of her heart against his thin shirt. Her forehead touched his chin, and he could feel the dampness of sweat on her brow.

The tension seemed to grow to overwhelming proportions, stifling and nerve-racking. The approaching figure was ominous, the furtive sounds menacing. Boardman moistened his lips. Now he was really up against it, but there was a humorous side to this. He was standing in a dark alley with an unknown woman in his arms, and death was likely closing in upon the both of them.

But the stranger passed by, feeling his way through the darkness with a hand pressed to the opposite wall. Boardman wondered what would have happened had he chosen their side of the alley and put a hand upon them. The woman drew back a little after the man had gone, and Boardman heard her great sigh of relief.

"Don't ask any questions," she said. "I can feel that you're full of them. Just listen so I can get away from here. It's too dangerous. If I've been missed I shall have to account for my movements. You've got to realise that this is too much for you. You're out of your depth. Nearly every other man in this town is working for the outlaws in one way or another."

"You're talking as if the outlaws mean something to me," he responded.

"That's obvious," she replied with a nervous laugh. "If they didn't, you wouldn't be here now. So stop trying to play games. Your life is in danger, and so is mine now. I'm trying to warn you off."

"Thanks for taking the risk. But I don't know you. I don't know what you're driving at. You say we have a mutual friend. Are you from the saloon? Did Josie send you?"

"That's right. She couldn't come herself. Moss watches her like a hawk. She told me to tell you to save yourself."

"Josie made her real feelings quite plain to me," he replied softly. "If she wants me to run then it must be safer for me to stay."

"You fool! Don't you know when a woman is in love with you?"

"Josie?"

"Certainly not me," she retorted. "I only saw you once this evening. I can understand why Josie is crazy about you, but you're not worth what she's risking." She paused. "I must go now."

He holstered his gun and took hold of her arm. She did not struggle.

"Listen," he said. "I loved Josie a long time ago. I threw her in jail when I could have let her go. But I figured that she had a lesson to learn. I tried to see her in jail but she didn't want to know me, and I can't say as I blame her. When I saw her earlier tonight she made it clear that she hated the sight of me. What's she doing this for? I can only think of one reason. She wants revenge."

"You've got her wrong, Boardman," the woman retorted. "I know Josie, and I know that she's taking this risk for you because she loves you. She would have come herself despite Moss and the others. I had to talk her out of it."

"Okay, so you've warned me. But I told Josie that I'd finished with the Rangers."

"She doesn't believe you. You're a lawman, and you're fated to die tomorrow as sure as the sun comes up."

He tightened his lips, staring at the pale blur of her face. He heard her sigh of impatience.

"Tell Josie that I'm sorry," he said. "I appreciate what you've tried to do, but I'm staying."

"Then I'll say goodbye to you," she retorted. "By this time tomorrow night you'll be lying in a casket in the undertaker's parlour. I'll tell Josie that I saw you."

Then she was gone, her footsteps echoing in his heart. He stood motionless, with the faint smell of her perfume in his nostrils, and he tried to get Josie out of his mind. Had she really tried to warn him off because she felt something for him? He recalled her face and what she had said in her room, and his mind went back several years to another part of Texas. He shook his head slowly, sadly, and pulled at his bottom lip with his teeth. She hadn't been fooled by his story that he had left the Rangers. Yet she had mentioned that fact to Pete Merrill. She had left the Coyotes know that he had been a lawman. But perhaps that had been a clever move. If they had found out later they would have wanted to know why she didn't mention it earlier.

He started retracing his footsteps to the hotel, and when he reached the back lots he hesitated. He wanted to see Josie, to talk to her himself when he could see her face and reactions. But he forced himself to forget the thought. He had to keep a clear head. He couldn't afford to let his mind become crowded with emotion. He would have to treat Josie as a hostile person, and expect that at some time in the future she would attempt to get her revenge on him. He reached the hotel without further incident and went to bed, but it was a long time before he went to sleep.

An insistent knocking on the door brought him back to reality, and he sat up, nursing his injured hand. He stared at the door for a moment, then got out of bed and pulled on his pants. He stamped into his boots and crossed to the door, lifting his gun from the holster as he passed the bedpost. He opened the door cautiously and saw Frank Quinn waiting outside.

"Ready for breakfast?" the rancher demanded. "How did you sleep?"

"Fine. I'll be with you in a minute." Boardman went back into the room and washed, then finished dressing. The rancher was in the corridor when he left the room, talking to one of his men, and they went down to the dining-room together.

Boardman was silent during the meal. He saw Moss and Josie come in and take a corner table, and although the saloon owner stared at him, the girl never looked in his direction. Quinn saw the direction of Boardman's glance, and moved his chair so that he could watch Moss without being noticed.

"He's got his eyes on you, Chet," the rancher commented. "I don't like it. I've got a feeling that they're gonna make a try for you some time today."

"I know they are," Boardman replied, but did not volunteer any more information. "I'm thinking that perhaps I'd better handle this from the other angle. I came to Burnt Hill in the hope of picking up a lead that would take me to the hideout. It's obvious now that I shan't be able to do that. So I'd better head out into the wilds and try to find the hideout for myself. There must be some movement out there by the gang, and I have enough patience to lie up and watch."

"You'll be making a fatal mistake if you try that," Quinn said. "I reckon some of that gang are waiting right now for you to show your nose outside town. You know what happened to you when Loman got to work. Well, the next time he ain't gonna just maim you. You'll be reaching for death when they drop onto you again."

"I can't afford to waste any time around here," Boardman said. "It may seem a bit like suicide to you, but it's my job. I'll go pay the Doc a visit and get my hand fixed, then I'll saddle up and ride."

"Maybe we can help you," Quinn said. "I can't tell you where the hideout is, but I can tell you where it ain't. I also better tell you that I've got some of my men watching a few of the trails I've found. The whole country is crossed by trails that honest men don't use, and I've had some of my crew out looking for strange riders, with orders to follow them. So far we ain't had any luck, but I'm still hoping."

"I'm glad to hear that some folk in the country are trying to do something about this menace," Boardman said. "It's a pity a lot more don't try. This situation wouldn't have got so much out of hand if everyone worked together."

"That's the fault of the sheriff," Quinn said. "Look, there's Wendell now, and he's gonna sit at Moss's table. Maybe that'll answer some of your questions for you. You've said you think maybe the sheriff is in with the gang. Maybe there's something in that."

"I'll find out, if I should live so long," Boardman replied. "Now I'd better go see the Doc. Will you wait for me?"

"I'll do better than that, I'll come with you," Quinn said. "Newman will stick around. I sent Parfitt back to the ranch to tell them at home that I won't be returning for a day or two."

They got up and left the dining-room, and Boardman felt Moss's hard gaze upon him as they departed. They paused on the sidewalk, and Boardman glanced around the sunlit street.

"I reckon you're making yourself some bad enemies, Quinn," he commented. "If Moss is in league with the gang then he's gonna make a report that you're siding me."

"They already know where I stand," Quinn said grimly. "I'm just waiting for the action to start. Last night after you went to bed I rounded up some of my old friends and tried to sound them out. I didn't let on about anything, you can bet, but I laid it on the line for them. I told them what we've got to do when the time comes. Most of them agreed to back me up. There are one or two big ranches in the country, and I know the owners. I'm gonna do some riding soon and put the same question to them. I reckon you'll be able to count close on a hundred guns backing you should you ever find this gang."

"I'm glad to hear that." Boardman started walking along the sidewalk, and the old rancher sided him. "But the most difficult job is gonna be to find that hideout and get those outlaws all together for a good fight. If they get wind of these preparations they're either gonna hit us first or they'll cut and run."

"They won't run," Quinn asserted. "Harper is too well set in around here. A lot of these smaller ranchers have thrown in with him. They warn him when a posse rides, and they feed him information. That's why I reckon a new approach will have to be made. The old method of finding the hideout and taking in a posse won't work here."

"That's all been taken care of," Boardman said. "I can't tell you anything more right now, Quinn, but you can rely upon it that the outlaws will get a real shock one of these days. A good plan was laid a long time ago, and that's why it's important for me to get a line on things around here."

"Some kind of a trap, huh?" The rancher's eyes shone. "I like the sound of that."

They went into the doctor's house, and Boardman spent a painful ten minutes, but he was relieved when the doctor told him that there was no sign of poison in his wounds. When the hand was rebandaged they took their leave again, and on the street Boardman spotted three riders swinging away from the hitching-rail in front of the Cartwheel Saloon. He didn't know why they should attract his eye, or why he watched them after that first searching glance, but he did watch them, and saw one, then another, ease the gun holstered at his waist.

"Those three riders coming towards us, Quinn," Boardman said out of the corner of his mouth, not taking his eyes off the approaching men. "They look like trouble to me."

The rancher stiffened, looked at the three men, then let his eyes rove away. He started to step away from Boardman, moving casually.

"I'll take them from the left if they're after our hides," he said quickly, and Boardman nodded.

The riders came a little faster, and dust rose around the hooves of their mounts. Boardman took up a stand beside a post, leaning his right shoulder against it. His left hand was tense as he lifted it casually to his hip. The riders kicked their horses and travelled a little faster. They came up quickly, and Boardman could see that they were priming themselves for trouble. They hadn't taken their eyes off him since reining away from the hitching-rail.

Then they were reaching for their guns, and Boardman caught the glint of sunlight on their naked steel. He set his left hand into motion, jerking his gun and thumbing back the long-eared hammer in one fluid movement. A Colt boomed, and splinters flew from the post at his shoulder. He didn't even flinch, and fired at the right-hand rider, aiming off to allow for the man's speed. He scored a hit and shifted his aim to the second man, and now the silence was gone and echoes were raging around the town. Smoke blossomed, and lead thudded into the building behind Boardman. A woman screamed, and along the street more than one dog started barking.

Frank Quinn was throwing lead, and the left-hand man tumbled heavily from his saddle and lay motionless in the slowly rising dust. Boardman fired at the centre man, hearing the crackle of a closely passing slug as the man fired his first shot. The right-hand man was out of his saddle, the horse veering away to the opposite side of the street.

Boardman worked his gun, and the centre man twisted sharply and then went over backwards. One of his boots caught in a stirrup and he was dragged through the dust by his bolting horse. The right-hand man fought to control his animal, and swung back to face the sidewalk. His gun came up, and both Boardman and Quinn cut loose at him. They drove him out of his saddle with a spate of rapid shooting.

There were a number of townsfolk on the street, and those who had not run for cover at the first shot were standing petrified in the attitudes they had adopted at the disturbance. Someone ran out into the street and stopped the bolting horse, and Boardman stepped off the sidewalk and walked slowly across to the nearer of the two prone figures in front of him.

Frank Quinn remained on the sidewalk, his gun in his hand and his eyes watching for further trouble. Boardman threw a glance at the hotel and saw Sheriff Wendell coming down the steps. The lawman half-ran towards him, and reached his side as Boardman bent to check the first of the two gunmen. He did no more than glance at the man to see that he was dead, and walked around the sheriff to look at the second. Both men were dead.

"What happened?" Wendell demanded.

"Don't you know?" Boardman countered.

"What the hell is that supposed to mean?"

"I'm a stranger in this town," Boardman said. "I'm only going on what I've been told. I guess you know all about me now. I reckon I don't have to explain anything. These three men made a play for me and Quinn, and lost out."

"I don't like the sound of that," Wendell said. "Maybe you'd better come across to my office and explain it."

"There's a leak in your office," Boardman said thinly, glancing around the street. Quinn was coming forward, still holding his gun, and following the rancher was his cowhand, Newman. Over on the sidewalk in front of the hotel, Josie was standing with Frederick Moss.

"What's it to do with you how my office is run?" the sheriff persisted. "I heard a rumour that you're a Ranger."

"Was a Ranger, and I guess old habits die hard. But I never did like a crooked lawman."

"Are you calling me?" Wendell demanded.

"There are six deputies working for you," Boardman stated. "I spoke to Pete Merrill last night. He was in the saloon, walking around as if he owned the place. He as good as admitted that he had friends in the law department, and so did Frederick Moss. I saw you at Moss's table this morning. I guess it ain't hard to put two and two together."

"That's so." Wendell smiled, but only with his lips. His grey eyes were hard and thoughtful. "Maybe you've forgotten that a good lawman will mix with anyone in the execution of his duties. How come you're so damned interested in the situation around here if you ain't a Ranger?"

"This." Boardman held up his injured right hand. "An outlaw did this to me, and three others held me. It's a helluva note when such a thing can happen, and afterwards a man has to listen to threats because he wants to meet the man who knifed him."

"Maybe we can get together," Wendell said. "This was good work. I hear that you came into the country looking for a job. Well, I'll offer you one. You can ride as a deputy for me if you like."

"I'll think it over." Boardman glanced at the silent Quinn, who was standing nearby reloading his gun. The rancher waited for Boardman to finish talking before he opened his mouth.

"Listen to me, Sheriff," he said heavily. "This is the last straw. I'm gonna stick around this town until the outlaws are dead or in jail. These three guys had the sign on them the minute we walked out of the Doc's place. Someone paid them to come for Boardman and me. This ain't the first time something's been planned for me, and I reckon it won't be the last. Well, I'm not gonna wait for the next. I can't always be lucky. I'm gonna raise a vigilante force in this town, like they did up north before the war. We're gonna bring some peace to this county if we have to string up a hundred bad men to get it."

"That's no way to talk, Quinn," Wendell countered. "It's dangerous. I don't hold with that kind of thing."

"There's a lot you ain't holding with," the rancher retorted angrily. "I don't see your department having much success with the outlaws. How much longer have we got to put up with them?"

"I'm doing my job the best way I know," Wendell said. He glanced around at the gathering crowd. "Listen to me, Quinn. You've known me for a lot of years, and until this gang started operating in this country I always did run a good brand of law. But this business needs a different touch. I'm working undercover now. When it looks like I ain't doing anything in particular against the outlaws it's because I don't want to raise any kind of alarm. But I've got a special deputy or two at work in the county, and I'm getting some facts together."

"There's a leak in your department," Quinn said. "One of your deputies is working for the gang."

"So I've heard," the sheriff snapped. "Well, I'll take steps on that right away. Maybe I know where to put my finger, too."

"Have you got any idea who these three are?" Quinn demanded, looking down at the dead men. "I ain't ever seen them around before. But then the country is full of guys like them."

"I've seen them around town, but they ain't been here long."

"New guns brought into the country," Quinn said bitterly. "You mark my words, Sheriff, this whole thing will blow up in our faces unless we do something strong about it. Where do these outlaws hide out? Who supplies them with their food? Who runs information to them? I've realised how it's only the big raids that are being made. They seem to know when the bank is shifting money or there's a gold shipment passing through from Arizona. It's about time something was done."

"I'm doing my best," the sheriff protested. "You know just how tough it is working in this kind of country. There's no organisation."

"There is," Boardman said, "and that's the trouble. It's all on the side of the outlaws."

"You put your finger on it," Quinn said eagerly. "We've got to get ourselves organised, Sheriff."

"You tell me how and I'll go ahead and do it," the lawman said. "But I don't like it. I sometimes think it would be better if they called the army in."

Boardman did not reply. He studied the faces of the dead men. The man who had stopped the bolting horse had led it back, and its rider was now hung over the saddle, blood dripping down one arm and trickling over the back of a slack hand.

"It looks like I've got to be ready for anything," he remarked.

"Are you planning on riding out?" the sheriff asked, and Boardman detected a note of eagerness in the lawman's voice.

"It's mighty tough country around here," he replied. "I guess I might pull out at that. Seems I ain't gonna get any satisfaction at all from the man who knifed my hand."

"I'll keep a tighter watch on the town," Wendell promised. "There won't be any more outlaws riding in."

Quinn turned away and Boardman followed him. They went back to the sidewalk, and Boardman paused to reload his gun. He gazed at the old rancher, and they grinned. Now there was a bond between them. They had stood side by side and fought a swift battle. They had come out on top, and now they were closer than brothers.

"You smacked lead into two of those sidewinders," Quinn said.

"Were they outlaws?" Boardman demanded.

"How can we say for sure?" Quinn sighed. He glanced around. "I've got a good idea to start the vigilante force I mentioned. Look at the crowd out there now. The shooting has drawn them. If I got a meeting going tonight I think I'd get a lot of response. It's worth a try. You ain't planning on leaving town, are you?"

"Not just yet," Boardman replied. "I think I'll go along and have another talk with Moss. I've got the feeling he knows who paid those three men to shoot at us."

"Do you want Newman to go along with you?"

"No thanks. I'll handle it myself. I work best alone."

"I reckon that depends upon the odds," the old rancher chuckled. "See you later then, and don't go wandering off the main street. If you get cut off you'll be in bad trouble."

Boardman thought about it as he went along the sidewalk, pushing through the crowd. He approached the Cartwheel Saloon and saw Moss and Josie ahead of him, just turning into the building. He saw Moss glance back at him before entering the place, and tightened his lips. When he shouldered his way through the batwings, Moss was standing at the bar, talking to a couple of tough-looking housemen, and Josie was nowhere to be seen.

The saloon owner turned as Boardman approached, and he smiled thinly, his blue eyes slitted and hard. One of the two men moved away, and Boardman took up a position at the bar that left his gun hand free and away from Moss.

"Well," he said with a smile. "You didn't waste any time, Moss, did you?"

"Do you think I was responsible for that shoot-out?" the saloon owner demanded. He sounded shocked, but there was grim amusement in his pale eyes. He studied Boardman's harshly set features, then beckoned for the tender, who slid a whisky bottle along the bar and followed it with a couple of glasses. "You're making a big mistake, Boardman." He poured a couple of drinks and pushed one in front of Boardman, who picked up the glass and held it out in a steady hand. "Listen, I threatened you because I figured that you were an ordinary cowpoke who drifted in. But now I see that I was wrong. Okay, so you're the law. I reckon you're gonna grab the country by its ear and shake the guts out of it."

"You're talking way above my head," Boardman said. "I saw those three guys come out of the saloon and mount up out front. I got it figured that you paid them for what they tried."

"Are you gonna have me arrested?"

"No. I don't believe in the law." Boardman smiled. "Especially the law around here."

"Wendell is a good sheriff."

"Yeah, but good for whom? He ain't got a good record against the outlaws, has he?"

"It's a tough set-up, as he's found out. It's more than a one-man job."

"Well, surely it's in the interests of men like you to help the law catch these outlaws." Boardman threw a glance at Moss's bland face.

"Sure, and I've told Wendell more than once that any time he gets the outlaws trapped he's only got to ask for my help and he can have it."

Boardman finished his drink and set down the glass. He declined another.

"How would you like to work for me?" Moss asked.

"Last night you were offering me a hundred dollars to get out of the country. This morning you hired three gunmen to take care of me, and now you want me on your payroll. What's behind this, Moss?"

"I figure that you and me should be friends. I think I could stand it having you around and Josie."

"I don't know so much about that. A jealous man is unpredictable. I don't think I'd have much future working for you. I reckon you want me where you can see me all the time."

"I pay good wages, better than you'd draw from that fool Quinn."

"I've found Quinn a very useful man," Boardman said. "He took care of some of the details out there on the street a short time ago. When is Pete Merrill coming in to see you again?"

Boardman was watching Moss's face in the mirror behind the bar, and he grinned when he saw that his unexpected change of subject took the saloon owner off guard. Moss set down his glass, lifting his gaze to meet Boardman's eyes in the mirror.

"What's your interest in the outlaws?" he demanded.

"I want to meet Link Loman again, and repay him for this." Boardman held up his injured hand. "Maybe someone should tell that Indian I can use my left hand. I hear he takes care of a thing like that."

"I reckon Loman has already heard what you've got to say," Moss retorted.

"If you'll tell me where the hideout is I'll ride out there and look him up," Boardman said softly.

"I could make a fortune by revealing that secret, if I knew it," Moss told him with a grin. "There's a helluva reward on the heads of that gang."

"Perhaps you never gave that a thought until now," Boardman said. "Think it over. It might be the way of ridding the country of these snakes."

Boardman turned and headed for the door. He reached the batwings before Moss called him back. When he turned, the saloon owner jerked a thumb along the bar.

"Come into my office where we can talk in private," he invited.

Boardman hesitated for the barest fraction before nodding. He went back along the bar, and Moss led the way. The saloon owner pushed open the door and Boardman entered the office. He took a seat so that he could face the door, and Moss smiled.

"Whisky?" Moss invited.

"No thanks. I don't drink that much. What have you got on your mind, Moss?"

"I can put you on to Loman, if that's what you want," the saloon owner said gently. He went to his desk and sat down. "I'm not sure of you, Boardman. I've got my doubts about you being an ex-Ranger. Maybe you're trying to work a fast one around here. Maybe you've even got Josie working for you again, like she did last time. It's a fact that a woman will never learn her lesson when it involves the man she loves."

"You're crazy," Boardman said, trying not to appear too emphatic. "I told you how it was between me and Josie. You give her some poison and you can watch her tip it into my glass when I ain't looking. But you've got something up your sleeve, Moss. If you hand Loman over to me, what do you get for it?"

"Loman has annoyed me in the past. If you can kill him then I'll be happy. But I don't think you can do it."

"Where can I find him?"

"There's a gold shipment leaving here tonight on the coach. It'll be a cinch that the outlaws will know about it. I've studied their tactics, and something seems to tell me that the coach will be held up at Aspen Crest. You can always find out where that is. Quinn can show you. Get out there and kill Loman."

"And me and Quinn will walk into an ambush and die," Boardman said with a smile. "I ain't that green, Moss. What's really on your mind? You want me out of the way for some reason, and you're racking your brains for the right way of doing it. If that's how you feel about me, you can always call me out and step into the street. That's legal enough."

"I don't do my fighting like that," Moss said, his eyes glittering. "But I've told you about Loman."

"How do you know that he'll be there?"

"He'll be there. I learn a lot in this business. But I don't think you're man enough to handle the chore. You've been shouting off your mouth about what you'd do to him, so now prove it."

"Just me and Quinn, huh? I suppose Loman is gonna rob this coach by himself, huh? You're still not coming clean with me, Moss. What are you up to?"

"Nothing." The word was almost hurled at Boardman. "Okay, so I've put you wise to something. It's up to you what you do about it. Now you can go. But leave by the side door. After what you did out there on the street you're likely to give this place a bad name."

Boardman got to his feet and moved to the side door.

He swung it open and peered out into the alley. It was deserted. He glanced back at Moss, who grinned at him, then went outside. He slammed the door and stood with his back to it for a moment. He stared both ways, wondering, and his mind was already whirling with what Moss had said. Where did the saloon owner get his information from? Was he trying to help the law because he believed that Boardman was still a Ranger? The information was vital if it were true, he thought, but told himself that Moss could not be trusted. Someone had paid three men to take a shot at him, and Moss was the obvious choice as the man behind it.

He started along the alley for the street, and had covered a few yards when a voice called to him from behind. He threw a glance over his shoulder and saw a man peering out of Moss's office. He halted and turned about, his eyes narrowing. The man emerged into the alley and stood with his feet apart. His swarthy features were almost completely shadowed by the wide brim of his greasy Stetson, but Boardman did not need the man to give his name. He recognised Link Loman without difficulty.

"I'm Link Loman, and I hear that you're hoping to meet up with me. Okay, so we've met. You've got a big mouth, Mister. Shut it and turn your gun loose. I'm gonna pin my knife through your gizzard."

Five

The outlaw flicked his wrist and a straying shaft of sunlight glittered on a naked blade. Boardman drew his gun, eyes slitted and nerves taut. He filled his hand and fired almost before the big Colt levelled. The crash of the shot struck the wall of the saloon and hammered back. Smoke belched, and Link Loman went back a quick pace. Boardman heard the hiss of a knife passing his right cheek, and set his teeth. Loman went down on one knee and pointed a gun at Boardman, who hadn't seen it being drawn. The outlaw's teeth were startlingly white in his dark face. Boardman pulled back his hammer, then released it, and dust spurted from Loman's stained check shirt.

Loman came up to his feet, tottering, and the gun in his hand was suddenly too big for his failing strength. He cursed Boardman, then spun and dropped on to his face. His gun flipped into the dust and lay glinting.

Boardman stepped out of the drifting gunsmoke, his eyes on the fallen outlaw. He threw a glance to the doorway of Moss's office, and heard the door close suddenly. He smiled tightly then, figuring that now he had something to work on. He slowly approached the fallen man, and peered intently at the contorted face. His lips pulled tight when he saw that Link Loman would never knife another victim.

There were footsteps at his back, and Boardman threw a quick glance across his shoulder. He spun and began to trigger his gun as two men opened fire on him.

He moved to the wall of the saloon and tried the door of Moss's office. It was locked. He triggered his gun again and one of the two men fell heavily. The other jumped back for the corner, and contented himself with emptying his gun at Boardman.

Hot lead screamed along the alley, striking around Boardman, and he felt the burn of a slug, then the sharp sting of a second. There was movement from the other end of the alley, and he looked towards the back lots. A couple of men appeared there and started throwing lead at him. He darted out and lifted Loman's gun, then hurled his weight at the side door. It shook but did not give, and Boardman ignored the pain in his hand. He tried to forget about the flying lead that thudded about him, but that was impossible, and he hit the door again, smashing the bolt fittings and crashing the door wide. He plunged into the office, lifting a gun to cover the desk, but Moss was gone and the office was empty.

Boardman ran to the door that led into the saloon and found it locked. Someone appeared at the side door, and a gun crashed. The slug pierced the panel beside Boardman's head, and he spun and sent a quick reply that caught the man in the doorway and hurled him off his feet.

Moving quickly, Boardman got out of the line of fire from the door and hurried to Moss's desk. He jerked open a drawer and saw a sixgun lying in it. He snatched it up as a shadow darkened the side doorway, and sent a shot through the panel. A man cried out and fell forward into the room, lying lifeless with a stream of blood spreading from his chest.

Boardman broke his own gun, placing Moss's on the desk in front of him. Loman's weapon was empty, too, and he pulled shells from his belt and loaded both weapons. He waited then, listening to the dying echoes of the shot and waiting for the next attack. There was a wild beating in his breast. Frederick Moss had overplayed his hand!

Tense seconds passed and there was no more shooting. Boardman was content to wait. He would see the shadow of anyone trying to enter the side door, and no one could get a shot at him from the entrance to the saloon because the desk was out of the line of fire. He could afford to wait because the sound of the shooting would bring townsmen.

He began to wonder where Link Loman had come from. How was it the outlaws could come and go as they pleased? He reckoned Frederick Moss would be able to answer that.

There was a hammering on the door leading into the saloon, then the sheriff's voice sounded. At the same time a furtive shadow moved in the alley, and Boardman cocked a gun, levelling it.

"Chet, are you in there?" a voice called cautiously, and he recognised Quinn's tone.

"Come in," he said, straightening. "Everything is under control."

The old rancher came in through the doorway, peering closely at the dead man on the threshold, and his cowhand, Newman, followed. They were both holding guns.

"So they made another try for you," Quinn said eagerly, his eyes glinting. "Three dead men. No wonder the Rangers only sent one man into this country."

Boardman smiled and moved around the desk. He holstered his gun, carried Loman's, and crossed to the saloon door and rapped on it.

"It's locked from your side, Sheriff," he called.

"Stand back," came the swift reply. "There ain't no key here."

Boardman moved aside, and a gun crashed. The lock on the door splintered, and then the door was thrust open. Sheriff Wendell came in, his bulk filling the doorway. He looked around swiftly.

"You again," he said, then glanced at the dead man in the doorway. "What happened?"

"Boardman did it solo this time," Quinn said. "We just walked in through that door, after it was all over. There are two more dead men outside."

"One of them is Link Loman," Boardman said. "I guess he heard about me wanting to see him again."

"What happened?" Wendell repeated.

"I reckon Frederick Moss will be able to tell us about that," Boardman said, and now the grin was gone from his lips and his face was set in deep lines. "Where is he?"

"Out in the saloon," Wendell said. "He was making for the front door when I came in."

Boardman stepped around the sheriff and made for the saloon, and Quinn followed him quickly. There were several housemen standing in a group, and most of them held weapons. But there was no sign of Moss.

"Where's Moss?" Boardman snapped. Quinn moved up to his right side.

"He left," someone replied.

Boardman turned to the sheriff. He was changed from the quiet, unassuming man that these townsmen knew.

"You've been complaining about not having anything to work on, Wendell," he snapped. "Go pick up Moss. He's probably on his way to the stable, or likely he's grabbed a horse from along the street."

The sheriff went quickly through the batwings, shaking his head. Frank Quinn turned to his gunhand and rapped out a terse command, and Newman followed Wendell.

"Now you're getting into your stride," the rancher said to Boardman. "Are you gonna tell me what happened in here?"

"Not just now," Boardman replied. "It'll all come out later. Right now I want Moss. He overplayed his hand, or his men couldn't back his play. There were four others shooting at me, and I nailed two of them. Did you see anyone out on the street or in the alley when you showed up?"

"No, and I figured to find your body in here," the rancher replied.

Boardman moved to confront the motionless group of housemen. He noted that the bartender was holding a shotgun, and some of the others were holding sixguns.

"You can put down those weapons," he told them. "In case you're wondering about my authority, I'll tell you that I'm a State Ranger. Get rid of those guns. This saloon is closed as of now, and nobody leaves the place until I've got around to questioning you all. Quinn, collect those guns they're holding, and check them. Maybe that guy down at the street end of the alley, who was throwing lead at me, ducked back in here."

The rancher went forward and quickly relieved the men of their weapons. He came back to Boardman, shaking his head slowly.

"No powder smoke on any of these," he reported.

Boardman glanced around the saloon and saw a group of women standing in the doorway leading to the dressing-rooms behind the stage. He saw Josie there, and let his gaze linger for a moment. Then his features hardened and he returned his attention to the men.

"Did anyone see where Link Loman came from?" he demanded. He studied the faces watching him, and spoke to one of the two men who had been standing at the bar with Moss when he had entered. "You were here all the time. You saw me go into Moss's office with him. Where did Loman come from?"

"I don't know," the man replied. "I must have been looking the other way."

Boardman nodded. He had expected this attitude. He heard the batwings swing open, and glanced in that direction. Sam Wendell was entering, pushing Frederick Moss before him. Newman, Quinn's cowhand, followed along behind.

"Here's Moss," the sheriff growled. "Now you tell me what this is all about."

"Ask Moss, not me," Boardman said, staring at the saloon owner.

"I've got nothing to say," Moss snarled.

"You'll soon change your tune," Boardman told him. "Sheriff, I've just told these men here so it'll be a secret no longer. I'm a State Ranger, and my job is to take the outlaws. I'll expect the co-operation of your department."

Moss laughed, and one or two of the other men joined in. Wendell shook his head doubtfully.

"I guessed you were a Ranger, Boardman," he said. "You know you ain't the first one to come here either. What makes you think you can break this gang?"

"The others didn't get Moss," Boardman replied. "But I've got the skunk. Are all your deputies in town?"

"Sure."

"Make sure they stay here. Keep them all on duty until I say they can go. Take Moss across to the jail, and the rest of these guys. Hold them until I can get around to questioning them. Have that mess in the alley cleaned up and the bodies removed. I'll make out a report this evening, and you can read it, Sheriff, before it goes to Austin."

Wendell took hold of Moss's arm and pushed the man towards the door. Newman covered the rest of the housemen and they went off in front of him. Quinn was about to follow, but Boardman spoke to him.

'Just a minute, Frank. Listen, you want to see the end of the Coyotes, huh? Well, this is your chance. You were talking just now about forming a vigilante force. No need for that now, but I could do with the men. Get around town and collect every man who's willing to carry a gun and fight the outlaws. Assemble them here, in the saloon. Keep them here until I want them to ride. You can check with the stable and get as many mounts ready to travel as you can."

"Leave it to me," the rancher whooped, almost running to the door.

Boardman drew a deep breath and turned to look at the saloon girls. Josie was still standing in the doorway, and he called to her. He moved to a small table and sat down as she approached, and after staring at him for a moment she sat down opposite.

"Still the same old Chet," she said bitterly. "Now I've lost another job through you."

"You should try to find an honest saloon owner," he retorted. "What can you tell me about Moss?"

"What makes you think I'm gonna tell you anything?" she demanded, and her blue eyes were bright and questioning.

"I think you will. You tried to help me last night, didn't you?"

"I was a fool," she said huskily. "I hoped you'd take notice of what was said and get out of the country. But I can see that you won't. So it's your funeral. I'll watch them bury you here in Burnt Hill."

"I hope not," he retorted. "What's your tie-up with Pete Merrill? Is he one of your friends?"

"None of those buzzards are friends of mine. It's just my hard luck that they move in my circle, or the other way around. So you've got the whole business sewn up, huh? How did you manage it this time without fooling some innocent young girl?'

He stared at her, his brown eyes serious. Her face hardened as she returned the gaze.

"I guess I got all this coming to me from you," he said at length. "It was a mean trick I played on you, but I wish you would believe that I really was in love with you when I arrested you."

"Sure." She laughed harshly. "So you loved me! Am I glad you didn't hate me! I drew two years as it was. I was a fool in those days, Chet, and you took advantage of me. Okay, it took me a long time to get over it, but I did. You don't mean a damn thing to me any more. I wish I'd never seen you again. Why the hell don't you try living in some other part of the country so I don't run into you?"

"I go where the crime is," he said. "I guess you do, too. I don't know why you get mixed up in all this business, Josie. You could make your own way well enough without tangling with outlaws and bad men. Now we've both got to forget the past. I'm a lawman trying to do my duty. You've got certain information that will help me rid this country of the outlaws. I need your help, Josie."

"You didn't ask for it the last time, remember? You played me for a sucker."

"Well, I'm asking you this time," he countered. "It's not for my sake, Josie. Just think of all the honest and innocent folk in this country. It's your duty as well as mine to put these outlaws where they belong."

"It's none of my business," she replied. "You've got Moss in jail now. Talk to him. Make that skunk talk."

"He's one of that gang, isn't he? He sure tried to get me killed today. Did you see Link Loman around here before he made his try for me? What about Merrill? When he was in here last night he said something about seeing you later. What did he mean by that?"

"You've sure got yourself a sackful of questions, Chet. Which one do you want me to answer first?"

"Okay, Josie." He stared at her for a moment, watching her expression intently, and there was nothing but determination on her set features. "I'll have to do it the hard way. Thanks, anyway, for sending the girl to warn me last night. I appreciate that.'

She gave a wry grin and got up. He watched her walk back to the doorway, and his thoughts stilled when he thought back into the past. He stared around the saloon and spotted the crowd of sightseers outside. He got to his feet and went to the door, pushing open the batwings and shouldering his way through the crowd. He crossed the street and entered the law office, moving through another curious crowd.

Inside the law office there were some more men. Boardman glanced around, counting the number of law badges, and numbered six deputies with Wendell. So one of these at least was a contact man for the outlaws! He wondered how he could flush the man out into the open.

Frederick Moss sat on a chair beside the sheriff's desk. Wendell was behind the desk, and the rest of the men from the saloon were standing in a corner, with four deputies watching them. Quinn's cowboy had gone, and Boardman moistened his lips when he took in Moss's jovial manner.

"You won't feel so happy when I've got through with you," Boardman snapped. He lifted his eyes to Wendell's expansive face. "Get the rest of these guys locked up until I want to talk to them. Have some of your deputies watch them. I don't want any stories concocted. I intend to get at the truth here, even if it means sweating it out for twenty-four hours."

He stood on the threshold and watched the deputies usher their prisoners out into the cell block. He studied the faces of the deputies, but saw nothing unnatural on any of them. He had it figured that the outlaws' contact should be getting a bit worried by now, but he intended riding this hard. It was the only way of making a breakthrough.

"Now listen to me, Moss," he began when the office was quiet. "You're in a lot of trouble, and it'll go hard with you unless you open up and spill the beans. I know you're mixed up with the outlaws. You'd better talk, and fast."

"You've got nothing on me," the saloon owner said with a sneer.

"Attempting to murder a lawman," Boardman intoned. "Harbouring known criminals. Those two charges will do to keep you on ice. If you don't collect ten years from them alone then I'll swallow my badge."

"I've got nothing to say," Moss told him. "I want to see my counsellor. I know my rights."

"You've got no rights until I say so," Boardman snapped. "I can play this as tough as I like, and you ain't got a leg to stand on. We're gonna bust this thing wide open, with your help or without it. It doesn't matter to me either way. But if you want to save yourself some time behind bars then you'll come clean and have us put in a good word for you at your trial."

"You're wasting your breath," Moss snapped.

"Okay." Boardman glanced at the sheriff. "Throw him in a cell, and I don't want him getting out of it. Even if he sees his lawyer and gets bail, you keep him here until I say he can leave."

A couple of deputies hustled the saloon owner to his feet and led him out to the cells. Moss opened his mouth, his fleshy face turning pale. He struggled and almost broke away from the two lawmen.

"You'll be sorry you ever set eyes on Burnt Hill, Boardman," he shouted as the door between the office and the cells was slammed.

"You're playing it tough," Wendell said.

"That's right. Do you know any other way to handle it?" Boardman considered for a moment. "Listen, Sheriff, we're up against one of the worst gangs in the West. We've got to do something, and fast, before they learn of this development. Are all your deputies here?"

"Yep, and no one is going off duty," Wendell said. "We'll see about this leak in my department. If one of these men is in the pay of the outlaws I'll see the colour of his guts before I get through with him."

Boardman reserved judgement on that statement. He let his mind run back over what had happened, and recalled Moss's talk in the office at the saloon before the shooting started.

"What do you know about the money shipments passing through here?" he demanded.

"I get to hear if there's a bigger shipment than usual," Wendell replied. "Why?"

"When I was talking to Moss in his office he was under the impression that I was about to die. I was pressing him for Link Loman's whereabouts, and he told me that a coach would likely be robbed tonight at a place called Aspen Crest. By now I reckon Frank Quinn has collected himself a mighty big posse I'm thinking of riding out with a couple of dozen men and setting a trap. It might work, and we could nab some of that gang. If we can get a couple of prisoners we'll soon make them talk, and the rest of the gang will be behind bars before they realise what's happening."

"That sounds all right," Wendell said.

"We've got nothing to lose by trying it," Boardman told him. "Where is Aspen Crest?"

"About twelve miles east of town," the sheriff said. "Would you like to handle this end while I ride with a posse? You reckon one of my deputies is a contact for the gang. Okay, so you stick around and watch them. It'll take the responsibility off me, and if anything happens here while you're around I can't be blamed for it. I take it that I'm under suspicion as well?"

"I'll stay," Boardman said, ignoring the last question. "You can ride with some of the men Quinn is collecting. I'll keep an eye on things around here. Perhaps you'll go along to the saloon and see how Quinn is making out. If he is there, tell him I want to have a word with him." The sheriff nodded and departed. Boardman paced the office, lost in thought. The cat was out of the bag. Word that he was a Ranger must have travelled the town by now, and it was likely that someone was heading for the hideout of the outlaws to spread the word. But he had Frederick Moss, and, unless he was mistaken, Moss would open his mouth before very long.

Yet he was not satisfied. He would have preferred to play the game the way it had been laid out for him. An ambush would have been set for the outlaws, and everything would have been neatly cleaned up. Now it was likely that the whole gang would disappear, and that meant five Rangers had died for nothing.

One of the deputies came out of the cell block.

"Where's the sheriff?" he demanded.

"He's preparing a posse to ride out," Boardman said. "I'm in command here now. What's the trouble?"

"I've got a chore to do. I'll have to leave here for a bit."

"What is it that's more important than this?"

"We've been having some small-time robberies about town," the deputy replied. "I've been watching, and I reckon I can pick up the man responsible. I've set a trap for him, and now I expect to get him. He's got to be caught red-handed."

"You can forget it," Boardman said. He didn't want anyone moving out. There was a leak in this office and he wanted to block it. "This is more important. The Coyotes are a powerful gang. There's no telling what they'll do when they hear that Moss has been taken. I've got it figured that Moss is their top man around here. They might even try to ride into town to bust him out."

The deputy went back into the cell block, his face showing his feelings, and Boardman wondered about that. He resumed his pacing, and shortly afterwards Quinn came in.

"Howdy, Frank. How's your end of the business going?"

"Fine, just fine," the rancher replied. "Wendell is picking out a score of men to ride with him. I told you I'd get nearly a hundred men to back you. Well, there's more than enough in Moss's saloon to handle the Coyotes. All we've got to do is find that hideout."

"That might be easier than we think," Boardman said, his brows indrawn. "You've heard that there's a leak in this department, Frank. Well, one of the deputies is mighty anxious to get off duty. This is what I want you to do. Pick six good men you can trust and tell them to hang around outside the jail. I'm gonna let these deputies go off duty. Some of the townsmen will have to stand in. I want every one of those deputies followed, and his movements noted. Can you handle that? If any of them leaves town I want to know about it. I'll do the trailing, and I'll have my fingers crossed. Perhaps you'll bring half a dozen men in here to take over. I'd like you to remain in command of them just in case someone decides to try and turn Moss loose."

"I was hoping to ride with the posse," Quinn said.

"You might find it more exciting here in town," Boardman told him.

"Okay, I'll stay here. Anything else?" The rancher made for the door.

"Yeah. Have my horse saddled up in case I need to leave town in a hurry. Come straight back with those men and I'll let the deputies go."

Quinn departed, and Boardman went to the sheriff's desk and sat down. He hoped that the swift change in the situation would panic one of the outlaws' contacts, and he was pinning his hopes on the deputy. There was a restless feeling inside him, and he got up and started pacing again. He didn't halt until Quinn returned with the special deputies.

"I've got those other men waiting outside, and they've got clear orders. The sheriff will be along here in a minute to talk over last-minute plans. He reckons he'll have to be gone within the hour in order to lay an ambush at Aspen Crest."

"I'll need a good man to stay with me," Boardman said. "If I have to start riding around the country I'll need someone to guide me. I'm a stranger here."

"Bill Newman is the man," Quinn told him. "He'll be along in a minute. He's saddling your horse."

Boardman liked the idea of having Newman along with him. The cowhand seemed to be a dependable man, and he would surely need someone in that category before this was done.

"I'll get the deputies on their way," he said, crossing to the cell block. "I want three of your men in here all the time, Frank. They can take turns. Keep the prisoners from talking among themselves, and they can make a note of anything that is said. If Moss sends for a lawyer, don't let them talk together alone. Don't take any notice of what might be said to you. Just follow my instructions, and no one else is to see any of these men."

"I've got it," Quinn said.

Boardman called the deputies out of the cells, and three of the specials took over. Boardman kept his eyes on the deputy who had asked to leave earlier, and figured that the man had something on his mind.

"Listen to me," Boardman told them. "I want you all to go off duty now. The townsmen will take over during the day. You'll be here tonight, so try and get some sleep before then. We've got to be ready in case an attempt is made to bust Moss out of here. We're not taking any chances. Okay, off you go."

The deputies departed, and Boardman stood in the doorway and watched some of Quinn's men begin their chore of trailing the lawmen.

He bit his bottom lip as he took in the activities along the street. Riders were coming from the stable and moving towards the jail.

They were some of the men who would ride with the sheriff to Aspen Crest.

"I reckon you're doing well," Quinn said at Boardman's shoulder. "I've never seen the town so het up before about the outlaws. I reckon you'll pull this off okay."

"I hope so." Boardman rubbed his chin. "It's about time we got organised. I hope I'm doing the right thing."

"So long as you're doing something, that's good enough," the rancher said. "It's been too long since strong efforts were made to take this gang."

Bill Newman came along the sidewalk, and paused at the door of the office. His weather-beaten face was stained with eagerness, his blue eyes bright with anticipation.

"Boardman wants you to ride along with him, Bill," Quinn said.

"It'll be a pleasure," the cowhand replied. "I've just saddled your horse."

"You'd better saddle your own and bring both of them back here," Boardman said. "If we ride out it'll be on the hop, and we can expect some action."

"I'll be right back," Newman said, turning back to the stable.

Sheriff Wendell came along the street at a fast clip, passing through the riders who formed his posse. He twisted in his saddle and shouted orders about provisions and water, and some of the possemen turned away to the big general store. Wendell pulled his bay to a dust-raising halt in front of the jail and stepped lightly out of the saddle. He grinned as he came up to where Boardman was standing, and remarked that he was about ready to ride out. Boardman told him exactly what he had done and what he proposed to do. The smile slowly died from Wendell's large face.

"If you do find the guilty deputy make sure he gets back here safe and sound," he said darkly. "I'll teach that snake to work behind my back."

"He'll see the inside of the jail all right," Boardman said. "But I'm hoping that he'll lead me to another contact."

"Which deputy was it spoke to you about trying to catch a thief?" Wendell demanded.

"I don't know his name. He's a tall fella, with a scar on his left temple."

"That's Jake Slattery." Wendell shook his head. "He ain't been a very good deputy. Likely he is the man you want."

"We'll soon find out," Boardman said. "But I don't think he'll make a move until you've left town with the posse."

"We're practically on our way," the sheriff retorted. "As soon as we get some grub and water. I hope I have some luck out at Aspen Crest. There's nothing like shooting a few outlaws to revive a man's spirits."

"You know how to run the job," Boardman said, "but try and get some prisoners if you can. There's been a lot happening in this country that won't ever come out unless some of the outlaws talk about it. I want more than the men who have been robbing with the outlaws. I want the men who have been helping them under cover."

"It's gonna be a big job," Wendell said. He saw some of his possemen coming out of the store. "Well, I'm off. Wish me luck. It's about time some of it came on to the side of the law."

"Good luck," Boardman said, and he and Quinn watched the posse mount up and ride off. When the street was deserted he looked around, wondering, and saw Bill Newman coming along, riding his mount and leading Boardman's. "Now it's my turn," he remarked to Quinn. "If that deputy is the man we want then he'll surely be making his move now."

"You could be right," Quinn said. "Here comes Ben Goward, and he was following Slattery when he left the jail."

Boardman waited tensely until the townsman came panting up. He had the feeling that his hunch would pay off. If it did then this could be the beginning of the end for the Coyotes.

Six

"Slattery just jumped on a horse and rode out of town," the man reported. "He headed north."

"What's out that way?" Boardman demanded, lifting a hand to Newman and beckoning. The cowboy kicked his horse and finished his ride at a run.

"Scar Calhoun's place," Quinn said eagerly. "I told you about his trading-post. There's been talk that Calhoun trades with the Coyotes."

"I'm on my way," Boardman said. He stepped off the sidewalk and ran to his horse, swinging quickly into the saddle. As he turned the animal he glanced back at the old rancher standing in the doorway of the law office. "Keep your wits about you, Frank," he called. "It's a tough bunch we're up against."

"You can leave this to me," the rancher replied. "You watch your step."

Boardman nodded, and with Bill Newman siding him he hit the trail north. They rode fast out of town, and spotted their quarry ahead. They slowed their pace to let the deputy draw away, and it was obvious that the man had a definite destination in mind from his speed. He did not bother to check his surroundings, but urged his horse on at a killing pace.

"It looks like he is heading for Calhoun's place," Newman ventured. They had been riding for over an hour, and the deputy had allowed his horse to settle into a tireless lope. "I've heard about that trading-post. It seems the outlaws use it at times. I've been there once. Calhoun has a meadow which he rents out to trail herds. It's a stop-over for the trail crews on their way north. Maybe I should try and get ahead of Slattery and hit the post from another direction. I could be in there having a drink when he rides in, and I'll maybe get a look at whoever he talks to, unless he leaves word with Calhoun himself."

"Do you think you can do it?" Boardman demanded. "I can stay behind Slattery. It wouldn't do for him to spot me until after he's passed on his word or he'll know I'm wise to him."

"I can make it okay," Newman said. "You say the word and I'll make a run for it."

"I don't know. If there's someone at this trading-post to carry the word onto the hideout then we want to remain strangers to him. If you ride in there it means you're gonna show yourself. No, I reckon we better play this smart, or try to."

"Okay. You're the boss." Newman narrowed his eyes as he peered at their quarry. "It ain't so far now to the post."

They continued, and Newman took the lead through the rocks and boulders that littered the trail. He reined up suddenly, and Boardman did likewise. They dismounted and left their horses with trailing reins. Newman led the way forward and they dropped to the ground and peered over a rise and saw the trading-post in the middle distance, set in the centre of a wide spread of grass. The high sun sparkled on a great stretch of creek water. The deputy was dismounting at a rail outside the sprawling, one-storey building.

"There it is," Newman said needlessly. "Now what happens?"

"We ain't gonna get any closer without being spotted," Boardman decided. "That's for sure. The only thing we can do is watch from here and try to nail anyone leaving in the next half-hour."

"And Slattery?"

"We can always pick him up," Boardman said. "We won't have anything on him unless someone leads us to the outlaws."

They sat waiting, only their heads above the rough ground. Boardman glanced at the sun. The time was way past noon. He wondered how the sheriff was making out, hoping that Wendell would have some luck at Aspen Crest. Time passed, and nothing moved on the flats outside the trading-post. The building itself looked deserted, and only the deputy's horse, standing hip-shot in the strong sunlight, gave them proof that there was life here.

"He's taking his time," Newman commented. "I reckon he should have put his horse in the shade."

A man appeared suddenly from the front of the house, and he led away the deputy's horse.

"They must have heard you," Boardman said with a grin. "You'd better keep your voice down."

They were all off a hundred and fifty yards from the trading-post, and Newman grinned. Boardman rubbed his chin thoughtfully. He would have given anything to have been somewhere close by when the deputy walked into the post. He wondered what was being said and felt anxiety build up inside him. But he was consoled by the knowledge that no one could ride away from here without being seen.

"Do you want me to ride on in there and see what's doing?" Newman demanded.

"I'd like to know what's happening, but I don't want you to show yourself. They're a cunning crew, and we've only got to tip our hand to warn them. We'll have to sweat it out."

The man who had led away the deputy's horse appeared with a change of mount, and moments later the deputy came out of the building and swung into the saddle. He came back across the grass, and it was obvious that he was returning to Burnt Hill.

"He's left word," Newman said. "Do we grab him when he comes by?"

"No. We'll leave him for later. After he's gone we're gonna sneak around to approach the post from another direction. If we see anyone leaving and heading for someplace else then we'll follow him on the off-chance that he's heading for the hideout. You better get back to our horses and move them. We don't want Slattery to know anyone is around. I'll stay here and watch for further movements."

Newman slid away from the crest and disappeared. Boardman kept low, watching the deputy, and the man came over the crest only yards away from him and went plunging down the opposite slope. Boardman didn't watch the deputy after that. He kept his eyes on the building out on the grass, watching for any movement. He heard Slattery's hoof-beats fade, and then silence returned. Shortly after, Newman came sneaking back.

"Seen anything?" the cowboy demanded.

"No. I'm wondering if I've made the wrong play." Frustration was rising in Boardman's mind. "I suppose I can take Slattery and beat the truth out of him. But I don't like to work that way."

Newman suddenly grasped Boardman's arm and pointed away to the left, and Boardman stiffened when he caught sight of half a dozen riders cantering towards the trading-post.

"Outlaws," he grated. "I'll bet my boots on that. Probably those ones who are gonna hit the coach at Aspen Crest."

"Now they'll get word of what's happened in town," Newman said.

"Yeah, and likely one of them will ride back to the hideout. I reckon I've got some more riding to do."

"What do you want me to do?" Newman asked.

"I still think we'd better stick together. If we find that hideout, one of us has to get back to town for a posse. There's nothing we can do about those men riding in there now. If they are after that coach then the sheriff will have to take care of them."

"Did that deputy hear about the coach raid when you told Wendell?"

"No." Boardman shook his head. "I kept that information for Wendell alone. Even the posse don't know where they're heading."

"Maybe we'd better head around to the left. That's where those outlaws appeared. If one of them rides back to the hideout with the news then he'll ride in that direction."

"That's a good idea," Boardman said. He slid back from the crest. "It'll take those riders another ten minutes to reach the post. We've got time to collect the horses."

They started back for their mounts, and Newman led the way to where he had hidden them. They were swinging into their saddles when a harsh voice called to them from behind.

"Okay, the pair of you. Lift your hands and don't try to get smart."

Boardman threw a glance over his shoulder as he lifted his hands, and clenched his teeth when he saw Slattery standing against a rock with a Colt in his hand.

"So you've got on to me," Slattery snarled. "Well, it won't do you any good. I don't have to head back to Burnt Hill for anything. Just get rid of your guns and we'll ride in and have a talk with Calhoun. Maybe he's got some ideas on what to do with a couple of long noses."

"How'd you know we were trailing you?" Newman demanded.

"I didn't, but I spotted your tracks heading this way when I started back, and I've got a habit of watching the ground as I ride. Those tracks you left were fresh, and I didn't see them when I came out. I didn't pass you either, so that meant you were lying up and waiting for me to pass you. Okay, now get rid of your guns and we'll start moving."

"So you're working for the outlaws," Boardman said.

"I don't have to deny it now," Slattery retorted. "You're wasting your time trying to beat this set-up. It's too big for the law to handle."

"Are you desperate enough to kill a Ranger?" Newman demanded.

"I don't have to do the killing." Slattery shook his head as he moved forward. The sunlight glittered on his law star. "And he'll be the sixth Ranger to die in this county. Once upon a time it was bad medicine to kill a Ranger, but nowadays it don't amount to much. Now get rid of those guns like I told you or you'll both bite the dust right there."

Boardman lifted his Colt and tossed it to the ground. Newman did the same, sullenly. The deputy told them to dismount and they quit their saddles.

"That's better. Now start walking thataway. Leave your horses where they are. I'll collect them later."

Boardman led the way. He walked through the rocks with Newman at his back. They came to Slattery's horse, and the deputy swung into his saddle.

"You know where the trading-post is," he said. "Start walking in that direction."

They climbed the slope and crossed the crest, and Boardman tightened his lips when he saw the half-dozen riders dismounting outside the low, sprawling building. Newman came up on his left, and spoke urgently from a corner of his taut mouth. "Should we try to jump him before he gets us into the post?" he demanded.

"No." Boardman threw a glance behind, and stared into the steady muzzle of a Colt. "He's just waiting for such a move. But we've got to be ready to take any chance that comes along."

"There won't be any chance at all with this bunch," Newman said morosely.

They were spotted before they reached the building, and there were nearly half a dozen men standing out front when Boardman and Newman walked up. Boardman had already spotted Pete Merrill among the bunched hard cases standing by the horses, and his quick eyes picked out other faces which had been on some of the wanted dodgers. His mind put names to some of them, and he drew a deep breath as Merrill stepped forward.

"Howdy, Slattery," the red-headed outlaw greeted. "We just got your warning from Calhoun. What's all this about?"

"I found them waiting on the trail," the renegade deputy said gleefully. "They must have followed me out of town. That guy there is another Texas Ranger."

"Yeah." Merrill turned his pale eyes to Boardman. "So you did meet Loman again, huh? Harper ain't gonna like it when he hears that you killed one of his best men."

"I'm sure sorry about that," Boardman replied. "Perhaps you should have told me the other night that Harper's feelings are easily upset."

"You've been raising hell, by all accounts. I reckon Harper will want to talk to you himself. So you've put Moss in jail. Well, that won't hurt him. He was getting too big for his boots. What else have you done since you got here, Ranger?"

"Why don't you ride into town and find out?" Boardman retorted.

"We're likely to do that," the outlaw snarled. "I guess this country will have to be taught a thing or two. We had everyone screwed down tight, but it only needs a guy like you to show up to start everyone reaching for a gun and calling for a clean-up. Well, we'll handle that. It's been tried before. Slattery, I need all these guys with me. We're on our way to do a job. You'll have to take these couple back through the hills to the hideout. Tell Harper what you know, and maybe he'll start the rest of the gang into town to bust Moss out of jail."

"Moss is finished around here now," Slattery said. "He was useful only so long as he could work undercover."

"Like most of the rest of you," Merrill retorted. 'Well, I've got to be riding. I'll have something else to say to you when I get back to the hideout, Ranger."

The six outlaws mounted and rode off, and Boardman heaved a sigh of relief. There would be a chance to jump Slattery between here and the hideout. The deputy swung out of his saddle. He didn't move within arm's length of his prisoners, and threw a glance at the rest of the men standing in front of the post.

"A couple of you could earn a few dollars by helping me," he said. "There's a couple of horses back there that need collecting. Someone get a rope so I can tie their hands. I don't want them to jump me.'"

"I don't want to get mixed up in anything like this, Slattery," a big man said, and glancing at him Boardman saw that his right eye-socket was empty. So this was Scar Calhoun. The man looked a hard case all right.

"You turn right round and take them two out of here. You took them so you handle them. The only reason the law ain't been able to close me down is because I ain't sided with the gang. I sell them supplies and booze, but that's how far it goes. The Rangers must have got wise after losing five of their men. It's likely that someone else trailed these guys from town. So get them out of here and be quick about it."

The deputy cursed, but the trader was adamant.

"I could make it tough on you, Calhoun," Slattery cursed. "I'm still a deputy sheriff, and if you make it hard on me then I'll return the compliment, never fear."

"Okay, one of you fellas go with him and help him get those two tied to their horses," Calhoun said. "But I don't want to see them around here again. I take too many risks as it is. Haul your freight, Slattery, and make it a long time before you show up around here again."

"I'll remember this," Slattery snapped. "I'll let the boss know how you feel."

"He already knows," Calhoun retorted.

One of the other men lifted his gun and came forward, and Boardman and Newman were made to retrace their steps. They went back to where their horses were standing and climbed into the saddles. While the deputy covered them with his gun the other man removed their rifles from the saddle-holsters and started binding them with the rope that Newman had carried with him. The cowboy protested bitterly when the rope was cut, and Slattery cursed him.

"You ain't got no need to worry about a rope," the deputy said. "You'll be dead and buried come sundown. Just shut your trap and we'll make it as quick as we can."

When they were tied to their saddles the deputy handed his helper a couple of dollars. Then he rode in beside Boardman. He holstered his gun and knotted together the reins of their mounts, securing a short length of rope to the bit of Boardman's horse and tying it off on his saddle-horn.

"So you wanted to find the hideout of the Coyotes, huh?" he demanded. "Well, I'm taking you there right now. Don't ever think that I won't help a Ranger." He chuckled loudly, and started forward.

"There's nothing lower than a renegade lawman," Boardman said. "You're worse than these Coyotes, Slattery."

The deputy leaned sideways and gave Boardman a full-blooded swing. His fist crashed against Boardman's jaw, and Boardman clenched his teeth, his ears singing. He fell silent, hoping that his turn would come.

"Just shut your mouth and keep it shut," the deputy told him. "You ain't got much of a future, I can tell you, but you don't have to make it worse than it has to be."

"Your turn will come, Slattery," Newman snarled. "I always figured you for a skunk."

"And you can keep quiet, Newman. I never did like you. Open your mouth again and I'll stop it permanent with a slug."

They rode on, and Boardman turned over in his mind the possibilities. It was hopeless attempting to get away from Slattery. In any case he wanted to find the hideout, and although their chances of escape would be lessened when they reached the gang's lair, there would be at least one opportunity of getting away. He had to be smart enough to recognise it when it came. He remained silent, noting the direction they were riding in and the landmarks. If he got away alone he would have to find his way back to town. He had to think of every eventuality.

The afternoon wore on. Boardman and Newman were thirsty and tired. But Slattery showed no signs of wanting to rest. He kept close behind them, urging them on whenever they slackened pace.

"You won't get away with this, Slattery," Boardman said once. "I suspected you in town, and Frank Quinn is wise to you. When you do ride back there you'll be arrested."

"I don't think so," the deputy replied. "No one can prove anything. You and Newman will have disappeared. It ain't got nothing to do with me."

"There are men who know that we set out to follow you," Boardman persisted. "You ain't so tough. When the sheriff gets to work on you he'll soon break you down."

"Okay, so I don't go back to town," Slattery said. "I don't have to. I ain't got no ties there. It was only a job of convenience. It helped us to keep an eye on what the local law was doing."

"So you really are a member of the outlaw gang?" Boardman demanded.

"That's right. Now drop it and keep moving. We've got a long ride yet. I want to get to the hideout before midnight. Harper has got to know about the change of situation."

"He'll find out about that soon enough," Boardman said. "This is the beginning of the end for the gang, Slattery. If you had any sense you'd see that and high-tail it to the nearest border."

"We're close enough to the Mexican border to be able to hang on here as long as we can," Slattery retorted. "We've had these scares before. You ain't the first Ranger to come on in here and try to take us."

"I won't be the last either," Boardman said soberly. "I don't understand the attitude of your kind, Slattery. You must know that you can't always get away with it."

"We ain't doing too badly right now," the renegade replied with a grin. "Now keep moving. You wanted to find the hideout of the Coyotes, didn't you? Well, that's where I'm taking you."

They continued, and Boardman shook his head slowly as he studied their rugged surroundings. No wonder the law hadn't been able to trace this callous gang! There was rock and wasteland here, and wide areas of ground that would not hold a hoofprint. A posse would need a lot of luck to track anyone through here.

The sun began to sink into the west, and Boardman thought about Aspen Crest. If Frederick Moss had been telling the truth about the stage hold-up then Pete Merrill and his party of outlaws would be in bad trouble right now. He tested the knots in the ropes binding his wrists, and winced at the pain in his right limb. They hadn't made allowances for his wound, and pain was throbbing dully through his hand and fingers.

Darkness came, and Slattery halted briefly to test their bonds. Boardman glanced at Newman, who shook his head hopelessly. Their feet were lashed to their stirrups. They couldn't move, and it would have been impossible to try to escape. They would have to wait, knowing that any slender chance would be all the more remote when they reached the hideout. It was likely that Harper would have the pair of them killed in cold blood. Men like the outlaws did not hesitate to murder.

Riding on through the night, Boardman twisted once or twice in his saddle when he thought he heard the sound of someone behind them. Slattery was leading them now, his figure black against the gloom. There was only the click and thud of iron against rock, the creaking harness leather and the stertorous breathing of their mounts. Boardman had been lost in his thoughts, yet his senses were alert to what was going on around him. Twice he thought he heard the crack of a hoof against rock, coming from way behind, and he listened keenly, but finally decided that it must have been an echo. The night carried even the slightest sound to a great distance, and his keyed-up nerves might be playing him tricks. There was no hope for him now. He would have to rely upon his own resources to save his life.

They entered a canyon, and black rock rose up sheer on both sides of them. Sounds were trapped and magnified a hundredfold, and flung back at them from the confining rock walls. Once more Boardman heard a furtive sound at his back, and twisted in his saddle, eyes probing the shadows but failing to spot anything. He shrugged and faced front again. His hopes of escaping were low. Even if he managed to get away from the gang he would find it impossible to find his way back to Burnt Hill in time to rouse out a posse and return.

A harsh voice challenged them suddenly, and then there was movement around them. The deputy called out his name and intimated that he had a couple of prisoners, and a man moved out of the black surroundings and peered at Boardman and Newman.

"Take them in then," a voice called. "Harper ain't here. He rode out at noon on a raid. You'll have to wait until he gets back, which will be about noon tomorrow."

"Anyone in at all?" Slattery demanded.

"Yeah. Half a dozen of the boys are around." Boardman perked up at the news, and threw a hopeful glance at Newman, but it was too dark to see the cowhand clearly. They had to be thankful for anything, and news that the gang boss was out meant that they might be kept alive until he returned. That would give two desperate men facing death a better chance of changing the situation. Boardman thinned his lips as he thought about it. He wouldn't hesitate to take any opportunity. He would kill with his bare hands if he had to. He knew the type of man he was up against here, and didn't need any telling that he would die as soon as they decided that he wouldn't be of any use to them.

He had been well briefed about this gang. He knew the number of robberies they had committed, the number of innocent men who had been killed by the Coyotes, and most of the names and histories of the permanent members of the gang. He would not be held by any scruples if he had to kill in cold blood.

They reached the end of the neck of the canyon, and the rocky walls fled away on either hand, encompassing a wide area of relatively flat land. There was grass underfoot, and then Boardman heard the sound of running water in the distance. He stared around, but was unable to make out any details in the darkness.

"Hold up there," Slattery suddenly commanded, and Boardman stopped his horse with his knees. The deputy swung out of his saddle, and Boardman noted the square shape of a wooden building just in front of them. There was no light from any windows, and he wondered just how many of the gang were still in this much-hunted lair. Then a door was opened in the building and a great shaft of yellow light split the darkness. A man stood framed in the doorway, and he demanded their identities.

"Jake Slattery," the deputy grunted. "I've got a couple of prisoners. One of them will interest you. He's a Ranger, and he killed Link Loman this morning in a fair fight. The hell of it is, Loman branded his gun hand a couple of days ago. This guy used his left hand to cool off Loman."

"Bring them inside," the outlaw commanded. "We've got someone here who will be mighty pleased to see them. Link's brother Blade rode in this morning."

Boardman clenched his teeth as he climbed out of his saddle when Slattery released him. Newman joined him, and they were ushered into the big cabin. Both prisoners blinked against the strong light, but Boardman glanced around quickly and saw five men in the building. One of them, resembling the dead Link Loman, was getting to his feet.

"What was that about Link being killed?" he demanded. "Who shot him?"

There was a sudden glint of lamplight as a knife appeared in the outlaw's hand, and he advanced quickly upon Boardman and Newman. Boardman drew a deep breath. This looked like the end of his trail.

Seven

"Lay off," Slattery snapped, stepping between his prisoners and the outlaw. "I don't care what happens to Boardman after Harper has seen him. But you know the rule like all the others. The boss will want to question this Ranger."

"He killed Link," the killer growled. "I'll finish him off."

"Sure," the renegade agreed. "But not right now. Have you got any grub in this place? I've been riding since this morning. I saw Merrill and his party at Calhoun's. They should have got that coach by now. Where's Harper gone?"

"Bank job in Morganville," one of the others said. "Make them two prisoners sit down over there in the corner. Better tie them up in case they try to start something."

"We'll feed them first," Slattery said. "They won't get away from here."

"No grub for the Ranger," Blade Loman said. "He'll die with an empty belly."

"Just stay away from him," Slattery snarled. "He's yours after Harper has seen him."

"Who's the other guy?"

"Cowboy. Worked for Frank Quinn. You know the Big Q ranch? You lifted a herd from there a couple of months ago."

"Yeah, and Harper says we're gonna take care of that bunch one of these days."

Boardman kept his ears open. He and Newman were made to sit at a table in a corner, and Blade Loman took a seat nearby, watching Boardman through slitted eyes. The outlaw's dark face was twisted with hatred, but it struck Boardman that Loman was not grieved by the death of his notorious brother. The man was holding his long-bladed knife, and did not miss a movement. Slattery sat down at the far end of the long table, and one of the outlaws pushed a big pan onto the stove.

"You'll have to take pot luck," he said. "We're getting a big low on grub. Harper reckons this part of the country is nearly played out, and he's beginning to plan to move on."

"It's just as well I ain't going back to Burnt Hill," Slattery remarked. "Where are we going next?"

"Nothing's settled yet," came the reply.

Newman was given food when it was ready, but Blade Loman took away the tin plate that was thrust under Boardman's nose. Slattery sighed and got to his feet.

"Blade, you leave that guy alone until he's handed over to you. He's my prisoner until Harper gets here. What's wrong with you, anyway? You'll want to fight him with that knife of yours, won't you? You wouldn't want us to think you're scared of him, starving him thataway, huh? He'll be so weak by this time tomorrow that he won't be able to stand up."

"Okay," Loman snarled. He thrust the plate of food back in front of Boardman, his dark eyes blazing with hatred and fury. "I guess I'll get my turn at you. Just keep yourself fit until I can start cutting you."

"Your brother did that," Boardman snapped. "Just turn me loose with a knife now and I'll take you on."

"Give him a knife, someone," Loman snarled. "I'll carve his heart out."

"Lay off," Slattery said impatiently. "Hell, don't you guys understand? That Ranger is valuable to the boss. There's no telling what he knows about the situation. The Rangers might be planning to move into this country in force. I figured that they'd given it up as a bad job after losing five men, but this guy turning up shows that they ain't finished. I always did say it was wrong to kill a Ranger. But the harm's been done now. Maybe it'll be a good thing if we do pull stakes and blow."

Boardman and Newman ate quickly, and kept exchanging glances. Boardman could see enquiry in the cowboy's blue eyes. Newman wanted to tackle these half-dozen outlaws, but Boardman was in no condition to fight with his bare hands. He pointed to his bandaged right hand, and Newman subsided. They would have to wait their chance.

After they had eaten Slattery came along with some rope and tied their hands. He indicated a door and ushered them through into a windowless room. There were several wooden bunks, and Boardman glanced around quickly, summing up the place. The walls were made of logs, and there was a wooden floor. The only exit was the door through which they had entered.

"That's right, take a good look around," Slattery said with a grin. "But you won't get out of here in a hurry. Even if you get the ropes off, there's Blade Loman in the other room, and he's gonna sleep right outside this door tonight. You'd better forget about escaping and get some sleep while you can. Harper and the rest of the gang will be back tomorrow, and afterwards you can get to work on Blade. But it won't be with guns, Ranger. Blade is real handy with a knife. Him and his brother were real artists with cold steel. You'll find that out tomorrow when Blade gets to work on you. It'll make a little fun for the boys. There ain't much out here to keep them amused."

Boardman did not reply, and eased himself down onto a bunk. Newman did likewise, and Slattery checked the knots he tied, then went out, closing the door and leaving them in darkness.

"Well, what about it?" Newman demanded. "Do you think we can tackle those six?"

"They're a big six," Boardman replied softly. "And I've only got one hand. But that won't stop me if you want to have a go. I reckon they will kill us after Harper gets back. It looks like I'm slated to meet this other Loman, and with a knife. I just hope they'll give me a knife. But you don't have to wait for certain death. Maybe we could get free in here and arm ourselves with a chair or something. If we rush them in there and start laying about with a club we might just turn the trick."

"I saw a belt and a gun on a chair in there," Newman said softly. "I reckon some of these guys will go to sleep. If I can work my hands out of this rope I'll make a try for that gun. I'll face any odds so long as I've got a weapon."

"That makes two of us," Boardman retorted. "We're standing right on the brink of death now, Newman, and we ain't gonna make it unless we help ourselves. No use sitting here and hoping that something will turn up. There's no one to help. We've got to do it alone and the hard way."

"I'm of the same mind," the cowboy replied quietly. "But if I've got to die then I want to go out fighting. We'll have a go."

Boardman was silent. He tested the bonds around his wrists, and gritted his teeth, cursing the wounds in his right limb. He was almost helpless like this, and told himself that it would have been a different story if he hadn't been knifed. When he thought of Blade Loman waiting for the return of Harper, he sweated, and fear trickled through him. He was not a coward, and his Ranger service could prove it, but lying here in the darkness, bound hand and foot, knowing that on the morrow a vicious killer would try to exact revenge for his brother's death, his nerves tightened until he felt the suffocation of real fear swelling inside him. But he had to cling to reason. If he let panic sweep him then the slightest opportunity of getting free would be wasted. If he froze he would be helpless, like a sitting duck, and then he would surely die.

"Are you asleep?" Newman demanded some time later. There had been dead silence in the room, although Boardman could hear the buzz of the voices of the outlaws in the outer room.

"No," he replied.

"I've managed to loosen my rope," Newman went on. "I reckon I've rubbed the skin off my wrists, but that don't matter. If I get free we'll make those skunks pay for this."

"I'm glad you came along," Boardman said. "I wish there was something I could do, but my right wrist is giving me hell, and I can't free myself."

"I reckon you'll do your share before this is finished. Leave this part to me."

Boardman waited, and tension slowly filtered into him. He was tired, could feel the drug of sleep dragging at his mind, trying to betray his alert senses. He kept his ears strained for sounds in the outer room, and guessed that the outlaws were not too worried about their prisoners. There were six of them against two unarmed men, and in their language that meant the prisoners had no chance. Boardman had to agree with it, too. Any one of those outlaws could pull a gun faster than a man could blink, and if he and Newman rushed into the outer room armed only with pieces of furniture they would be shot down before they managed to subdue more than one or two of the outlaws. It seemed to be certain death, but there was an outside chance of success. If they just sat and waited for the morning then they would surely die, and there was no percentage in hoping for a miracle.

"I can get my left hand out of these ropes now," Newman said suddenly. "I reckon we better wait for a bit though. They won't be sitting up all night, surely. Some of them will sleep. If they come in here we can deal with them first. If we can get our hands on a gun apiece it'll be a different yarn to spin."

"You can say that again," Boardman told him. "Okay, we'll wait a bit, and hope we get some of the breaks when we start."

The silence was intense. Boardman strained his ears, and could make out the voices of the outlaws. He had been in some tight spots before, but this was the tightest, and he held out no hope for success. They were slated to die, and it would help them not at all to make this trouble for their captors. All they could do was take one or two of them along for bad company.

His keen ears suddenly picked up the distant echo of a shot, and he stiffened. He heard another echo, then there was silence. He lay listening for a long time, but heard no other disturbance. Then he spoke softly to the cowboy.

"Did you hear that shot?"

"Yeah, I figured it was my ears, but you picked it up, huh?"

"One shot," Boardman said.

"That could mean anything."

"I guess you're right. We ain't gonna get any help around here."

The silence filled them with apprehension. One gun would have made all the difference, Boardman told himself. He thought about the situation, drawing upon his experience in the hope that something might come up that would show him a way to beat these outlaws. But the simplest thing would be to get free and to lay his hand on a gun.

There was a commotion suddenly, and Boardman stiffened as he listened to the raised voices in the outer room. He heard Slattery's nasal tone, and the thick voice of Blade Loman. But he could not make out what was being said. Then the outer door was banged and there seemed to be less voices talking inside.

"Something's up," Newman said. "Some of them have gone out."

They listened, hoping against hope. The outer door banged again, and then there was silence in the cabin.

"I think they've all gone out," Newman whispered hoarsely. "I'm gonna get out of these ropes now and take a quick look."

Before he could move the door was thrown open and light streamed in. Then Blade Loman came in carrying a lantern, which he hung on a nail driven into a post. His dark face was set in harsh lines, his eyes slitted and glittering. His knife was in his hand, and Boardman bated his breath when the outlaw slowly approached him and pressed the point of the long blade against his throat.

"You've got it coming to you, Ranger," he snarled. "You're gonna feel the length of this blade in your guts."

"Where have the others gone?" Newman demanded. "I heard a shot some time ago. What's happening?"

"Don't build up your hopes," the outlaw growled, grinning. "Some crazy fool sneaked in and shot one of the guards. But he won't get away."

"Jed Marsden," Boardman said through his teeth. "I'd forgotten about him."

"Yeah," Newman retorted. "Some of these outlaws killed his wife and son, didn't they? Well, I hope he sneaks in here and gets them all."

Loman went across to the cowboy and prodded him with the blade of the knife. Boardman twisted his neck and watched the outlaw, cursing the tight rope around his wrists. He'd take a chance on the knife if he could get free, but he was powerless. He listened to Loman reviling the cowboy.

Then Newman was making a grab for the outlaw's knife. The cowboy had got his left hand free, and must have been working on the right even when Loman was in the room. He seized the outlaw's knife hand in a powerful grip and swung his feet off the bunk. His legs were roped together, but he didn't need his balance. Newman was not a tall man, but powerfully built, with wide shoulders and heavy arms.

Loman yelled thinly when pressure was applied to his arm. Boardman struggled with his ropes, but only succeeded in hurting his injured hand. He was forced to desist, and lay watching the struggle, one eye on the door. If any of the outlaws entered now it would be the end of them.

Newman was breaking Loman's arm. The outlaw was down on his knees, beating at Newman's chin with his right hand, his knife in his left, and Newman had secured an unbreakable hold on the outlaw's knife hand. Boardman watched with bated breath. Newman was incredibly strong, and fear and determination had added to his strength. There was a sharp sound, dry and sickening, like the crack of a stick being broken against a man's knee, and Blade Loman screeched in sudden agony. The knife fell to the floor, glinting in the lamplight, and Boardman stared at it.

Newman's right fist sledged against Loman's jaw and the outlaw crumpled soundlessly. The cowboy grunted as he reached for the knife, and the next instant he had slashed through the ropes binding his legs. He went at a run into the big room, leaving Boardman to stare after him. Then he came back, and there was a cocked Colt.45 in his hand and a big grin on his rugged face. He came quickly to Boardman and slashed through the rope binding the Ranger.

"You can have the gun," he said, passing it over. "The cartridge belt is in there. I can use a knife as well as this guy. What do we do now, Boardman?"

"Tie him," Boardman ordered, cocking the gun, then checking it. "Let me get that cartridge belt. Then we'll see if there are some more guns around." He grinned and slapped the cowboy's thick shoulder. "You'll do to ride any river with, Newman."

He went through to the big room and buckled the cartridge belt around his waist. For a moment he stood looking around, then went to a corner and picked up a Winchester. He handed it to Newman when the cowboy came through, and Newman started searching around, finding a couple of boxes of shells in a drawer.

"Okay, so now we've got a chance," he said, checking the rifle. "But you're the boss. What happens now? We're outnumbered about three to one. There are five of them left here. I didn't see them all at the entrance to the canyon, but I reckon there were at least two there."

"I saw two," Boardman replied. "But don't forget that Jed Marsden is around somewhere. He's a mighty mean guy, and I wouldn't mind betting that right now he's sneaking in on the rest of them."

"What are we gonna do?"

"We've got to secure the rest of them here," Boardman replied. "Then I figure that one of us should ride back to town for a posse. There's no telling when Pete Merrill will get back, if he managed to slip the sheriff's posse. I reckon he'll be in some time tomorrow morning. Harper will be back tomorrow too. It's gonna be a tight thing, to get a posse back in here to wait for the gang's return. But that'll be the best way of handling it. They won't expect trouble in here."

"I'll do the riding, if I can find a horse," Newman said. "But you call any tune you like. I'm ready to go along with you. I'm telling you one thing though. Now I've got a gun in my hand they'll have to kill me before I drop it. I ain't been too happy these past few hours."

"That makes two of us," Boardman said grimly. "Come on, let's go see if we can get some horses. Do you think you can find your way back to town from here?"

"I'll make it," Newman said confidently. "What will you do?"

"Stick around here. If the gang does get back before you show up with a posse they'll realise that something's gone wrong and they'll pull out again. But now I've found them I ain't letting go. I'll follow them clear into hell and back if I have to."

"That's a dangerous chore," Newman said. "But if you do have to leave then try to make some kind of trail for us to follow."

"Leave it to me. Better put out that light. Then we'll get moving. Stick close by me until we find the rest of these guys. I want them alive if possible, but don't be too cautious. If they start anything let them have it."

"No need to tell me twice," Newman said. He blew out the lamp and Boardman cautiously opened the door.

There was a moon, and pale brilliance made the shadows deceptive. The sky was filled with cloud, slow moving and beautiful, and the breeze blew steadily down from the surrounding peaks. There was silence, an emptiness that was too peaceful. There were men somewhere around, crouched and patient, deadly and ready to deal out death. Boardman heard the soft breath of Newman as they moved easily from the big cabin and started away from the building.

Why had there been only one shot? Boardman wondered about it. Loman had said someone sneaked up on the guards and attacked them. He recalled that he had sensed someone trailing them when Slattery had brought them in. There had been echoes of hoofbeats, and the unexplainable feeling that they were being watched by unseen eyes. Had it been Jed Marsden, the grieving rancher from Mason's Crossing? If it were then the outlaws were in for a tough time. Boardman narrowed his eyes as he stared into the shadows. This half-light was deceptive beyond the range of twenty yards. He did not want to walk into trouble now.

Newman touched his left shoulder, and Boardman halted and dropped to one knee. The cowboy pointed to the left, and Boardman peered in that direction. He saw several horses, and nodded, placing his mouth close to the cowboy's ear.

"I wonder where the saddles are kept," he said softly.

"They must have a bridle on at least," Newman said. "But let's try and grab the rest of these outlaws. Then we can look around at our leisure."

"I reckon they must have headed for the entrance. It's not much further ahead." Boardman stared at the ghostly rock walls rising up to the night sky. Ahead was the narrow passage that led to freedom. But he wouldn't be leaving yet, he told himself. He would be satisfied if Newman got away to fetch the posse.

A shot cracked sharply, and Boardman's keen eyes spotted the flash of the weapon. It came from the narrow passage that led out of the canyon, and there was an immediate reply from three or four guns.

"Whoever he is they've got him pinned down now," Newman observed. "Let's go take a hand."

Boardman snaked forward, and they made it unnoticed to a cluster of rocks. Shooting was rattling out, throwing strings of echoes into the vast space of the sky. Red and orange flashes winked viciously, and there was the screech and whine of tortured lead as some of the slugs ricocheted off hard rock.

As they closed in on the trouble-spot, Boardman saw that there were four guns firing at a fifth which was spurting rapidly from the cover of a hole in the wall of the canyon. That meant some of the others were trying to sneak in close. Boardman estimated that there were at least half a dozen of the outlaws left, unless Jed Marsden, if it was the half-crazed rancher, had killed some more of them. He edged closer, with the undaunted Newman keeping near him.

"We'd better start shooting," Newman said, when they were in a position behind the half-circle of guns hemming in the single defiant weapon. "If we call on them to throw down their guns they are gonna get to hell out of here, and then we won't be able to nail them."

"I don't like cold-blooded shooting," Boardman replied, "but in this case I think you're right. Let's hit them."

The cowboy opened fire almost before Boardman spoke, and one of the outlaws uttered a sharp cry and pitched sideways. Boardman cut loose with the Colt, and the next minute the initiative was with them. Boardman saw the figure of Slattery make a sudden movement into the canyon passage, and he flicked his Colt in that direction and blasted the renegade. Slattery crumpled and did not move again.

The single gun trapped by the canyon wall redoubled its shooting, and by the time Boardman reloaded the fight was over. The shooting stopped and they listened to the echoes grumbling sullenly into the distance. Newman started to get to his feet, and the gun over by the canyon wall loosed off a single shot. Newman yelled in sudden pain and clutched at his right shoulder as he dropped back quickly into cover.

"Hold your fire over there," Boardman shouted, and his voice echoed. "We are not outlaws. This is Chet Boardman, Texas Ranger. Is that you, Jed Marsden?"

A gun hammered from the left, and Boardman hurriedly dropped to cover, hearing the strike of lead close by. He triggered his already smoking Colt, and saw a figure stagger several yards, then fall. He waited for the echoes to fade before calling again, and this time he kept his head down.

"Marsden, is that you over by the wall?"

Silence followed the dying echoes of his strong voice. Boardman tightened his lips. He knew that Marsden was half-demented with grief for his family. He felt great sympathy for the rancher, but he wanted some cooperation now.

"Marsden, this is Chet Boardman, the man you met on the trail a few nights ago. Link Loman, the outlaw, stuck a knife through my hand. You must have seen me and the cowboy in ropes today, being brought in here. You followed us, didn't you? Well, we got free and the outlaws are finished. There are no more in here right now. The others are out on a raid. They won't get back until some time tomorrow."

Boardman listened until the echoes of his voice died away. There was no reply from the spot where the single weapon had been in action. Boardman sighed. Time was getting short, and he wanted a posse back here to take care of Harper when he showed up with the rest of the gang. Suddenly he caught a faint movement over by the canyon wall. Then a harsh voice called to him.

"Okay, Boardman, this is Jed Marsden. Sure I followed you in here today. I'll be around, too, when those other Coyotes show up."

"Come on out here and talk," Boardman said. "I can do with some help to take this gang. If you start shooting before they get into the trap I want to set then they'll likely get away."

"They won't get away," the rancher called, chuckling harshly. "And you ain't taking them to jail neither, Ranger. They killed my family, and by hell I'll get them all. If you need a horse there's one in the entrance where I got the guard."

There was the sound of a boot scraping rock, and afterwards silence. Jed Marsden had gone. Boardman shook his head slowly. Here was a complication that he could have done without. He didn't want Marsden running around loose. The man was likely to start shooting the instant he saw the outlaws, and that would put paid to any plan Boardman might make for capturing them.

Newman got cautiously to his feet. He was gripping his right shoulder, his rifle on the ground. Boardman took hold of the cowboy's left elbow.

"Are you hit bad?" he demanded.

"I don't think so. The slug went right through. I'm bored, that's all. I reckon I can make it back to town. But let's check these outlaws before I go. You don't want any of them sneaking around after I'm gone."

They went carefully through the rocks, checking the fallen men. They found seven outlaws, including Slattery, who was dead, and only one of the others was breathing. He had taken two bullets in the chest and didn't appear to have any chance of surviving.

"He's cashing in right now," Newman commented, and they squatted helplessly beside the outlaw until he died. When the man was dead, Newman moved impatiently. "I guess I'd better get moving if I'm going to make town in time," he said callously. "I'll have to keep my eyes open for any of these killers wandering around."

"Let me take a look at your shoulder first," Boardman told him. "It's a helluva long ride to town, and you're losing blood fast by the looks of it."

The tough cowboy pulled off his neckerchief and handed it to Boardman.

"Just bind me tight with this," he said carelessly. "It'll hold me until I can get to the Doc."

Boardman attended to the man's wounds as best he could. Then Newman collected a gunbelt from one of the dead outlaws and buckled it on. He picked up the Winchester, and they started along the rock passage, coming presently upon the horse that Marsden had mentioned.

"I'll get there as fast as I can," Newman promised. "You just keep out of the way if they return before the posse gets here."

"Do you think anyone will be able to follow your directions for finding this place?" Boardman demanded.

"I'll draw them a map," the cowboy said. "I took particular note of the trail this trip. The posse will get here, but I'm wondering if they'll be able to do it in time."

"Leave me to worry about this end of it," Boardman told him. "I know one thing for sure; you won't be coming back with the posse. I just hope you'll be able to hang out until you hit town, and be careful of Calhoun's place."

"Okay." Newman climbed into the saddle and thrust the Winchester into the boot. He reached down awkwardly with his stiff right arm, and Boardman took it briefly. "Watch your step, Ranger," the cowboy said, and then he was gone, hoofs rattling and sparking on hard rock, and Boardman stood immobile until the sounds faded and silence returned. Then the loneliness of this great place covered him, touching him with its spell, and he checked the gun he was holding and started back into the canyon.

There was a lot for him to do. When dawn came he would have to remove the evidence of the fight. He wanted any returning band of outlaws to come right into the canyon. He strode back to the cabin, keeping his eyes open for Jed Marsden, but there was no sign of the demented rancher.

The cabin was in darkness, as he and Newman had left it, and Boardman struck a match as he entered. There was a very dangerous man bound up in the smaller room, and he tightened his lips as he thought of Blade Loman. The killer was the only outlaw left alive in the hideout right now. Bending over the lamp, Boardman lifted the chimney to light the wick, and the next instant a heavy blow struck the back of his head. He fell forward, overturning the table, and the lamp crashed to the floor. Boardman felt some of the oil saturate his bandage as the glass smashed, and then the kerosene burst into angry, roaring flames. His bandage caught fire, and he rolled over, shaking his hand. He felt the fierce heat of the quickly spreading blaze, and thrust himself around, catching a glimpse of a hatred-filled face as Blade Loman grappled with him.

"You killed my brother," the outlaw yelled furiously, and dropped upon Boardman, his strong fingers closing around Boardman's throat. "I'll see you in hell before you get out of here."

Boardman beat at the outlaw's face, using his injured right hand, and pain flashed through the two knife-wounds in the limb. He groaned, could feel the heat of the spreading flames against his neck. The outlaw's weight was pressing him against the floor, and for a moment he could not move. His breath was stifled in his throat by the cruelly squeezing fingers, and pain burst frenziedly inside his skull. Lights seemed to flash before his eyes. He lifted his right hand and tore ineffectually at the outlaw, but made no impression on the man's attack. Then he thought of the Colt, holstered on his left thigh, but when he felt for the weapon he found the holster empty. The gun had fallen out of the leather when he hit the floor.

Loman was yelling like an Indian, and Boardman felt his senses fading. The heat from the fire was blistering, and he cringed, but could not move. The frenzied face above him was dark and ruddy in the leaping flames, the wide mouth gaping and yelling. Boardman felt his strength going, and knew great despair. He was finished, he realised. This cruel outlaw would get revenge for his dead brother, and the injustice of the situation started a spark of fury through Boardman's failing mind. Was there no justice in this world?

Eight

With a desperate heave, Boardman arched his back, pressing both hands flat against the floor. Loman yelled as he sailed forward, and the stranglehold broke. Boardman gasped for breath. His eyes felt as if they had been started from their sockets. His head was spinning, his mind blank now. He could feel pain in his hand and bursting agony in his neck and head. He heaved again as the outlaw struggled to remain upon him, and this time he threw Loman completely off him. The outlaw went skidding head-first into the now raging fire. Boardman twisted around, and as he turned he saw that the saturated bandage on his right hand was aflame.

He pushed himself to his knees, and was shocked to see that the fire was now engulfing one wall of the cabin. Loman was springing to his feet, and threads of bright fire were clinging tenaciously to the outlaw's clothes. Loman's hair was burning, and, screaming like a savage, he hurled himself at Boardman. He thudded against Boardman, and they went sprawling. Boardman choked on the whirling smoke, and grabbed at the outlaw. He lurched upwards, gaining his feet, and threw a heavy left punch into Loman's face. The outlaw replied with a flurry of wild swings, and Boardman staggered backwards.

Loman followed him, yelling and screeching in pain, and Boardman saw that the outlaw's shirt was burning. The killer slapped at his clothes, then ripped his shirt and tore it away from his dark flesh. Boardman hit him again, using both hands, and the pain that burst loose in his injured hand made him sink his teeth into his bottom lip. The bandage was still burning, and he set his teeth and threw himself forward at the outlaw.

Loman met him with both fists flailing. The flickering, flaring light of the fire lit up the interior of the cabin, staining everything with a dancing red sheen. The roar of the engulfing flames sounded angry and urgent. The floor was alight, and smoke billowed thickly. Boardman kicked viciously at the outlaw, and caught his man on the left knee. Loman went down, rolling in the flames, and sprang up again with a hoarse cry on his lips. Boardman hit him with a left swing that sent the outlaw staggering backwards into the fire, and for a moment Loman was completely hidden by flames and smoke. Then he came rushing out of the inferno, and Boardman caught him again with a straight left to the chin.

The outlaw used his weight and impetus to hammer into Boardman. A hard fist smacked solidly against Boardman's left temple and he reeled sideways. He straightened, using his right hand to fend off the outlaw, and he could see by the fiery light that Loman was badly burned. The killer grabbed Boardman's right hand and swung him viciously, pulling him forward and twisting him, and Boardman had to go. He whirled like a top and fell backwards. Flames raged around his feet. Smoke blinded and choked him. He almost went to the floor, but managed to keep his feet moving under his body. He maintained his balance and tottered between life and death as he staggered into the very heart of the fire. His breath was taken. The heat was terrific. Flames leapt at him like living matter. The crackling and snapping of burning woodwork was loud and menacing. He compressed his lips and tried to hold his breath, and whirled and hurled himself back out of the inferno. He could feel the skin scorching on his face, felt the heat through his riding-boots, and put down his head and sprang forward towards the door of the cabin and the cool night beyond. He collided with Blade Loman as the outlaw made a dash from the doomed building.

Boardman lowered his head when he saw Loman ahead of him, and grasped at the outlaw's waist as he struck and butted viciously. Loman went straight to the ground, tripping over the doorstep, and Boardman fell to his knees beside the outlaw. He thrust himself up and kicked at Loman's head. The outlaw groaned and slumped, and Boardman kicked again, deliberately and without mercy.

The cool air seemed to torture his palpitating lungs and he dropped to his knees beside the killer. His eyes were streaming, and his chest was rough with smoke. He gasped and spluttered, trying to control his trembling limbs. He looked at his right hand through a shimmering veil of tears, and saw the breeze fanning the now smouldering, blackened bandage into fresh flames.

He pushed himself to his feet and went back to the doorway of the cabin. The interior was now well alight, and he was amazed at the speed with which the fire had spread. He saw his sixgun on the floor and rushed inside and scooped it up. If he didn't have a gun then he was finished. He burnt his fingers on the hot metal, and threw the gun outside, turning quickly to follow it. As he crossed the threshold on his way out the far wall collapsed with a shower of sparks and a sullen roar, and the rush of hot air towards him was like the lick of a serpent's tongue.

Boardman dropped to his knees again, hanging his head, his chin digging into his chest. He was done. His senses were whirling, and the roaring sound in his ears threatened to take his senses and drop him into a black pit. He could see Blade Loman moving slightly, quivering as returning consciousness also brought pain. He picked up the Colt, still hot to his fingers, and rapped the long barrel against the outlaw's skull. Loman fell limp again, and Boardman sat down and stared at the fire.

By degrees his strength returned. He pushed himself to his feet, holstering the gun, and removed the thong from the bottom of the holster and used it to bind Loman's hands. The outlaw came to as he was moved, and lay groaning. Boardman slide his hands under Loman's shoulders and dragged him away from the fire. He dropped him in the grass several yards out from the cabin.

"Water," Loman croaked. "I'm half burned to death. Give me some water."

"Get to your feet," Boardman said hoarsely, coughing and choking. "I'm in the same condition as you. There's a creek over there. Let's go."

The outlaw arose, cursing when he found his hands bound behind his back. Boardman followed closely, ready for any movement the killer might make. But Loman was concerned only with getting to the water. He shambled along, and smoke still wreathed in his clothes. His hair was singed and there were blisters on his back, chest and arms.

Boardman let the outlaw go into the water, then moved several yards away before slithering down the bank and splashing in the shallows. He drew his gun and removed the gunbelt, placing them on the bank. Then he ducked himself in the water, gasping at the shock and feeling blessed relief spreading over him. He drank and spat, then floundered to the bank, and Loman came out of the water like a drowning rat and flopped down, groaning and cursing.

"I hope you're satisfied now," Boardman said, panting as he buckled the gunbelt around his waist once more. He threw a glance at the furiously burning cabin. "It's gonna be tough on the both of us until the posse shows up."

"Get me to town," the outlaw moaned. "I'm burned up. I'll die unless I see the Doc."

"You'll stay here with me," Boardman told him. "You started this, Loman, and you'll have to put up with it until this chore is done."

"The pain is killing me," the outlaw snarled.

Boardman looked at the blackened bandage on his right hand, and could see fresh blood soaking through it. He had opened up his wounds, and the pain in his hand was worse now than when Link Loman had first stabbed him. He clenched his teeth, and began to feel the first cruel pangs of coldness striking through his wet clothes. His chest felt raw. His head ached, and his throat was swollen where Loman's brutal fingers had dug into his neck.

"You won't die yet," he retorted. "You'll go mighty quick though if you try to jump me again. Be warned. You're my prisoner, and if you only look like you're planning to tackle me, I'll put a slug through your skull."

"I'm done for," the outlaw gasped. "Ain't you got any decency? Untie my hands so I can die in peace."

"You'll live until they hang you," Boardman said mercilessly. "Is that cabin the only place you outlaws have got around here?"

"There's a shack a couple of hundred yards that-away," Loman said slowly. "It's Harper's place. He bunked there alone. He's got whisky there. God, I could do with a drink!"

"On your way then, and don't try any tricks or I'll bore you. Get up and make tracks."

The outlaw got unsteadily to his feet and stumbled forward. Boardman followed warily, although the man's hands were tied behind his back. He felt all in, and realised that it was going to be a long, hard night. He glanced back at the fire, and saw showers of sparks soaring away on the breeze. He tightened his lips, knowing that his plan would be doomed to failure if there were any more outlaws in the area.

The shack stood small and ominous in the darkness. Boardman tried to moisten his dry lips with the tip of his tongue, but guessed that there was no moisture left in him. Loman reached the door of the shack and turned to face him. Boardman drew his gun and waggled it at the man.

"There's a lamp inside, I guess," he said wearily. "I ain't got a match. I lost mine back there. Have you got any?"

"In my pocket. This one."

Boardman approached the outlaw and jabbed the muzzle of the Colt into his side. He felt in Loman's pocket and found the matches. He backed off and opened the door of the shack.

"Stand where you are," he snapped. "If you take a step in any direction I'll shoot you in the belly."

"For God's sake get in there and find the whisky," Loman snapped. "I'm nearly dead on my feet."

Boardman holstered his gun and struck a match as he stepped into the shack. He saw a lamp on a table and moved towards it, glancing back to watch the outlaw. Loman didn't move. Boardman lit the lamp and motioned for the outlaw to join him. The killer came into the little building with lagging steps and sank down on a chair.

"Find the whisky," he choked. "For God's sake get the liquor."

Boardman checked the outlaw's bonds before grabbing at the bottle of whisky that stood on a shelf. He studied Loman as he uncorked the bottle and pushed the neck between the man's eager lips. Loman was badly burned. His flesh was seared and scorched, and there were large blisters on his shoulders, back and chest. His eyebrows were gone, his hair singed and shrivelled. He was black and dirty, his dark eyes burning savagely in his taut face. When he choked on the whisky, Boardman took away the bottle, and Loman cursed him.

A gulp of whisky took some of the smoke out of Boardman's throat, and he sat down at the table and dropped his head into his hands. He drew a deep breath. He couldn't take much more of this, and the chore was not over by a long rope.

"What about some grub?" the outlaw demanded.

"You were eating when I was first brought in," Boardman said. "That's all you'll have until morning. There's a bunk over there. Get on it and try to sleep. I'll see about getting you into town as soon as I can. But give me any trouble and you'll never make it."

Loman looked as if would argue, but dragged himself over to the bunk and sprawled upon it. Boardman took a coil of rope from a nail on the back of the door and went across to him. He bound the man securely, and relaxed when he went back to the table. He took another long pull at the whisky bottle, and felt much better.

Examining himself, he found that his eyebrows were gone. When he touched them they powdered between his trembling fingers. There were blisters on his neck, and his hair was brittle and hot. His hands were burned, the fingers patchy with damaged skin. He looked at the burned bandage covering his injured hand. There was dull red blood showing through the blackened material, and he started unwinding it, wincing at the slight movement. He bared the two wicked-looking wounds, staring at them while his stomach muscles tightened. They were red, swollen and angry looking, and he turned the hand over. Dark blood had congealed now, and he felt suddenly faint and sick. He closed his eyes and listened to the roaring sound in his ears. He thought he would pass out, but the bout went off and he got unsteadily to his feet and looked around for something which could be used as a fresh bandage.

He found a clean shirt in a saddlebag and tore it into strips. He rebound his wounds, then took another drink from the bottle. His eyes felt heavy, and were burning like coals in their sockets. He stared at Loman. The man was breathing heavily, his eyes closed, but Boardman did not know if he slept or not. He searched the shack thoroughly and found a Winchester rifle in a cupboard. There were two boxes of shells for the weapon, and he filled his pockets, loaded the rifle, and took it with him when he left the shack. He closed the door gently and shot home the bolt on the outside.

The cabin was almost burned out now, the fire just a heap of bright red ruins in the moonlight. Boardman took a deep breath and stared around, wondering if Jed Marsden had seen the fire. But there was no sign of the demented rancher, and Boardman supposed that he had made camp somewhere and was sleeping, content to wait for dawn before continuing his vendetta against the outlaws.

Where was Bill Newman right now? Boardman wondered. Had the sheriff managed to take Pete Merrill and the crooked party who had ridden out that day with the intention of stopping and robbing the coach at Aspen Crest? He gazed around through narrowed eyes. This was the most difficult and dangerous chore he had ever undertaken. There were so many points to be covered. The gang was split, and he was here in their hideout, alone and almost at the end of his rope. Would Newman be able to send a posse back here? Would the law party arrive before the returning gang boss? Could they set an ambush in the hideout?

Boardman felt tiredness seeping into him. He almost dropped where he stood. Weakness was rife inside him. His legs were trembling, and there wasn't a part of his body that didn't hurt. He leaned his back against the front wall of the shack and stared across the canyon. There was the smell of smoke on the breeze, and he hoped that it would dissipate before the outlaws started returning. Some of these men were more cunning than an animal, and they seemed to be able to sense danger and a trap.

He placed his right hand across his chest. The pain did not seem to be so intense with the limb in that position. He pushed back his Stetson and let the wind blow into his face. There were slow thoughts in his mind. He hadn't done so badly, he told himself. In the couple of days he'd been in the county he had broken open the gang. He had accomplished more than anyone else, even if he had taken a beating doing it.

He watched sparks flying from the burnt-out cabin. There had been a lot of men in the past trying to find this hideout, and most of them had died. Now he was in a position to capture the gang, but the completion of this job depended upon others. If Newman managed to get to town and set a posse on the way here! If the posse could find its way here, and arrive before the outlaws returned! He tried not to think of what would happen if the outlaws showed up before the posse. He was here alone, and to make matters worse he had a prisoner. If Luke Harper got here and saw the burned-out cabin and the dead outlaws, the whole gang would hightail it out of the country, and then they might never be caught.

There were some precautions he could take, he thought tiredly. He could take his prisoner and hide in the rocks across the canyon. Then if the outlaws got back before later tomorrow he would be in a position to observe them. He decided that was what he should do, and the sooner the better. There was no point in taking unnecessary risks. All he would do was throw away his life needlessly. He turned to enter the cabin, and as he moved his eyes picked up a changing pattern of shadow out there in the deceptive moonlight. He froze instantly, his breath dying in his throat, and he strained his ears for any sound.

Tension crawled in upon him, and he did not move as he studied the ground before him. He had seen something move, and now his tiredness was forgotten, his aches and pains and worry thrust into the background.

He eased his Colt out of the holster, holding it steady in his left hand. The Winchester dragged against the wounds in his right, but he did not move. Nothing betrayed his presence.

After some moments he began to think that he had made a mistake, that his nerves were playing him tricks. Then he caught the movement again, and it was as if scales were suddenly removed from his eyes. He could see the figure of a man quite clearly, crawling towards him, and for a moment he stared in fascination, held spellbound in shock. Was it Jed Marsden? Or had some of the outlaws already returned? He cocked the Colt, tensing as he did so.

There was the sound of leather scraping a rock, and it came from around the right-hand corner of the shack. The short hairs on Boardman's neck lifted, and he swallowed the lump that constricted his pulsating throat. It couldn't be Jed Marsden. There were several men here.

He eased himself down to one knee, placing the Winchester gently on the ground at his side. He knew that he would have to throw a challenge before matters got out of hand. He moistened his dry lips, and drew a deep breath.

"Hold up out there," he called suddenly, and heard the echoes fly. "Declare yourselves or I'll shoot."

"This is Pete Merrill," came the immediate reply. "Who's that? I don't recall your voice. What's been happening in here?"

"This is the law," Boardman replied unhesitantly. "Better throw down your gun, Merrill, and surrender. I've got a posse here. We've been waiting for you."

There was an orange flash, and a bullet smashed into a log behind Boardman. He listened to the crash of the shot and the string of echoes fleeing away. There was a movement at his right, and he saw the figure of a man appear around the corner of the shack. He flicked the muzzle of his gun in that direction and fired almost without thinking. The flash illuminated him, and he dropped flat as Merrill sent two hammering shots in search of his flesh. The man at the corner took a jerky step forward and plunged onto his face. He never moved again.

Boardman held his fire. He could not see Merrill now. But his mind was working at top speed. The fact that the outlaw was here with his party proved that the sheriff had lost out at Aspen Crest. But Boardman had no proof that Merrill had held up the coach there. He had gone on the word of Frederick Moss, and the saloon owner might have been lying. If that were the case then Merrill had another four men around here somewhere, and they would be closing in on the shack right now.

A gun hammered four times from the left, about fifty yards out from the building, and Boardman heard the slugs tear into the front wall above his head. He wasn't in a good position here. They could get him easily from the corners. He edged forward, taking the rifle with him. If he got inside the shack he could hold them off. The thick timber walls would give him some cover, and there was only one room in the shack. They would have to cross open ground to get at him.

Merrill spotted his movements and guessed his intention. Three guns suddenly cut loose at him, and he was forced to lie flat and return fire, aiming rapidly at the erupting muzzle flames before him. He cursed his damaged right hand. If he could have used the rifle to the best of his ability he would soon have had these men stretched out. But he kept the long gun beside him for an emergency. He didn't want to hurt his right hand by using the rifle unless he had to.

He moved again, and reached up and opened the door of the shack. Lead snarled at him, splintering the door and boring through the wall. He rolled inside and slammed the door, getting to his feet and hurrying to the window. He smashed out the glass pane and emptied his Colt at the gun flashes.

Now he took up the rifle. He had to remain cool. He had to do more than fight off these men. He had to take them prisoner. The shooting would sound for miles in this country, and he had no idea where the rest of the gang was. Luke Harper could be on his way back right now, and if it were so another Texas Ranger would die trying to nail the Coyotes.

He fired awkwardly, using the trigger finger of his right hand, gritting his teeth at the pain brought on by the movement of the hand. He missed with the first shot, but the second must have scored a hit for a man yelled hoarsely, and his gun didn't fire again.

There was a lessening of the shooting, and then a gun cut loose from farther back. One of the outlaws sprang up and started staggering away, and the intruding gun fired a second shot and the outlaw fell. The echoes died and an uneasy silence returned.

Boardman moved back from the window, still peering out, and his brow was wrinkled with a frown. That last bit of shooting must have been done by Jed Marsden. The sound of shots must have drawn the rancher from his hiding-place. Now he had arrived to exact his revenge. Boardman sighed harshly. He waited.

There was a flurry of shooting out there in the silver shadows, and none of the lead was directed at the shack. Boardman dared not fire for fear of hitting Marsden. He waited tensely while the shooting rolled and echoed. The fight was moving slowly, and darting tongues of red fire marked the positions of these men locked in a life and death struggle.

Then the silence rolled back, but still Boardman waited. There was no movement out there, no sign of life, and the stillness was ominous and brooding. Blade Loman, tied to the bunk, suddenly spoke harshly, and Boardman started nervously. He had forgotten about Loman.

"You might as well throw down your gun, Ranger," the outlaw told him. "You won't get away from here. I heard Merrill's voice just now. You can't beat him."

"The shooting is over," Boardman replied. "Merrill hasn't won. There's a man out there whose wife and son were murdered by someone in this gang. He's been on the trail of the Coyotes for more than two weeks. He's making a good job of wiping you all out. He just took a hand out there, and I think he's done for Merrill and the others."

"Harper will be back at any time. If you've got any sense you'll get the hell out of here before he shows. What can you do on your own?"

"I don't know," Boardman confessed. "But I'll have a go when they do show. I'm not letting this gang get away now."

"They'll walk all over you," the outlaw jeered. "You're a damn fool, Ranger."

"Hey there, the shack," a harsh voice suddenly yelled, and Boardman recognised Jed Marsden's hatred-filled tone. "Are you alive in there?"

"Sure, Marsden," Boardman replied. "Do you want to come in?"

"I don't want no truck with the law," came the terse reply. "I've just killed these gunmen out here. There ain't none of them left alive. You'd better stay put in there. I'm shooting anything I see skulking around. I'll handle these Coyotes for you. This ain't the lot we got here. There's some more acoming, ain't there?"

"Most of the gang is out on a raid," Boardman replied. "Why don't you come in? We'd have a better chance of getting the lot of them if we did this together."

"No dice. I ain't taking any prisoners, and that's what you'll want to do, Ranger. I'll tell you this. There ain't one of these guys getting out of this alive. When the others show up I'm gonna start shooting. Don't you get in my way. If you try and save some of these outlaws for the law I'll plug you with them."

Boardman shook his head. He didn't like the sound of that. "We're on the same side, Marsden," he called.

"I ain't got no one on my side," the rancher replied harshly. "I asked the law for help a couple of weeks ago and didn't get it. Now I'll handle this chore my way. Stay under cover until the sun shows. Then don't get in my way."

"Just watch where you throw your lead," Boardman warned. "I'm expecting a posse to show up from Burnt Hill any time after dawn."

"They'd better keep out of this," the rancher replied. "I ain't doing this for fun nor for money. I want to kill every last one of those Coyotes, and I'm gonna do it."

Boardman remained silent. He caught a glimpse of a shadow moving out there, and shook his head. He felt sorry for Marsden. The man had become demented through grief. But the law had to do this grim work, and the outlaws had to be given a chance to surrender. He hoped that Marsden wouldn't complicate matters when the dawn came.

He realised that there was no need for him to stand guard while the rancher was out there in the canyon. Marsden wouldn't let anyone within a mile of the shack. He sighed, sagging against the wall. He could not afford to take any chances.

It was a long night, but it passed, and Boardman was standing in front of the shack when the sun came up. He remained motionless until full daylight came, and saw several prone figures stretched out in the area before the little building. There was no sign of Jed Marsden, and no movement anywhere in the canyon.

Boardman walked slowly around the shack. There was a dead man lying just before the right-hand corner. He studied the canyon, judging it to be five hundred yards across at its widest point, and nearly a thousand yards long. There was plenty of ground for hiding in, and he knew that he could disappear quickly if the outlaws showed up. There was flat land and grass around the creek, and he counted nearly a score of horses grazing around.

Recalling the approach yesterday, he could understand why the local posses had failed to find this place. The entrance to the canyon was only a few feet wide, a winding passage that had been cut through the high rock thousands of years before. From a distance the entrance was invisible, searching eyes baffled by the many out-flung faces of drab rock. It was a good hideout.

He looked around for sign of Jed Marsden. He went back into the shack and checked Blade Loman's bonds, satisfied that the outlaw had not succeeded in getting loose. He didn't want another battle like the one they'd had in the burning cabin the night before. Then he left the shack again, ignoring Loman's demands for breakfast. He started across the canyon to check on the burned-out cabin and the entrance to the canyon.

A cursory glance at the heaped, still smouldering ruins of the cabin showed him that he was wasting his time here. He went on, deathly tired, staggering at times, the rifle heavy in his left hand, the right hand almost useless. There was a deep-rooted pain in the hand this morning that seemed to penetrate the very bones of the limb. He wondered if gangrene was setting in. The wounds had taken some rough treatment since his arrival here.

He reached the entrance of the canyon and made sure that none of the dead outlaws could be seen. He didn't want anything to scare off Luke Harper when the gang boss brought in the rest of the gang. He kept a close watch on his surroundings for the killer rancher, although he did not think that Marsden would attack him.

Satisfied that nothing could alarm the outlaws should they come in, Boardman was turning to head back to the shack when his keen ears detected a faint thundering sound. He paused for a moment, frowning, trying to place it. Then he realised it was the beat of many iron-shod hooves upon hard rock. He darted into cover, ducking down behind a rock that was shared by the dead Deputy Sheriff Slattery, whose vacant eyes stared glass-bright at him like the pale windows of an empty house. He drew his Colt and waited. Was this the posse or the outlaws returning?

Nine

The hoofbeats drew nearer, echoing mightily in the narrow passage, and the sound was picked up by the curving faces of the rock, amplified and hurled across space. Boardman took a shuddering breath. If Newman had gotten back to Burnt Hill all right then this could well be the posse. He hoped so. The outlaws riding in now would ruin everything. They would check the burned cabin, take a look in the shack and find the bound Blade Loman, and that would be it. Loman would tell them everything, and they would know that only two men faced them here in their own lair.

A rider appeared, coming at a canter, and then there was a whole bunch of men spilling out of the narrow passage and moving up to form a watchful group. Boardman thinned his lips as he looked at unshaven, tough faces that had stared up at him from different wanted posters. He recognised the sharp features of the gang boss, Luke Harper, the stubbled face and glaring dark eyes of Hank Larkin, and counted fifteen outlaws in all. The party reined up only yards away from him, and he could hear their loud voices as they talked.

"I don't like this," Harper snapped. "Where in hell is the guard?"

"The cabin has gone," another retorted. "Look at that heap of ashes."

"One of you stay here," the gang boss directed. "Keep your eyes open, and warn us the minute you spot trouble. Perhaps a posse found its way in here. Come on, the rest of you. The shack is still standing. Let's get over there and find out what's been going on. It's likely that one of the boys got careless with his matches and burned down the cabin."

The outlaws spurred forward, their hard eyes missing nothing as they hammered away across the canyon. One of them sat his horse for a moment, watching them. Then he dismounted and moved to a rock, sitting down and taking out the makings.

Boardman crouched silently, his thoughts racing. What should he do? There were fifteen of them. He couldn't take on all of them. Then he stiffened with horror when he thought of Jed Marsden. The rancher would start shooting as soon as he got them spotted. Boardman raised himself a little and peered around, looking for sign of the rancher, but saw nothing to warn him of the man's presence. He looked into the canyon and saw the outlaws reining up to stare at the ruins of the cabin. He moistened his lips. Very soon now they would know what this was all about, and Boardman's guess was that Harper would get out of here as fast as he could make the entrance.

He removed the gunbelt from the dead deputy sheriff, knowing in his mind that he could not remain in hiding and let this scourge of the country pass him by. He would have to do what he could to detain them. The entrance was only a narrow passage, and they wouldn't be able to come at him fast. If he could get up into the rocks on the rim above the entrance he ought to be able to hold them in here for a time. If a posse was on the way and getting near they would hear the shooting. It would hurry and guide them. But first he would have to deal with this guard Harper had left.

Boardman glanced into the canyon again. The outlaws were now riding for the shack. He knew that he had to make his decision immediately, else there would be no time to get into a good position and prepare for battle. He stood up suddenly, his lips thin, his eyes hard, and he was only a few feet from the lounging outlaw. The man caught his movement and swung quickly, his rugged face paling when he saw the grim figure and the levelled gun.

"Sit still," Boardman told him. "I'm a Ranger, part of a posse, and there's no escape. But you don't have to die. Just lift your hands and keep still."

The outlaw obeyed, and Boardman started moving in towards him. He was barely a yard away when a rifle cracked and echoes thundered. The outlaw jerked, uttered a cry, then pitched sideways to fall upon his back. Blood was spurting from a hole in his side.

Boardman threw a quick glance around. He saw smoke puffing from a rock high up, and then caught a glimpse of Jed Marsden. The rancher was grinning insanely.

"Get yourself up on the other side," Marsden yelled. "I can't handle this bunch alone. If we're on the same side then get your weapons ready."

Boardman threw a glance towards the distant shack. The outlaws had reached there, and some of them had dismounted. He could see all faces turned in his direction now, and they would be wondering at the shot. He went forward and took the dead outlaw's rifle and Colt, securing the gunbelt, and he checked the saddlebag on the horse, finding a couple of boxes of 30-30 shells for the long weapon. He picked up his own rifle and started for the rocks at the entrance to the passage. He began to climb, groaning as he struck his right hand, and, burdened as he was with the extra weapons and shells he slipped and sprawled heavily several times.

Marsden started shooting, and Boardman paused to dash sweat out of his eyes and peer at the shack. Half the outlaws were already coming back towards the entrance, and Marsden was too impatient to wait for them to draw into effective range. He was standing and shooting wildly.

Boardman continued to climb. He had spotted a ledge some twenty feet above the floor of the canyon, and when he reached it he dumped the extra weapons and peered around. He commanded an excellent view of the canyon, and could prevent anyone from entering the passage or leaving by it. He pulled at a big rock and set it on the edge of the ledge. There was plenty of room for movement up here, and, glancing up, he saw the rim-rocks some twenty feet above his head. One thing was certain, he told himself grimly, settling down and spreading his ammunition within easy reach, he was in a good spot here, but when the outlaws came up he wouldn't be able to move. He would be pinned on this ledge whatever the outcome.

He crouched then, watching. There were about a dozen of the riders coming back towards the passage, and Marsden was still shooting wildly. Each shot echoed about four times, and Boardman listened, his mind blanking out as the time for action approached. He knew it would be no use asking these men to surrender. He was going to have a tough fight on his hands to contain them here in the hope that a posse would show up before things got too hot.

The riders came into range, but Boardman held his fire. He saw one outlaw pitch from his saddle as Marsden found their range, and the others drew their guns and started replying. The noise was overwhelming. It crashed and rolled like thunder, the echoes mingling with the fresh reports, and Boardman cocked his rifle and prepared to start shooting.

Marsden was crouching now, throwing lead with reckless abandon, and his fierce attacks made the outlaws dismount and seek cover in the sprinkling of rocks where the victims of the previous fight lay in cover. They came creeping forward, and Boardman waited patiently, watching them angle towards the spot where Marsden was laying. They were covered from the rancher, but exposed to Boardman.

The rancher was shouting at him to join in the shooting, and a couple of the outlaws were watching the surrounding rocks for other guns. Boardman closed his left eye and poked his rifle over the ledge. He drew a bead on the nearest outlaw and fired, and the man never knew what hit him. He slumped on to his face and lay still.

Boardman swung his weapon, reloading quickly, and started throwing lead at the creeping figures almost below him. They had covered themselves from the angle of Marsden's murderous fire, but they were open to Boardman's screeching slugs. He hit three of them before the others realised that there was another man here. Then they took notice of the true situation, and he failed to spot them.

Lead came striking at the ledge, making him draw back, and he thrust his left hand over the ledge and emptied the Colt in reply. He had two Winchesters, three Colts, and a great number of shells. He reloaded and kept up a hot fire, using both sides of his cover to try and get the outlaws to think that there were more than just two men holding this vital passage. All forward movement ceased in the rocks, and then he saw the outlaws moving back. The rest of the outlaws were coming at a dead run from the shack, and by now, Boardman thought grimly, Luke Harper would know what he was up against. He took up a rifle and started shooting at the newcomers, and they returned fire, moving in quickly and dismounting, running for cover in the rocks and sending out a heavy and accurate fire. Marsden was reckless, Boardman observed. The rancher was throwing lead everywhere, aiming at all the spurting puffs of gunsmoke marking the positions of the outlaws, and more than once he scored a good hit. The outlaws had split into two parities, one taking on Marsden and the other shooting at Boardman. The rocks around Boardman were streaked with lead deposits from the hammering, ricocheting bullets, and he kept low, picking his fleeting targets as they showed and replying when he had a sure shot. He saw an outlaw or two drop under the impact of his speeding lead, but the rest kept up a heavy fire.

After several minutes the intensity of the shooting faded a little. The outlaws settled down, aiming carefully, and Boardman could hear the smack of lead against the rock in front of him. He kept low, using his Colt now, pushing his hand forward. He and Marsden had the advantage, and as long as they could keep the outlaws back from their positions they could command the fight. It was early in the day yet, and the posse should be arriving soon.

Boardman reloaded, and edged to the right of his cover to observe. Smoke was puffing up from various rocks, and he could see that a dozen of the outlaws were still in the fight. He wondered what their thoughts were. Blade Loman would have told them that a posse was on its way. Harper would soon be pushing his gunmen forward to clear the way. The gang boss wouldn't want to be around when a posse of about forty rode in.

The volume of fire suddenly increased, and Boardman ducked and reloaded his guns. When he peered out again the outlaws were coming forward, darting from cover to cover, blazing away frenziedly in an attempt to make him and Marsden keep their heads down. Boardman threw a quick glance across at the rancher's position. Marsden was shooting rapidly. He was down in cover now, but uncowed by the heavy fire directed at him. Boardman resumed firing, and the outlaw attack failed. The heavy shooting, sent at them from a high angle, pinned them down, and by degrees the shooting lessened until it died away.

Boardman was content. All he wanted to do was contain these men until the posse showed up. But Marsden was of a different mind. Boardman heard the rancher's harsh, hatred-filled tone ringing out.

"Come on, you murdering skunks," the rancher yelled. "What are you waiting for? Had enough already? You guys ain't getting out of this place alive. Do you know who I am? I'm Jed Marsden from Mason's Crossing. Remember me, Harper? It was my wife and kid got killed a couple of weeks ago. So come on and try to get past me. I swore I'd get all of you, and that's what I'm gonna do."

An outlaw started throwing lead at the rancher's position, and he showed himself carelessly to Boardman, who took quick aim and squeezed his trigger. The outlaw jumped, then sprawled, and didn't fire again.

"That's the stuff to give 'em," Marsden yelled wildly. "We've got them pinned down here. We can take all day to knock them off."

"Marsden, listen to me," Boardman called. "I'm a Ranger. If these men want to surrender to the law then you've got to hold your fire."

Marsden showed himself briefly, and his gun cracked. The slug struck the rock behind which Boardman was crouching.

"You listen to me, Ranger," he yelled in a high-pitched tone. "I said none of these skunks is gonna come out of here alive. If you want to join them then start shooting at me. I don't care how many I've got to shoot. They're all gonna die."

"You damn fool!" Boardman yelled in reply. "Keep your shots for the outlaws. We haven't got them bottled up yet for sure."

Marsden laughed crazily and returned to shooting at the outlaws. Boardman shook his head. This could have finished right way. The outlaws would surrender if they thought there was no chance of escaping. But Marsden intended killing them all, and after hearing his maddened voice the outlaws wouldn't consider surrendering, and Boardman did not blame them.

Harper sent some of his men forward in an attempt to get to the high ground where Boardman and Marsden were lying. Six of the outlaws were down in firing positions, three shooting at Boardman and the other three hammering slugs at Marsden. Boardman kept low, watching four outlaws coming through the rocks towards him. The fire was so heavy about him that he dared not show himself. But Marsden was not so cautious. The rancher was shooting rapidly, and Boardman saw one of the outlaws making for the rancher suddenly spin and fall.

When the four drew closer, Boardman eased the muzzle of his Colt around the rock. He ignored the splattering lead now, the angry, heart-stopping screech of tortured slugs flying off at a tangent from the canyon walls. He took careful aim, waiting, and when he had a perfect target he squeezed the trigger. The outlaw dropped and the others went into cover. The shooting increased, and Boardman ducked again and waited it out.

His ears were ringing from the crashing of the shots. The canyon walls seemed to trap the sound and hurl it from face to face. He reloaded automatically, and peered cautiously for another target.

He suddenly recognised Blade Loman moving forward, and sunlight pierced the curling gunsmoke and glittered on the long blade of the knife in the outlaw's hand. Come and get me, Boardman thought, and his finger tightened around his trigger. He kept low, content to wait this out.

Marsden suddenly uttered a loud shriek and dropped out of sight. Boardman thinned his lips, staring across at the rancher's position, but he saw nothing of the man, and his brown eyes turned bleak when he saw the outlaws who had been concentrating on Marsden turn their attention to his position. The increase in shooting at his spot was frightening, and when he raised himself and risked a glance around his cover he saw four more outlaws snaking forward to attack him. He thrust out his left arm and started blazing away with a Colt, emptying the weapon at their scurrying figures. A bullet burned his left elbow and the Colt spun out of his hand and clattered down to the ground twenty feet below.

Boardman ducked back, snatching up another Colt. He checked his arm and saw a red furrow along the forearm and across the elbow. Even as he watched, blood started to fill the wound and spill on to the hard rock. The shooting faded then, and a harsh voice called to him.

"Ranger, I'm giving you a chance to surrender. Come on down from there and I'll let you go. I'll give you a horse and you can get to hell out of here."

Boardman grinned tightly, thinking of Blade Loman. The killer wouldn't let him leave if he wanted to. He moistened his lips.

"I reckon you're the one who should be asking to surrender," he replied, watching the ground below for signs of a rush. "I'm the law, and you're trapped."

"You can't hold out against us," the voice continued. "You've got a couple of minutes to make up your mind."

There was silence now, but the heavy sounds of shooting still hammered in Boardman's ears. He checked his guns, glad of the respite, and didn't take his eyes off the stretch of bare ground below. He couldn't afford to let any of the outlaws get by that. He spotted Loman again, and the killer was sneaking through the rocks, crawling on his belly. Boardman waited, and when Loman made a sudden rush to get across the open ground and into the rocks at the foot of Boardman's position, Boardman snapped off a shot that tore through Loman's left thigh. The outlaw screeched and whirled back into cover. There was an immediate fusillade of shots, and Boardman started throwing lead again, aiming quickly at the fleeting figures that sprung up and rushed forward.

Then Marsden's wild voice was yelling exultantly, and the rancher's Colt cracked rapidly. Boardman saw outlaws falling, and threw a quick glance of amazement across the narrow space to where the rancher was kneeling on his rock and pumping slugs at the milling outlaws.

Marsden downed three of the bad men before the others recovered from their shock and dropped back into cover. The shooting died, and Marsden's eager voice was calling out.

"Thought you'd got me, huh?" he demanded. "Well, you ain't the only ones who can pull snaky tricks. Now that's evened the score a bit. Come on, you Coyotes, show yourselves. I've got plenty of slugs left."

The shooting started again, and Boardman opened up at three different outlaws who were foolish enough to show some part of their bodies. He drilled two of them, then fell to watching for Harper and Loman. But he guessed that Loman would be fully occupied with his fresh leg wound.

Harper let the shooting rage on for several minutes, then called for a halt. Boardman reloaded and waited. There was silence from Marsden, and glancing across Boardman could see nothing of the rancher.

"Ranger," the gang boss called. "I'll do a deal with you."

"No deal," Boardman replied. "You can throw down your guns any time you like, but no deals."

In the ensuing silence Boardman checked his guns. He didn't relax his vigilance, and his narrowed eyes were sore from the drifting gunsmoke and the brilliance of the sun. The heat was packing among the rocks now, and he was exhausted and dry. Lifting his eyes briefly he caught the sparkle of the creek, and tried to moisten his lips with a dry tongue.

This was stalemate, he thought, but it also meant that he must win. The posse should be showing up soon, and then the gang would have to surrender. But there was Jed Marsden to think about. The rancher was practically out of his head, and it was likely that he would start shooting at the posse if he thought he could not get a shot at all the outlaws.

A Winchester crackled quickly, and glancing down Boardman saw three of the outlaws making a run for the bunched horses at the far end of the cluster of rocks. Marsden had spotted their movement and was shooting rapidly. Whipping up his rifle, Boardman joined in the shooting, and in the instant his attention was taken from the stretch of bare ground below him two outlaws dashed across it and disappeared from sight beneath him. The outlaws making for their horses dropped to cover.

Boardman yelled at Marsden, and the rancher showed his bearded face for a moment. Boardman pointed over the ledge at the foot of the rocks below him, and Marsden spotted the outlaws. His rifle came up and cracked again, and Boardman watched the smoke puff and drift. He tried to work out how many of the outlaws could be left, and figured that less than half of them remained. He grinned tightly when he realised that whatever happened the Coyotes were finished as a gang.

Marsden stopped shooting, and waved at Boardman, who nodded. He could not blame the rancher for this bloodthirsty revenge. He would have likely done the same thing had he been in Marsden's boots. The rancher resumed firing at the surviving outlaws.

Boardman kept glancing at the passage leading out of the canyon, hoping to spot something of the posse, but nothing moved, and there was no dust to mark the approach of a group of riders. He returned to the task of watching for the outlaws.

Marsden cut loose again when he spotted movement, and Boardman tried to see the effects of the shots, but dust was flying down below, mingling with the drifting gunsmoke as the last of the outlaws kept shooting. There were not so many guns firing upwards now, Boardman could see, and he guessed that Luke Harper would be getting very worried. The gang was finished. They had failed to break out, and now their numbers were depleted they could not snatch the initiative.

Marsden suddenly uttered a yell, and glancing in his direction Boardman was horrified to see the rancher straighten then pitch forward and fall twenty feet to the ground. The outlaws immediately riddled the sprawled body, and then the weapons were turned on Boardman. Lead came screaming as the outlaws, heartened by the death of Marsden, tried to intimidate Boardman with an overwhelming volley.

Boardman crouched, grabbing at the two rifles and the brace of Colts. All weapons were fully loaded, and he waited for the rush that must come. He tightened his lips and slitted his eyes when he spotted three outlaws making a dash for their horses, but he watched the stretch of ground below. They had tried this trick before and it had failed, but now there was only one man above them, and they could hope. That was about all they had left.

He started shooting at the three men, brought one of them down, and was ready with a second Colt when two men made a dash across the open space below. He emptied the Colt at them, throwing six slugs, and they both staggered. One fell in his tracks and lay writhing. The other fell, rolled, and vanished beneath him. Boardman snatched up a rifle, unmindful now of the pain in his knifed hand. He triggered the Winchester, and his slugs tore at the two men making for the horses. There was heavy shooting directed at him from below, and he caught sight of Harper kneeling in the open and hammering away with a Colt.

Boardman hunched his shoulders and kept at it. He swung his rifle to cover Harper, but the gang boss ducked out of sight. Boardman lifted the other Colt and emptied it at the two fleeing men. One of them dropped, and then he had to reload. In the following silence he peered around, hoping to catch a glimpse of the posse. But there was nothing.

The outlaws had become reckless, but he had thinned out their odds considerably. He didn't think there were more than three or four left untouched by flying lead. But they were still a dangerous party. They would be desperate now, and he expected them to make a break. He listened in the awful silence, and could hear echoes rumbling in the vast distance.

A movement to his left attracted his eye, and he thought it was the posse coming. Then a bullet thudded into his cover, ricocheting under his chin, and he felt a flash of pain where it nicked him. Blood dripped from his face, and he glanced around quickly. One of the outlaws had flanked him, and he guessed that the second of the two who had tried to cross that stretch of bare ground below had finally succeeded. He looked for movement, and a bullet tore through the flesh of his waist, just above the left hip. He groaned and swung a Colt, hammering shots at the puff of smoke erupting between two rocks. The outlaw had got up to his level, and now Boardman was in real trouble. He picked up a rifle, peering down at the surviving outlaws in the rocks, and saw that they were already making for their horses. There were three of them, and one was Luke Harper.

Another bullet came from the man who had flanked him, and Boardman caught sight of the outlaw's head and right shoulder. He fired the last two shots from the Winchester and saw the man slide sideways and lay prone. Then he reloaded.

There was pain in his body. He tried to move, wanting to get to his knees in order to throw lead at the last of the outlaws as they came pounding towards the passage in a wild bid to get free. He held a Colt in his left hand, struggling to sit up, but his legs seemed paralysed and there was no strength left in him. He had to rest his gun hand on the rock, and his sight blurred when he tried to get the blob of the foresight lined up on the nearest rider as the man came thundering forward.

The three outlaws started shooting, but Boardman was past worrying about flying lead. He concentrated on the rider under his gun and fired, the gun bucking powerfully and jumping from the rock. The rider swerved, but came on, and Boardman fired again, teeth bared, every nerve screwed up tight, and he saw the horse leap and break its stride, then go slithering to its knees. The animal shrilled in agony, and the rider went sailing over the beast to land in a heap and lie still.

Luke Harper was firing two Colts, guiding his horse with his knees, and the outlaw leader was yelling his defiance. Boardman pushed his Colt forward. His Stetson jumped from his head as Harper's searching lead tore through the crown. Blood began to drip from Boardman's face, seeping out from under his hair. He fired at Harper and saw the gang boss throw away one of his guns. The other swung back to aim at Boardman, who fired again, and then Harper was pitching from his saddle. He hit the ground hard and lay still, one foot kicking slightly before relaxing.

The third rider reined up, lifting a rifle, and the quick blasts of the weapon seemed to go on and on. Boardman snapped his last shot at the man, and saw him jacknife and sprawl sideways, hands clutching at air as he went out of his saddle. Dust spiralled up from the impact of the body with the ground. Then the silence came back.

Boardman slumped against the rock. He looked around slowly, his eyes narrowed to the merest slits. There was no movement below. The smoke was blowing away, vanishing like magic under the push of the wind. Bodies were scattered around, and none of them showed signs of life. The stillness and the silence seemed overbearing after the racket of the fight.

He pulled himself into a sitting position, dropping his gun. Blood was running down his face, smearing him with its sticky matter. He gingerly felt for the wound at his right hip, and found a messy hole through the soft flesh. He could move his left leg only with difficulty and great pain. He gave up the idea of trying to get down from his position. He would have to wait for the posse to show up. They would have little enough to do now, for it was obvious that the outlaws were finished.

He must have passed out, for when he opened his eyes again and came back to hazy awareness his body was stiff from the burning heat of the sun, which was directly overhead. He pushed himself up into a sitting position, and blood was dry upon him. When he stared down at the ground he saw more than a score of men moving around, collecting the corpses of the outlaws. He grinned crookedly when he saw the extra-tall figure of the sheriff and the smaller shape of Frank Quinn. The two were standing together in the clear space, staring around.

"Up here," he croaked hoarsely, but his voice could not carry. His throat was dry, constricted, and he had the feeling that he was floating on air. None of the pain in his battered body was sharp. Everything seemed to be out of focus.

He lifted a hot Colt, found it was empty, and tossed it over the edge. It hit the ground a foot in front of Frank Quinn, and the old rancher and the sheriff spun, lifting their Colts. Boardman saw their expressions change when they spotted him, and the next instant the sheriff was scrambling up towards him. But the whole canyon suddenly began to spin. The earth and the sky revolved, twisting and whirling. Boardman stared into the sheriff's large face as the lawman came on to the ledge. Then blackness hit him like a falling curtain. When Wendell lifted him gently he was unconscious, but there was a faint grin on his blackened face. He didn't need to be told that he'd made it. The outlaws were being tied to their saddles, and they proclaimed the fact with their sightless eyes and dead bodies. It was the bitter end of the Coyotes.

Printed in Great Britain
by Amazon